THE WHITE ROAD

Also by Sarah Lotz

The Three

Day Four

THE WHITE ROAD

SARAH LOTZ

First published in Great Britain in 2017 by Hodder & Stoughton
An Hachette UK company

1

Map by Rodney Paull

A CIP catalogue record for this title is available from the British Library

Hardback ISBN 978 1 473 62457 3
Trade Paperback ISBN 978 1 473 62458 0
Ebook ISBN 978 1 473 62460 3

Printed and bound by Clays Ltd, St Ives plc

Hodder & Stoughton policy is to use papers that are natural, renewable and recyclable products and made from wood grown in sustainable forests. The logging and manufacturing processes are expected to conform to the environmental regulations of the country of origin.

Hodder & Stoughton Ltd
Carmelite House
50 Victoria Embankment
London EC4Y 0DZ

www.hodder.co.uk

For Charlie

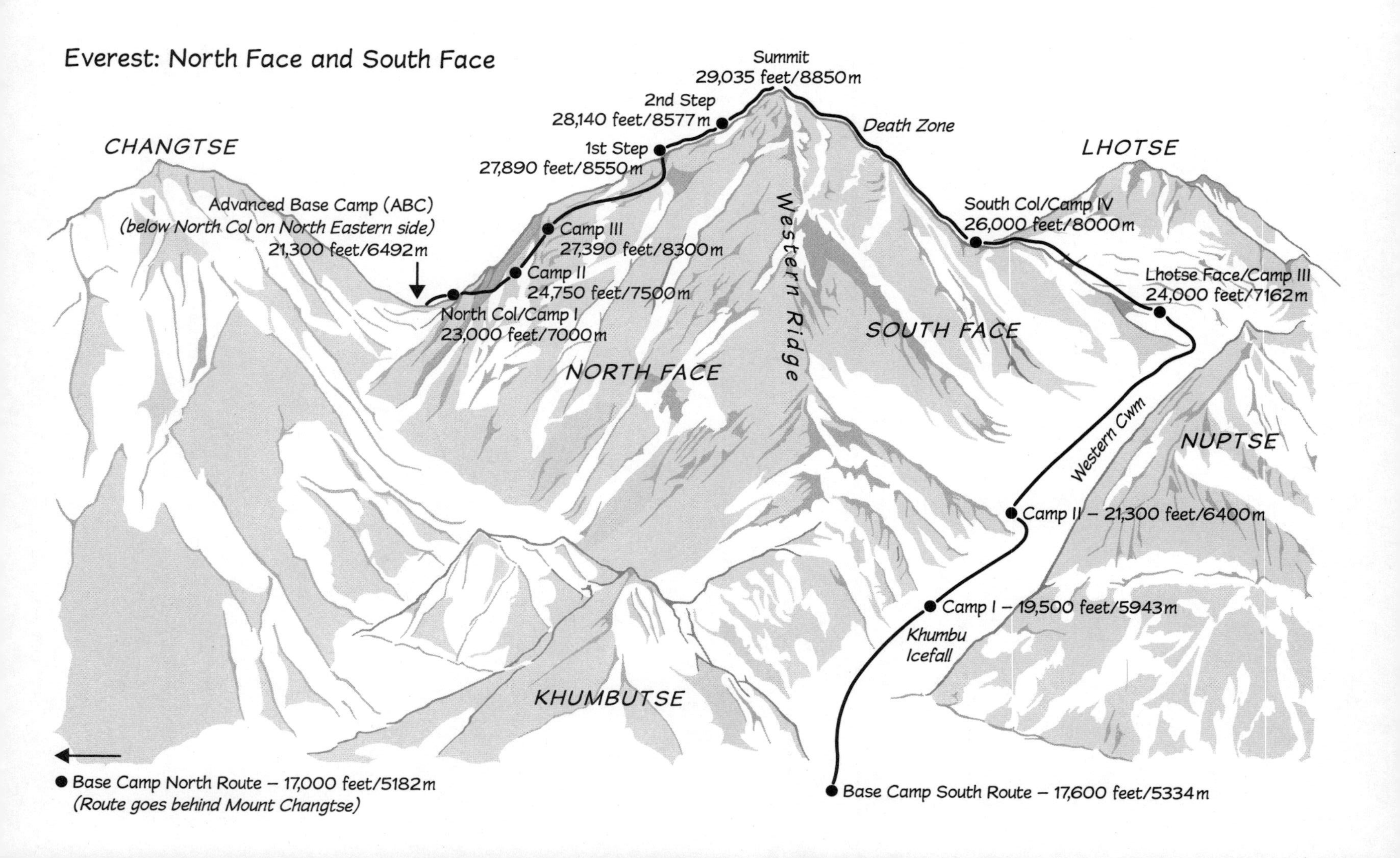
Everest: North Face and South Face
Summit
29,035 feet/8850m
2nd Step
28,140 feet/8577m
Death Zone
1st Step
27,890 feet/8550m
CHANGTSE
LHOTSE
Advanced Base Camp (ABC)
(below North Col on North Eastern side)
21,300 feet/6492m
Camp III
27,390 feet/8300m
South Col/Camp IV
26,000 feet/8000m
Camp II
24,750 feet/7500m
Lhotse Face/Camp III
24,000 feet/7162m
North Col/Camp I
23,000 feet/7000m
Western Ridge
SOUTH FACE
NORTH FACE
Western Cwm
NUPTSE
Camp II – 21,300 feet/6400m
Camp I – 19,500 feet/5943m
Khumbu
Icefall
KHUMBUTSE
Base Camp North Route – 17,000 feet/5182m
(Route goes behind Mount Changtse)
Base Camp South Route – 17,600 feet/5334m

To: TCAKES@journeytothedarkside.com
From: simonpieman66@gmail.com

Hi T,

No easy way to say this, but I'm going back to Tibet. Yeah. Back to the mountain, though I swore I never would, remember? Leave for Heathrow in 5. How's that for casually dropping a bombshell? I've tried everything else, T, and going back is the only way. Got to the point where it's this or a padded cell.

If I don't make it home, there's a dropbox file you should check out. Sounds ominous, I know, like I've gone full B-movie: *If you're reading this then I'm already dead* . . . Password is 'fingersinyrheart06'. Anyway, read it. Or not. Up to you. Do whatever you want with it. Just needed to tell the truth. Put the record straight, you know?

Farewell and adieu, mate.
Aka
So long, and thanks for all the fish.
Si

PART ONE

Simon

December, 2006

I met the man who would save my life twice – and ultimately destroy it – on a potholed road in the arse-end of the Welsh countryside. He was sitting on a kitbag at the side of the lane, a trio of crushed cider cans at his feet. Morning mist still clung to the snow-dusted hills surrounding us, but all he was wearing on his top half was a Harley-Davidson T-shirt.

I pulled up next to him and wound down my window. 'Ed?'

A curt nod.

'Hi. I'm Simon.'

'You're late, lad. I said eight.'

'Sorry about that, got a bit lost. All looks the same round here, doesn't it?' I gave him my best self-deprecating grin – it usually thawed the frostier punters at the coffee shop where I part-timed. It didn't work on Ed.

He jabbed a finger at the rutted track snaking through a wooded area on the opposite side of the lane. 'Pull into the trees over there. Don't want the car to be seen from the road.'

'Wilco.'

Wincing as branches scraped along the paintwork, I slid Thierry's Ford Focus beneath the limbs of a broken tree. My breath smoked as I climbed out, stretched, and waited for Ed to join me. I was chilled to the bone (the car's heater had packed up just outside Newport), and already cursing myself for setting this thing up.

He threw his bag next to the car and gave my hand a rough-palmed shake. Close up, he had the swollen nose and florid skin of a career alcoholic. Baby-fine hair wisped over his scalp. I put him at around sixty. *Do you really want to follow this grumpy old sod down a hole, Simon?*

'Where's your car, Ed?'

'Don't have one. Hitched here last night.'

'All the way out here?' Quite a feat: apart from a stoical sheep, he was the only living thing I'd seen in the last hour. He smelled like he might have slept rough; a cured-meat fug wafted off his clothes. 'I could've given you a lift, picked you up somewhere.'

'It's no trouble.'

'Well, I really appreciate this.'

A sniff. 'So you want to go down Cwm Pot, then?'

'Yeah.'

'To film the caves.'

'That's right. Like I said in my emails, I'm interested in what happened down there in the eighties. Thought it might make a good documentary.' Bullshit of course, but I wasn't going to tell him the real reason I wanted to explore the caves until I had a clearer idea of how he might take it.

'Caves are off-limits. Have been for twenty years.'

'I know. That's why I got hold of you.'

'Dangerous, too.'

Fuck's sake. 'Yeah, Ed, I know.'

He smirked as if he knew something I didn't. His irises were dark, the whites around them tinged with yellow – pickled-onion eyes. 'You got my money?'

Tell this prick you've changed your mind and get the hell out of here. Good advice, sensible advice, but I ignored it. It had taken serious legwork to get to this point, and I wasn't about to throw in the towel. After hearing about Cwm Pot and its grisly history, I'd spent days scouring caving forums looking for a guide, finally coming across Ed, the only caver who openly admitted sneaking into the caves. He was clearly a miserable old git with a drinking problem, but the other cavers on the forum deferred to him, so presumably he knew what he was doing. I gave him the three hundred quid we'd agreed on. He counted it, taking his time. 'And an extra fifty for the equipment.'

Bastard. 'That wasn't part of the deal.'

'It is now.'

'Twenty.'

'Twenty-five.'

He smirked again as I handed it over. Now I had to make this work. Half a month's rent had disappeared into the pocket of his filthy jeans, as well as next week's food and beer budget. 'You brought gloves and boots like I told you?'

'Yeah. Wellies and washing-up gloves, right?' Not exactly the outdoor gear I was used to.

He dug in the bag and handed me a helmet, a head torch, a ratty belt with an old-fashioned karabiner attached, a yellow rubber exposure suit, a pair of kneepads and a blue fleece undersuit that resembled a giant Babygro. 'Put that on first.'

He pulled his T-shirt over his head and I tried not to stare at the wormy scar bisecting his concave chest. That and the grey hair furring his limbs made him look older, vulnerable, less of a hard-man. 'What you waiting for, lad?'

Not wanting to look prissy by retreating to the car to get changed, I used the exposure suit as a makeshift mat, stripped off and gingerly shucked the fleece suit over my legs. It held the same cured-meat pong as Ed.

'What happened to you, lad?' He was eyeing my own cluster of scar tissue, a network of raised white flesh criss-crossing my left shoulder.

'Climbing accident. Eight years ago. Smashed up my ankle, femur and collarbone. Fractured my skull too.' A stupid, avoidable accident. I'd been showing off in front of a group of hikers, free-climbing an easy first pitch at Cwm Silyn – the kind of training-wheels route I'd have cruised through when I was a kid. I'd got cocky, miscalculated what should have been a no-brainer grab, and then the ground was rushing up to meet me. 'Two months in hospital.' I rolled up the suit's bottom cuff and pointed out the keloid bumps where the pins had fused my ankle together.

Another grunt. A sign of respect? Impossible to tell.

The yellow outer-suit was a size too small and nipped at my armpits and crotch, but it was surprisingly effective at keeping out the cold.

Time to get the guy onside – I was about to spend the day doing some seriously dangerous stuff with him, after all. 'So, Ed. How long have you been—'

'How old are you, lad?'

I blinked, wrong-footed. 'Uh . . . twenty-eight.'

'Think of yourself as a pretty boy, do you?'

'What? Why would you say that? No.'

'Married?'

'No.'

'Girlfriend?'

'No. What's all this got to do with—'

'Not one of them pillow biters, are you?'

'No!' *Great – homophobic as well.*

'You sure you can handle this?'

'The caves? I think so.'

'You think so?'

'I know so.'

'It's not some tourist day out. Gets technical. Dangerous.'

'I can handle myself.'

'Caving experience?'

'No, but like I said in my emails I've been climbing all my life.'

'Don't tell me, some namby-pamby weekend outings, am I right? A trip up Snowdon and a fiddle around Ben Nevis's botty?'

'I know what I'm doing. Among other things, I've done the Aiguilles and I was leading out on VS routes at sixteen.' Pompous, and an exaggeration, but so what? He was pissing me off.

'The Aiguilles, eh?' A sneer. 'Means nothing to me.'

My irritation flipped into anger. 'Look, I've come a long way to do this. If you don't want to guide me down there, just say so and give me my fucking money back.'

A cackle, a flash of tea-coloured teeth. 'No need to lose your temper.' He belched. 'Get a move on. Want to be out of there before dark.'

'Sure you don't want to give me a hard time for a few more minutes?'

'Nah. You're all right, lad. Before I took you down there, I needed to know you had a backbone.'

'Seriously? You were messing with me?'

He winked. 'Get off your high horse. You'll do.' He took a hip flask out of the waterproof bag slung over his shoulder, knocked back a slug and handed it to me. I wasn't a fan of hardtack, especially that early in the morning, but I surreptitiously wiped the spout and drank anyway, stupidly pleased that I'd passed the Ed test.

Back then, whenever I met someone new, I used to do this thing where I'd try and figure out their film or TV character equivalent – a dumb mental tic that started when I was in hospital recovering from the climbing accident. I knew immediately that my best mate Thierry was Ray, Dan Aykroyd's character in *Ghostbusters* (American, pudgy, nerdy, endearing); Cosimo, my manager at Mission:Coffee, was Tony Soprano (mercurial, morbid, a mouth-breather with major mommy issues). Ed was easy. He was Quint, the unhinged, predatory shark hunter from *Jaws*. Same cruel smirk and scar fetish.

He rolled a cigarette while I fiddled with the helmet-cam's waterproof case, attaching it to the helmet with clumsy fingers.

'That going to work down there?'

'Absolutely.' Another lie. Thierry and I had bought the camera off a dodgy, debt-ridden motor-cross enthusiast who used to come into the coffee shop. Even in ideal conditions, its quality wasn't great, I hadn't tested it properly in limited light, and I wasn't sure that the case, which I'd bought on the cheap and modified, would actually work. 'How likely is it that we'll get wet?'

'Should be fine.' A sly smile. 'Unless you fall in.'

'Fall in what?'

'Just keep your wits about you, and mind you don't get me on your film.'

'You camera-shy, Ed?'

'Just mind you don't, lad.'

I tried the helmet on for size. The weight of the camera made it droop to one side, but it would have to do. I collected the

Snickers bar I'd bought for elevenses from the console, locked the car, and hid the key under the wheelbase. I thought about sending Thierry a text, something along the lines of <about to head into hell with Quint, farewell & adieu>, but it was unlikely I'd get a signal out here.

Ed made for a bramble-strangled stile, scrambled over it and headed up the sloping field beyond. I followed, my boots crunching on frosted grass and sheep shit. Despite being bow-legged and decades older than me, he set a cracking pace. By the time I caught up to him, I was puffing.

'How far is it?'

'Entrance is two miles or so.'

'That far? Couldn't we have driven closer?'

He gave me a sideways look. 'You're not in London now, lad. After we cross this section, we'll be trespassing. Keep an eye out for the farmer. He's come at me with a shotgun before.'

'That bad?'

'Doesn't want the hassle if people run into trouble down there. Happened more than a few times over the years.'

'How many times have you been down Cwm Pot? Since they closed the caves, I mean.'

'A fair few.'

'And you don't worry about the caves flooding?'

'I know what I'm doing. Know the signs.' He paused and looked up at the low concrete slab of the sky. 'Think it'll hold, but there might be run-off from the snow if it warms up later.'

Thanks to the booze and the fleece Babygro, my body was warm, but the crisp air made my lungs ache, and I trudged on in silence. We slurped through a shallow ford, and I trailed him across another couple of fields, through a barbed wire fence – a 'no trespassing' sign hanging from its tines – and down towards a rocky outcropping. A stream frothed and burbled alongside it, edged with a fringe of startlingly green moss. After another short and slippery trek down a path, we came to a rock face with an opening about the size of an oven door. This was barred by a padlocked gate with a cracked and fading 'danger, no entry' sign on it. He hung back while I got an establishing shot, then whipped out a Swiss Army knife and picked the padlock in seconds.

'Where did you learn how to do that?'

'Never you mind. In you get.'

I squeezed my body through the opening, and crab-walked into a sloping cavern. Ed relocked the padlock ('Don't want to advertise that we're down here'), clicked on his headlamp, pushed past me, and disappeared into the mouth of a rough-hewn vertical tunnel at the far end. I peered into the tunnel's throat, the beam of my head torch unable to penetrate much of the blackness. The ladder bolted to the wall was showing its age, and to reach the top rung, I'd have to swing my legs into the abyss and drop down more than a metre. Ed was already slithering down the mossy rungs like a ferret.

'Stop playing with yourself, lad!' his voice echoed up, punctuated by the thunk of feet on metal rungs.

I rolled onto my belly, and inched down until my toes hit the top rung, fingertips clinging to the edge of the hole until I had no choice but to commit. There was a bladder-weakening moment when I teetered, unbalanced, and then my legs took my weight and I was able to wriggle down until I could grip the top rung with my hands. *You used to be able to do this shit in your sleep, what happened to you?*

The fall happened. The bones had healed, but my confidence was still shattered. In hindsight, I suppose part of my motivation for heading down Cwm Pot was to see if I *could* still handle myself.

The washing-up gloves gripped the metal surprisingly well, as did the wellies I'd bought from a discount store the day before. The lower I went, the more comfortable I became. Then my left foot stepped down into nothing. I bent my head and directed the light between my legs, revealing the stony floor a couple of body lengths below me. There was no sign of Ed. Muscles straining as I took my weight on my arms, I let my legs dangle, counted to three and dropped, careful not to land awkwardly on my ankle. There had to be another route out: I doubted I'd be able to reach the sheared-off end of the ladder even if I stood on Ed's shoulders. 'Ed? Now what?'

'There's a crack at the base.' His voice was reedy, as if it was coming from miles away. 'Get down on your arse, and slip through it feet first.'

True enough, there was a ragged fissure in the rock to my right. I wriggled through a short lumpy passage that dipped abruptly, and before I could arrest myself, plopped onto the floor at Ed's feet, landing on my tailbone.

'Ow. Thanks for the warning.'

Ed cackled. The sound didn't echo. Rather, the air seemed to swallow it.

I stood up and took stock. We were in a church-sized chamber, the ceiling arching above us in graceful waves, several walls adorned with the dripstone cascades of calcified rock in muted shades of red and bronze and gold. I'd imagined there would be a dank, dark odour of rot and stale water, maybe mould, but I couldn't smell anything at all. I breathed in, sniffing the air like a dog – still nothing. It was slightly warmer than outside. The sound of distant water whispered in the background, and every so often came the musical plink of globules dripping into shallow rock bowls. 'Impressive.'

'They were going to open it to the public back in the eighties, then those lads died down here. Put paid to that.' He led the way to a tunnel that branched off to the left. 'Time to go off-piste, lad.'

'How long will it take us to get through?'

'About three hours to the Rat Run if you don't mess about. Then another hour or so to get out. We'll exit about a mile from where we started.' Up until the mention of the Rat Run I'd successfully managed to keep claustrophobia at bay, but now it began to nip at me. 'Cwm Pot is known for its aptly named "Rat Run", five hundred metres of some of the tightest squeezes in the UK', was how the sadistic caving guide I'd consulted put it.

The tunnel's roof tapered down, forcing me to lurch along like a hunchback, and ended at a jumble of mid-sized boulders. A scramble over these led into a more impressive conduit, the rock around us diminishing up into velvety blackness, the sloping floor peppered with scree. The burble and spatter of water was always with us. I double-checked the camera was secure, mindful that I only had an hour and a half of battery life. I'd have to be picky; especially if I got the chance to capture the footage I was really down here for.

The tunnel widened again, roomy enough for us to walk side by side. 'Where are you from, Ed?' Sometimes his voice had a Yorkshire burr; at other times it morphed into something less distinct.

'Lived all over.'

'And you usually do this alone?'

'Ay.'

'So what drew you to caving?'

'Been doing it off and on all my life, lad.' He turned and tapped the side of his nose. 'It's one of the places they can't get you.'

'Eh? Who can't get you?'

'Them, lad. *Them.* You know who I mean. Blair and Bush and those other fuckers. They can't track you down here, lad, with their CCTV and their satellites and their electromagnetic signals.'

Was he trying to psych me out again? I waited for the accompanying cackle. It didn't come. *Shit.* Now it wasn't just the thought of squeezing my bulk through a sodden rock fissure that made my bowels clench. Ed wasn't just a grumpy old codger with a drinking problem, but a bona fide nutter. But as we walked on, I caught him glancing slyly at me. I honestly couldn't tell if he was messing with me for some twisted reason of his own, or if he was genuinely deluded.

Go back, go back, make some excuse.

It wasn't just the practicalities that kept me moving forward – I'd never get back up that ladder – but my ego. Conspiracy nut or not, I couldn't bear the thought of Ed's scorn if I backed out now. Instead, I changed the subject. 'So they would have come this way? The lads who died down here in the eighties?' Lads. I was picking up his speech patterns.

'They would. One route in, one route out. I was part of the rescue team.'

'Really?'

'Oh ay. Only cavers can rescue cavers. No good sending anyone else down. Don't know what they're doing, see?'

'It must have been horrible.'

'Oh it was *horrible* all right, lad,' he spat, reminding me more than ever of Quint. 'Couple of us almost drowned as well. Had to dam that stream up top, but it wouldn't hold.'

We'd reached an enormous pile of boulders, the evidence of a long-ago cave-in, stacked to the top of the chamber. They looked impassable, implausible, like a movie set. 'Boulder choke,' Ed said, matter-of-factly. 'Stay close. Going to be tight.' He glanced at my belly. 'You're going to wish you'd given the pies a miss, lad.'

He scaled the rocks closest to us, then posted his body through a tiny V-shaped opening, twisting his torso mid-manoeuvre. His light was far brighter than mine, and the second he slipped through the crack, shadows closed in on me. I hesitated, unsure that I would actually fit through it. It was all right for Ed. Ed was wiry. I had wide shoulders and a gut gestating a Guinness baby. Aping him, I corkscrewed my bulk through it, rock scraping my belly and back, trying not to think about the tons of impervious material above and around me. I detected a faint guff of sulphur as my suit rubbed against limestone – the first whiff of anything I'd had down here. Once through the opening, I had to contort myself through a lumpy U-bend, haul my body up a short vertical shaft, then scramble along a narrow funnel. Ed could do this on his hands and knees; I was forced to do an inelegant belly wiggle, pushing myself along with my elbows and toes, and all the while trying not to bash the camera on any outcroppings. Still, it wasn't anywhere as difficult as he'd led me to believe. *Fuck you, Ed.*

The going for the next half-hour or so wasn't challenging either: another hands-and-knees crawl, a squirm through a couple of eye-holes, and then I was birthed out into one of those roomy chambers. Niggles about hiring a nut to guide me aside, I was beginning to enjoy myself. I decided it was best not to ask him about the bodies – not now that he'd revealed himself as a possible member of the tin-foil hat tribe. Instead, I'd concentrate on filming the Rat Run, and get Thierry to add creepy music and subtitles hinting at the caves' tragic history: *A Trip down Cwm Pot, The Caves of DEATH*, or something.

Ed was waiting for me at the base of a wide vertical face, which was riddled with ridgelines. Halfway up it, an elongated slender mouth bisected the stone, a rusty chain hanging in front of it.

'Took your time, lad. You ready for the next bit?' He pointed at the mouth with a gnarled finger. 'Got to climb up there, grab the chain and post yourself through that gap there.'

I could sense he was waiting for my reaction. From our vantage point the aperture looked too narrow to admit anything more substantial than a newspaper. 'Sure. No problem.'

He snorted, clearly seeing through my fake bravado. 'I'll go first, shall I?'

'Yep.' My mouth was dry.

He hared up the crease at the side of the wall, monkeyed across a ledge on the balls of his feet, and then, in one smooth movement, lunged, grabbed the chain and slotted himself feet first into the gap. He wriggled his way inside it, disappearing into the darkness beyond.

He'd made it look easy, and it was at first. The climb up was effortless, as if the cracks and ledges were purpose-made rather than random acts of nature, but when I reached for the chain and trusted my full weight to it, it jerked as if it was about to come loose from the bolt holding it in place. Heart in my throat, I pin-wheeled my legs upwards, catching the edge of the mouth with my toes, my head and torso hanging vertically down, brain filled with images of my head cracking open like a watermelon on the rock below. If the chain came loose from its mooring, that would be it. Moving my hands up the chain to eke my body into a better position, I managed to slot my feet inside, then my legs. *Thank fuck.* There was just enough room for me to squirm my body further into the gloom, but I had to remove the helmet to prevent the camera scraping against the low ceiling. Using my bum and shoulder muscles, I wormed my way along, the stone above me a hair's breadth from my gut. The top opened out, and I slid the helmet back on. Now I was able to shift my body around, roll onto my front and crawl head-first along a passageway to where Ed was waiting for me, a savage smile on his face. 'Careful here, lad.'

'Oh *shit*.' The end of the tunnel dropped down to an inky abyss, a good three storeys below. The route down gave the impression of being as smooth as a sheet of glass. As my head-lamp swept it, I fought a twist of vertigo, although I'd never had an issue with heights before.

Again he was watching me slyly. 'Shouldn't be a problem for a climber like you. Not one who's done the *Aiguilles*.' He didn't suggest a belay. In any case, we didn't have any rope.

And then he was off, dropping down, fearlessly taking a direct route, clinging to the rock like a spider. I watched him carefully, trying to memorise the handholds he chose.

'Come on then, Chris Bonington, let's see what you're made of.'

Dry-mouthed once more, I turned on the camera, my inner voice unhelpfully ad-libbing, *caught on camera, the last tragic moments of Simon Newman's life*, rolled onto my front and felt for the first toeholds, hoping to Christ that the limited light created an optical illusion, and made it appear more challenging that it actually was. *You can do this*. I couldn't allow myself to get gripped – frozen midway between moves. Traversing across was the best plan, and I paused while I scanned for the first grab. Within seconds, muscle memory kicked in, and taking my weight on my legs, I shone the light down and across for the next handhold. As with the previous face, they were fairly evenly placed. *Step down, traverse again. Take it slow, solve the problem.* Down and across, down and across. I took my time, fully absorbed in what I was doing, grateful that my ankle didn't appear to be taking any strain. My thighs shook when I finally reached the base. And I was flushed with something else: euphoria. It was a basic climb, but I'd nailed it. The first real climb I'd done since the accident. I switched off the head-cam and turned to grin at Ed. 'That was actually—'

My spine exploded with pain as I was slammed into the crag behind me. Before my brain could fully comprehend what was happening, Ed had a hand at my throat, his fingers pincering my windpipe, his full weight pressing against me. 'Why are you really down here!' he spat in my face. 'Who sent you, who sent you!'

I'm not totally useless in a fight, but I fought the instinct to lash out at him, go for his eyes, head-butt him maybe. That wasn't an option. I had to calm him down; I was God knows how far underground and needed him to guide me out of here. The pressure on my windpipe increased – it hurt like a bastard – and I put my hands up in surrender. 'Please, Ed!' my voice squeaked out. 'Calm the fuck down. Please!'

'Why are you really here?' Spit flecked my skin, and I had the horrible feeling that he was about to lean in and bite me.

'I want to film the bodies for a website!'

The raw, agonising pressure on my windpipe eased. He stepped back, muttering to himself. I gagged and rubbed at my throat. 'Ed, I swear—'

'Quiet, lad.' He coughed, turned and spat. 'What website?'

'Me and my mate Thierry run it. It's called *Journey to the Dark Side*, and we've started doing this thing where we film creepy places and banter about them and put the clips up on the net and I heard about the caves and the disaster in the eighties, and a rumour that the bodies of the men who died back then are still here.' I was babbling like an idiot, but I didn't care. 'I wanted to film them. That's it. I swear that's the truth. It's not for a documentary and I'm sorry I lied about that, but I didn't realise . . .' *I didn't realise you were such a fucking nutter.* 'You believe me?'

We stood there, me breathing hard, him staring at me with

those pickled-onion eyes for at least a minute. I couldn't read his expression. It was muddy, unfocused.

I prepared myself for another onslaught. This time, I decided, I'd fight back; hit him with everything I had. If I fought him off, could I climb back up the traverse? Yeah, probably. But then what? I mentally tried to map the route we'd taken here. Christ, I just didn't know if I'd be able to retrace my steps, never mind get back up the ladder. I'd been following him blindly.

Then he let out one of his cackles.

'You believe me, Ed?'

'I believe you, lad. Had to be sure you weren't one of *them*.'

'I understand that, Ed.' *Oh Jesus*.

The flask emerged. We passed it back and forth, the cheap burn of the alcohol flushing away the irony after-tang of adrenalin, and making me feel vaguely sick. Again he was watching me with a wicked half-smile on his lips. I still couldn't decide if Ed's conspiracy bollocks and violent outburst were put on to freak me out. The thought wasn't a comfort: Ed was either a psychopath who was toying with me for sadistic reasons or a paranoid schizophrenic. The raw ache in my throat was easing, but my spine throbbed from being slammed against the rock.

'So. You want to see the bodies, you say.'

No. I want to get the fuck out of here and away from you as fast as possible. Too late for that, I was stuck with him. Might as well make the best out of a bad situation. 'Is it true? Are their remains still down here?'

He nodded, a trick of the light deepening the grooves in his face. 'Course they are. Think about it. You can't take a body out when it's this deep underground, lad. Not out of a network like this.'

I tried to imagine dragging a corpse through the snug spaces we'd been through, managing to make myself feel even sicker. 'And you know where they are?'

'Parents of the lads got the remains moved up to a chamber in the late eighties. They were going to seal it in with concrete, but then the landowner petitioned to have the whole system closed for good, so they didn't see the point. You want to film them, you say?'

'Yeah.' Only now it seemed stupid. Obscene.

'You seen a dead body before, lad?'

'Yes.' *Don't go there.* But I couldn't stop the image of Dad flooding in. Lying there behind the grubby hospital curtain, his face muscles slack, an emptiness about him that had badly scared my ten-year-old self. Still scared me, if I'm honest.

'Me, I've seen plenty. Belfast. Bosnia. Been all over.'

'You were in the army, Ed?'

'Seventeen years, lad.'

Bosnia. When was that, early nineties? I should know. 'Why did you leave?' *Apart from the fact that you're certifiably insane or a psychopath. Or both.*

'Had to get rid of me, knew their plans, see? Knew what they were really up to.'

Conspiracy theory alert, keep him on track. 'Is it possible to see the bodies? Can we get to them?'

A crafty look. 'Ay. I can show you, lad. Shall we say an extra hundred quid?'

I didn't have an extra hundred quid, but I'd cross that bridge when we got out of here. 'Fine.'

The next section was easy. A short belly-wriggle, another boulder choke, and then the air was alive with the gush and chatter of water. We sidestepped down a scree slope to where a fast-moving stream gurgled into a tunnel. Ed crouched next to it. 'Water's higher than I'd like.' He sniffed. 'Should be okay, long as we don't fuck about. You getting cold feet, lad?'

'No.'

'You will soon.' The cackle turned into a liquid coughing fit that doubled him over. After another of his delightful hawk-and-spit combos, he stepped into the stream and sloshed ahead. I followed, the current coiling and pulsing against my calves. The floor dipped, I stumbled, and water spilled over the lip of my boots, soaking my socks, the sudden shock of cold making me gasp.

'Watch where you put your feet, lad, there are sinkholes here that go straight down to hell.'

We rounded a corner and edged past an inky sump pool. 'Watch this bit, it can be a right arse-clencher.' He clambered up onto a slender ledge skirting the stream, then stepped across, straddling it, one foot either side. I did the same, praying that my weak ankle would hold my weight and the wellies wouldn't lose their purchase on the slippery ridges. As we shuffled along, we crept incrementally higher, until we were a good six feet above the frothing stream below us. Falling now would be a disaster, and I had to remind myself to breathe. Ed paused and pointed upwards. Stalactite shapes dripped from the ceiling: a cluster of slender straws, larger fangs, weird alien ribbed fans. But I wasn't there for the geological marvels.

'Ready for the Rat Run, lad?'

'It's here?'

'Ay.'

He lurched across to an outcropping on the right, leaving the stream behind, then squirrelled over a jumble of rocks and through one of those tapering eye-holes.

I turned on the camera – my hands were trembling, so it took a while to get it right – took a deep breath, then copied Ed's moves, making a stupid yipping sound when my left foot slipped as I reached across, almost sending me slithering back into the water.

The Rat Run started off mildly as if it was trying to lull me into a false sense of security, with a hands-and-knees crawl that wasn't particularly taxing, but made me appreciate the kneepads. Ed was waiting for me at the end of the tunnel.

'Next bit gets a bit tight, lad.'

The understatement of the year – a squeeze through a gut-crushing aperture led into a tight space that couldn't have been more than a foot high. Forced to twist my head to the side to fit, my cheek a breath away from the damp scree, I scraped along it, so constrained that the only way I could get any traction was by pushing with my toes and using my fingers as leverage. After five minutes of this my busted ankle started screaming. Every so often I'd feel the rock above me press against my back and buttocks with heavy hands. My whole body started to tingle unpleasantly and I was more aware than ever of the weight of the rock above me. The effort it took to squirm along stole my breath, and soon I was panting. Rivulets of sweat stung my eyes.

The tunnel opened up for a glorious section where I could use my elbows and knees to propel me along instead of my digits, then squashed in on itself once again, the roof jutting down, a brutally low slab that seemed to go on forever. Even Ed was having difficulty eking his way through here, his boots scrabbling on the loose ground to get purchase. The tingling in my limbs increased as my energy leached away; I had to keep pausing to get my breath and strength back. The ceiling lifted enough for me to raise my head to ease the ache in my neck, but there was far worse to come: an impossibly tight cavity that twisted up and around a bend. Ahead of me, Ed was halfway through it, grunting and swearing, his legs kicking frantically before he finally made it through. I let my head drop onto my arms for a few seconds. My mind kept latching onto horrible images: a cave-in further on that would trap me forever in this constricted space; Ed dying in front of me, blocking the route ahead; a show-reel of what had happened to those lads down here . . .

Stop it.

Gathering my remaining strength, I posted my head and shoulders through the gap, but there was only enough room to slip one arm through the awkward orifice. I felt around for a handhold on the other side, hoping to find something to latch onto that would help haul me through it, but my fingers were unable to grip the slippery surface beyond. I kicked as hard as I could, managed to nudge forward, fighting to breathe as the rock strangled my ribcage. I tried to back up, but I was jammed, one arm through, the other wedged at my side, like a swimmer caught mid-crawl. I pushed with my toes. Still nothing.

'Uh, uh, uh.' There was no doubt about it. Trapped. I was

trapped. The panic came then, hot and quick. 'Ed! Ed! Ed! I'm stuck!'

'Relax, lad,' his voice floated back to me. 'You can get through it. Panic is the enemy.' He sounded calm, almost caring. As unlike Ed as I could have possibly imagined. It helped.

Breathe, breathe, breathe.

There's always a moment on any challenging climb when you reach a tipping point – a no going back moment. To deal with these, my old outreach climbing instructor, Kenton, an ex-Special Forces guy with zero sense of humour and the ability to put the fear of God into us without raising his voice, told us to empty our minds and focus. Panic and hesitation weren't an option – not if you wanted to survive. No one could get me out of this but me. I could give in to the terror, or I could fight.

I let myself go limp. Breathed in again. Forced myself to empty my mind, lose the image of the crushing weight above and around me.

My left ankle and toes protesting, I pushed. Nothing. *Don't panic. You can do this. Take it slow.* Pushed again. And this time I moved an inch. *Keep going.* Another push, another inch. Then, slowly, incrementally, I was able to twist my body around and free myself from the band of rock imprisoning my ribcage. Now able to wiggle my left arm through, I could use both hands to help my poor toes do the work. Body half free, I dug with my elbows, wriggling like a snake until my gut and legs followed. *Thank fuck.* I took five, huffing like a steam train, waiting for my galloping pulse rate to slow. But another seemingly endless body-hugging squeeze lay ahead, smothering the relief at my narrow escape.

Once more I propelled myself along using my toes and fingers. The floor was far damper than what I'd experienced so far, and I spat out a mouthful of gritty mud which scraped against my teeth. I couldn't shake the sense that I was dragging myself through the smuggy intestine of a huge animal. The hollow sound of water pulsed below us. Ahead of me, Ed turned on his side to slip through yet another of those limited cracks. Thankfully,

I was able to lug myself through it with relative ease. It opened into a conduit that would allow me to use my elbows to propel me along.

'This is where those lads died,' Ed shouted above the water's gurgle. 'Two were found here, one tried to get further.'

Thanks for that, arsehole. Panic gnawed again as I inched along, once more imagining getting stuck, the air running out, the caves flooding, racing against time to escape. *They'll never be able to dig you out of here, Simon. Stuck. You'll be stuck forever.*

Finally we came to a kink in the bowel, a space high enough to sit up in.

'Turn around, lad.' The roar of the water was louder and he had to yell to be heard. 'Don't want to go down here head-first.'

I did as he instructed and, wriggling along feet first on my bum, followed him to the end of the tunnel, which dropped down into the stream. Legs shaking from adrenalin and exertion, I flopped down into it. The water, which now reached over my knees, immediately flooded the boots. That vicious shock of cold made me gasp again, but it soothed my aching calf muscles.

'That's it, right, Ed? We're done with the Rat Run?'

'What?'

I repeated the question, raising my voice.

'Ay. Wasn't too bad, was it?'

Ed stopped dead and gestured to an outcropping on our left. 'Got to go up now, lad. They're up there.'

'The bodies?'

'Ay.'

It was what I was down here for, but the haul through the Rat Run had sapped my strength, and my leg and arm muscles were throbbing like sore teeth. I longed to be back in the relative warmth of the car, and en route home for a pint and a bacon sandwich. *You're here now. Just do it. The worst is over.* Fortunately there was an overhang two thirds of the way up that provided enough leverage for me to heave my bulk up to the crack at the top. The opening meant another one of those body-contorting squeezes, but it was a piece of piss compared to what I'd just been through. A hands-and-knees scuffle along a lumpy tunnel led into an oblong chamber the size of a box room, only one section of the curved ceiling high enough to sit up in. Blood-warmed water sloshed around the bottom of my boots. I considered tipping it out, decided not to bother. I paused to catch my breath, and let the light drift around the space.

'There's nothing . . .' And then I saw them: a jumble of shapes that I'd mistakenly taken to be rocks at the far end of the chamber. They weren't at all what I'd been expecting – I'd been harbouring a mental picture of perfectly preserved bodies like those dug up from peat bogs. Two of the skulls were face to face as if they were kissing. One had a shaggy look to it, as if the flesh had grown fur, the other was covered in delicate strands of dried skin as if it had been encased in a pair of ripped stockings. Again there was no smell. Tentatively, I waddled closer and let the headlamp dance over the rest. They hadn't been placed with much care: an ulna nestled against the brown curve of a pelvis, and what had to be a partially collapsed ribcage sheathed in rotting fabric. Other limbs were clad in the tatty remnants of what looked to be wet-suit material, and desiccated finger bones were scattered around like pebbles. A lone helmet lay, upended like a turtle shell, in the rocky corner behind the bone mound. The water's grumble was ceaseless: the sound they must have heard before they died; the sound they'd hear forever. And I thought, *this isn't horrible or gross, it's sad.* I also thought: *Thierry is going to fucking love this.* I turned off the camera, half hoping that the footage wouldn't be useable. All I knew about the victims was that they were students, part of an ad hoc caving club from the University of Warwick. They'd hitched out here for a laugh, a touch of adventure, never dreaming that thanks to the weather, fate, whatever, they'd end up like this, forever stuck in a cave with some arsehole crawling into their mausoleum so that he could film them and put them on the Internet. I gave myself a mental shake. I was being morbid. Philosophising about the randomness of death and the ethics of what I was doing wouldn't do these guys any good.

I jumped as a splash of brighter light heralded Ed's appearance at the chamber's mouth. He was shaking his head, sending the light in wide arcs. His face was drawn, the light once again scoring those thick black lines around his mouth. I prepared myself for one of his tirades – or worse. He said something that was swallowed up by the watery backdrop.

'What?'

' . . . trouble!'

I shook my head, pantomiming that I couldn't hear him.

'We're in trouble.' And then it hit me: he wasn't about to go off on one; he was scared.

'Why?'

'Water's rising. Weather must have broken.'

'How bad is it?'

He shook his head once more. Rivulets of water ran off his suit.

'How bad, Ed?'

'See for yourself.' He backed up, giving me just enough space to slip past him. I scrambled along the tunnel, thunking my hip on an outcropping, and stuck my head through the gap. The roar of the water was almost deafening, and my face was hit with rogue spatters. *Jesus.* It looked as if the maelstrom had almost reached the Rat Run's exit. How was it possible that it had risen so fast? But I knew it was possible: of course I did. I'd just been looking at the evidence of what it could do.

What I did next was inexcusable. I slipped my legs feet first through the crack, feeling around for the ledge, intending to climb down to get a better look and a shot of the raging water. I was cocky after how well I'd navigated the other tricky sections – typical of me – but I missed my step and then I was sliding, out of control. The shock of cold as I hit the water feet first was heart-stopping, so icy that my brain first registered it as boiling hot. There was a detonation of pain as my ankle hit rock, I lost my balance and the force of the water – which now reached above my chest – pushed against me, sweeping my legs out from under me. Fingers of freezing water found their way past the collar of the exposure suit, and I involuntarily took a breath, choking as water scoured my lungs. I flailed for the nearest rock, scrabbling for purchase, but the churning water forced me under again. Then, something tugged roughly at my waist, heaving me backwards. Panic muddying my mind, I fought against it, until it hit me that it was Ed hauling on the waist belt. I coughed up a gout of water; my throat, already raw from Ed's attack, was now on fire, and I could do little to help him fight the torrent that was beating against us.

Ed gave an almighty tug on the belt, and pressed me against the face that led up to the lads' chamber. 'Get back up there!'

I couldn't seem to get enough air into my lungs and the route up was as slippery as glass. I tried twice to get purchase, but kept slipping back. Then I felt Ed boosting me up, his hands under my left foot. I pulled myself through the opening, threw myself along the tunnel, and collapsed when I reached the mausoleum. Still coughing and struggling for breath, I scrunched across to the pocket where the ceiling was roomier. I didn't give a thought to Ed right then – I barely registered him arriving behind me.

Finally I was able to find my voice.

'How long until it subsides?' Again I had to shout above the crash of the water, a challenge as it hurt to speak and my teeth were chattering.

'*What?*'

'How long until we can get out of here?'

'Could be a day. Could be a week.'

'A week?' My first reaction was, ridiculously: *I've only taken one day off work.*

I tried not to look at the bones, but something made me take off my gloves, reach over and touch them. Now they felt alive, clammy and warm. I was shaking violently. I could actually feel the cold worming its way deep into my core.

'Get out of those clothes, lad.' He was already stripping off his suit.

He was right. Keeping the wet clothes next to my skin was a

one-way ticket to hypothermia. I kicked off my boots – a mistake as water gushed onto the already damp floor – and wriggled out of the PVC suit and sodden fleece under-suit. My socks and boxer shorts clung clammily to my flesh; I stripped those off too. The cave's crumbled floor biting into my buttocks, I scrunched my knees up to my chest.

The light dimmed, and it took me a second to realise that Ed had turned off his headlamp. He reached over and tapped mine.

'Turn it off. Need to conserve the batteries.'

'No!' It was an instinctive response, every inch of me balking at the thought of being left in the dark.

'Do it.' It wasn't a threat exactly, but I doubted he would take no for an answer. And he was right: of course we had to conserve the batteries. I took off the helmet, flicked the switch, and pure, liquid blackness engulfed us. There was nothing for my eyes to focus on, and for a few minutes they played tricks on me, forming shapes out of nothing, creating bright circles of light that couldn't exist. The lack of visual stimulation was disorientating, faintly nauseating and seemed to amplify the chatter of the water.

I jumped as I felt Ed's cold body sliding in behind me, his thighs either side of mine, his arms curling around my ribcage. *Oh God.* I kept absolutely still as his breath tickled my neck, the cold squish of what had to be his genitals pressing against the base of my spine. 'I'm not sure you should do that, Ed.' He didn't respond – maybe he didn't hear me above the clatter of the water below. It had been years since I'd done a first-aid course, and I was fairly sure that two hypothermic people this close together would make things worse. But the chill inside me hurt, a solid insistent ache, and I couldn't see how it *could* get any worse. He started rubbing at my arms and legs, as if he was an impatient parent towelling a child after a bath. The friction helped, and the squeamishness at being so close to him faded as the cold became a manageable ache: deeply uncomfortable, but no longer painful. As the violent shivering subsided, my brain turned its attention to the massive fucking pickle I was in.

Okay. Don't panic. Thierry knows where you are. The directions

Ed sent are on the laptop. He's not stupid, he knows how dangerous the caves are, one of the reasons he didn't come with you. If you're not back by midnight, tomorrow morning at the latest, he'll sound the alarm.

A weight on my shoulder as Ed rested his scratchy chin on it as if we were lovers. The situation would be hilarious if it wasn't so deadly. I was no longer scared of him; he'd saved my life, and in any case, the horror of our situation made his psychotic breaks or whatever they were pale into insignificance.

'Does anyone know you're down here, Ed?' My throat protested as I raised my voice above the water's clamour.

'No, lad.'

'My mate's expecting me back around nine tonight. Reckon he'll call in the cavalry then.' I was trying to sound optimistic, but there was a thread of panic in my voice. 'Could rescuers get down to us?' I had to repeat the question twice.

'No. Not even the divers would make it through the Rat Run. Too narrow, see.'

'Can't they come in through the other side? You said it was an hour to get out from here.'

'Current's too strong. You felt it, lad.' His grip relaxed as he let loose a wracking, lung-searing cough.

'You okay, Ed?'

'Ay.' He cleared his throat and coughed again, his ribcage thrumming behind me.

'You saved my life.'

No response.

'I said, you saved my life.'

One of his grunts. Another cough. I prayed I was imagining the fine spatter of fluid on my shoulder.

And then it hit me: *Fuck.* The bodies. 'The water can't get up here, can it?'

'Oh ay. Fills the whole system when it goes.'

'Shit.'

That was why the remains were such a random mess and weren't preserved by the pure air down here; over the years water must have licked and nudged at them. Drowning hurt. Everyone said it didn't, that it was peaceful, but that was bollocks. The CIA used waterboarding as a torture tool, didn't they? And I could still feel the razor-blade burn caused by water going down the wrong way.

We sat like that, wrapped together in silence for God knows how long. My thoughts were jumbled, mostly fluttering over and over rescue scenarios and desperate denials at what was happening to me. The darkness was so complete that I couldn't tell if my eyes were open or shut. The panic ebbed, leaving not acceptance but lethargy in its place.

And then, voices, I could hear voices! And more than one – a chorus of people calling out to us. They were coming, Ed was wrong, they were coming! 'Hey!' I screamed, ignoring my tender throat. 'Hey! We're up here!' I twisted my body out of Ed's embrace, and lunged in what I hoped was the direction of the cave entrance, my elbow smacking into some part of his body. 'We're here!'

Rough hands grabbed at me, fingers digging into my flesh.

'Let go, Ed! Voices! I can hear voices!'

I was hauled back, pinioned in a headlock, and his voice rasped in my ear: 'Lad! Lad! It's just the water. Listen.'

I struggled against his grip, then my brain caught up with what he'd said. I listened. He was right. Of course he was right. Rescuers couldn't have made it down here this quickly – if at all. *Who's the mad one now, Simon?* What I'd thought was a chorus of voices, the chattering and chortle of five or six people, was simply the thundering of the water rushing beneath us. Yet despite this, for several minutes afterwards I was certain I could make out words hidden in the watery clamour; it was tantalising, like listening to a conversation through a wall. There was an isochronal rhythm to it too, haunting, cruel and mesmerising: *We're coming for you, Si. We're coming for you, Si.*

Ed released me, and shifted back into position behind me, his furred limbs locking around me, and now I couldn't shift the image of being in the clutches of a giant hairy spider. He started to rub at my limbs once again, yet this time, (although in hindsight I could have simply fallen foul to the lurking madness at the edge of my mind), there was something wrong about the way he was touching me. His fingers seemed to linger on my thighs and biceps. It wasn't sexual, exactly, but intimate, as if he was massaging me for pleasure rather than warmth. And he was saying something to himself, mumbling. I couldn't bear it. I didn't care if I pissed him off.

'Can you stop that, Ed?'

I half-expected him to ignore me, or freak out again, but his fingers stilled immediately. I scrunched my knees up into my chest, and buried my face in them, tasting the salt of my skin.

This is how you're going to die, Si: drowning in freezing water with the dead, or starving to death embraced by a crazy ex-squaddie.

No. I can't die like this. Not before . . . not before what? I fulfilled my potential? What potential? Self-pity came dribbling in as I thought about Mum, imagining her hearing about my death. She was living in Australia, close to my sister Alison, and was happily re-married to an actuary. I hadn't seen her or Alison for four years. I hadn't spoken to her for six months. Would she miss me? Maybe she'd even be relieved. No more requests for loans; no more worrying about the black sheep of the family. This drifted into musings about my funeral, only there wouldn't *be* a funeral as there wouldn't be a body. *You can't bring bodies up from this deep underground, lad.* Maybe Thierry would organise a wake or memorial service at Mission:Coffee, where we'd worked for the last two years, and where we'd met. Thierry. I couldn't help but feel a pulse of anger at him – I wouldn't be down here at all if it wasn't for the website, which had been his idea. It had grown after he'd decided to post online the stupid banter we used to trade to keep ourselves sane during work, mostly silly 'top five' lists and pop junkie stuff: 'the top five movie monsters you'd least like to shag'; 'five of the most disappointing horror movie endings'. This was a few years before Buzzfeed made listicles ubiquitous, and before long we'd gathered a modest following. Then Thierry suggested that seeing as our grubby flat was situated in the heart of Whitechapel, we should film an 'alternative virtual Jack the Ripper Tour', taking the piss out of the Ripper industry in the area. It was a hit – especially with our US subscribers – and *Journey to the Dark Side* was born. The 'top five' material anchored the site and brought in a steady stream of hits, and every so often to boost circulation we'd take day trips to film graveyards and the haunts of notorious serial killers, overlaying the footage with satirical banter. It was while I was researching our next outing that I stumbled upon Cwm Pot; Thierry loved the idea of featuring it, but flatly refused to join me, citing his 'fat nerd' status as an excuse.

Ed let out one of his rumbling coughs once more.

'You okay, Ed?'

No answer.

'Ed?'

'Quiet down now, lad.'

Was the water's grumble louder? Would it come in a rush, tossing us around the chamber as if we were socks in a washing machine, or would it creep in slowly?

Think about something good.

I scrolled through my mental hard-drive, hitting on the trips I'd taken years ago with the outreach climbing programme for 'difficult teens'. At her wits' end after I'd been caught shoplifting for the third time, Mum had signed me up for it without telling me; she'd had to threaten me to go the first time. But despite myself, I loved it. There were weekly training sessions at an indoor climbing centre, monthly outings to Snowdon (Ed was right about that), and once, the mind-blowing excitement of a jaunt to Chamonix and a glacier exploration, learning how to use crampons and an ice axe. If we had time after our sessions, Kenton would take us to a pub, and we'd sit outside in the beer garden with Walkers Cheese & Onion crisps and pints of Coke. Crammed around a scratchy wooden table, dappled by sunlight, muscles aching, the sound of laughter and football floating out of the pub's windows, the smell of beer in the air, we'd unpick every move we'd made, over and over again. It was the happiest

I've ever been. But these recollections weren't potent enough to stop my brain looping back to dwell on other, darker things.

If I get out of here, I'll do something with my life. I'll go to church, yeah, I'll go to fucking church, okay, God? If I get out of here, I'll say sorry to everyone I've ever hurt. I'll help the homeless, I'll volunteer at a soup kitchen. Just don't let me drown. Don't let me die here. Let them get to us before that happens. I'd screwed up so many things in my life, floated along for years. Bobbing in whichever direction the tide took me – a porter in a hospital, waitering, bartending, construction. I was a completely different person from the kid who wanted to be the next Andy Kirkpatrick. But I didn't have the dedication. Didn't have the single-mindedness for that sort of career. The fall at Cwm Silyn had almost been a relief. It wiped out any chance of failing at something I really loved. Self-sabotage. Self-destruction. Sitting there, inches away from Ed's furry embrace, I delved far deeper inside myself than I ever had before, and I didn't like what I found. I knew what Ed was the second I saw him, but still I followed him. Some part of my brain must have known something bad would happen. Some part of my brain *wanted* something bad to happen.

The voices in the water came back. Now they were saying: *Fingers in your heart, lad, fingers in your heart, lad, fingers in your heart, lad.* Nonsense words. *I'm going slightly mad.*

And along with the voices came the cold again. Now I envisaged ice crystals deep in my marrow, like a disease – a cancer. I couldn't imagine ever getting warm again, or what that felt like. A fact I'd read in an old SAS manual popped into my addled mind: survival is all about the threes. Three minutes for oxygen. Three days for water. Three weeks for food. *Food.* Now that the adrenalin had waned, I was starving, couldn't remember ever being so hungry. I started fantasising about my mum's lamb-neck stew. A Big Mac, fries, a Coke. KFC nuggets. I could almost taste them. Bizarrely, I began to crave a tuna and cheese toasted sandwich, something I don't remember ever eating. There was something nibbling at the edge of my mind, and then I got it – the Snickers bar! Of course. I frantically patted the rocky ground around me for my suit. It was caught on one of the bones, and my fingers brushed against it. The three men lying just feet from me, brown-boned and jumbled, wouldn't have gone through this. It was quicker for them, trapped in the confines of the Rat Run when the water surged in. Jesus. I didn't even know their names. I'd been planning on filming them and putting them on the Internet, and I hadn't even bothered to learn who they were. They'd saved us. If I hadn't stopped to film the bodies, then the water would have caught us out too. The dead had saved our lives.

Another nonsensical thought drifted in: *a skeleton walks into a pub and asks the barman for a pint and a mop*. I half-laughed, half-sobbed, and Ed tightened his grip on me again. This time I didn't resist. I was too cold. I relaxed back into him, barely shuddering at the grizzled feel of stubble and skin on my shoulder. I dragged the suit's slippery wetness onto my lap, located the Snickers bar in the inside pocket and unwrapped it. It was squashed and frozen, but that first explosion of sweetness on my tongue was sublime and comforting. I broke off a piece for Ed, turned, patted his face and slid it into his mouth as if we were lovers, as if, for a second, we were tuned to the same frequency. He grunted his thanks. I knew I should ration it, but we ate the lot in one go. I even licked the inside of the wrapper.

Ed moved away from me – the cold where the heat of his body had been felt like a slap – and then the flask was being pressed into my hand. The brandy burned, giving me the illusion of warmth for a few seconds. I handed it back.

I dozed. Woke. Dozed again. Now I was thirsty, the cheap booze drying out my mouth. Dozed again. It was easier. My bladder throbbed, but I ignored it, scared to move and let in the bone-crushing cold again.

Fingers in your heart, lad.

Seconds, minutes, hours later (who knows? I'd lost track of time – the bleakness and blackness swallowed it up), Ed disentangled himself, and there was a sudden flare of brightness that stung my eyes, making them water instantly, as he switched on his head torch. I turned to look at him; his eyes were black holes, his skin far too white. He shouted that he was going to check on the water level – and then he was gone. As his light disappeared, the chill in my core intensified. I was alone in the dark, deeply aware of the dead next to me.

How long did I wait for him to return? I don't know. It should only have taken him a few minutes to crawl to the edge of the tunnel. I counted to a hundred, thinking, *He's gone for help. He's gone to get help. That's it. Then why didn't he say so? Because he's a nutter. You can't trust him. You're on your own.*

He's left you and he's not coming back.

'Ed!'

The light returned, piercing my eyes again. But my relief at his reappearance was short-lived.

'Well? Is the water still rising?'

'It's still bad.'

'Fuck.'

'Will it get up here, Ed?'

He didn't seem to have heard me.

'Ed? Will we be okay?'

He was mumbling to himself, but I couldn't make out what he was saying. He shone the light around the space, and scrabbled through his discarded clothes. He turned to look at me and said something else I couldn't catch.

'What?'

'Where is it?'

'Where's what?'

'The flask.' He spat out the words.

'I don't know. I gave it back to you.'

'You're lying.'

Oh shit. He was really becoming agitated now. 'C'mon, Ed. Don't lose it again. Not now, please.'

Then he pounced, the helmet and head torch slamming into my shoulder. I fell back onto the bones, my hand catching on one of the skulls.

'Ed! I seriously don't need you to go all mental on me again!'

He paused, removed the helmet, and with one of his nasty grins, turned off the light.

The darkness was heavy with intent. 'Ed? I—'

Stars danced in my vision as something cracked against my head; blood and water roared in my ears as I curled myself into a ball, the bones digging into my flesh. Blow after blow landed on my back as he screamed something unintelligible at me. He wasn't going to stop; I'd have to fight back. I twisted onto my back, and lashed out with both legs, pistoning outwards, feeling them connect with softness – his gut? I didn't move for several seconds, using up all of my energy to gauge if Ed was going to come at me again. I sensed, rather than heard him moving away from me. The space around me felt empty.

Gingerly I shifted off the bone bed, damp stone once again cutting into my bruised naked skin, and curled into a ball. I was shaking. A ball of fear and misery lodged in my chest. I didn't dare move, ears straining for any sign that he was about to launch another attack on me. Everything ached. But I didn't have the energy for constant hyper-vigilance. Eventually I gave in to the exhaustion, and shut my eyes.

I slept. Woke. And knew immediately that something was different. The roar of the water had quietened. *Fingers in your heart, lad.* I uncurled my limbs.

'Ed?'

Had he left me again? I didn't know which was worse: the constant threat of him lashing out at me again, or being alone in the darkness.

I inched forward to where I estimated he must be, and reached out a hand. I touched something cold and unyielding and snatched it back. 'Ed?'

It took all of my resolve to reach out once more, my fingers grazing over furred, cold flesh. 'Ed?' And then I knew.

No, God, no, God, no, God. Light, get light. A frantic feel around for my helmet and the lamp attached to it. Fumble, fumble. Click, and then the bloom of light. Eyes streaming, I made myself look at him.

He was lying on his back, staring up at the ceiling. His lips were blue, his skin grey, his face muscles slack. He was empty. Gone. *Like Dad, he's like Dad.*

I gagged, tasted brandy-flavoured bile.

I doubled my fists and slammed them again and again into his chest, using the top of his scar as a reference point. I tipped his head back, opened his mouth – oh God, his jaw muscles were already stiffening – and breathed into him, his cold lips rubbery against mine. Gagged. Spat. Tried again.

Rubbing at my mouth to scour away the feel of him, I sat back on my heels. Over in their corner, the skulls grinned at me.

My bladder woke up again, painful and insistent. Unsure I'd have the strength to climb down onto the ledge and pee into the water, I knee-walked over to the far end and let rip. Gagging at the smell, I chucked stones and dirt over the greasy puddle.

Then I returned to Ed. There was nothing left to do. I covered his face with his fleece suit, and used the yellow exposure suit as a shroud for his body.

I turned my back to him, and buried my head in my knees once more.

Turn the light off.

No.

You have to.

I reached for the helmet, and with a huge effort of will, flicked the lamp's off switch. Darkness drew me in. I counted to five hundred, allowed myself ten seconds of light, then switched it off once more. I did this again and again, but the transition from light into blackness never became easier.

On my fourth light-to-dark changeover, the second the light died, I felt something dance across my thigh – a whisper of breath. I yipped and turned on the light, shone it around, pulse pounding.

Nothing.

Just your imagination.

But when I made myself turn it off once more, I felt it again. Stronger this time. The water whispered, my heart thundered, and my fingers shook as I groped for the on switch. How to describe it? I guess it was like playing the world's most terrifying game of grandmother's footsteps. Whenever I turned off the light, something seemed to shift in the air around me – as if the lads, or Ed (*Ed is dead*) were inching closer to me. It had to be my imagination playing tricks on me, but my traumatised mind was incapable of rationalisation: it felt so *real.* Too real. Once I even dragged the fleece suit away from Ed's face to double-check he wasn't fucking with me and pretending to be dead. I couldn't risk running out of battery power, being left in the dark with no hope of a break from it. I had no choice but to turn off the light.

But there were worse things than the dark. The next time the blackness crept over me, a slippery voice hissed: 'Fingers in your heart, lad.'

I screamed, fumbled for the light, a terror as visceral as the cold inhabiting my bones washing through me. Whatever I was sensing now felt dirty, poisonous, pitiless.

Fuck, fuck, fuck. Get out of here. Go.

Can't. I'll die.

You'll die anyway, lad. Fingers in your heart.

Stay or go, stay or go, the voices in the water were now whispering. But that was it. Why hadn't I noticed it before? They were whispering, not clamouring. Still poisoned by fear, I scrabbled out of the chamber, along the tunnel and peered down at the water below. The Rat Run's exit was still submerged, but I was certain the water level had dropped – I could see a slick tideline a foot above the stream on the rock opposite.

Ed said it would take an hour to get out. An hour. Only an hour. *Unless you get lost. You don't know where the hell you're going, do you?* I had two choices. Risk trying to get out, which could result in drowning or wandering around under the earth until the batteries in the head torch died, or I could stay in the cave with Ed and the dead and that creeping, unbearable presence and hope against hope for a rescue. I can't explain how profound the loneliness was at that second. I'd go through something akin to it in the next few months, but right then it was all-encompassing.

I'd felt something in that cavern. A malevolence that was telling me to get the hell out of there. *Pushing* at me, almost.

I made my decision. Returning to the mausoleum, and trying not to look at Ed's lumpen shape, I pulled on the achingly cold fleece suit, then the outer-layer and boots. My socks and underwear were still sodden so I didn't bother with them. Being clothed comforted me slightly, made me feel less vulnerable. The watery voices (the crowd) were chattering again, but now I couldn't tell if the sound was coming from the water or inside my head.

The camera had plenty of battery life left, but I hadn't checked to see if it was broken or not after its dousing. There was one last thing I had to do before I left. Frigid fingers switched it on – the light blinked red, so presumably it was okay – and turned it to face me. 'Hey. Um . . . This is Simon Newman and I'm in trouble. The guy I was with has died and I can't stay here. I have to get out. Fuck, I don't know what to say. Mum, I'm sorry I'm such a disappointment. I'm sorry I wasn't . . .' *wasn't what?* 'I'm sorry. You'll be the last person I'll be thinking of if I don't make it out.' *Christ.* No one gives you lessons on what to say in this situation. I tried to unclip the camera so that the last words might have a better chance of being found if I didn't make it, but my fingers were shaking too badly to remove it from its casing. I took Ed's helmet instead – the light was stronger in any case – and left mine where it was.

That feeling came again, the sense that something poisonous was on its way. I shone the light around, over Ed, over the bones. Something deep and primeval awoke inside me and shrieked at me to get moving. And I knew that I would rather drown than stay in that cave any longer.

I crawled along the tunnel, and then carefully stepped onto the ledge above the stream. A return through the Rat Run was out of the question, and I wouldn't be able to fight against the current before my strength gave out, so my plan was simple, albeit potentially deadly: let the water guide me out.

I stared down at the frothing mass below me. Subjecting myself to another freezing dousing was the first obstacle. Once in, I'd need to wedge myself against the walls to stop from being swept away.

Do it. Don't think about it. Do it.

I did it. No mental preparation could have protected me against the shock of the water's icy embrace, a chest-high ice bath that ripped the breath out of my lungs. The current wasn't as insistent as it had been, but it still shoved against my back, the suit helping to keep me buoyant. Keeping one hand on the wall next to me, I bobbed along, the water streaming around me.

This isn't too bad.

The relief at being out of the orbit of whatever was in that cave was enough to keep me calm at first. Then it began to dawn that the top of the channel, once a roomy body's height above me – was gradually funnelling lower. I arced the light upwards. *Oh shit, oh fuck.* In less than fifty feet I would have no more than a foot of breathing space. The walls either side of the stream were sheer – there were no more outcroppings like the one that led up to the death chamber.

Go back!

I couldn't – I didn't have enough strength to fight against the current, and whenever I tried to arrest my progress, the force of it threatened to tip me off balance. My only hope was that the roof would lift again before the space ran out. I rolled onto my back, let myself bob along head-first, and pressed my hands against the channel's roof to slow my progress. The suit doing its bit to keep me afloat, I stared at the rocky waves above me, praying that they wouldn't drop any further.

My prayers went unanswered.

Within minutes, I had barely five centimetres between the tip of my nose and the roof, and I was in danger of inhaling the water that lapped around my cheeks. Palms flat on the stone above me, I reached behind, using my fingers as eyes, desperately seeking an air pocket up ahead. They touched only stone. A second later my helmet thunked into rock. *Oh God, oh no.* No more air. I'd have to duck down under the bulge, pray that the ceiling opened up again further on.

I couldn't do it. I couldn't. The current prodded at me, but I was able to hold my position. I tried to edge myself back along the tunnel, sodden fingers tearing into the rough ceiling – I'd left the gloves behind in the cave and my softened nails were ripped to the quick – but the water's strength was unyielding and swept me back against the rock bulge.

This was it. This was it. Death. A tsunami of terror, and then, suddenly, with no build-up, a pure sense of calm came over me. It was as if I'd moved beyond fear and exhaustion, and into a realm where I literally didn't give a shit. No, it went beyond even that. It was almost a state of grace. A tranquil, beatific feeling.

I counted to three, took a deep breath, and pushed myself under, my fingertip eyes guiding me along. The bulge ended and I floated up, back into an air pocket, utterly serene. I kept going, and when I reached another air-stealing lump, I once more drifted under it. I liked this new me. This panic-free, blasé Simon Newman, pulling himself through a watery tunnel, using his fingers for eyes. My mind latched onto this, turning it into a soothing mantra: *Fingers for eyes, fingers in your heart, fingers for eyes, fingers in your heart.*

How long did this go on for? No idea. I looked up after one of my underwater sorties and realised that the ceiling was more than a metre above me, and the current was no more than a gentle prod. I should have been euphoric at this, but I was still in the grip of that curious calm. I flailed my body around until I was facing forward again. My head torch danced over the sloping face to my right, and I made out a suitcase-sized opening midway up it, the rocks around it worn smooth.

A way out?

My gut said it was worth a shot.

I almost slid back into the water on my first attempt up the face – the liquid sloshing around in the inside of the suit unbalanced me – but the New-and-Improved Simon urged me to take my time. I unzipped the suit and watched dispassionately as water cascaded out of it. Then I got going. The conduit I was in could lead somewhere, it could lead nowhere, it could suck me into the bowels of the earth never to return – did I care? Did I *fuck*.

The tunnel seemed to switch back on itself, then tapered into a crawl space. Even doing another arduous fingertip-and-toe shuffle wasn't a big deal. A slippery climb up a boulder stack led to a casual scramble through a rock formation that was as intricately ribbed as an HR Giger sketch. At the end of this, there were two possible channels to take, one steeper than the other.

Which way, Ed, you fucker? Blithely, I chose the left, the steeper of the two.

A long hands-and-knees slog followed, but I was confident I was going in the right direction – don't ask me why. I was dimly aware of a chattering in my head – my teeth again.

It was then that the head torch dimmed. I froze, momentarily snapped out of that laissez-faire state. Then it flared again. I got moving with more urgency. Now that I'd left the water behind, each warren I chose took me higher up. I blindly posted my body through cracks, and belly-squirmed along low shafts. I was moving simply by instinct.

I ended up in a sloping, U-shaped chamber, the floor littered with stones. But this time, there were no obvious exits. I lurched up and down the scree slopes like a ball-bearing in a salad bowl, looking for a way out, convinced the light was going to die at any moment.

Drawing on the vestiges of that strange calm, I shut down the growing panic, and slowly swept the light over the lumps and bumps in the rock walls, not easy as the cold had its teeth into me now and I was shaking violently. Then I saw it: a crack, just large enough for a body to squeeze through. A climb through the guts of another of those boulder chokes and then I was looking up and into a pipe, my numb brain registering that it was concrete – manmade. Someone had built it into the rock – it had to be the way out. It was smooth, and there were no handholds cut into it, but I could chimney up it, or I could if I had any strength. *C'mon, c'mon, c'mon.* I squirmed up into it, leaned back and propped my feet against the other side. I'd done the back and foot manoeuvre more times than I could count; it was one of the first things Kenton had taught us. I took my time, but my body wasn't willing, and I made slow progress. Then I spied the raggedy stem of a rope a couple of feet above me. I lunged for it, but my hands were bloody blocks of wood, and I couldn't reach it. My thigh muscles were now jitterbugging at the strain of keeping me from plummeting back down the pipe. I wouldn't be able to hold the position for much longer. It was almost funny. I'd be trapped forever, lodged in a chimney like a hypothermic Father Christmas.

And then, the light died. It was the last straw. I laughed – I actually laughed. What else was there to do? Eventually my legs would give in and I'd fall back onto the rocks beneath. Maybe I'd survive. Maybe I wouldn't. I was cool with that. Copacetic.

Again, I have no clue how long I stayed wedged there. I must have dozed off, because the next thing I remembered was the sound of muffled voices.

It's just the water.

A small, rational part of my battered mind woke up. *There is no water here. You left the water behind, remember?*

Speak.

I'm here. 'I'm here!' The cold had tightened its fist around my damaged vocal cords, and I barely made a peep. I tried again. 'I'm here!'

Light blazed down on me, the shock of it almost causing me to lose my balance, and a line from an old movie came to me: *Go towards the light, Simon.* Hope gave me the strength to move again, and I pushed with my legs, lunged for the rope, caught it, its rough surface abrading my tender hands, which were black with dried blood, and hauled myself further up the pipe. The voices came again, and I knew for sure they weren't the voices of the water, with their slippery madness, but real, human voices.

And then I was being dragged towards the light.

I'll never forget that first hit of outside air – it smelled foul, like inhaling sewerage, a huge contrast to the purity of what I'd been breathing below in the caves – but my memories of what happened immediately after I was hauled out of the pipe are fuzzy-edged. I was vaguely aware that it was dark outside, although the halogen lights set up around the exit hole had given me the illusion of daylight at first. People were shouting over the distant grumble of a generator, and figures rushed towards me, encircling me, their faces shadowy blurs. I know I fell to my knees, feeling a flush of warmth as someone thrust a tin mug of hot tea into my hand. I looked down at it – I couldn't hold it steady, and most of it slopped onto the grass. Someone else wrapped me in one of those rustling silver blankets.

Voices bombarded me with questions: 'Is there anyone else down there? How many? You're okay, mate. You're safe now. How many down there?'

'Give him space.' A thin-faced man sank to his haunches in front of me. His forehead and cheeks were smeared with mud. 'Come on, mate,' he said in a thick Black Country accent. 'Is there anyone else down there?'

I sipped the tea – oh God, it was warm and sweet and wonderful – then gulped the rest. I forced myself to speak. 'Yes. One. Ed. He's dead though. He's dead he's in the cave with the dead boys he's dead.'

'This is important, lad. Take it slowly now. You certain he didn't make it?'

I nodded. And then I couldn't seem to stop bobbing my head up and down. 'Sure.'

'How did he die?'

I killed him when I lashed out at him.

No you didn't. He moved away from you, remember? 'Heart attack, I think.' I burbled out a near-incoherent account of my half-arsed attempts at CPR.

The fellow clapped me on the shoulder. 'Okay, mate.' Drizzle drifted down, feeling almost warm after the frigidity of the water down there. The man with the Black Country accent – who I later learned was a caver named Keith, one of the men who'd hauled me out of there – stared up at the sky. 'Got out just in time. They've been damming the stream up top on the other side. If the rain picks up . . .' He didn't need to say any more. 'Come on. Let's get you out of here.'

It took Keith and his burly helper two tries to get me to my feet. Then followed a slow stumble across a field and down to where a cluster of 4X4s were parked. I was helped like an invalid into the back of a Land Rover that stank of rubber. 'Get him down to the lane, Mike,' Keith said. Then he disappeared into the rainy night.

The Land Rover lumped its way across another couple of fields, through a quagmire of tyre-churned mud, and across to where an ambulance was waiting. I was shaking violently again, the tea sloshing in my stomach, and I had to be half-carried out of the vehicle.

Headlights blinded me, more dark figures rushed towards me, more questions were fired at me: 'Are you Simon Newman?' 'How did you get out of there?' 'How are you feeling?' Lights – camera lights, I learned later – were flashing and popping, and someone yelled, 'Leave him alone!' And then: 'Si!' The crowd parted and Thierry was waddling towards me, anorak zipped up to his neck, water spots on his glasses.

'Thierry?' I couldn't quite allow myself to believe it was really him.

'Dude! Jesus, Si. You look terrible.'

I opened my mouth to say something, and then jagged, raw sobs exploded out of my chest. I couldn't stop them. I hadn't cried since I was ten, when Dad had his stroke, and Mum came to school to pick me and my sister Alison up from school. The memory of the three of us heading to the hospital on the bus is crystal clear: the winter rain outside, the condensation on the windows, Mum and Alison on the seat behind me holding hands, me sobbing silently all the way there, feeling as if a chasm had opened up where my heart should be.

Thierry sat next to me in the ambulance while I howled, tapping my shoulder and saying 'dude, dude, dude', over and over again, while a paramedic – a meaty guy who took the spectacle of me crying like a two-year-old in his stride – wrapped a blood pressure cuff around my arm and dabbed at my lacerated hands. The crying jag had emptied me out, as if I'd dislodged a stone in my throat.

Thierry told me later that seeing me so broken had shocked him to the core. He'd always considered me as tough, able to handle anything – it was how I saw myself – and he hadn't known how to deal with it. And it was only later that I learned that he'd come through for me, raised the alarm and insisted on a search party when I hadn't returned any of his calls or made it home by two a.m. He'd stayed up, desperate for news, finally borrowing a car from Cosimo, and driving to Wales. I'd been down Cwm Pot for almost thirty-six hours, escaping at around seven p.m. Most of what I pieced together came from the news reports Thierry saved for me. There was a shot of me huddled in the ambulance in the *Daily Mail*, my face a muddy blob, editorials on dangerous sports and health-and-safety issues, sound bites from the rescuers. I had no idea of it at the time, but the scale of the operation had been huge, most of it centred around the entrance, and a desperate attempt to dam the swollen stream. When I'd found my way to the exit, a recce from that side had only just been organised. Cavers and mountain rescue teams had flocked to Cwm Pot from all over the UK, rushing there in the middle of the night, working round the clock in shifts.

The rain continued to fall unabated for three days. It would be a week before it was safe for anyone to reach the mausoleum safely. If I hadn't felt that malevolent push, that overwhelming sense that I had to get out of there, it's doubtful I would have survived. The cold would have killed me, or I would have been forced to do unspeakable things to stay alive.

I don't remember being ferried to hospital, but apparently I was out for a good twenty-four hours. I was treated for hypothermia and dehydration, and my skin became a hyena-spotted pelt as multicoloured bruises bloomed all over my body.

When I was discharged, Thierry drove me home like a new husband ferrying a heavily pregnant wife. Even now, after all that's happened between us, I'll never forget how good he was to me then. On paper our friendship shouldn't have worked. I was a tearaway who'd grown up in a tiny West Midlands flat, destined to minimum-wage my way through life; he came from a family of over-achievers where failure wasn't an option – his WASP dad was an entertainment lawyer, his French-Mauritian mum an obstetrician – and after a trust-fund childhood spent in LA, he'd scored a place at MIT. He'd toed the line until his sophomore year, when he fell in love with a British girl he met online. Ignoring his parents' threats to cut him off, he dropped out, and travelled to London. His parents made good on their threat, and when his relationship imploded, leaving his heart smashed, he was too proud to return home and admit his folks were right. I suppose we bonded over the fact that both of us were untethered, broke and broken. I helped get him laid, he helped top up my intellect, getting me into Alan Moore and Terry Pratchett. Calling me 'dude' all the time had started as a joke, after I took the piss out of his faux surfer dialect, which was at odds with his nerdish exterior. I know now that his desperation to make the website a success was fuelled by a burning need to prove himself to his parents. It overrode everything else.

I was careful with myself for a while, aware that my mental carapace had been ripped away, leaving a tender endoskeleton that would bruise easily. On more than one occasion I almost told Thierry what I'd felt down there – the sense that something was pushing me out of the cave – but I didn't have a clue how to articulate it without sounding like I'd gone mental. Besides, I didn't want to pick over it in case I ripped off a scab that wouldn't heal. Instead I slept a lot, craved cigarettes, although I've never been much of a smoker, and binged on instant gratification food – McDonalds, Burger King, chicken madras – I couldn't get enough. I stayed away from booze and dope, scared that intoxication might smash through the denial I was building around the events. I didn't have nightmares in those first few days, but every time I lay down and closed my eyes, the gush of water whispered in my ears.

Thierry was out when the police came to the flat to collect another statement from me. They travelled up from Wales, two rotund fellows with identical side partings and egg-sandwich breath. I made them coffee that they didn't drink and tried not to shake as they informed me that the water had subsided enough for a caving team to safely reach Ed's body. My gut producing pints of acid, I listened as they told me the police surgeon who'd accompanied the team had confirmed that it was 'more than likely' that Ed had died of natural causes. Inside, I deflated with relief.

'How did you get hold of this man?' the older of the two asked.

'A caving forum. He'd written a few short posts mentioning that he'd sneaked into the Cwm Pot caves, saying that it wasn't right they were closed to cavers. I joined the forum, sent him a message asking if he'd be willing to guide me through them, gave him my email address and that was it.'

'You never met him previous to the incident?'

'No. And we only emailed back and forth a couple of times. Basically all he said was that he'd guide me down there for three hundred quid, and he'd supply the equipment. He sent directions and a time and place to meet and that was it.'

'You didn't know anything else about him?'

'Nothing except for what he'd written on the forums. I shouldn't have gone down there with him. I know that now.'

I could see on their faces how stupid they thought I'd been. After all, what sort of pillock heads down a notoriously dangerous caving network with a complete stranger? I thought back to the flash of insight I'd had about myself down there; decided it was best to lock that in the mental vault along with the rest of the shit.

'How did he seem to you when you were down there with him?'

'Seem?'

'His state of mind.'

'A bit all over the place. He seemed paranoid or something.'

'Did you have an altercation?'

'Yeah.'

'That became violent?'

I couldn't swallow. 'Not violent exactly.'

Simon Newman, we are arresting you for the murder of . . .

'Well Mr Newman, you should prepare yourself for something of a shock.'

I was suddenly convinced they were going to say, we lied to you about Ed, Mr Newman, *he's aliiiive.*

But no. They were going to tell me that Ed was a monster.

Edward James Ferry. Fifty-nine. He had been in the army; he hadn't lied about that, although he wasn't on active duty, but a lackey in the catering corps. No family, no dependants. A history of violence, alcohol abuse and heart disease – the most likely cause of death. He'd been a member of several caving clubs over the years, all of which had kicked him out for 'erratic behaviour'. And then this: he was discharged from the army after accusations that he'd attempted to abduct a ten-year-old girl when he was based in Germany.

I listened to this, my pulse beating sickly.

He'd saved my life. He was a monster.

For now, Ed's body would stay in Cwm Pot's watery depths, interred with the three lads from Warwick University. I felt sorry for them: they hadn't asked for a roommate.

No charges would be laid against me for trespassing or wasting police time, although the cops made it clear that I'd better consider my spelunking days to be over. They said they'd let me know if the coroner were to request my presence at an inquest, then I dictated a statement, signed it, and that was that. I thought I was done with Ed.

He wasn't done with me.

Eventually, I had no choice but to go back to work. I'd been dreading it, but there was something reassuringly normal about the warm gust of coffee that greeted me when I walked into the store. Even the annoying décor – the walls cluttered with photos of multiracial couples gurning at lattes, and maniacally happy

Colombians running their fingers through coffee beans – was comforting in its familiarity. The shop's statement: *Coffee is our Mission. Ethics is our Promise* made no real sense, but the punters seemed to like it, probably because it made them feel less guilty than going to Starbucks, and there was rarely a lull in business. My stint at Mission:Coffee was only supposed to be a filler job until something better came along or the website took off, but it was convenient – a twenty-minute walk from the squalid flat I shared with Thierry in Whitechapel.

Thierry had filled the staff in on all the gory details, and on my first day back I was treated like a minor celebrity. Even Cosimo, the mercurial manager with the Tony Soprano tics, reined in his usual mafia-like management style and was fairly pleasant. But eventually things started to nudge their way back to normality.

It didn't last long.

I was on shift when Thierry burst into the store, shoving his way to the front of the queue. 'Dude! They've sent the camera back! I've got the footage!'

I stared at him stupidly. 'Huh?'

'I've got the camera back. The head-cam.'

'But I left it down in the cave.' *With Ed. And the others.*

The suit I was serving harrumphed. The other people in the queue were happily eavesdropping.

'Listen, Si, you mind if I see what's on it?'

The floor dipped, a needle-sharp pain lanced the back of my skull, and then for an instant I was back in the watery tunnel, eyes looking up at stone, feeling that malevolent *push* again. Nausea blossomed, my chest closed in. Then Thierry's voice floated tinnily into my consciousness. 'You okay, dude?'

I didn't want to hear any more. Couldn't. 'Later, Thierry, okay?'

'Sorry, Si. Shouldn't have said anything, not while you're at work. Only, it's just . . . do you mind if I see if there's anything worth using?' Eyes bright, almost feverish. I'd never seen him like this before.

The cloying stink of sugar syrup and coffee wasn't helping with the nausea. I swallowed. 'Do what you want.' I sucked in a breath, and my stomach settled.

'Thanks, Si.' And then he was gone.

With a monumental effort I turned my attention back to the irritated banker-type I'd been serving when Thierry interrupted us.

I clicked over to automatic pilot for the rest of the day: *steam, hiss, double macchiato. You want cream with that? Have a great day. You're welcome, coffee is our mission. Steam, hiss, scoop, bang bang.* The faces of tourists, distracted workers, business types, lonely elderly men and women, ebbed and flowed. I don't know how I got through it.

I stayed way past my shift, helping Cosimo cash up and close, reluctant to return home. Why did I say that Thierry could look at the footage? A large part of me prayed that the camera had been damaged. Just the thought of watching anything I'd managed to capture down there made my gut corkscrew.

It was coming up to Christmas in the city, usually one of my favourite times of the year – I'm a sucker for the lights and cheesiness, the barely controlled hysteria and excitement of the Christmas rush – but I might as well have been walking to the gallows. Getting wasted was suddenly attractive again, but thanks to Ed, I didn't even have enough for a pint.

When I got home, Thierry was at the desk in our tiny lounge-cum-kitchen, earphones on, fingers skittering over his keyboard. I didn't dare glance at the monitor; I didn't want to know. The room stank of dope and its usual dirty-socks fug.

Thierry was so absorbed that I had to shout to grab his attention.

He jumped and spun round in his chair. 'Oh hey, Si. You gotta see this. It's fucking hectic, dude.'

A stone formed in my gut. 'It wasn't ruined?'

He shook his head.

'How did you even get it? Who sent it?' This should have been my first question when he bustled into the coffee shop, only I was too busy having a panic attack to articulate it.

'Don't get mad, but you know when I wrote to those guys who pulled you out of the caves to thank them? Well, I kinda mentioned it to them. Said that if they happened to find it we'd appreciate getting it back, and one of them was with the team that went down there with the cops, so . . .'

And there it was, the camera itself, sitting next to the ashtray on the desk. I didn't feel much of anything looking at it. It looked fine. It looked as if it had got off lighter than I had.

'Won't the cops want to see it?'

A shrug. 'Maybe. Listen, Si. Some of the stuff on here . . . It's really dark, man. You want me to run it for you? Quality's crap, but it's useable.'

'No.'

'You sure? There's like . . . you left a message at the end.'

'Yeah. I told you about that. I thought I was going to *die*, Thierry.'

'Dude. I really think you should see it. That guy you were with—'

'Ed. His name was Ed.' *Ed. Ed is dead.*

'Yeah, him. Well—'

'I don't want to see it, Thierry. I don't want to hear about it. I'm serious.'

'Dude. I think this could be big. It scared the shit out of me.'

'I know. I was there.'

A pause. 'Oh yeah. Forgot. They sent something else.' He dug in a padded envelope at his feet. 'This isn't yours, is it, Si?'

He was holding the flask. Ed's flask. A whooshing in my ears; my stomach flipped. 'No.'

'It belonged to the dead guy?'

'Yeah.' I couldn't look at it. 'Can you put it away?'

'Sure.' He slid it in a drawer and I was able to breathe again.

'Look. Dude. The footage. I'd really like to use it.'

'No way, Thierry.'

'C'mon, dude. Why not?' He was sweating. Desperate.

'Are you serious, Thierry? *Why not*? I thought I was the insensitive one.'

'I'm sorry, dude. I know I'm coming on strong here. And I know you went through hell down there, but surely you should get something out of it? C'mon, when have I ever asked you for anything? Seriously, my gut is telling me this could be big. You know how hard I've worked to get the site off the ground.'

Emotional blackmail wasn't usually his style. But he had a point. He did the majority of the back-end stuff for the site, as well as posting the daily listicles, replying to comments and sparring with trolls and doxers. He also tirelessly pimped us out to other online sites and blogs. Letting him use the footage was really the least I could do. And if I didn't actually watch it, what was the harm? My eyes kept straying to the drawer containing the poisonous flask. I wanted to grab it and throw it out of the window.

'Okay. But you can't use anything with Ed on it. I promised him I wouldn't film him.'

'Okay. But I can use the other stuff?'

'Fine.'

He jumped up, almost strangling himself with his headphone wires, and threw his arms around me. He reeked of dope and nervous sweat. 'Dude, you're a legend.'

'Whatever, Thierry. Listen, I need to lie down.'

'You feeling shit again?'

'Just knackered.'

'Cool.' His eyes were already straying back to the screen. 'Listen, I'll let you know when I'm done.'

'Don't worry. Do what you want with it.'

'Sure you don't want to see it first?'

'I'm sure, Thierry.'

'It's like, the light down there did some freaky shit. There's a bit where—'

'I don't want to see it, okay?' I almost lost control, lashed out at him. 'Sorry. Just keep it to yourself, okay?'

Occasionally I find myself wondering what would have happened if I *had* looked at the unedited footage then. Would things have been different? Maybe, maybe not. But desperation aside, there was something off about the way Thierry was looking at me, and I should have paid that more heed.

That night, the second I lay on the bed and shut my eyes, my ears once again rang with the ghostly voices, the gush of the water. Then, my voice came smoking into the room: 'You'll be the last person I'll be thinking of if I don't make it out.' It shouldn't have been that distinct – the crash of the water in the background should have muffled it. Just my mind playing tricks – it had to be. Thierry was a competent editor, but he wasn't that good.

I grabbed Thierry's iPod, and crept beneath the duvet. I lay there numbly, playing 'Ace of Spades' by Motörhead on repeat.

I opened my eyes, blinked, but couldn't see anything but blackness. I was on my side, curled into a foetal ball, something digging into my thigh. I shivered. I was cold, naked, assumed at first I'd kicked the duvet off, turned out the lights without remembering I'd done so. I shifted position, patted the area around me, but instead of the comfort of sheets my hands touched a rough surface, then slid over what I knew were slippery, mildewed bones, *nuh-huh, no no no no.* With a sickening rush of terror and certainty, I knew that my escape had all been a fantasy. I was still down there. I was still down there, in the cave, with Ed. Then it came: cold flesh, furred with hair, snaking around my chest, squeezing and rubbing. Next, a drumming in my ears: *Fingers in your heart, lad. Fingers in your heart. You're coming with me.*

Body paralysed, my bladder let go, the gush of hot fluid hurling me out of the cave and back into my room. The blackness was replaced with faint light; the chatter of water became the patter of Thierry's fingers on his keyboard. My heart wouldn't slow, breath squeaked in through my closed throat. I didn't dare move in case I was dragged back down there. And I didn't move, not until the urine-soaked sheets turned cold.

Tentatively, I touched my sides, half expecting to feel Ed's flesh still there. *Sit up. Turn around.*

Nothing. Of course there was nothing.

Careful not to let Thierry hear me, I ripped the sheets off the bed and bundled them into a ball. I chucked them in the corner of the room and piled dirty laundry on top of them. The terror ebbed away like a slow poison.

I crawled back into bed and plugged in the earphones again. Thierry was now playing Lux Aeterna, which he'd nicked off the soundtrack to *Requiem for a Dream*, over and over again. He used it as a backing track every chance he got, and it didn't help with the dread that had taken root in my gut. I didn't dare drop off again. I sat up all night, waiting to be dragged back into the cave again.

I knew from listening to him all night that Thierry had worked right through, but he bounced into my room at seven thirty as if he'd had a good eight hours of sleep.

'I've done it, Si. Uploaded it.'

I managed a grunt. It was impossible to feel worse than I did already.

We were both on shift that morning. I was groggy and grumpy from lack of sleep and still reeling from the too-real cave flash-back. Fuelled by the power of caffeine, and on a high after his night's work, Thierry was as chipper as always. When Cosimo nipped out for a fag break, Thierry sneaked into his office to check on the clip's progress. He walked back to the counter looking dazed: 'Dude. *Dude*. DUDE. You're not going to believe it. Thirty thousand views. Thirty fucking *thousand*. And you should see the comments. People are going nuts for it.'

'Seriously?'

'Yup.'

He grabbed my arms and spun me around. 'I told you, Si. I fucking *told* you!'

The implications of this could be huge for us, and Thierry's excitement was contagious. I pushed away the residual horror and shame of last night's bed-wetting episode and convinced myself to go along for the ride. This was big. It could be our break, and in the days before YouTube and Twitter became ubiquitous, the fact it had gone viral so speedily was a major coup.

The hits racked up. We thought they would peter out, but it

was cross-referenced and shared on countless blogs, and made it to 4Chan where boards sprang up discussing whether it was faked or not. The next few days were heady, exciting, and the aftershocks of what I'd been through dribbled away. I still hadn't watched the edited footage, entitled (as I knew it would be) 'The Real-Life Caves of Death', but Thierry and I took it in turns reading the comments. Our subscriber numbers had shot up, and we were pulling in thousands of unique hits a week. The pressure to come up with another gut-puncher of a stunt for the site was building; Thierry was still writing the listicles, but we needed to capitalise on our success.

Then, on Christmas Eve, this appeared on the site in the comments section:

> My husband and I request that you take down this video. It is disrespectful to the dead. My son Nigel was one of the boys who died that day in Cwm Pot. It sickens me to see that you are displaying his body and those of his friends without a care for the hurt it may cause. Please take this video down at once.

'Shit.' Shame slimed through me. I'd spent thirty-six hours with this woman's son and the remains of his friends, and I still hadn't bothered to learn their names. 'We'd better take it down, T.'

I expected Thierry to agree with me. I'd always considered him to be alive to the feelings of others, unselfish, a softy. Unlike me, I suppose. Sure, I'd been taken aback by how desperate he was to upload the footage, but his instincts about it had been right on the money. Instead he snorted and looked at me as if I'd lost my mind. 'No way, dude. It's still pulling in traffic. We'd be mad to take it down now. We're so close to getting advertisers on board.'

'It's not right though, Thierry. Imagine if that was your kid.'

'Are you kidding me, Si? Since when have you turned into Mother Theresa?'

Since when have you turned into a heartless bastard? 'That could have been me down there, T.' And another thought: *maybe it is me down there*. That slippage I'd felt on the night Thierry edited the footage was still fresh in my mind. *I'm a dead man dreaming he's alive*. But that was simply the result of watching too many movies. I wasn't living in *Jacob's Ladder*. Here's where I should say: *the reality of my situation would end up being far worse than any scriptwriter could dream up . . .*

'It wasn't you though, was it, Si? We've earned this, dude. *You* earned this. Don't you see how close we are to getting what we want?' There was a fanatical gleam in his eye: Thierry was more like his ambitious parents than he knew, fuelled by the burning desire to succeed.

Hating myself, I let it go. We scrolled through the comments below it in tense silence:

Sorry for yr loss lady

They shouldn't of been down there in the 1st place

Do a dangerous sport that's what you get

No but it is disrespectful

Yr all idiots as its obviously fake

So gross like have u guys seen the pictures of the people that die on the mountains there's one of this guy I think it's in like south America or something and hes coming up out of the ice and he's wearing a suit and they think he was a drug dealer or something and he fel out of a plain

What are you on, *man?*

Its true you should check it out

And then this: *seeing as the guy who made this film likes dead people so much he shuld go to Everest as its the highest graveyard in the world. There are dead bodies everywhere up there*

Thierry was watching me.

'What?'

'*Dude*. You *should* go to Everest.'

'Don't be daft, Thierry.'

'I'm serious, Si. Think about it. It makes sense. You've been way deep underground, and got some awesome stuff. Now you should go up to the highest point on earth and do the same. It would be great for the site. I know it sounds crazy, but think about it.'

'I've thought about it. You've lost your mind.'

'Give me one reason why not.'

'Christ. Okay, I'll give you a shed load of reasons why not, T. One, it costs thousands of pounds to get there, thousands of pounds that we don't have; two, it's as dangerous as a bastard; three, I don't have the skills – I've never been at really high altitude.'

Thierry flapped a dismissive hand at all of these. 'But isn't it one of your dreams, Si? What climber doesn't want to conquer, like, the highest mountain in the world?'

'I'm not a climber any more, Thierry, in case you haven't noticed.' I thought back to my painful self-assessment in Cwm Pot. 'I honestly don't have the skills.'

The desperation I'd seen in him after he'd viewed the caving footage for the first time was back. 'You don't have to get to the top. Just bring us back some good stuff like with the caves.'

'You basically want me to almost die while filming some dead bodies on a mountain.'

'You got it.'

'You're a sicko, Thierry.'

'Yeah, yeah. If I can get the cash together, will you go?'

Everest. Frozen turds and fractured egos was how I pictured it. I vaguely recalled reading an article years ago about the impossibility of repatriating the bodies of climbers who died on the high peaks. *You can't take a body out when it's this deep underground, lad.* Thierry was right about the warped symmetry. 'Sure. Why not?' He'd never get the cash together; we barely had enough for the rent. And agreeing to his insane plan would shut him up.

Big mistake.

PART TWO

Juliet

I know now that there's no chance I'll fall into the trance-like state that usually comes after several hours of hard going. Instead I concentrate on the creak, chink, creak of my crampons biting into snow, the musical jangle of my harness, the huff of my breath. We've crossed the South Col, and I estimate we must be nearing the flat area before the Balcony, where the climbing will become mixed. From there, I will lead out. It's an unusually clear night, so clear that the stars reflect on the snow, something I would find beautiful if I could erase my worries about Walter. He's moving with more care and concentration than usual. Then he stumbles, goes down on his knees. He turns, taps his oxygen mask. I nod, miming that I will check his regulator. It's clogged with rime, and it's difficult to clear it with the bulky over-mitts. I don't remove them, won't, not even for a second. There's nothing I fear more than frostbite. I take my time, working in the underwater light cast by my headlamp, pulse thudding in my ears as I bend my head to focus. Walter nods wearily, a sign that the gas is flowing again. I make sure the canister is secure in its place in his pack and we continue. Occasionally my light catches on the rope this season's commercial expeditions have fixed along the route. We won't touch it.

Step, step. Crunch, creak. My breathing is steady; my lungs ache, but this I can handle.

~~And that's when I feel it: a sense that someone is behind me. At first I check that I haven't inadvertently overtaken Walter. I haven't. Of course I haven't. The dark lump of his body hulks up ahead of me. I stop, make sure my feet are firmly planted, and turn, my hood and balaclava obstructing my peripheral~~

~~vision. Far, far below me, pinprick lights move upwards like sluggish fireflies. Another team, probably the Enviro Group, is making its way up the col, but the climbers are too far below me to be the cause of the disconcerting sense that I'm being watched. Whatever it is feels as if it's lurking just over my shoulder. I turn again. Nothing. Hypoxia is always a fear for me as I don't use gas, but I can't detect any other worrying symptoms that I'm succumbing to AMS or oedema: my coordination isn't compromised; my thought processes aren't muddied.~~

~~It's not me I should be worrying about.~~

Something's wrong. I can no longer see Walter ahead of me. I miss a breath, feel the burn in my lungs as I fight to draw in enough air. He's lying on his side, his knees bent, his oxygen mask skew. I pothole my way towards him, fall to my knees next to him, recoiling at the liquid edge to his breathing. Fluid in his lungs. Pulmonary oedema. He's been trying to hide a cough from me since we left base camp; it's why he chose to use gas – unusual for him. I should have fought harder at Camp III to make him return to lower altitude, but he insisted we take advantage of the weather window to summit. And I wanted to believe he was fine. I let myself believe it. We both know how important this climb is for my career. In the eyes of the public and the sponsors you're chopped liver unless you've 'conquered' Everest and K2. It's as if our other, far more challenging achievements mean nothing to anyone but a tiny elite.

I try to position the oxygen mask back over his mouth. He slaps wildly at my hand.

'No, Walter.'

I try again, and he bats me away again.

I don't panic. Not yet. I don't give up until I manage to get him to take a few breaths of oxygen.

The light is coming now, its lavender glow gradually revealing the exposure falling away below us. I have to get him down the mountain, and quickly. It's his only chance. Yet still I don't panic. Walter is invincible. We've dodged death countless times. 'Come on, Walter. Up, up, up.'

He rips the mask off his face. 'Don't,' he gasps. 'Don't, Julie.' He tears the protective goggles from his eyes. I've never seen him truly scared, not even when we heard the first crump-thud of the avalanche that should have killed us on Broad Peak, but now his eyes are wide, his mouth slack. He's looking past me, at something above my shoulder. He groans and curls into himself. I beat at his body, the exertion turning my chest into a fireball.

I collapse in on myself then. I feel like I'm falling, falling. Because I know, deep inside, that he isn't going to get up again and—

DAY 1, Everest Base Camp, Tibet

Forgotten how fantastically unsubtle the sunset can be in the Himalayas. Sat outside my tent this evening, watching as the light on the North Ridge turned from golden, to blue, and then black as if it was under the control of a literal-minded celestial light designer. For an instant the wind ceased, and I could finally hear myself think.

Still find it strange that we were able to drive straight into base camp. Should be relieved we didn't have to hike in, but can't forget that the Rongbuk Base Camp Road is another example of the Chinese regime's systematic plan to colonise, control and access every inch of Tibet – not even Everest's flanks are safe from its stranglehold. And the atmosphere on this side of the mountain feels darker than it did last year on the south, although this could just be a reflection of my mood. After spending 2 days in Kathmandu and 4 in Lhasa and Tingri with the other climbers sharing the permit, I'm still on the outside, looking in. Can't blame them. I'm the one who's being mardy. *Cheer up, Juliet pet, you've got a face like a smacked arse.* My hackles are always up these days, and after the vicious interpersonal conflicts Walter and I witnessed 2 years ago when we were in the Karakoram, I'm wary of letting my guard down and getting sucked into group dynamics. The plummeting temperatures chased them all back into their tents after a hasty supper, and they haven't emerged since.

They are:

Andrej and Sem Danielsen, Norwegian, brothers, tall, spectacled, look like twins, often find them looking at me curiously as if I'm an alien species. They've done the Vinson Massif and Aconcagua.

Lewis Day, American high-altitude climber/skier. Laid back, long hair, young, personable. Climbed McKinley twice. First time in the Himalaya.

Tom Baskin-Heath, a fellow Brit. Reeks of old money. Says he's climbed Kilimanjaro and plans on doing the Seven Summits, which he mentions at every opportunity. The first thing he said to me was: 'Good God, are you *the* Juliet Michaels?' Taken aback, I was short with him and he now treats me with exaggerated politeness. He must have read all the bad press about me (but does he believe it???). Reminds me a little of Graham, has a similar Eton drawl and casual elegance, but I mustn't project. Graham says I'm an inverted snob, and I am, it's true.

Wade Thorpe, American, affable. Some sort of investment consultant. Spends his summers crawling over Mount Rainier, but has little high-altitude experience. Says climbing Everest is his 'life's ambition'.

Eri Aka, Japanese. Superb reputation – was a member of the '92 all-woman Annapurna 1 team. She's as reserved as I am, and so far we've been tiptoeing around each other like extremely polite cats. She understands English but rarely speaks it. Getting the impression that this isn't cultural diffidence, rather that she prefers to be an observer.

Anyway, futile to worry what the others think about me. I won't be climbing with them, just sharing the base camp facilities. Should be grateful to be here at all. It's all down to Aussie expedition leader Joe Davis, who offered me a discounted place on the permit at the last minute (it still sucked up every cent of the book advance, but have to believe it will be worth it). Walter didn't approve of the commercialisation of Everest, he hated the notion that 'any bugger with a chequebook could bag the summit without putting in the hours', but he would approve of Joe, who doesn't suffer fools, knows how to run a camp and likes a drink. And Joe has put in the hours. He's topped out on Everest 3 times, and lost 2 teammates and a fistful of toes during an attempt on Nanga Parbat. Joe didn't mention the controversy around Walter's death, but got straight into discussing likely summit dates and the pros and cons of a bid from this side as opposed to the south. Camp III here is 1000 feet higher than Camp V on the Nepalese side, so I'll be spending longer in the danger zone above 26 000 ft. Without bottled gas, this means higher risk of hypoxia and my dreaded frostbite, which should be the least I should expect.

~~Couldn't have tried from Nepal again, not with Walter's body still there~~

Tadeusz, Joe's guide, a young craggy-faced Pole with an equally impressive record, has the air of someone who is more at home in the mountains than in 'civilisation'. Jangbu Sherpa, Joe's sirdar, is reserved and competent, but is dubious about me hauling all my equipment up to the high camps myself, without using gas, Sherpa support or the fixed ropes. Perhaps he's right.

My list:

- Summit and salvage my reputation. ~~PROVE I can do this.~~

Write the bloody book and get paid the balance of the advance.
- Finalise the divorce.
- Pull Marcus out of that shite school.
- Find a place for Marcus and me to live.

I can do this.

I CAN DO THIS

DAY 2

Eri joined me on an acclimatisation hike around camp this morning. Environmental groups have been cleaning up the mountain since 1990, but the glacial stream that cuts through the moraine is still rife with toxic froth and clogged with cans. People are shite, aren't they? Decided to head up to George Mallory's memorial. Surprised myself by crying as I read his plaque. Not like me at all. Mallory and Irvine's remains are still on the mountain somewhere, their secrets buried with them. I choose to believe that they did make the summit in 1924, wearing their layers of tweed and silk and fighting with their obstinate oxygen equipment. Everest wasn't one of Walter's goals, he wasn't one for climbing in other people's footsteps, but he knew everything about the mountain's history. I've never forgotten him telling me that Mallory liked nothing more than to whip his kit off and prance around naked – even in the freezing Himalaya.

Eri, bless her, didn't seem to be embarrassed at my show of emotion.

Felt wiped out when I returned to the tent. It's not just the altitude. Tried to re-read what I wrote about Walter's death. Couldn't get past the first sentence. It was oddly painless to write, probably because I vomited it out and didn't think too hard about what I was putting down. The publishers are very insistent that this climb and what happened last year should form the meat of the book. At least I've made a start.

Have to admit I'm still in the mental crevasse I fell into after Walter died. Losing him has left me unbalanced, a car missing a wheel. I'd give anything to hear his voice. I know exactly what he'd say if he knew how my life had unravelled since he died: 'Don't let the bastards grind you down, pet.' ~~Can't bear the thought that his body is still there, on the other side of this bloody BLOODY mountain.~~ ~~And I'm still angry at him for dying. Furious. Pain and fury, not a healthy mix. And not just because I was so unfairly blamed for his death. He's left me in a terrible position no no can't write that even just for my eyes only it makes me sound selfish and petty~~. It can take years to recover from a loss. Mam never got over Dad's death; it's what killed her in the end. And everyone knows the bond between climbing partners is more intimate than that between lovers. There's a deeper trust that grows when you're hanging from pitches in extremis, starving and freezing and shitting in front of each other. Just after I met Graham, he accused me of sleeping with Walter (oh the irony), too dense to see there was nothing sexual about our relationship. And yes, Walter and I were as close as two people could get, so I understand why Graham found this threatening, but Walter wasn't into women. Wasn't really into men either. Makes me sad to think that he'd spent too long in the company of macho arseholes to accept that side of himself, and certainly we never spoke about it. I want to say that the mountains were his one true love, but that's trite and he would have told me not to be so bloody daft.

~~I wish I knew what he saw just before he died.~~

Need to move on. If I don't have a clear head, I'll fail. Walter is dead. And I have to shed the ever-present guilt about Marcus. Tried to call him from Kathmandu, but the old sow in the school office refused to pull him out of class to let me talk to him. With only an hour before we were due to leave for Lhasa, I raced through Thamel, collecting gifts so that I could send him a parcel, prove to him that I'm thinking about him. I dithered, ended up buying a cheap T-shirt with a yak on it and a tiny teddy bear that reminded me of Chewie, the toy that was his constant companion when he was three, although he's ten now, hardly a baby. Hate myself for not trying harder to see him before I flew out. It all happened so quickly.

Tomorrow I'll leave all this self-pity behind. ENOUGH.

DAY 3

Slap slap slap goes the wind against the tents, making the prayer flags spiral and the guy ropes thrum. No plume on Chomolungma today, a sign that the mountain's destructive jet stream is dying, and the ridge is preparing for our assault. On the Nepalese side, the mountain hides behind Lhotse and Nuptse's friendlier peaks, but here its messy pyramid looms thuggishly behind camp, taunting us.

Spent hours organising my tent, ensuring that everything I needed, head torch, spare gloves, water bottle, Kendal Mint Cake, Walkman, books and this bloody notebook were exactly where they should be. I refuse to see my desire for order as obsessive. Being organised helps my state of mind, gives me the illusion of control.

Otherwise, feeling good. Strong. Positive. Itching to start the trek up to advanced base camp and begin stocking the high camps, but will wait until after the puja ceremony out of respect for the Sherpas.

Had a surprisingly good time in the mess tent last night. Joe broke out the beers, and I felt myself thawing as we sat around swapping war stories. Booze goes to my head at altitude, and after a couple of drinks we were all getting rowdy. Only Posh

Tom and Captain of Industry Wade didn't join in. Joe's tales are the stuff of legend, but the Danielsen brothers (we've taken to calling them 'the Scandis') and Lewis (who gets flirty when he drinks) have been through their own scrapes as well. Lewis spent 2 days buried in a snowdrift after plunging through a snow-bank while skiing off-piste, and kept himself alive by singing Bob Dylan songs. It was only when someone decided to investigate who was doing a terrible rendition of 'Just Like a Woman' that he was rescued. Even Eri opened up, and told us matter-of-factly in her halting English about the notorious 3-day bivouac she endured after topping out on Dhaulagiri (south pillar route). On their descent from the summit, she and 3 teammates were forced to huddle on a narrow ledge when the weather closed in. All survived, and only 1 was seriously frostbitten – a miracle. She's a real pioneer. She and her team had to scratch for the money for that expedition, and were so broke they ended up sewing their own bivvy sacs and sleeping bags!

Then Tom said, 'What about you, Juliet? You must have some stories.' He was smiling his supercilious smile that makes me think of Graham. No way was I going near last year's horror or the near miss on Broad Peak, so I told them about my down suit blowing away with our tent when Walter and I were hunkered down on Cho Oyu – my first big peak.

Tom piped up again, asking me if my choice not to use supplementary oxygen was because I wanted 'to be known as the first woman to summit Everest without using gas'. The booze had made me chippy, and I quoted Messner at him, saying that in my opinion all mountains should be climbed 'by fair means' – without oxygen, and without relying on the backs of the Sherpas. Poncy of me, but sometimes you have to give as good as you get.

In fairness to Tom, 'firsts' are important in this game, especially when it comes to sponsorship. If I succeed, this could open more doors for me on the speaking circuit, give me my independence without having to grovel for money from Graham. It could erase all the terrible press I've been getting, prove that I am capable of climbing a big peak, unsupported. Suspect I've made an enemy, but it isn't the first time, and I have far more important things to worry about.

DAY 4

Camp a hive of activity as yak herders squabble with expedition sirdars, and porters gather to ferry equipment up to advanced base camp.

After breakfast, Joe, Tadeusz and I planned my acclimatisation strategy:

- Hike up to Advanced Base Camp (ABC) at 21 300 feet
- Acclimatise for a few days
- Head up the North Col to Camp I (23 000 ft)
- Night at Camp I
- Back to ABC
- Back up to Camp I
- Night at Camp II (stock camps) (24 700 ft)
- Back down to base to gather strength
- Repeat above
- Back up to ABC
- One night at Camp II
- One night at Camp III (27 400 ft)
- Summit
- Back to Base Camp
- HOME

It helps having it laid out so clearly.

Atmosphere frosty in the mess tent this evening. People are nervy about the climb/weather ahead. Tom and Wade are keeping themselves to themselves, and the Scandi brothers are having issues

– Sem is worried about Andrej, who is coming down with tonsillitis. Could be a bad setback.

Puja ceremony tomorrow, and then my first trip up to ABC. Need to be strong for this. Must sleep.

UPDATE: More bad news. More pressure I don't need. Joe has heard from his connections on the Nepalese side that the German alpinist Stefanie Weber is also going to be making a bid to be the first woman to summit without using supplementary oxygen or Sherpa support. Not what I wanted to hear. Joe says the weather is bad on that side so not to worry too much. I admire Stef but I desperately need her to fail. Turning this into a race will only cloud my judgement, but it could be that I will have no choice.

DAY 5

Bad day that started with a BAD omen.

Couldn't find Walter's ice axe, the only possession of his that I brought to the mountain, so couldn't place it on the chorten to be blessed during the puja ceremony. (Yet, when I returned to my tent, there it was, next to my foam sleeping-pad.)

After the lama's blessing, which is meant to appease the mountain spirits before our assault on Everest's flanks, Jangbu drew me aside, saying there was someone who wanted to talk to me. Bemused, I followed him into the kitchen tent, which, as ever, was clouded with cigarette smoke. (Another pang of loss – smoke always makes me think of Walter.)

Dawa Sherpa, a guide attached to the Korean team, was waiting for me there. A kind face, good English, had a calmness about him that I associate with Tibetan Buddhists. He got right into it, telling me that he'd heard I was here, and that one of his cousins,

Ang Tsering, had been guiding on the Nepalese side of the mountain last year when Walter died. Not only that, Ang Tsering was part of the Enviro Group, the first team to come upon us when Walter ran into trouble. How to describe what I felt? *A cold finger ran up my spine, a fist clutched my heart, my breath stopped.* Clichés all, and none came close. I remember Ang Tsering. Of course I remember him. I can still hear his voice: 'Move, didi, move, lady. Can't help him. Go down now.'

The rest of his team continued their ascent, but Ang Tsering stayed with me until thoughts of Marcus slapped me out of my grief, and I got moving. He saved my life. I never thanked him.

And then came another shock: Dawa said his cousin had been killed in an avalanche while guiding on Manaslu last September. Ang Tsering left behind a wife and 2 children, and the insurance is a pittance. Here am I, bleating on about how hard done by I am, when Ang Tsering's family have lost everything. I promised to do what I could for them when I returned home. It will be the least I can do.

It's another reason to succeed and gain financial independence. <u>I can do this.</u>

Seeing I was upset, Tadeusz was kind in his unsentimental way when I bumped into him as I was leaving the kitchen tent, and later Eri came to see why I hadn't pitched up at the mess tent for supper. Their concern helped, but showing weakness makes me feel less like myself.

Plus, nerves are kicking in now. I'll be hulking 40 pounds of equipment up to ABC tomorrow. 12 miles. Have to remember this is nothing compared to the loads the Sherpas and porters will be lugging up there. Not as fit as I'd like to be, but this is a mental, not a physical game.

Can't let myself obsess about how Stef might be faring on the south side. Latest news is that not even the ice doctors have made it through the Ice Fall yet, so it's doubtful she's even started her acclimatisation rotations. Stef can't be seen to use the fixed ropes, but surely she won't try to make it through the Ice Fall before the Sherpas? When I met her briefly in Cham all those years ago, she didn't strike me as a risk-taker. She's steady, pragmatic, and doesn't have the additional emotional baggage that I will be carrying.

DAY 7, Advanced Base Camp

Made ABC yesterday in good time, but was so shattered that putting up the tent and collecting snow to melt for tea took me almost 2 hours. Managed to eat something this morning although have no appetite. Feet are swollen. On some climbs even my face balloons when I'm at altitude, as if I've been pumped full of air. Moon Face, Walter used to call me.

For the book??: *On the Nepalese side of the mountain, the first obstacle Walter and I faced was the notorious Khumbu Icefall, a treacherous two-hour scramble over crevasses and under the shadowy danger zones of the unstable, towering seracs. But here, on the north side, the first section is all about stamina rather than skill. The route up to advanced base camp is technically unchallenging, but every bit as gruelling as I'd been told. The path switches back on itself, snaking up and down, and sometimes disappearing completely – often I only found my way by following the trail of yak droppings. As I made my way higher and higher, nauseous from the rapidly thinning air, my back began to sob from the weight of my pack. My lips were cracked and numb from the wind and dry air, and I bit down on the grey dust kicked up by the yaks' skittering hooves. I thought ahead to the climb, to the immense challenge that lay before me. Stocking the camps will be a truly Sisyphean task, yet my heart soared: I was on my way.*

Too much? Too arsey? I can't very well write that all I was thinking as I put one foot in front of the other was: 'this is shite, this is shite, this is shite'. Readers don't want the truth, they want a triumph against the odds, not an old cow cursing her way up a hill.

Stopped at the Indo-Tibetan team's tent at interim camp halfway for a breather. They were all very friendly, especially the two women on their team. They offered me tea, but I couldn't accept. From here on in I have to be seen to be doing this completely unassisted.

~~There was something else. Something I've been putting off writing about. Something I can't possibly put in the book, but can't ignore. Just past interim camp, the hairs at the back of my neck started to prickle as if someone was staring right at me. More than once I turned to look behind me to see if someone was following me or if the porters and yaks I'd passed when I crossed the glacial stream had caught up to me. They hadn't. I couldn't shake it until I reached the edge of camp.~~

~~It was the same feeling that came over me just before Walter collapsed.~~

DAY 8

Slept surprisingly soundly – adapting to the altitude well, only woke once in the night with a very mild headache. And a good day today. Social!

During a camp recce, ran into Pauline Zierzinger, an American alpinist I met briefly at last year's disastrous conference in Banff. She's a bit 'up herself' as Mam would say, but who isn't on the mountains? Good to see a familiar face and talk about the minutiae of the climb ahead, and I appreciated that she skipped over last year's events. Got the impression there are also tensions in her camp, with big personalities jostling for position. We discussed her worries about her new over-boots and my concerns about the stove fuel lighting in the high camps. She was also the bearer of good news: says she's heard that the poor weather on the south side isn't letting up. Pauline knows Stef well and says she's surprised she decided to attempt the climb at all as she broke her wrist recently. Echoing my own misgivings, she warned me about the dangers of making this a race to the top. She's right, but the fact is, if I don't make it up there before Stef then this whole expedition will have been for nothing.

Gave her some of the baby wipes I always use for 'washing'. She's been using ones scented with cologne – they've brought her nethers out in a rash!

~~This is hard to think about but can't shake the feeling that~~

DAY 11

Eri is the first of Joe's team to make it to ABC. Ha!

~~Getting the feeling that NO~~

DAY 12

Can't deny it any more. Can't shake the feeling that something (someone??) is in my peripheral vision all the time, a dark shadow on my left side. Keeps giving me a jolt. Could just be tiredness – struggled to sleep last night, which was a blow after the first good nights here. Queasy, and have a niggling cough.

Felt like companionship, but I won't use Joe's mess tent here. It's vital vital vital that I do this completely unsupported. Rumours flare quickly here, and I don't trust Tom.

Andrej made it to ABC, but Joe and Tadeusz are very concerned about him. Looks like he could have bronchitis, which will ruin his summit bid. Sem is distraught, doesn't want to do this without his brother. I know how he feels. Really felt Walter's absence today. A hollow ache in my stomach.

DAY 13

Took a recce to the aptly named 'crampon point' at the foot of the steep North Col. It's only a mile outside camp, but altitude is really hitting me now, there's a tell-tale tug in my lungs and a constant headache. Cough is worsening. The route up to Camp I will be a steep but easy climb on ice (some rotten) and snow, but that sense that someone's watching me is growing. It's not just uncomfortable, it feels – what's the word – almost dirty. No, not dirty, intrusive. As if I'm being spied on.

So similar to what I felt just before Walter died.

Need Walter to balance me out. *Stop being so daft, pet.*

~~There will be trouble ahead. I can feel it in my water~~

DAY 14

Spent the day preparing for tomorrow's slog up the North Col to stock Camp I.

Tadeusz suggested I leave early before the sun hits the snow on the col and turns it claggy. He says he doesn't know how Stef is doing. He's lying. He and Joe and their team of Sherpas are well connected and soak up climbing gossip like sponges. Part of me is angry with him for not being transparent, part of me is grateful. He and Joe are trying to protect me. We all know that this kind of pressure is a one-way ticket to poor decision-making. People have died on the mountain for less.

The feeling I'm being watched is still there. Is it stronger? I think so.

DAY 16

Back at ABC after 1st overnight stay at Camp I.

Glad I followed Tadeusz's advice and left early – I was boiling after an hour. Easy but very monotonous climb, and in places the col was so steep it felt vertical. Used Walter's ice axe, which pulled me through. It's an area prone to avalanche, but this worry barely entered my head. I had other things on my mind.

For the book: *To get to the camp itself, I had to climb beneath an overhanging serac the size of a row of terraced houses (and yes I did pick up my pace as I moved through its shadow). From there the smattering of tents at ABC looked as small as Monopoly pieces. Again it took every ounce of strength to set up camp and collect enough snow to melt for tea. Had no trouble lighting the stove – my greatest worry. Around me were signs of previous expeditions: the wind has sandblasted the icy surface to reveal half-buried wisps of canvas and nylon, prayer flag flecks, Poisk bottles and plastic. The weather remained kind, rare for this high on the mountain, the light crisp and amplified. I was the only westerner there, but there were three Sherpas setting up camp for their teams nearby. I could tell they were keeping an eye on me, which was comforting. Tried to eat, but could only manage a few bites. Food tastes so different up here. I feel like I need to add salt to everything, and find myself craving curry and sugar. I never eat chocolate when I'm at home; for me, it's mountain food.*

Barely slept, but will have time to rest before tomorrow's climb up to Camp II.

If it wasn't for the continual presence of it, I would have been triumphant.

Because it's getting worse.

There were 2 Sherpas fixing ropes on the col as I made my way up it. But for an instant, when I paused to look back down the slope, I counted 4 of us. When I counted again, only 3.

Something was niggling at me, and I was grateful to Mrs Ryan, my old English teacher, for making us learn T. S. Eliot's *The Waste Land* by heart (I used to bloody hate that poem). Dug in my memory and unearthed these lines:

> *Who is the third who walks beside you?*
> *When I count, there are only you and I together*
> *But when I look up the white road*
> *There is another one walking beside you*

Exactly what I felt yesterday. Clearly remember Mrs Ryan telling us that Eliot was inspired by explorer Ernest Shackleton's tale of being shadowed by a ghostly figure in the Antarctic. He and his companions were at the very limit of their endurance, their lives in danger, when he became convinced that a mysterious being was trailing the group. An extra man. Another man. A fourth man, when there should have been only 3, although Eliot used poetic licence in the poem and changed it to 'the third who walks beside you'. Is what I'm feeling a version of Shackleton's 'Third Man'?

Have to remember that the sense that someone or something other is with you is common on the mountains and in extreme and life-threatening conditions (only my life isn't being threatened here, is it? ~~Is it??~~).

BUT Shackleton spoke of his invisible companion as a benevolent being who wanted only to soothe him and help him stay alive. Mine doesn't feel like that. There's a nastiness to it. An edge. Uncomfortable. Like a foul smell.

~~And in the poem, isn't the Third Man meant to be death??~~

Is it the stress of the solo climb ahead that's getting to me? Am I trying to conjure up a companion to join me? ~~Walter???? No no.~~

Or worse: could it be hypoxia or the beginnings of cerebral oedema, my brain swelling and making me delusional? No. There are no other symptoms: no loss of balance, no dizziness, and the horizon is staying where it should be.

Apart from the cough that I can't shake, physically I feel better than I have any right to feel.

Worried that the higher I go the more intense it will get. ~~Perhaps it's a warning that I shouldn't go higher.~~

Tomorrow up to Camp II.

~~Can't give up although I want to. Too many people depending on me now.~~

DAY 18

Back from Camp II

~~BAD~~

Battered by wind and spindrift on the way up the col this time.

And worse than the wind, it was there, my Third Man, dogging me every step of the way. Lingering like a bad smell, hovering in my peripheral vision, which was partially obscured anyway by the edge of the goggles. Took a real effort of will not to keep stopping, turning and trying to catch it out.

One good thing – en route, I easily passed Wade, Tom and Lewis who were inching their way up using the fixed ropes. Lewis whooped, but I could sense the resentment from the others as their egos took a knock, and this helped fuel me forward. The Sherpas guiding on the slope laughed and shouted: 'Hey, didi, you carry like a man!'

Weather grew worse when I reached Camp II. Fought hard again to dig a platform for the tent, tying it down with extra rope I gathered from the site. It's exposed, this camp, the howling wind revealing yet more of the faded scraps of fabric and rubbish and ~~bones no not bones why did I write bones???~~ oxygen bottles of earlier attempts. I was alone up there. No other climbers have made it this high yet. Felt very small, a flea on the back of the mountain. After the avalanche on Broad Peak, I am more aware than ever that it could shake me off any time it chooses.

Even in the bad weather, the view of the North Ridge from here is both alluring and daunting. By a trick of perspective it looks easily within my grasp and capabilities, yet I know it will still take 2 days of hard climbing to reach the summit. Could make out every obstacle on the ridge, including the treacherous Second Step.

Knew I was in for a night of fractious sleep as the wind slammed and screeched against the tent and my lungs fought the thin air.

Storm blew out in the middle of the night, and I drifted off. Woken by a slapping sound. It wasn't the wind – it was irregular, yet considered, as if a hand was striking the tent's sides. Groggy, I found my headlamp, unzipped the tent and looked out. The cloud had come down, and the light didn't penetrate more than a metre of its foggy depths. Chilled, both inside and out, I couldn't shake the sense that I wasn't alone, that something was there, watching me, biding its time.

Kept the light on until dawn. Didn't sleep again.

Seriously worried I could have AMS.

Must go down. Really should make 2 more trips up to the high camps, but instead will trust I've acclimatised enough.

It's a risk.

Joe and Tadeusz still being cagey about Stef's progress. The weather must have eased up on the Nepalese side by now. Didn't push them. Have enough on my mind as it is.

DAY 20

Last night at ABC.

Slept badly, waiting for it to come, dreamed (?) I heard the crunch, crunch, crunch of cramponed feet walking around and around the tent. Wanted so badly to talk to the others about this, seek out Eri or Tadeusz maybe, but CAN'T.

DAY 22

Back at base camp. Walked down yesterday.

He – it – followed me down. I could almost hear the scrape of its footsteps on the talus. Barely felt the cold bite of the air, which is roughening my skin and cracking my lips. I was so distracted I almost forgot to keep myself hydrated.

But when the towering ice pinnacles that loom above interim camp came into sight, the feeling disappeared. It was gone. He was gone. Because I'm certain it's a he. Why? I don't know. It just feels male. Relieved that it's left me, but this does imply I'm showing signs of hypoxia. When I go up again, will it return?

It helped that the lower I went, and the thicker the air became, the more my body rejoiced. Physically, I'm in good shape. Mentally, I can't deny there is a problem.

DAY 23

Usually forget dreams as soon as I wake. Can still remember every detail of last night's:

Walter and I are back on Broad Peak lying in our tent, the wind screaming around us, feeling as if we could take flight at any moment. Walter falls asleep, but I can't, I'm pressing my body onto the rough ground, as if my weight will anchor us against the force of the wind. Then comes a thud, thud, thud CRUMP – don't know what it is at first, but then Walter starts yelling: 'Don't, Juliet, don't! Avalanche!' There's a BOOSH as the force of the impact hits and I'm falling, tumbling, out of control, my bewildered brain convinced that I'm underwater, being pummelled by a giant wave. Then I stop. It's instant, a jolt that winds me. I sit up, all is white and I don't know where I am, but I do know I can't find my gloves. Panicked, I dig and dig and dig with my bare hands through snow that feels and smells like hot, buttery mashed potato, unearthing Chewie, Marcus's teddy bear. I hold up my hands and watch as they gradually turn black, like a time-lapse video of a flower rotting. I can't breathe: my air passage is packed with snow, and as I try and claw it out, my blackened fingers crumble. I beg Walter to help me, but he's not there.

I woke up gasping for breath. The first thing I did was double-check I had my spare gloves and boot-warmers close to hand.

The dream only faintly echoed what actually happened in those terrifying seconds on Broad Peak, but even now, wide awake, I can still feel an ache in my throat as if it really had been compacted with snow, and my fingers won't stop tingling.

DAY 24

Pauline's team is taking a break from its acclimatisation schedule and she came over to see me, bringing a piece of cake (it tasted like sawdust, but I ate it anyway – appetite is back now I'm at a lower altitude). She says that she's heard that Stef has completed her first acclimatisation run but doesn't know what shape she's in.

Will Stef pass Walter's body when she finally makes her lonely way up to the summit? It goes against the Sherpas' beliefs to touch the recently dead on the mountain, so it's unlikely anyone rolled Walter into a crevasse. ~~He could still be there, lying on his side, his eyes frozen open.~~

Trying to distract myself with the book:

It's strange now to think that when I first met Walter I found him intimidating. He was part of the elite band of older, fearless climbers who used to hang out at Brigham Rocks. Gnarled, tough and with a thick Sunderland accent, we were all in awe of him and the fact that he refused to climb with aids, whatever the route's difficulty. I couldn't believe my luck when he took me under his wing. He was the first to see my potential. He was my buttress when Mam and Dad died. Supported me when I said I wanted to try for the big peaks. He never came out and said it, but I knew he was disappointed when I married Graham and gave up climbing to look after Marcus. But he knew I'd be back. He waited patiently for me to return to the mountains. He knew I couldn't stay away. He was right.

~~He wouldn't have been there last year if it wasn't for me. But he would have wanted to die on the mountains. He wouldn't have coped with a spell in an old folks' home, a gradual withering of his limbs.~~

~~What did he see before he died?~~

DAY 25

Cloud came down this morning. Spent the day in my tent.

At the beginning of my career, I was known as the 'Angel of the Alps', a tabloid nickname that stuck after I did five back-to-back solo climbs in one season. But the approval turned sour after Marcus was born and I continued to climb, especially when Walter and I made our first forays into the high peaks. Rumours abounded that he was the one who did all the heavy lifting, and despite my history of solo climbs and the fact that I led out most of the time, they said that without him I wouldn't be capable of managing a flight of stairs, never mind a 26 000-foot peak. Worse, we were accused by one of the Spanish teams of faking our summit of Broad Peak. We proved it later, but the damage was done. There's something about me that sets people against me. It became de rigeur to attack my choice to climb without oxygen, putting myself at risk 'even though I was a mother', and the crueller of the opinion pieces hinted that my ambition was directly responsible for Walter's death. They said that he was too old to climb – he was only in his mid-fifties – and I pushed him into it. So unfair. So cruel. So hurtful. I went from being known as the 'Angel of the Alps' to the 'Angel of Death'.

Too much? Too defensive? But I need to address this in the book.

Dark thoughts keep niggling. Why didn't Walter ever publicly repudiate the claims that I was the weaker partner after we returned from Broad Peak? This burned Graham, and perhaps he was right to be angry about it. I made excuses for Walter, saying that public opinion didn't matter to him and that no one with any sense would believe the shite the papers print anyway. Perhaps Walter would have said something if I'd asked him to. Why did I never ask? ~~Perhaps I was afraid of what he'd say. Where did this come from? He was my rock.~~

The others have just returned to base camp. All made successful recces up to Camp II, including Andrej, who says he's feeling stronger. Good to see them. Even Posh Tom was pleasant to me.

DAY 26

Spent more time with Eri today. The weather up on the high camps was far worse for them than it was for me, but she's positive that the whole team will make the summit. Came so close to telling her about my Third Man. Still concerned I might have been displaying the first signs of cerebral oedema, which would explain why it has disappeared now that I'm at lower altitude.

We traded photographs. She had loads with her, which surprised me. I'd assumed she was a loner, but there she was, with a group of smiling climbers outside the Yak and Yeti in Kathmandu; posing with her parents and brothers and sisters; surrounded by a bunch of laughing women, barely recognisable in a dress and make-up. We laughed about this. I shrug off my femininity when I'm in the mountains. Longing for a bath and clean clothes won't help you get up the mountain.

I only had one photo with me, taken last year with Marcus at a school function. We both look forlorn and vaguely traumatised, as if we've just been snapped after escaping a wartime atrocity. What was I thinking bringing that one?

DAY 27

Woke with another cough. It's unusual for me to get ill this low on the mountain. Hope I haven't caught the Scandi boys' illness.

Tadeusz and I spoke privately about my decision to remain down here until my summit attempt. It's not ideal. I should really make another acclimatisation trip up to ABC and the high camps before I prepare for the summit. I won't. I can't. I've heard through the Sherpa grapevine that weather on the south is deteriorating again, but I resisted the urge to ask about Stef's progress, although the temptation is strong. I have to climb at my own pace.

On the bright side, that feeling that I'm being stalked is gone, but need to get perspective before I go back to the high camps. It shook me. It shook me badly. It was too close to that poisonous sense I had just before Walter collapsed. Is there a connection? Just hypoxia? A delusion? My imagination out of control, making up excuses to give up the attempt? I just don't know.

Later, on the way back from the toilet tent, I overheard voices – Tom and Wade's. Didn't mean to eavesdrop, but I caught my name. Tom was complaining that Tadeusz and Joe were giving me preferential treatment by allowing me to summit ahead of everyone else.

Tom squirmed when he saw me. Before he could hit me with his bluster, I told him in no uncertain terms that no one was 'allowing' me to do anything.

He got the message.

It left a bitter taste in my mouth. I thought we were over all that.

DAY 28

Dark clouds are gathering, but not over the summit.

Coughed non-stop last night, decided to rest and read in my tent and monitor it. Just before lunch, Joe called me into the area of the mess he uses as an office, saying that Graham was on the satellite phone. Sick with anxiety, all I could think as I left my tent was please don't let anything have happened to Marcus.

It wasn't Marcus, but the news wasn't good. Graham's been getting non-stop calls from some 'oik' (his words) at the *News of the World* asking about my 'return to Everest' and if it was true I was 'planning to take needless risks to prove a point'.

He also said there were reports about Stef's bid, and apparently the papers are pitting us against each other. The journos hate me, but maybe this could work in my favour and there will be some nationalistic pride at the thought of me getting to the top before Stef. God, I hate thinking like this.

I told him that no one, except for him and the publishers (in whose interest it was to have exclusive rights to my account of this climb) knew of my decision to return to the mountain, and asked if the hack had mentioned who his source was.

Graham said, 'Think it's someone on your side. They know whose base camp facilities you're using and said you were "acting like you owned the mountain".'

Tom. It had to be Tom.

Thankfully they haven't bothered Marcus, and Graham said he'd alerted the school just in case.

And then his voice softened and he said, 'Whatever we've been through, you know I want you to succeed, don't you?'

Taken off-guard, I felt a lump form in my throat – he sounded so much like the old Graham. The one who'd been there in the old days before the bitterness and resentment set in.

I told him that I was going to wear my 'lucky' down suit. The one he'd had specially made for me before Walter and I left for the Karakoram. Bright pink, not my style, but it did the job. I regret not wearing it last year.

When he hung up, the rage came.

I knew by the tense silence that greeted me when I stormed into the dining area that everyone had overheard my conversation.

Wade and Tom were sitting together at the end of the table. I don't remember exactly what I said to him, the red veil had come down by then, but I know I threatened him and called him a 'posh entitled shite'.

Eri bent her head and looked at her hands, not wanting to get involved. The others, including Lewis, who I thought was an ally, watched in frank enjoyment: a fight to break the monotony.

I can't let this sort of interpersonal conflict derail me. I should be used to it by now. I've fought hard to get this far. Clashed with egos both big and small over the years.

DAY 29

The atmosphere in the mess tent is now as bitter as the wind at the high camps.

Feel guilty for kicking off, but have to remember life is more intense at base camp: tempers flare over the stupidest of things. Is it the proximity of danger? The high stakes? The lack of luxury? The boredom that comes from waiting for a weather window? When Walter and I made our first and only foray to the Karakoram, the other teams who were hiking in with us had started bickering before we'd even left Askole. We cut ourselves off from them and didn't get involved. Perhaps this was why they turned on us after our ascent of Broad Peak, and accused us of not reaching the 'true' summit. They assumed we thought we were above them. They resented us, like Tom resents me.

DAY 30

Should have been back at ABC by now. Cough is still hounding me, but I'm losing the aftertaste left by it, which is enough to keep me on track.

Discussed summit dates with Joe. The 10th looks good. He says he's hearing reports that Stef is being accused of using the fixed ropes and ladders in the Ice Fall. Felt a blast of relief at this, then hated myself. I, of all people, should know what this feels like. The press have accused me unjustly in the past of being dragged up mountains by Walter, and I shouldn't rejoice that another climber is getting the same unfair treatment. He also told me that reporters are now calling his sat phone directly. So far he's fielded 6 calls. Bloody bloody Tom.

At least the anger stops me obsessing about it.

Will need to say something about my marriage in the book, readers like gossip and scandal. But what? It wasn't always rocky. I was charmed by Graham's smooth good looks at first, impressed by the fact he was the CEO of Tally High Mountain Gear. Mam warned me against marrying him, said we were too different, said he spoke 'like he had a broomstick up his arse'. She was right. His family were as different to ours as you could get – Tory, Barbour-jacketed, saddled with a festering country house, generations of debt and an inbred sense of entitlement. People used to stare at us, trying to figure out what this willowy, handsome bloke saw in short and squat me. He was supportive of my career until Marcus was born, and then the resentment set in. I escaped to the mountains – my version of infidelity; he was more traditional in his betrayals. And Walter was always my rock, my ally. Poor Marcus was stuck in the middle. Why did I listen to Graham and allow him to be sent to that bloody awful school? I know why. I can at least try and be honest with myself. Six years I spent at home with him, my life on hold. Watching from the sidelines as other climbers snapped up sponsorships, made first ascents. And I wasn't getting any younger. I gave in too easily when Graham suggested that Marcus attend his old boarding school, despite it conjuring up images of buggery and bullying, despite the crippling school fees that ran us deeper into debt. I convinced myself I was just being an inverted snob like Mam. Convinced myself that he was getting a good start in life. Mam and Dad knew the value of a good education, made sure I went to a good school and didn't get spat out by the system, that's what Graham and I were doing for our son. But something died in Marcus's eyes when we dropped him off for his first day.

Hang in there, Marcus.

DAY 31

~~Very worried that~~

~~Think it might be time to call off~~

~~Start at the beginning~~

Eri and Sem asked me to join them on a hike to the tented camp on the outskirts of base camp. I half-expected them to bring up the bad atmosphere at camp, but they kept schtum. Good. I know I lost my temper, but I refuse to believe I'm being unreasonable.

As we reached the road, that familiar, sickening feeling that there was someone else hovering in the fringes of my vision suddenly swamped me. I turned to the side, and this time, I was sure I caught a glimpse of a figure dressed in a mustard-coloured down suit, its face a misshapen bulky smudge. I blurted: 'Who's that next to Eri?'

Sem said, 'Huh? There is no one.'

Sem was right. No one was there. No one at all.

Fighting nausea, I made my excuses and returned to my tent.

~~Losing it, I'm losing it~~

~~That or I'm being stalked, being haunted~~

DAY 32

No dreams, but woke feeling a deep sense of unease. Knew something bad was going to happen today and it did: it's back.

Saw it outside the mess tent this time. It was only there for a second, but that was long enough for me to see why its head was so bulky and malformed: it's wearing an old-fashioned oxygen mask, tubes snaking from its mouth. But the rest of its gear, its boots and mustard-coloured down suit, appeared to be modern. ~~This mishmash of old and new gear means it can't be the angry spirit of a climber who died on the mountain, surely?~~

It could just be an altitude-induced hallucination. It's unlikely at this relatively low altitude, but it's possible this is all it is.

~~Either I'm being haunted, I'm hypoxic or I'm mad. Which one is worse?~~

Fighting for distractions. The anger at Tom helps.

Update: overheard Tadeusz and Joe discussing Stef. She's been seen at Camp 3. Is she on her second rotation? Has she shaken off the accusations? Good for her, bad for me. I will have to up my game if I want to succeed. I don't have a choice.

DAY 33

Downsides to giving up the summit:

- Will lose book advance and get heavily into debt
- Won't be able to support Marcus, and Graham will use this to his advantage and might go for custody
- Doubtful I'll get sponsorship for another attempt if I fail now so could be my last chance, and if Stef makes it first I can forget that
- Press will have a field day
- Could be final nail in my career's coffin
- Won't be able to help Ang Tsering's family

No. I can fight through this.
Don't let the bastards grind you down, pet.

No it today.

DAY 34

Returning from a solo hike this morning, discovered that Walter's ice axe was missing again. Eventually found it pushed under my sleeping mat. Definitely didn't put it there. Someone (it? Tom?) has been in my tent. Paranoid that vital equipment had been removed, I packed and repacked my rucksack, the fear building and building.

Please let it be Tom. Thought about confronting him, but know in my gut it isn't him.

It was behind the toilet tent this evening. I blinked and then it was gone.

~~I so badly want it to be Walter. But why does this presence feel so *dark* if it's him?~~

DAY 35

Not sure how to feel about this. Was ensuring I had everything I needed for tomorrow's hike up to ABC, when Tom came to my tent. He's a tall man, but he looked small today. His dark floppy hair, usually hidden under a hat, was striped with grease.

He said: 'Juliet, can we talk?'

I wanted to tell him to do one, but I was curious. We walked to the back of the kitchen tent, where we wouldn't be overheard. And he said: 'I owe you an apology, Juliet. I was telling the truth about not saying anything to the press, but it seems one of my acquaintances back home hasn't been quite so discreet.'

Turns out he'd been blabbing about me to one of his friends, who'd spilled the news of my climb to the tabloids.

I should have enjoyed seeing him squirm, but I didn't. He said that he'd only 'vented' because he was hurt that I'd treated him 'with disdain' from the start of the expedition. I could hardly say it was because he reminded me of my cheating husband, could I?

We left it at that.

But this means he definitely wasn't the one who sneaked into my tent and moved Walter's ice axe. Could I have just hidden it and forgotten I'd done so?

And I have to admit that the anger at him was helping keep me focused. I almost miss it.

Tadeusz says that two Italians are planning to summit at the same time as me. I'm glad. At least I won't be alone up there. ~~*You won't be alone up there, pet. IT will be with you.*~~ He was vague as usual about Stef's progress, but I could see he was concerned about it. She must be doing well. If I am going it has to be soon.

Told Tadeusz and Joe that if I run into trouble, they're not to send anyone after me. I will not have the Sherpas risking their lives to save mine.

~~I wonder if it's true that you only have a finite amount of luck in life. Buddhists believe that most people are born with the date of their death predetermined. But what happens when you dice with death, taunt it? Does it taunt you back?~~

I can't let this rattle around in my head any more. I need to rest. I need to eat, I need to be strong.

~~Doing this for Marcus. Doing this for Ang Tsering. Doing this for me.~~

Who is the third who walks beside you?

Simon

To: TCAKES@journeytothedarkside.com
From: sibaby@journeytothedarkside.com
Subject: The Eagle has Landed

Hey T,
So I made it. Kathmandu awesome, people are excellent & v friendly.

I'll meet the other expedition members tonight at the 'welcome dinner', but Tadeusz & his lady met me at the airport. Tadeusz is a badass. Think Rutger Hauer in Blade Runner. *His GF Ireni is the team doctor and base camp manager & is Swedish and cute, looks a bit like a sexy hamster. Oh yeah, what did you say to them about my climbing experience to get me on the permit? Ireni seems to think I'm some kind of prodigy.*

Will send an update tomorrow but then might not be able to email for a bit as on Wednesday we'll take the 'Friendship Highway' (it's seriously called that) into Tibet and then drive to Nyalam and Tingri for a few days to acclimatise before we drive to base camp. Two Kiwi guys I met in the visa queue say these towns are pretty shitty & to be prepared.

Can you believe we're actually doing this?

Idea for a listicle: 5 of the grossest flesh-eating diseases?

Adios, and speak again when I'm on the mountain
Si

The bougainvillea crawling up the courtyard walls tickled the back of my neck; shouts, laughter and the buzz of passing motorbikes floated in from the street. I helped myself to a bottle of San Miguel from the ice bucket on the table, wishing I'd thought to down a fortifying shot of whisky before I left my room.

I'd been the last to arrive at the welcome dinner, and as I weaved my way towards the table I picked up on the stiff atmosphere – the awkwardness of strangers who were surreptitiously checking each other out. Along with Tadeusz and Ireni, there were three men in their forties or early fifties; a skinny, spectacled guy in his twenties who I immediately dubbed Depressed Harry Potter, and a slender thirtyish woman with a strong serious face and cropped hair like Mia Farrow's in *Rosemary's Baby*. Not my type. All eyes were on me as I squeezed in between Depressed Harry Potter and a grizzled guy who gave me a yellow-toothed grin. We'd be spending almost two months together, and first impressions were crucial. I'd already decided on my strategy. I was going to be an exaggerated version of Charming Si, the persona I turned on at the coffee shop (the one that had totally failed to charm Ed): witty, modest and a great listener.

Tadeusz stood up and broke the news that due to the Maoist demonstrations that were spreading through the city, we'd be leaving for base camp a day earlier than planned to avoid any trouble. One of the older guys sitting opposite me, an American with an oblong head and an expensive haircut, held up a hand. 'We're not in danger here, right, Tadeusz?' He mispronounced Tadeusz's name – Tad-esh instead of Tad-ay-esh.

'No, Robbie. But it is best that you do not go outside Thamel.'

Robbie nodded and gave Tadeusz a wave as if to say: 'You may continue.'

No one looked bored as Tadeusz outlined our itinerary in his accented English, stipulating when and where we were to deposit the gear we wouldn't need on the four-day journey, all of which would be stuffed into personalised storage barrels and ferried to base camp ahead of us. He spoke confidently, catching everyone's eye at some point. He came across as someone who didn't miss a trick, someone whose trust you had to earn. *You'll have to watch yourself with him, Si.*

Robbie broke in again to ask about Sherpa support.

If Tadeusz was irritated by this interruption, he didn't show it. 'We will meet Mingma and Dorje, the Sherpas who will climb with us, when we get to base camp. Dorje has summited Everest six times; Mingma has summited nine times.' The older guy next to me whistled through his teeth. 'They are very experienced and are very good guys. Now, I know you have the member list that I have sent out' – I cursed myself for not studying it properly – 'so you know the names of the others, but let us go around the table, and you can tell us more about yourselves.'

Unsurprisingly, Robbie went first. A low-rent version of Tom Cruise, with dinky manicured hands and an ego the size of Canada, he was some sort of scientist or doctor, had climbed Denali twice, and was attempting Everest for the second time. He'd tried the year before from Nepal with a different company, and blamed his failure to top out entirely and at length on the shortcomings of the tour operator. *Ladies and gentlemen, I think we've found the dick of the group.*

Next up was my friendly, yellow-fanged neighbour, a Scot named Malcolm Fey who owned a chain of pet supply stores. Malcolm also liked to talk, and although not as cocky as Robbie, oozed a similar level of self-confidence. He'd topped out on Mount Cook in New Zealand and Cho Oyu, and had also tried and failed to summit Everest from the north last year. He didn't say why he'd turned back.

Then came Howard Perrin, the last in the trio of middle-aged men at the table. His erect posture, barrel chest and bulging eyes reminded me of someone – and then I got it. *Holy shit, it's Hannibal Lecter.* But appearances can be deceptive: an accountant based in Boston, he told us in a shaky, high-pitched voice that this would be his third – and final – attempt to climb Everest. The Nepalese side had beaten him twice and almost wiped him out financially.

So far three of my teammates had extensive high-altitude

experience, and yet all had failed to top out. *Don't panic. You're not here to summit the bloody thing.*

I'd almost forgotten about the serious-looking woman until she spoke up. Like Tadeusz's, her voice held the trace of a Polish accent: 'I am Wanda Florczak. I am originally from Poland but I live now in Saint-Gervais-les-Bains in France, where I work as a ski and mountain guide. I have summited Cho Oyu, Pumori, Aconcagua and Manaslu without using supplementary oxygen, and I have reached eight thousand metres on Dhaulagiri. It is my first time attempting Everest.'

She somehow managed to say all this without sounding egotistical. A stunned silence followed, and Ireni smirked. Malcolm leaned into me, gifting me with a waft of beery halitosis, and said: 'Five eight-thousand-metre peaks without gas.' He left out the 'not bad for a chick', but it was written all over his face. Even Robbie looked impressed. Then, and this is going to sound bizarre, it was as if Wanda morphed in front of me, and I thought, *she's actually quite hot.* As I took in her wide mouth and grey eyes, I couldn't understand why I'd thought her unattractive in the first place. I racked my brain for her celebrity double. She didn't have one. She was unique, although years later I'd see Tilda Swinton in something, and think with a jab of pain: *that's her. That's Wanda.* Not in looks exactly, but in presence. She had that *thing.*

Then it was my turn: *Hi, I'm Simon Newman. I'm here because I'm hoping to film a bunch of dead climbers so that my mate can exploit their deaths on a website. I spend my days serving coffee to rich arseholes like you, and I have no fucking idea how I'm going to deal with this whole thing.* I couldn't compete with their climbing achievements, but I could give them the full Charming Si treatment: 'What an act to follow! Hi, I'm Simon Newman. I live in London, and I'm a filmmaker and website developer – well, I'm trying to be one,' – a small, modest chuckle – 'and I'm really looking forward to getting to know all of you. Can I just say that all your accomplishments are really impressive.'

Except for Wanda, who I couldn't read, and Mark, who had travelled somewhere internally, they all seemed to buy the act.

Ireni clucked her tongue. 'Simon, there is more to you than this.' She looked around at the others. 'Not only has he climbed Cerro Torre' – (not true, but I knew enough to fake it) – 'but he has also done a solo winter ascent of the North Face of the Eiger' – (absolutely, utterly untrue). *Thierry, you utter, utter bastard.* The least he could have done was research a lesser-known climb that couldn't be so easily verified, or say I was part of a team or something. I couldn't believe he hadn't warned me about the extent of his bullshit to get me on the permit. No, actually I *could* believe it. It was my own fault for letting him do all the admin. Wanda perked up a little and Malcolm gave me a nod of respect.

There was a pregnant pause. I drained my beer to mask my panic, and helped myself to another one.

'You ever been above eight thousand metres?' Robbie drawled at me.

'Only in a plane.'

He turned to Tadeusz. 'Isn't high-altitude experience a requirement to join the team?'

I smiled inwardly as Tadeusz gave him a belated Rutger Hauer death stare. 'Do not concern yourself about Simon's experience, Robbie. Everyone will be monitored closely and their climbing skill will be tested on the fixed ropes on the col. I must make it very clear that if I do not think you have what it takes, and I mean *any* of you, then you will not be given a chance to summit.'

Finally it was the turn of Depressed Harry Potter, real name Mark Pratchett, who mumbled something in a British Home Counties accent about climbing the Mont Blanc massif, then stammered and trailed off, his face red. Good – it was reassuring to know there was another Everest newbie on the team. Before Robbie could jump in with another snarky comment, Ireni stood up to outline the symptoms of acute mountain sickness, which could lead to the potentially fatal horrors of pulmonary and cerebral oedema. She really did resemble a pretty Scandinavian hamster, her chubby cheeks and slightly protruding teeth a contrast to her partner Tadeusz's chipped glass features. They'd held hands under the table while we introduced ourselves, so their differences were clearly working out for them. As Ireni expanded on the more gruesome details – lungs and brains drowning in fluid, blood turning to syrup – my eye kept straying to Wanda. She caught me staring a couple of times, but this didn't seem to embarrass her. I wasn't the only one checking her out: Robbie was also giving her sideways glances, and every time Mark looked in her direction his cheeks turned crimson.

Ireni finished her spiel and we drifted into general conversation. If it weren't for the spectre of the ridiculous Eiger lie hanging over my head, I might have enjoyed myself; small talk and banter were Charming Si's comfort zones.

I'd clocked that Mark was the only one who wasn't helping themselves to the frosted San Miguel on the table. 'Not a drinker, Mark?'

'No. Not really.'

'Where are you from?'

'Hertfordshire, originally.' His accent may have been public-school posh, but he didn't appear to have any of the confidence that often came with a privileged background.

'What do you do when you're not climbing mountains?'

'I work as an instructor at a centre in the Peak District. Teaching climbing and kayaking to troubled youth.' He spoke in a monotone, looking down, avoiding eye contact. And then there was the old-fashioned wording: 'troubled youth'. The kids on my outreach project would have eaten him alive. Kenton kept us in line with a clip round the ear; I couldn't imagine Mark even raising his voice.

'That's how I got into climbing. I joined an outreach project when I was thirteen.'

'Really?'

'Yeah. I was a troubled youth.'

'Right.'

There was an awkward pause while I waited for him to say something else. He didn't.

Malcolm nudged me. 'Do I know you, son?' I shuddered inwardly at the 'son'. It was too close to an Ed-ism for my liking.

'Don't think so.'

'You look familiar.'

'One of those faces, I guess.'

'How come your name wasn't on the members list?'

'Signed up at the last moment. Apparently someone cancelled, so Tadeusz let me take their place.'

'Oh aye? So it was a last-minute decision, was it?' Malcolm didn't approve. I didn't blame him. Sensible people spend months or even years preparing for a trip to Everest. My route to the mountain had been crazy by anyone's standards. 'Always been a dream of yours to climb the big one, has it?'

Well actually Malcolm, a bloke left a message on our website saying it was the highest graveyard in the world, and my mate thought that filming a few corpsicles would be a cool way of racking up hits. I went along with it because I'm a moron. 'Yes. Since I was a boy.' I gave him a Charming Si grin. Time to inject some truth into my growing smorgasbord of lies. 'Wasn't easy getting the cash together. Had to sell the car.' This was true; the sale of Thierry's Ford Focus had paid the deposit. I hoped this sacrifice would impress him.

'That why you chose to climb from Tibet instead of Nepal? Because it's cheaper?'

'Partly. And because it also poses unique challenges.' *Bullshit.* The sole reason Thierry had chosen the north side was because it cost substantially less than climbing from the south. 'And you, Malcolm? Were you on Tadeusz's expedition last year?'

'No. I was with a different outfit. Chose to go with Tadeusz this time because he's got a good rep. If anyone can get us up there, it's him.'

'Was it the weather that stopped you summiting last year?'

A cagey expression flicked over his face. 'Turned back at the base of the Third Step. Topping out is only half the battle, son. You've got to get down again.' He cleared his throat with a phlegmy rumble. Another Ed-ism. *He's not Ed.* 'So the Eiger, eh? Which route did you take? The nineteen thirty-eight one?'

Oh bollocks. 'Yeah.'

'Now tell me, how did you find the Brittle Crack?'

'I got lucky really, Malcolm. It was one of the good years, so

I didn't encounter much rotten ice.' Would that do? No. He was looking expectant. *Change the subject.* I wracked my brain for another climbing story I could segue into. There was the time my mate Chris and I had hitched to Calais, spent two days making our way to Chamonix and scaled the Aiguille Verte. Boosted by this, we naively thought about climbing the Bonatti-Zappelli route on the Eckpfeiler face, but we ran out of food on the second day, and limped back to Biolay, defeated. That wouldn't do. *Think. Change the subject.* And then I got it. 'Truth is, Malcolm, I'm a bit nervous about what's ahead. Had a bad fall a while ago.'

I pulled the collar of my T-shirt aside, revealing the Cwm Silyn scars, hoping they would steer the conversation away from my astonishing ascent of one of the world's most notorious climbs. They did. I was almost grateful to Ed for that.

Malcolm shook his head. 'You think that's bad? Well, son, let me show you what can happen on the high peaks.'

He bent down and started unlacing his boot. I tried to trade glances with Mark, but he was staring intently at his fork. And then Malcolm swung his foot up onto the table, although it was less of a foot and more a misshapen block, with no lumps where his toes should be. Conversation around the table ceased. We were all thinking the same thing: *Please don't take your sock off.* 'Lost them on Mount Cook.'

'Wow.'

'Oh aye.'

'That's quite something, Malcolm.'

'Frostbite. And all because of an ill-fitting boot.' He beamed. 'Still got them.'

'Got what? Your boots?'

'My toes, son. Got them off the surgeon and preserved them. Keep them in a jar in the garage. Wife won't have them in the house.'

'Why the fu— Why would you do that?' All I could think was: *wait till Thierry hears about this.*

'They're my toes, son. Why shouldn't I keep them?'

Adesh, the guy who owned the hotel, chose this moment to

come in with a tray of dhal bhat, chicken curry and rice. He carefully placed the food on the table.

'Eat up, everyone,' Ireni said. 'You will lose much weight on the mountain.'

The foot disappeared, along with my appetite. I tried to catch Wanda's eye, but she was lost in conversation with Ireni and Tadeusz at the cool end of the table. I still couldn't understand why I'd thought her plain, or figure out exactly what it was that drew me to her. She came across as reserved, self-contained, standoffish, and couldn't be more different to the glamorous, hard-partying girls I usually went for.

As we ate, Robbie and Malcolm dominated the conversation, trying to out-macho each other with tales of derring-do, but to be fair, Robbie couldn't compete with Malcolm's missing digits. Howard interjected occasionally, Mark didn't say a word, and Wanda contented herself with the food – she ate twice as much as the rest of us. I also got the impression Tadeusz was silently assessing us; again I reminded myself to be on my guard.

Wanda finished her plate and stood up, gave Ireni a hug, said a curt 'Good night' to the rest of us – interrupting Robbie who was droning on about scaling a frozen waterfall – and strode out. The men at the table appeared to deflate, partly out of relief that their egos (and dicks) could have a rest. Because no one had missed what I'd picked up: Wanda had something. Tadeusz and Ireni made their excuses shortly afterwards.

Adesh brought us another bucket of beers, and eager to avoid another Malcolm interrogation, I turned back to Mark.

'Is this your first big peak, Mark?'

'Yes.'

'Me too. Looks like we're the virgins of the group.'

Robbie raised an eyebrow. 'What's this about virgins?'

'I was just saying that seeing as it's my and Mark's first time on the mountain, you guys are the veterans, and we're the virgins.'

Howard chuckled at this.

'Yeah? Well you'd better not jeopardise my chances of

summiting.' Robbie grinned, showing his teeth. 'Only kidding, fellas.' But he wasn't joking. I could see that.

'Why would you think we would jeopardise your climb?' Mark said, surprising all of us with a flash of steel. 'You're the one who's failed to make it up there before.'

Robbie bristled. 'I'm just saying I'm not here to babysit anyone.'

'And I'm not *asking* you to babysit me.'

'Come on, guys, keep it friendly,' Howard said with a nervous laugh. Malcolm had gone quiet.

Robbie held up a hand. 'Just saying that I've had experience of this kinda thing before. Last year there were a couple of guys on the team who didn't have what it takes. Slowed all of us down.'

'It's up to Tadeusz who summits or not,' Mark said. 'And I won't slow you down.'

'Good. I'll hold you to that, *mate*,' Robbie said in a crap attempt at a British accent. 'Going to be bad enough with all the dirt-bags clogging up the high camps.'

'What?' Mark said. The blood had now diffused from his face, as if the effort of standing up to Robbie had worn him out.

'Dirt-bags. The climbers who come to the mountain without backup or adequate preparation. Use the fixed ropes without paying for them, leech off the other teams, don't have any climbing support and expect to be rescued when they run into trouble. They give the mountain a bad name.'

If Thierry had had his way, *I'd* be one of those climbers. Mindful of Ed-Gate, I'd put my foot down and insisted he shell out for me to join a reputable guided expedition.

'Shit happens on the mountains,' Robbie carried on, reluctant to let his dirt-bag bugbear go. 'The only way to do it is to sign on with a good commercial organisation.'

'So you think that only rich people should be allowed to climb Everest?'

'Not what I'm saying, Mark. I'm saying that the mountain should be regulated and only experienced climbers should be allowed to attempt it, with the proper support, of course.'

Mark muttered something that sounded like *whatever*, and left the courtyard without saying goodnight. I was glad to see he did have some backbone, but I remember thinking that I didn't want to be saddled with him – he was too downbeat for my taste. I wasn't sure I wanted to be saddled with any of them, except for maybe Ireni and Wanda.

While Malcolm and Robbie resumed their battle of the egos, now debating which side of the mountain was the most challenging, Howard moved into Mark's vacant seat. 'That scene was tense, hey, Simon?'

'Yeah.'

'Can get like that on these trips.' He was slurring, flabby cheeks flushed from the booze. Despite his resemblance to literature's most famous cannibal, I reckoned Howard was probably the least likely out of all of us to kill or eat another human being. 'You got a reason for doing this, Simon? Climbing Everest, I mean?'

'Yes. Because it's there.'

He wasn't listening. 'Me, I've got to do it this time. Third time lucky. Been my ambition since I was a kid.' Howard was an over-sharer and had things he had to get off his chest. He'd gone into debt to pay for the climb, putting his marriage under strain. 'But,' he confided in a loud whisper that could have been heard across town in Durbar Square, 'I'm pretty sure she's screwing someone else. You see, Simon,' – he was the type of guy who used your name as often as possible in conversation – 'I'm doing this for me, you know? Know I've got it in me to succeed this time.' On and on he went. I let my mind wander to Wanda. What were the chances? I thought about the journey ahead. How would I handle the altitude? Was I fit enough? Doubtful, I'd only had a couple of months to get into shape, using the flat as my gym, haring up and down the stairs, a rucksack of Thierry's second-hand climbing books on my back. *What if it all goes wrong like it did in Cwm Pot?* No. I couldn't think like that. I'd got through the trials of Ed and the caves, and I was a different person to the Simon Newman who'd been a mewling mess down in Cwm Pot; I hadn't been hit with another panic attack or plagued by an Ed nightmare since I'd started training for the mountain.

And this was going to be our ticket to the big time. Thierry was sure of that. To fund it, he'd borrowed thirty thousand dollars from his parents on the proviso that if the website wasn't generating an income in six months, he'd return to the States and pick up their dreams for him. He had everything on the line. He was counting on me.

The dubious morality underpinning our plans didn't nag at me, not in the run-up to the expedition at any rate. Sure, that message from Nigel's parents occasionally haunted me, a faint echo at the back of my mind, but that was it.

After Malcolm's display the night before, which underlined how easy it was to misplace digits on the mountain, I decided to blow some of my meagre funds on a backup pair of over-mitts. Thierry and I had missed a trick here. Thamel is riddled with second-hand climbing stores, and we could have saved a fortune if I'd waited to kit myself out in Kathmandu. After breakfast, Adesh gave me directions to a shop where he said I'd get a discount.

I didn't pick up any of the political tension Tadeusz had spoken about as I rambled through Thamel's touristy warren. I'd only ever travelled to France and Ibiza before, but I felt weirdly at home in Kathmandu, getting a kick out of its dusty, sometimes acrid air, the constant honking of car horns, the rickety colourful tenements, and the death-wish dance performed by the scooters and motorbikes that zipped through the narrow streets. Shopkeepers called out to me as I passed, friendly without being pushy. The occasional group of westerners, smug that they'd made it this far off the beaten track or bewildered by the lack of ATMs and pavements, threaded their way through the crowds. After backtracking several times, I found the hole-in-the-wall store Adesh had suggested. Indri, who turned out to be Adesh's cousin, a handsome man with outrageous eyebrows, was a champion haggler, and I ended up buying a pair of salopettes I didn't need as well as the gloves.

On my way back to the hotel I bumped into Ireni, who greeted me like an old friend. 'It is good to have met you after all of our emails, Simon.'

Thierry's emails – please don't let this be awkward. 'You too. And I appreciate you letting me on the team without high-altitude experience.'

'Tadeusz would not have let you on the permit if he did not think you had a good chance, Simon. He has built up his business from nothing and his reputation is everything. It has been a hard struggle for him to do this. He does not take risks with people.'

We pressed ourselves against a wall to avoid being flattened by a mother, father and two kids sandwiched on a moped.

'How did you and Tadeusz meet?'

She smiled. 'We met two years ago, at base camp on the Nepalese side. After I finished my hospital training, I joined as a support hiker and doctor for a Swedish expedition. I was only there to be a friend to the climbers, but I became more than a friend to Tadeusz after one day.'

'Love at first sight?'

She laughed. 'Yes.'

A stab of envy. My longest relationship had lasted three months, and although I'd thought I'd fallen in love several times, it only ever ended up being lust, petering out after a few weeks.

'I think we have a good group this year,' she said.

'What's the story with Mark?'

Her expression became guarded. 'What do you mean?'

'I tried to talk to him last night but didn't get very far.'

'He is shy, I think. Also, he was supposed to be climbing with someone else who dropped out. You took their place.' She changed the subject. 'Wanda is very focused. Very determined. You like her?'

'Don't really know her.'

'I saw that you were looking at her last night.'

'Oh God. That obvious?'

'That obvious. It is very good that Tadeusz gets her on this expedition. If she summits, then it is likely that she will get full sponsorship. The North Face, maybe.'

In climbing terms that was pretty much the equivalent of scoring a million-dollar recording contract or winning the lottery. 'She is a rising star.'

A rising star who no doubt had a boyfriend (or girlfriend). I pictured a slick, fearless alpinist, the kind of character *Outside* magazine would profile.

I asked Ireni what she thought about Robbie.

'He is a little over-confident, perhaps. But Howard is a *very* good man.'

Howard, aka cuddly Hannibal Lecter.

'And Malcolm?'

'Ah, Malcolm . . . ugh! That thing that he does with his toes. I hope he will make it this year. Everyone has a reason for climbing this mountain. What is yours, Simon?' The same question Howard had asked me last night.

I gave her the 'boyhood dream' spiel, and an exaggerated version of the fall at Cwm Silyn, spinning a story about how I was fighting to regain my confidence. 'I suppose I'm trying to prove something to myself.'

Ireni was no fool, but I'm a good liar. Always have been.

'Do not worry, Simon. We will look after you.'

'I'm not worried.'

And I wasn't. Not then.

To: TCAKES@journeytothedarkside.com
From: sibaby@journeytothedarkside.com
Subject: Kill Me Now

I fucking hate you, dude. Arrived at base camp day before yesterday after journey from hell. Started to feel sick soon as we left Kathmandu. Then followed 4 days of Exorcist-grade puking, not fun on a long drive on a winding, shitty road next to a precipice. Ireni says I probably had severe food poisoning.

Here's the lowdown:

It's so very very cold. Hurts to BREATHE. Have to keep my water bottle in my sleeping bag at night or it freezes.

Base camp basically looks like a giant stony parking lot on which hundreds of nutters have decided to set up giant igloo-style tents. Ireni says it's the busiest season ever. Chinese camp is huge – even has a posse of bored military guys guarding it.

Teammates still mostly a bunch of dicks. Been hanging out with a cool French couple from one of the international teams who have some seriously good coffee, so at least I'm getting a decent caffeine fix.

Yeah, we've met the Sherpas we'll be climbing with, but they're now up the mountain helping to fix ropes so that everyone else can pull themselves up. Gyaluk, the guy who runs the kitchen, is completely cool but can't cook for shit. Get woken every morning by Ngima, Gyaluk's awesome assistant, bringing me a flask of 'Sherpa tea'. Feel like a colonial throwback.

Internet is shit even though the Chinese team have set up a communications tower.

Leave for advanced base camp in a few days after the puja ceremony (where a Buddhist priest is shipped in to say a blessing to the mountain gods asking them not to wipe us out). 12-mile hell walk. Tadeusz says we have to hike a couple of miles every day to acclimatise. Fuck that shit, but can't say no as he scares the crap out of me.

Been filming the toilets along the journey & here, because DUDE, holy shit they're bad. Our toilet tent is a blue barrel with a stone plinth over the top. Thinking we can do a 'Five Worst Toilets in the Universe' thing for the site.

Did I say I hated you for sending me here?

Got your emails and links, but can't download anything as Internet too slow & like I said I was feeling like death. And NO I don't accept yr apology for the Eiger bullshit. You could have screwed us there.

No leads on what the hell I'm going to film but will dig around

CAREFULLY & see what comes up.

Laters

'Gotta take a break,' Howard gasped, before collapsing on his arse in a patch of snow-covered talus.

Oh thank you, Jesus. Using my pack as a cushion I slumped next to him, my ankle whimpering in relief. Despite wheezing like a couple of obese chain-smokers, Malcolm and Robbie were pretending they weren't knackered. Mark wandered several metres away from us and hunkered down, unsteady on his feet. He'd surprised us all when he'd accepted my invitation to join our acclimatisation hike. He'd been conspicuously avoiding Robbie since their clash in Kathmandu.

We'd only been walking for an hour, but thanks to the altitude – we were well above five thousand metres, way higher than I'd ever been – my body was insisting it had just run a marathon. On the plus side, after three days at base camp, the headache that had dogged me since our stopover in Nyalam was fading, and my gut no longer felt like a couple of rats were fighting inside it. I made myself drink half a litre of Gyaluk's trademark sugary tea and passed the flask to Howard. We'd set off after breakfast, intending to explore the path we'd take to advanced base camp in a few days' time. We hadn't got far. The camp's glacial valley was peppered with stones, all of which happily lurked, waiting to turn the ankles of the unwary, but by far the hardest thing to cope with was something I'd never really thought about before: breathing. Never had I been so aware of my lungs and exactly what they went through to keep me alive. It didn't help that the freezing air was sharper and drier than anything I'd experienced before – it scoured my throat with every breath.

'Shame we can't see her today.' Howard sighed like a man suffering from unrequited love. The sky had dropped, cloaking the valley in cloud, and only the grim grey feet of the mountain's surrounding foundations were visible.

'Why are mountains female?' I asked no one in particular.

'Because they're a bitch to climb,' Robbie said.

Howard's sycophantic laugh turned into a coughing session.

Far as I was concerned, Everest should be male, the type of huge, intimidating bloke who said, 'What the fuck are you looking at?' before nutting you. It dominated the skyline as if it had elbowed the neighbouring peaks out of its way.

'Sherpas call her the "Mother Goddess of the Earth",' Malcolm said, full of himself as usual.

'Gyaluk says it's also known as "Unshakable Good Elephant Woman".' *Take that, Malcolm, you smug bastard.*

'You getting in tight with the Sherps, Simon?' 'Sherps' – typical Robbie. He, Malcolm and Howard tended to patronise Ngima and Gyaluk, talking too loudly at them and leaving out pronouns. *Tea, make tea now, okay?*

'They're cool.'

'Yeah. Except I reckon Gyaluk's doing his best to give us food poisoning.'

'Food's not *that* bad.' It was. Gyaluk had to be the only cook in the world who could make lentils and chicken taste like aftershave. 'How come you didn't join one of the high-end teams, Robbie? The ones with gourmet food and heated mess tents?' He clearly had the cash. His equipment was state-of-the-art.

'Tadeusz has got a good rep. Got every member of his team up there last year.'

Time to do some digging. 'Ireni says last year was a really bad year for the mountain. People were just like, stepping over bodies on their way to the summit.'

Robbie snorted. 'You try and help someone when you're in the death zone. It's impossible. You've barely got the energy to sort yourself out.'

'Is it true that some of the bodies have been there for so long that climbers use them as landmarks?'

Too obvious? Had I gone too far? Mark was looking at me as if I'd just farted in the Vatican.

'Oh aye,' Malcolm said. 'That's true enough.'

'Why doesn't anyone remove them?'

'Not as easy as that, Simon,' Robbie said. 'They're frozen to the ground. Have to chip them out. And then there's the danger factor. Heard that some teams charge thirty thousand dollars to retrieve a body. The Sherps don't like to touch them. Goes against their beliefs. There's one that's been up there for years, known as Green Boots. You musta heard of him.' I had. Thierry had unearthed his story during his 'highest graveyard in the world' research. He'd died high up on the mountain in 1996, and his body remained curled outside a cave, his lime-green climbing boots bright against the snow cloaking his body. He wasn't one of our goals. There were pics of him all over the Internet and we needed something no one else had.

'Tsewang Paljor,' Mark said.

'What's that, Mark?'

'That's his name. Tsewang Paljor. Not "Green Boots". Have some bloody respect, Robbie.'

'Whoa, Mark. Wasn't me who gave him that name.'

Mark stood up abruptly and walked off, slipping on a patch of snow in his haste to get away.

'Mark!' I called after him. 'Where you going?'

'Back,' he said without turning around.

Robbie shook his head. 'What the hell is that kid's problem?'

'Boy's got a point,' Malcolm said. 'Got to respect the mountain. Got to respect those who've died on it. Seen it myself. Two Ukrainians died last year up at Camp III. Wore themselves out after trying for the summit, ran out of gas, didn't have the energy to get back down. Died right there in their tent.'

'They still there?' I asked, trying to sound casual. Thierry had mentioned something about a couple of Eastern European or Russian guys who'd bought it last season.

'Could be, if the storms haven't taken them. Got to prepare yourself for that, son. Won't be the only ones you'll come across.'

This news was exactly what I'd been digging for, but instead of feeling chuffed, an image of the Cwm Pot lads slid into my mind, bringing with it a roll of nausea.

Malcolm clapped me on the shoulder. 'Dig deep inside yourself, son. You'll be fine.'

Thanks, Dad.

Robbie sighed. 'Last year I was so close I could smell the barn. Gonna do it this year if it kills me. If I'd bought an extra bottle of oxygen I could've made it.'

We'd heard it all before. Even Howard, Robbie's loyal sidekick, looked panicked at the prospect of another 'coulda, shoulda, woulda' monologue. He got to his feet. 'Let's head back.'

We retraced our steps, picking our way carefully along the path that led to the edge of the glacial valley, the sounds of camp life – the rumble of equipment trucks, and a mix of Bollywood and rock music – drifting in on the wind. En route we passed a cluster of yaks waiting to be loaded with supplies to be ferried up to advanced base camp. With their woolly coats and delicate legs I'd thought them cute and exotic at first, but they lost their charm on the days when the sun melted the mounds of frozen droppings. The smell was pungent enough to cut through my dulled senses.

The hike had half-killed me, but I wasn't in the mood to head back to my tent: I needed to sluice the Cwm Pot imagery from my mind. 'I'll catch you guys later.'

'Where you going?' Howard puffed.

'Caffeine run. Going to see if Claude and Elodie have the coffee on.'

I peeled away before Malcolm could offer to join me. After my first night here, when I'd lain in my sleeping bag trying not to vomit, cursing Thierry and longing for my own bed, Charming Si had rallied, and I'd become the unofficial ambassador for our camp, taking daily recces to visit the other teams. The only camp I actively avoided was a high-end American-based operation, mainly because it had a film crew attached to it. Having splurged on high-altitude boots, oxygen canisters, down suits, airfares and the fifteen grand it took to join Tadeusz's team, Thierry and I had run out of funds and we were forced to buy a camcorder on tick (no way was I going to use the Cwm Pot helmet cam again). It was fine for our purposes, but as I was supposed to be a 'filmmaker', I didn't want to give myself away with my comparatively crap set-up.

Claude, who was as slim and chic as his wife, welcomed me with cries of: 'Ah, Simon! You come for café?'

He made me an espresso in his battered moka pot, and we shot the shit for a while. He and Elodie were climbing dirt-bag style, with minimal facilities and no Sherpa support, but they knew how to live. Like Wanda, they both worked as ski guides, and every year they scrimped and saved to fund what they called 'an adventure for living'. They'd been to the Vinson Massif, and next year were planning to join a round-the-world yacht crew. God knows why such cool people liked hanging out with a freeloader like me; it may have been because their camp was populated with Robbies and Malcolms.

My upbeat mood and caffeine buzz took a knock when I returned to camp and spotted Wanda sitting outside her tent, laughing and chatting in Polish with two guys who I found out later were planning to paraglide from the summit. How could I compete with that? In any case, I'd blown any chance of hooking up with her on the drive in. She'd seen me at my lowest ebb: puking my guts out and begging for someone to make it stop. I slunk into the mess tent and used Tadeusz's laptop to send Thierry a one-line email: 'got a lead on a couple of dead Russians'.

Malcolm had warned me on the drive in that base-camp life could get boring, and I hadn't believed him. But as we waited for the next chapter – the hike up to advanced base camp – time started to drag.

I spent a fair amount of time in the Sherpas' mess tent next door. It was warmer than ours, which made up for the fug of cigarette smoke and the hum of boiling lentils from the kitchen tent attached to it. Ngima didn't speak any English, but he was permanently upbeat, even when Gyaluk shouted at him, which he did on an hourly basis. Wanda was clearly Ngima and Gyaluk's favourite. They called her 'didi' – 'sister' – but otherwise, she kept everyone, Tadeusz and Ireni excepted, at a distance. The only time she spoke to me directly was on the day of the puja ceremony. Tadeusz had encouraged us to place our equipment next to the chorten – a stone plinth that Gyaluk and Ngima had erected – so that the lama could bless it, and I caught her eyeing my gear. Compared to her battered

Edelrid harness, my stuff looked shamefully new. 'You use switch-blade crampons, Simon?' I loved the way she said my name: *see-moan*.

'Sure. Always use them.' *Bullshit*. They were the type Chris and I had used on our aborted Aiguilles trip and I'd gone on the recommendation of the bloke in the climbing store.

'You don't have a problem with them in the soft snow?'

'No. I like their versatility.'

I'd find out later that the crampons tended to suck up clogs of snow, forming dangerous icy crusts at the base of my boots. I was unreasonably chuffed that she'd spoken to me – it put me in a good mood for the rest of the day.

Thierry had given me a copy of *The Mammoth Book of Mountaineering Disasters* as a joke, but I didn't crack it. I discovered that Mark had brought along a pile of Terry Pratchett's Discworld books, so I revisited these instead, using him as my not-so-mobile library.

'It's cool you have the same surname, Mark.'

'Huh?'

'You and Terry Pratchett.'

'Oh. Yes.' Dragging a word out of him was like getting a smile out of Cosimo: you had to work at it. I wasn't alone in attempting to pry him out of his shell; Malcolm and Ireni also gave it a go. He hadn't joined us again on our hikes, and only emerged from his tent when Gyaluk called us for supper. The only person I saw him talking to at any length was Tadeusz. Depressed Harry Potter was a closer moniker than I realised, and Mark's downbeat attitude needled Robbie in particular.

'You figured out what's up with Mark, Simon?'

'How would I know?'

'He's your friend, isn't he?'

'I don't really know him.'

'Tell him to cheer up. Whenever he walks into the mess tent, the temperature drops.'

I'm not sure why, but I felt a compulsion to defend Mark, which made me half-resent him. 'He's okay.'

'Yeah? Don't think he should be here. Don't think he's got what it takes. Reckon Tadeusz made a mistake letting him on the team.'

And then followed a Robbie-style monologue about 'focusing and overcoming life's obstacles'. His conversation rotated exclusively around his mountaineering and ice-climbing achievements; he rarely spoke about his personal life or his job. I'd assumed he was involved in some sort of Big Pharma operation, but according to Howard he worked with stroke victims. I couldn't imagine anything worse than Robbie with his pathological one-upmanship showing up at my bedside after I'd suffered a cerebral event: *So you've got no feeling in your left arm, huh? If you think that's bad, let me tell you about the time I was climbing Denali and the weather came down . . .*

Howard seemed to shrivel as the days passed, becoming a ghost of the nervy, friendly guy I'd met in Kathmandu. He was like a camel, storing up all his energy for the climb ahead.

I did my best to avoid Malcolm. I wasn't worried that he'd try and weasel out any more damning details of my fantasy Eiger climb – I knew how to divert him from that thorny track – but he'd got into the habit of cornering me and dispensing unsolicited advice: 'Now, Simon, let me show you the best way of using the ascender with your over-mitts and hand-warmers. Now, Simon, don't forget to put sunblock on the inside your nostrils as the sun will reflect upwards off the snow. Now, Simon, you want to think about how you're going to pose on the summit when they take your photo, you only get one shot at it . . .' Blah blah. He would go on for hours if I let him.

I fell into a routine: woken with a welcome flask of tea. Some kind of rudimentary wash. Breakfast. One of Tadeusz's killer hikes. Nap. Lunch. Another nap. A wander over to Elodie and Claude's tent for an espresso, the Spanish team's camp for a slice of Serrano ham, or the Indian team's mess for some chai. Back home to listen to music or read. Supper. Join in with the inevitable whinge-fest about supper. Game of poker with Robbie and Howard. Rinse and repeat. And every evening, if it was clear, I got into the habit of layering up and wandering to the edge of camp to watch as the sun died behind the mountain and shadowy fingers crept over the north ridge. Base camp was becoming the new normal. It was only when I read Thierry's emails that I remembered why I was actually here. It wasn't to socialise. It wasn't to climb. I told myself to dig around for more information on the dead climbers I'd started to think of as 'Thierry's Ukrainians', but I kept putting it off.

I didn't dream.

We convened in the mess tent before dawn, a surly gathering of shivering, silent wrecks. As I filled my flasks with diluted Tang and sugary tea for the slog up to advanced base camp, I noticed Malcolm had a phlegmy cough, and Mark was paler than usual, the white anti-radiation cream on his lips giving him the look of a weedy, unfashionable vampire. Only Wanda radiated any energy.

Outside, porters were gathering in the glacier, strapping gas bottles, boxes and tubs of equipment to their yaks' sides, and as we set off, the mountain was bathed in a golden glow that gave it the illusion of being warm and inviting. I slathered my face with sunblock, remembering to smear it inside my nostrils (*thanks, Malcolm*). My pack, containing a down jacket, extra gloves and the litres of fluid I'd need to keep me hydrated on the long walk up to advanced base camp, already felt like a small angry child on my back. The air held its usual spiteful bite.

We clumped together at first, before finding our own pace. Wanda was always ahead of me, moving gracefully, the bright red of her jacket appearing and disappearing like a beacon. Mark, in his yellow and black, trailed behind, with Howard, Malcolm and Robbie bringing up the rear. It was clear where to go, cairns were built along the path that looped through the talus, and the ragged scraps of prayer flags were still visible from previous years. Occasionally I'd hear a looping whistle behind me, the crunch of skittering hooves, and I'd have to scramble out of the way to allow a bunch of yaks and their porters to pass. The yak herders' hardiness put us all to shame; several were wearing little more than trainers, jeans and light jackets. But it was the yaks I really felt sorry for. Every so often I'd come across a bright splash of blood where the rough ground had bitten into their feet. I paused and filmed some of this for Thierry; he'd probably subtitle it *Blood on Death Mountain.*

The wind picked up, blowing fine grit into my mouth that coated my teeth. I picked my way through a gulley that never seemed to end, and across an undulating rocky snarl that punished my ankle with every step. Every so often came the belly rumble of a mini stone avalanche. The path didn't take a direct route, but maliciously switched back on itself, rising and falling. As I crossed a glacial stream the colour of milk, the naughty child on my back grew into a troubled youth, biting into my shoulder muscles and kicking my kidneys.

You're not going to make it, Si. You haven't got what it takes. When he was manipulating me into doing this, Thierry had gone on and on about how Everest was a piece of piss to climb: *blind guys have done it; guys with no legs and shit.* But you needed true grit to do this. You needed a compelling reason. And I didn't have one. I wasn't here to prove something to myself like Malcolm; to fulfil an ambition I'd had since I was a child, like Wanda and Howard. Even trophy hunter Robbie, who was climbing for purely egotistical reasons, had more motivation than I did. I was here to capture some salacious footage for a website, and it wasn't enough. My only hope was that the summit would pull me into its radar like some kind of granite Death Star.

I trudged on, cursing Thierry, cursing Tadeusz, cursing the world. My feet became their own entity, divorced from my body. My lungs now felt like they'd been pierced by knitting needles. I almost burst into tears of relief when I spotted the yellow tents that made up interim camp – the halfway point. Behind them towered a jagged jaw of immense ice shards. I didn't pause to take in the spectacle; all I cared about was taking the weight off my feet and back.

I spied Wanda sitting next to a pocket of herders brewing tea, their yaks stamping impatiently, and made my way over to her, trying to mask my exhaustion.

'Mind if I join you?' My voice squeaked out like air through a leaky balloon.

'Of course.' Her eyes were hidden behind huge old-fashioned aviator sunglasses.

Alone at last. Only I couldn't spare the breath to talk to her. I collapsed onto my pack and rotated my ankle. My thighs shook, a hangover-grade headache pulsed at my temples. I downed half a litre of juice and crammed peanut butter crackers into my mouth.

Wanda ate two energy bars in quick efficient bites, then neatly rolled the wrappers and placed them in her pocket. She did everything gracefully and economically; I had crumbs smeared all over my face. Again: too tired to care.

'Hey!' A far fitter climber than me was heading straight for us at speed. With his blue-black stubble, chic red scarf and Polaroid sunglasses he could have walked out of a climbing couture advert. *Bastard.* He nodded in my direction and leered down at Wanda with a *hey, how you doing?* grin. I gave him an Ed-esque grunt.

'There is a man in trouble down there,' he said. 'I think he is with you? He is wearing a yellow jacket.'

Wanda glanced at me. 'That could be Mark, no?'

'He sits in a ball. He would not speak when I ask his name.'

'How do you know he's with us?' I asked.

'I think I have seen him with you before.' Another sultry glance at Wanda that she didn't reciprocate. *Good.*

'Is he hurt?'

A Gallic shrug. 'I do not know.'

'Okay, thank you,' Wanda said.

'You are welcome.'

Miffed that Wanda had been impervious to his charms, he wandered away.

Wanda got to her feet. 'We must go and check on him.'

Really? I honestly didn't know if I could stand up, never mind stage a rescue mission. And Mark was hardly a mate. But how could I say no without looking like an arsehole?

Wanda was already striding off without checking to see if I was going to follow. I shouldered my pack and gave chase – stupid, as anything more arduous than a slow walk kicked the breath out of my lungs.

I was still huffing asthmatically when we ran into Howard and Robbie five minutes later. Before we could ask them about Mark, Robbie blurted: 'This is bullshit. We should be taking a break at interim camp. Staying the night so that we can acclimatise properly.' I secretly agreed. Unlike many of the other teams, we had to do the entire trek in one go. It was our first trial by fire. If we didn't make it, then Tadeusz reserved the right to chuck us off the summit team.

'Tadeusz knows what he's doing,' Wanda said, voice cold.

'Yeah? You sure about that?'

'Yes. I am sure.'

Howard nervously adjusted his rucksack's strap.

'Have you seen Mark?' I said, before the Robbie vs Wanda stand-off could escalate.

'Yeah,' Robbie said. 'Looked a bit rough.'

Wanda shook her head. 'You did not stop to help him?'

'We stopped, but he didn't want to know. Told him to go back down.'

'How far away is he?'

'Not far.'

And then she was off again.

'Laters,' I said. Howard gave me a weary thumbs-up.

We spotted Mark's yellow and black shape after another five minutes of backtracking over ankle-biting talus. He was sitting at the side of the route, his head buried in his arms. Glad of an excuse to rest again, I slumped down next to him. 'Hey Mark.'

No reaction.

'Mark.'

He lifted his head and mumbled something.

'Come on, mate. You feeling ill?'

'Can't do this. Tired.'

Wanda shook his shoulder. 'Come, Mark. We are halfway. We must move to make it there before it gets dark. You must come with us, Mark. Or you must return to base camp.'

My brain latched onto this immediately: *Hey, Si, you could offer to accompany Mark back down. In fact, you could give it all up, head back to Kathmandu with its lovely, lovely bars and beds and beers and warmth.* But Thierry's thirty thousand dollars hung over my head. He was counting on me. And what would Wanda think of me if I threw in the towel?

You got through the caves. You found something in yourself and you got through it. You can get through this. The caves and Ed didn't have a place here; I shoved them back in the mental strongbox where they belonged. 'Come on, Mark, mate. You can't give up now. I can't be the only virgin on the mountain.'

'Huh?' Wanda gave me a look.

'Not that kind of virgin. It's just a stupid joke.' I thought about explaining it, but decided against it. Talking was robbing me of my breath again. *Hurry up, Mark, you fucking loser.* No way did I want to be wandering around the mountain when the shadows came down. 'Come on. This is the easy part.'

'What Simon says is true. Come, we will walk with you. I will take your pack until you feel stronger.'

'No, I'll take it,' I jumped in, thinking, *seriously, dude?* But I couldn't let her carry it without looking weak. She was tall, but I outweighed her by at least thirty kilos.

Mark removed his sunglasses. His eyes were red-rimmed. 'I'll be okay. You go on.'

'No. We will not leave you.'

I decided to take a leaf out of Thierry's *Mammoth Book of Emotional Blackmail*: 'Yeah, mate. You want to screw up our chances of making it to ABC? You want that on your conscience?'

It seemed to do the trick. A soul-crushing sigh, and then: 'Okay.'

Wanda helped him to his feet. 'So you will walk?'

'I'll walk.'

'You have been drinking enough, Mark? You are hydrated?'

'Yes.'

'Then let's go.'

Gone was the concern. This was an order, *my way or the highway*. Mark gave me a wry glance, and thankfully shouldered his own pack. I wasn't sure if I'd make it up there with two angry children on my back.

I paused to down another half litre of sweet, lukewarm tea.

The sugar-boost pepped me up, and my headache quietened. We hauled back through interim camp without stopping, striding past Robbie and Howard without a word, Howard lamely calling, 'You okay, Mark?' in our wake.

After that, the only thing that kept me going was the dread of looking weak in front of Wanda. Even Mark, who shuffled along with his head down like an inmate being dragged to the electric chair, had more oomph in his step than I did.

We came to a wide pathway that meandered through an ocean of serrated ice teeth; I was too wiped to take more than a passing interest in the way the light bounced in glorious blue waves across it. 'This part is called the miracle highway,' Wanda said.

'Yeah, because it's a fucking miracle if you can make it through here without wanting to kill yourself.' It took me half a minute to huff out this lame joke, but Mark parped a laugh all the same.

Wanda lowered her sunglasses, and we shared a smile, relieved that he'd snapped out of his funereal mood.

There was another brief bright spot when we stopped for a bathroom break, Wanda on one side of the trail, hidden behind a cairn, Mark and me on the other. As we peed in unison, he said in his usual monotone, 'Don't cross the streams,' – a *Ghostbusters* reference that Thierry would have dug. I didn't have the energy to laugh, but it was good to know he had a sense of humour.

Wanda put in her earphones and I followed her example. *Just keep going until you get to the end of a song.* Then another. And another. This worked until I hit a playlist Thierry had loaded for me entitled, 'Si's Climbing Soundtrack'. There were a few good tracks on it: 'River Deep Mountain High', 'Country Roads', 'The Misty Mountain Hop', but then it slid into dubious territory: 'Rocky Mountain High', 'Green Green Grass of Home', which didn't exactly have the oomph of say, The Prodigy. So it was that I arrived at ABC, my ears ringing with Julie Andrews singing 'Climb Ev'ry Mountain'. It was oddly fitting.

Like the sadist he is, Tadeusz had placed our camp way above everyone else's. The light was taking on a violet hue as we stumbled past other teams' cook tents, inching our way to the tip of ABC's shallow, bowl-shaped expanse. Wanda led us towards our mess tent – a grubbier version of our base camp facilities – where we downed sugary tea, hot chocolate and vegetable soup. God knows what would have happened if my tent hadn't been erected for me; I barely had the oomph to remove my boots. Perhaps I would have just flumped down outside, a Gore-Tex snow angel. Nor did I have the energy to feel smug that we'd beaten Robbie and Howard (Malcolm would arrive two hours after everyone, narrowly avoiding spending a night out on the mountain). I apologised to my ankle, which was swollen, and the rest of my body, which felt simultaneously lighter now that the obese teen on my back was gone, and heavier because it ached like a rotten tooth, made myself drink another litre of sweet tea and water, and passed out.

I lurched awake a couple of hours later, gasping for air, heart thudding, a tight band restricting my lungs. Panicked, I felt around for my head torch. *Relax. Chill. You're fine. It's just the altitude.* I sucked in air, thumped my chest and dug in my pack for ibuprofen. My water bottle had frozen (I'd forgotten to keep it next to my body in the sleeping bag), so I was forced to dry swallow them, the tablets razoring my raw throat. Shaky, I lay back down, pulling my sleeping bag over my head. My breath's condensation had turned the inner lining of the tent into an icy ecosystem. The wind hissed around me, whispering on the tent's sides.

You made it. Relax, dude. You're fine. It's all fine.

I slept. Still I didn't dream.

I emerged out of my tent like a maggot squirming out of an apple. Crystalline light gunned into my retinas, and I squirrelled back in to root around for my sunglasses and down jacket. Even this relatively mild action left me breathless.

No one else from my team was out and about yet. I shuffled into the cook tent to greet Gyaluk, who was cheerfully arguing with Ngima and smoking, and after downing a litre of juice, I dragged a camp chair to the snowy, stony pocket in front of my tent, and sank into it to check out what I'd missed last night. It was the first time that the true scale of the Himalaya really hit me. Changtse, Everest's smaller cousin, towered behind camp, and I stared up at its grim, snow-flecked face, feeling as insubstantial as an ant on a dining-room table. Finally, the zip in the tent next to mine slid down, and Mark's head emerged. His lips were cracked and the bum fluff on his chin looked faintly ridiculous – as if he'd stuck it to his face in an attempt to look older.

I handed him my flask, and we sat in silence until Gyaluk called us for breakfast. Tadeusz was finishing a bowl of porridge in the mess tent, and he nodded to us, then headed outside to fiddle with his radio. No one else pitched up. Ngima brought us bowls of fried potatoes and eggs swimming in a paddling pool of grease. My stomach tipped over.

Mark pushed his plate away.

'Not hungry?'

'No.'

'Me neither. It's just the altitude.' Malcolm and Ireni had warned me I'd lose my appetite up here. I hadn't believed them – I've always been a greedy bastard. But you could have put a bacon sandwich in front of me right then, and I wouldn't have been tempted.

Mark cleared his throat. 'Listen . . . thanks for yesterday, Simon. For coming back for me. I'm sorry I was such a burden.'

'You're not a burden, mate. We're in this together.'

'Well, thanks. I know I haven't been . . .' his voice trailed off.

'Weird to think we're not even halfway to the summit, isn't it? That hike almost killed me.'

'Yeah.'

I popped a piece of cold potato into my mouth, and made myself chew and swallow it. It was like eating wallpaper paste; my taste buds had disappeared.

Mark let his hands dangle between his knees. 'Can I tell you something?'

'Course.'

'It's just . . . I'm not going to the summit.'

'Don't be like that, mate. You'll be fine once you've acclimatised. Get some drugs or something from Ireni if you're feeling rough. Robbie uses Diamox – it's supposed to help.'

'No. You don't understand. I'm not here for that. The summit, I mean.'

'What you here for then? The ambiance?'

A pause. 'Can I trust you, Simon?'

I should have said: *No. Absolutely not. Of all the people in all the world you shouldn't trust, I am top of the list.* But of course I didn't. I was curious. 'Course you can, Mark.'

A deep sigh. 'I won't be going to the summit because I have to see my mother.'

At first I thought I'd misheard. 'Come again?'

'My mother. She's up there. On the mountain.'

My brain was running at half its usual speed. 'Eh? You mean she's on another team?'

'No.'

Then I started to worry that maybe he – or I – was having some sort of altitude-induced delusion. 'Are you feeling okay, Mark?'

'I'm fine.' Vehement. A touch of the steel I'd seen on that first night.

'Okay. I'm still not—'

'She's dead, Simon. My mother. She died up there, on the mountain, years ago. Her body is up there. That's why I'm here. I'm going to go and see her.'

The penny dropped. 'Fucking hell.'

'Yeah.'

'When did she die, mate?'

'Twelve years ago. Nineteen ninety-five.'

My knowledge of Everest's history was sketchier than it should have been, but I didn't remember hearing about a British mountaineer named Pratchett – it was the kind of name that would stick in my head. Thierry would know; he'd spent a fortune on second-hand Everest disaster books. And I couldn't think of a reason why Mark would be lying about this – it was way too left-field.

Malcolm lurched into the mess tent like an extra from *Dawn of the Dead*, and before I could pry further, Mark disappeared.

Juliet

DAY 38, Advanced Base Camp

I've been physically broken before. Mountains have a way of stripping you to your core. That's what Walter was: a person permanently stripped to his core. But I've never been mentally challenged like this.

He – it – came again last night. Crunching around my tent, tapping on the nylon sides. Trembling, I shone my light around the interior, saw a bulge in the tent's side above my head as if it was leaning on it. The others were only a scream away. Joe was only a radio call away. But I can't let on that I'm being hounded. Hunted.

Never been so lonely.

No.

Can't give into the fear, although it's so different to anything I've felt before. Walter was adamant that there's nothing weak about feeling afraid. Fear keeps you vigilant, gives you an edge. But this runs deeper, as if the usual concerns about crevasses, avalanches, even the horror of getting frostbite, are only skin deep. This goes right to my core. Would it be easier if I knew what it – he – wants?

~~What did Walter see before he died? Did he see the Third Man? What if Walter blames me for his death? He wouldn't have been there if I hadn't~~

It helps to picture Marcus and me in a cottage, a small place, 2 bedrooms, nestled in a valley in the Peak District. We have a dog, a terrier with a whiskery chin. Starlings live in the roof. It's chilly in winter, but we make do.

I build this house and hope it's enough.

Tomorrow up to Camp II.

DAY 40

Failed to make Camp II yesterday. Feet are swelling badly. Throat is also sore. Cough has once again embedded itself in my lungs, and I'm hacking so hard I'm in danger of breaking a rib. If he/it is Death, then it's not playing fair, chopping away at me, grinding me down, stacking the odds for itself.

But it didn't come last night. Marcus's cottage kept me safe.

Heard via radio that Stef has given up her bid for the summit. Should be rejoicing. Can't. Too broken. Barely feel the loss of this added pressure. Now it's me against myself.

DAY 42

Made it to Camp II this time. Hard, hard going. The wind jostled me, racing up like a train from the North Col.

I've started furnishing the cottage. I have a white wicker rocking chair in the corner of my bedroom. The bed is brass, the metal dinged here and there. None of the furniture is new. A soft, faded patchwork quilt serves as a coverlet. Last night I crawled beneath the quilt and slept.

He didn't come.

DAY 43

The countdown has begun. Joe is confident I'll have a good weather window in 2 days.

The others are now at ABC, but will only think about summiting in a week or so. Andrej, Sem, Wade and Lewis are all strong. Tom has come down with Andrej's chest infection. Feel no triumph at this. I'm past all that. It seems so petty now. My world has shrunk to nothing but the mountain and it.

Eri is also taking strain physically – says her back is giving her trouble. If stoical Eri is complaining about it, she must be in agony. I hope she finds the strength to make the push, I truly do. When she arrived she sought me out, tapped her chest, and said, 'Don't let it go here, Julie.' She wouldn't, or couldn't find the words to explain what she meant. The climb? The altercation with Tom? The bad press? The Third Man? (But how could she know about that?) Whatever the meaning, they were wise words, but too late.

Tadeusz is also worried about me. He keeps saying, 'If you climb with oxygen it is still good, Julie.' I keep telling him I'm fine. Strong. Each time it sounds more like a lie. I'm hurting.

Joe, I know, trusts me to make the right decision.

DAY 45

he's back shouldn't be able to hear the crunch of his footsteps but I can and round and round he goes and the wrongness of it is so so very real slap now goes his hand on the tent oh please don't come in

The worst has happened. Last night he – it – came into the tent. I didn't dream it, I wrote about it. I saw him clearly, I touched him.

He shouldn't have fitted inside the tent. But he did. I could hear the hiss of his synthetic suit fabric as he shifted position, although the buffering of the wind should have smothered it. I fumbled for my head torch, praying that the light would banish him. Praying that it was Tom, or one of the others, but the tent was still zipped up, so how did he get in? I shone the light on his face. The skin around his old-fashioned oxygen mask was black with frostbite: pure black, there's no colour more terrifying than what cold does to skin. His hands were bare, black as pitch and curled into frozen claws.

He, it, edged closer. I dropped the torch. Did I scream? I don't know.

He shucked over and squatted on my chest. Slowly lowered his weight. I couldn't breathe. Clawed, cold fingers forced their way between my lips.

Then, he was gone.

The dream house's walls weren't strong enough to keep him out.

Desperate to believe it's just altitude and loneliness tricking my brain. But his fingers in my mouth . . . I can taste them still. Salty, cold, bitter, like ashes. No. Real. He's real.

Walter always had a second sense for people who were climbing for the wrong reason. Are my reasons the right reasons or the wrong reasons? Is the Third Man trying to tell me something? Is it a warning? Is he telling me not to climb? Not to continue? Is my subconscious doing this, finding a way to let me know I'm not strong enough?

~~There's a part of me that doesn't care. That wants to go whatever the outcome. A part of me that wants it all to end no no no~~

Am I going?

~~maybe the dead don't haunt us. We haunt them. It wasn't just fear in his eyes at the end, there was also blame~~

When he comes tonight I will look behind the mask. I will keep the house in my head and I will make myself look. I have to know. *Who is the third who walks beside you?*

~~If it's Walter~~

Simon

I lasted three hours before I told Wanda about Mark's mission to find his mum. I tried to justify it to myself with a wishy-washy caveat that she'd been great with him when he'd collapsed on the trek up to ABC, but let's face it, sharing Mark's secret was the perfect excuse to spend time with her. And I was curious. From eavesdropping on various conversations, Wanda clearly had an encyclopaedic knowledge about the mountain's history. She'd know who died on Everest twelve years ago. Could I have just waited to ask Mark who his mother was? Sure I could, but the lure of Wanda was too strong.

When Mark disappeared for a nap after lunch, I went for it. Like the others, Wanda had emerged only briefly for something to eat before heading back to the warmth of her sleeping bag. The tent flap was open, but I called out to her rather than rudely sticking my head inside.

'Yes?' She was sitting cross-legged on her sleeping mat, fiddling with her harness, her earphones in. She didn't look charmed to see me.

'Can I have a word?' Thankfully the wind had picked up and thwacked and rustled against the nylon, so we wouldn't have to keep our voices down. ABC wasn't as plush as base camp, and far more cramped; our tents had barely a foot of space between them. On clear nights we'd be able to hear every word, fart and snore from the others. 'It's important.'

She removed her earphones and waved me in, scrunching to the side. Unlike mine, which was already a chaotic mess of clothes, gear and snacks, Wanda's tent was rigidly organised. I clumsily knocked the rime from my boots, took them off and shuffled in, head grazing the domed ceiling. They really were strictly one-woman tents, and we were only inches apart. I prayed I didn't have bad breath, grateful that the altitude seemed to blunt the sense of smell.

'Is it Mark? He is okay?'

'Yeah. Well, kind of. Listen, you know loads about Everest's history, right?'

'I know some.'

'Were there any British female climbers who died on Everest in nineteen ninety-five?'

'Eh? Why do you want to know this?'

'I'll get to that in a minute. Please, Wanda.'

She scrunched up her nose. She was already getting a mountain tan. I found out later that she was younger than she looked – my age in fact – but years of exposure to mountain air had prematurely aged her. If anything, the fine lines around her eyes and mouth made her sexier, and I was struck again at how different she was to the type of girls I usually went for. 'Ah, well of course there was Juliet Michaels.'

The name was vaguely familiar. 'And she died on this side of the mountain?'

'Yes. You do not know of her? You should, Simon. Like you, she is British and she also did a solo ascent of the Eiger.'

Careful. 'I've heard of her of course, but I don't have a great memory. What else can you tell me about her?'

'Why do you want to know?'

'It has something to do with Mark.'

'What?'

'You first.'

She frowned again. 'Okay. Well, she is a legend of course and ah . . . there is a word that means she goes first?'

'Pioneer?'

'Yes. Of course. Thank you. It is very similar in Polish. Sometimes I have problems as English is my third language. First Polish, then French, then English.' Jesus. Her English was fluent. I didn't even have a second language. Well, I could swear in

Romanian (thanks to Gergo, a former co-worker), but that was about it. 'Juliet did five back-to-back solos in one season in the Alps, and she was one of the first women to summit Broad Peak. She died during her second attempt at Everest. The year before this she tried from Nepal.'

'Right. Well I think she's Mark's mother.'

She said something in Polish that sounded like a curse word, and then: 'Explain.'

'He told me he was on the mountain to pay his respects to his mother who died in 'ninety-five. It has to be her, right?'

'He does not have her name.'

'They could have different surnames, or he could be using a fake name.' Of course – it was obviously fake: Pratchett, the *Discworld* books. The altitude really had dulled my synapses. 'How did Juliet die? Did she fall or something?'

'No one is sure. I think the last time they heard from her she was at Camp III preparing to summit. She disappeared. Perhaps Mark comes here to search for her.'

'I got the impression he knew where she was.'

'I have not heard that they have found her body. You are sure?'

'Nope. Not sure about anything.'

'Poor Mark.'

'Yeah. He asked me to keep it to myself, but seeing as you were there yesterday, I thought you should know. I think he needs all the friends he can get right now.'

She gave me a slow, crooked smile. 'You are a kind person, Simon.'

'Me? No I'm not.'

'You are. I am sorry. I feel bad. I have misjudged you.'

'What – did you think I was a bastard or something?'

'No. Not a bastard.' A shrug. 'I thought you were someone who just wants to play and was not serious about the mountain. A person who wastes time.' *Jesus, sugar-coat it, why don't you?* But I had to admit she'd seen right through me. 'You helped him yesterday, and you do this today. Not everyone would do this. Who else knows this about him?'

'I'm pretty sure Tadeusz and Ireni must know' – that would explain Ireni's caginess about Mark in Kathmandu, and his and Tadeusz's intense pow-wows – 'but no one else, far as I know. Like I said, he wants to keep it quiet.'

'Perhaps he does not want the story to get out and the newspapers to know. Juliet was very famous in her time, very controversial. It explains why he has been so upset. Should we tell him that I know?'

Selfish Simon piped up: *Tell her no. That way you'll have an excuse to feed her information.* I shut him up. I was the new Simon, Kind Simon. 'Yeah. That's probably best. I'll tell him.'

There was a slightly awkward silence as she looked at me in a 'we're done here now' fashion.

I didn't want to leave. *Think of something else to say.* 'What were you listening to?'

She handed me her iPod. I struggled to keep my face straight as I thumbed through an eclectic and random mix of show tunes and movie soundtracks: *The People Versus Larry Flynt*, *The General's Daughter*, Music from the Films of Alfred Hitchcock, The James Bond Collection, *Harold and Maude*, *Funny Girl*, *Fiddler on the Roof*, *Hairspray*, *The Umbrellas of Cherbourg*, *Cabaret*, *The Wiz*, *Seven Brides for Seven Brothers* and horror of horrors, *Annie*.

'Show tunes?'

'Yes. I like movie soundtracks and music from the theatre.'

'Seriously?'

'Yes, seriously. You think this is dumb?'

'No. I'm just . . .' *So she wasn't perfect after all.* 'It's cool.'

A shrug as if to say: *I don't care if you think it's cool or not.*

Nice going, Si. One step forward, two steps back. 'I'll see you later then.'

'Yes.'

After narrowly avoiding kicking her in the face during my clumsy exit, I drank in a gulp of oxygen, and burrowed into my own tent. Remorse came whispering in. I'd sworn to Mark that he could trust me – he was clearly in a lot of pain – and I'd failed him for my own selfish reasons. *You're a shit.* Fortunately, the effort of breathing and trying to keep warm – my body was snug in my sleeping bag, but the tips of my ears seemed to be permanently frozen – numbed the true extent of the guilt I should have been feeling. I knocked back another two ibuprofen to fight the headache pulsing at my temples, and napped.

I woke when Gyaluk called us for supper. I hadn't had a chance to tell Mark that I'd blabbed to Wanda, but I made sure I was sitting next to him as the others trickled in. It wasn't hard. Robbie, Howard and even Malcolm appeared to shift away from him as if they sensed weakness; he was the wounded animal in the herd. He looked frail and wasted, and barely glanced at me.

'Glad to see you made it here, Mark,' Robbie said, managing to sound both patronising and insincere. He didn't look any worse for wear, unlike Howard and Malcolm, both of whom were listless, the grey stubble on their jowls ageing them.

'Thanks,' Mark mumbled without looking up from the table.

'It's only going to get harder from here on in.'

'Was it dark when you *finally* arrived at camp last night?' I asked sweetly, which shut him up. I knew he wouldn't stay down for long.

The food that evening was one of Gyaluk's better attempts, some kind of curried chicken that only tasted mildly like it had already been eaten, but no one except Robbie and Wanda managed more than a few mouthfuls.

'Got to keep your strength up,' Robbie said to no one in particular. 'When I did Denali the first time, there was a guy with us who hardly ate anything and he . . .' Blah blah.

I nudged Mark and whispered: 'Sorry about this, mate, but I told Wanda about your mum. I won't tell anyone else, I swear.' I expected him to be seriously pissed off at me, but instead he just nodded resignedly. 'Hang back later so we can talk.'

'What's the big secret?' Robbie piped up, cutting his story short.

'Mark here was asking me if it's true you have one of those micro-penises, Robbie.'

Howard almost spat out his drink, and Wanda snorted a laugh. Malcolm didn't react; like Mark, he was picking at his food.

Robbie gave me a black look. 'You're a funny guy, Simon.'

'Well, you did ask.'

Ireni came in and said she wanted to test our blood oxygen levels and general health before we headed up the North Col. She'd lost some of her pep – the altitude was taking its toll on her as well.

Malcolm sloped off to bed early, but Robbie and Howard seemed to linger like a bad smell for ages, before finally making for their own tents.

The second they were gone I turned to Mark: 'Listen, mate, I'm really sorry I told Wanda.'

'It's okay. I won't be able to keep it a secret forever.'

The three of us scrunched up together at the end of the table. Wanda got straight into it. 'Was Juliet Michaels your mother, Mark?'

He showed no surprise that she'd figured this out. 'Yes.'

'She was an incredible woman.'

Mark nodded and looked down at his hands.

'Wanda said that no one knows if she made the summit or not,' I said.

'That's true.' He dragged in some air and coughed. 'No other climbers were attempting to summit on that date, but two Italians were at Camp II, waiting to go up the next day. They didn't see her. She never returned to her tent.'

'Sorry, Mark.'

'Actually, my name is Marcus. My real name is Marcus Michaels.'

'Pratchett after Terry, right?'

He nodded and blushed. 'Tadeusz knows, so does Ireni, but I didn't want anyone to know who I was, so I changed my name. Maybe the press wouldn't care, but it would make a good story, wouldn't it?' His voice slid into bitterness. 'Marcus Michaels, on the trail of his dead mother. You can still call me Mark though. It's what I used when I was at school.'

'Like I said, I won't tell anyone else.' He gave me a loaded glance – I didn't blame him. 'And you can trust Wanda.'

'You are here to look for her?' Wanda asked. 'How can you hope to find her?'

'I know where she is.'

'How?'

'Last September, a team were up on the north-east ridge looking for the body of Irvine.'

'Oh yeah, George Mallory's partner,' I broke in, eager to prove to Wanda that I did know *something*. 'He died on the mountain in nineteen twenty-five, right?' The discovery of Mallory's disturbingly frozen-in-time corpse in 'ninety-nine was the cornerstone of Thierry's 'convince Si to go to Everest' campaign: *The first website to publish pics of Mallory's body got so many hits it* crashed, *Si.*

Wanda shook her head. ''Twenty-four. Go on, Mark.'

'They didn't find Irvine, but they found my mother.'

'How do they know it was your mother?'

'They didn't, not at first. But when they got back home they looked into who it might be. She always wore a bright pink down suit. She was famous for it. It was made by my father's old company before it went bust.'

And that's when I started shaking. The others didn't notice. I hadn't had a panic attack since I'd thrown myself into training for this trip. I thought they were a thing of the past. *Fuck.* I punched my thigh and made tight fists. *Judder, judder, judder.* That sense that I wasn't quite present, the same feeling I'd had after Cwm Pot, was creeping in. I became hyper-aware of my breathing. Cold fingertips danced up my back. My heart thudded. *Thunk, thunk.* I bit the inside of my cheek, releasing a salty gush of blood, and the act of doing something visceral helped. *Don't go back into the caves. Don't. Don't. Don't.*

Mark's voice floated back in. ' . . . and then my father told me they'd found her.'

Wanda placed a gloved hand on Mark's forearm. 'Ach, that must have been a terrible thing for you.'

'Yeah.' He wiped his nose, leaving a trail of snot on his sleeve. 'Ugh. Sorry. I'm a mess.'

'You are allowed to be a mess, Mark.'

'Dad asked them to keep it quiet. Not to go to the press. I have the coordinates of where she is.'

'Did it look like she made the summit?'

The panic attack was losing its grip. I could speak again. 'Does that matter? She died.' It sounded harsher than I intended.

'It would mean that she was the first woman to climb Everest without supplementary oxygen,' Wanda said, slightly defensively. 'Stefanie Weber had that honour. She summited without using supplementary oxygen a year later, in 'ninety-six. But it is true that this would only stand if Juliet had made it down alive.'

A clammy hand gripped my neck again. *Stop it.*

'They don't know if she made the summit,' Mark sighed. 'It's impossible to tell. From the position of her body, the most likely outcome is that she slipped from the third or second step on the ridge and tumbled into the catchment basin below. She could have fallen either on the descent or the ascent. They took photos but' – he swallowed – 'but my father wouldn't let me see them.'

'She had much trouble from the newspapers when she was alive, didn't she, Mark?' Wanda said.

'Yes. She didn't use oxygen, and some people thought it was selfish of her to take unnecessary risks like this, especially as . . . especially as she was a mother. She was under a lot of pressure.' His voice had gone back to its flat monotone. 'That's why I'm here. I want to find her, maybe . . . I don't know, say goodbye. It's just . . .' He shrugged, leaving the sentence unfinished.

'You are not going to the summit as well?'

'No. Just to find Juliet.' The use of 'Juliet' or 'my mother', rather than 'mum', was clearly a way of distancing himself. 'That's why Tadeusz let me on the team even though I don't have any high-altitude experience or achievements like you, Simon.'

I squirmed inwardly.

Wanda said something under her breath.

'What?'

She ignored me. 'Of course I should have known this. I know that Tadeusz was working for Joe Davis on this side for many years. He must have known your mother.'

'Yes. He was a guide on the 'ninety-five expedition. I reckon . . . I think he let me join the team because he knew her. He knows what I want to do. He's not easy to talk to, is he?' Understatement of the year. I glanced at Wanda. She, Ireni and Tadeusz were tight. 'Anyway, so Tadeusz says I'll go up with everyone to Camp III, then traverse across from the Exit Cracks rather than head up to the summit.'

Camp III. The last stop of Thierry's Ukrainians. My gut lurched, and I bit the inside of my cheek again.

'You are going by yourself, Mark?' Wanda asked.

'No. Tadeusz is going to send Mingma or Dorje with me. I . . . it's not . . .' He looked up. 'Excuse me,' he said primly, 'but I think I'm going to be sick.' He got up and hurried out of the tent.

Wanda didn't speak again until he was out of earshot. 'I feel very sorry for him.'

'Yeah. Me too. He was only ten when his mum died.' The same age as I was when Dad died. 'Must have messed him up good and proper.'

'Poor Mark.'

'Yeah.' I shifted in my chair, still shaky after my panic attack.

I want to get something out of the way. When Mark told me about his mum, I didn't immediately think, *wahey, a backup corpse for the site if Thierry's Ukrainians don't work out.* Even I'm not that crass. I'll admit to being swept along by Mark's story; I'll admit that it gave me a great excuse to connect with Wanda. But I won't admit to that.

The day after Mark poured his heart out to us, Wanda offered to give him an ice-climbing refresher course so that he could get his technique down before we headed to 'crampon point' and up the North Col. I'd been planning to join them – it had been over nine years since I'd last climbed on ice and I'd take all the help I could get – but I was troubled in the night with another upset stomach. I'm not going to go into the details of how awful it is to get that sick at altitude, except to say there was a moment when I actually considered soiling myself rather than leave the warmth of my sleeping bag. I don't think it was anything I ate this time, just my body rebelling to the altitude. Several of us were suffering from nausea.

I lay sulkily in my sleeping bag while they prepared to head out. Mark stuck his head into my tent before they left. He still resembled a fifteen-year-old suffering from a vicious hangover, but he appeared to be happier and more 'alive' than usual, as if confessing the real reason behind his climb had lightened his load.

'Get you anything before we leave, Simon?'

'A new digestive system would be nice.'

'Ha. I've finished *Good Omens* by the way. You can borrow it if you like.'

'Cheers. Maybe later when I feel less like death.'

Bored and miserable, I snuck into his tent barely half an hour after they left. I told myself Mark wouldn't mind if I snagged something to read – he'd offered, hadn't he? – but really, I was curious to see his set-up. As I'd suspected, his tent was as organised as Wanda's, his books, headlamp, pee and water bottles all tucked into the inside pockets, his clothes rolled in his rucksack as if he was planning to make a hasty getaway. I was about to leave when I spied the corner of a hardback notebook peeking from beneath his sleeping mat. Double-checking to make sure none of the other members were hanging around, I slid it out. It was wrapped in plastic, its moleskin cover worn away in places to reveal the white padding beneath. I assumed it was Mark's journal at first, and I'll admit to being curious to see if he'd written anything about me. Promising myself I'd just take a quick peek, I sat on his sleeping mat and riffled through it, struck by the angry crossings-out and spidery handwriting. The last two pages in the book had been ripped out, leaving ragged edges clinging to the spine.

I'm not going to say that a chill ran through me as I read it; I was already freezing, dressed for a quick nip to the toilet, not an extended sit down in the doorway of someone's tent. When I finished, I brushed out the snow I'd fuffled in, grabbed *Good Omens* to use as an excuse if anyone had seen me crawling in here, and carefully slid the journal into its place underneath the sleeping-pad. Back in my own tent, it took me a while to get warm. It took me a while to stop obsessing over what I'd read.

What really got to me of course were Juliet's experiences with 'it' – the Third Man. They chimed with that unsettling *thing* I'd felt down in the caves. Something had been down there with me after Ed died; something had pushed at me. And Juliet had written that her 'presence' was malevolent. Like mine. She'd felt it before her climbing partner had died, and then again, when she was here.

And then there were the fingers, those black frostbitten fingers. *Fingers in your heart, lad.*

Almost immediately, I began to think of her as a kindred spirit – someone else who'd had a bizarre and disturbing experience in an extreme environment. The most logical explanation, that she was as nutty as a caveful of Eds, wasn't one I wanted to accept. It was clear that she was under a great deal of pressure to be the first woman to summit unaided, tortured by her climbing partner's death the year before, and probably depressed. Trauma upon trauma. *Sound familiar, Simon?*

Sensing the first threads of a panic attack, I fought it with my new cheek-biting defence (stupid, really, as cuts and abrasions wouldn't heal at this altitude). I had too many questions roiling around in my head to give in to it. I managed a small cup of noodles for lunch, and feeling stronger, I layered up and ventured outside. I sat in a sagging chair, and stared blankly at Changtse's apocalyptic sprawl.

Presumably Joe Davis or Tadeusz had sent the journal back with Juliet's belongings. I couldn't imagine how Mark must have felt when he read it for the first time.

Did I suspect even then that Juliet's tragedy could provide the answers to what I'd experienced in Cwm Pot? Fuck knows. But what she'd written had chimed with me.

'Heard you were sick, son,' Malcolm said, making me jump. He dragged a chair next to me. I wasn't in the mood for a dose of paternalism, but nor did I want to be alone. Part of me wanted to discuss what I'd discovered with Thierry. *Got a lead on a dead mum.* No. Mark wasn't exactly a friend, but telling Thierry would blow the lid right off the whole thing. *Not only is Juliet dead, she's famous – the perfect storm as far as Thierry's concerned. But that's what you're here for, isn't it? You've struck gold, dude.*

Malcolm harrumphed. He'd been telling me something, and I hadn't been listening.

'Can I ask you a question, Malcolm?'

'Go on.'

'Have you ever had any strange experiences on the mountains?'

'Like what, son?'

'I've been reading up on the great explorers,' I paused as if to imply, *like you*, 'and lots of them say they experienced freaky things – hallucinations and the like. You know, like Shackleton seeing that extra man in the Antarctic.'

He chuckled. 'Oh aye, Simon. The Third Man factor. Happens a lot. And you must know the story about Frank Smythe, of course.'

'Remind me?'

'He tried to summit Everest on the south side in 'thirty-three I think it was. Well, he was so convinced he was being followed by an imaginary climber that he even offered him a piece of his Kendal Mint Cake. Also saw teapots dancing in the air in front of him. Very famous story.'

'It's caused by hypoxia, right? Lack of oxygen to the brain?'

'Could be the altitude, son, could be the cold, could be exhaustion. Brain's a funny thing.' He chuckled. 'Could be wee guardian angels for all we know.'

'So it doesn't necessarily mean you've gone ment— mad, does it?'

'I hope not! You were asking if I'd ever experienced anything like it. Well I did. Happened on the day before I summited Pumori. There I was, heading for my tent, when I was suddenly convinced I was walking down a supermarket aisle, and that Molly had asked me to get some oven chips. My Sherpa, Tashi, picked up that I wasn't quite right, checked my oxygen, and it turned out the valve had iced over.'

'How long did it last?'

'Time's different up there, son, but it couldn't have been more than ten minutes until Tashi realised I had a problem with the oxygen flow. You'd be hard-pressed to find a climber who hasn't experienced something like that.' He grimaced, and stretched out his toeless foot. 'Took a beating on the hike up here. It's why I took so long to make it.'

'Aren't you worried that you'll lose something else to frostbite, Malcolm?' Into my mind jumped a picture of him in his garage, polishing a row of neatly labelled jars, each containing a different body part. Most of them were the colour of charcoal. I chased it away.

'Can't let myself worry about that kind of thing, son. No place for that up here.'

'Why do you do it, Malcolm? Put yourself through this?'

Another chuckle. 'My wife can't understand it. She says I do it because life's simpler at base camp. All you do is eat, sleep, climb. Less stress in a lot of ways. Last year, while I was here, my eldest son was caught shoplifting, the daft wee sod. I didn't have to deal with that.' His expression changed. 'But it's not that. I think of it like this. There's a thread that attaches itself to you when you're up there, in the zone. It tugs and tugs and unless you make an effort to sever it, it'll keep pulling you up there until it kills you.' His voice was raw. Poetic. A different side to the Malcolm I was used to.

'Summit fever?'

'Aye. Call it that if you want. Turning back last year was the hardest thing I've ever done.'

'Why did you?'

He hesitated before he spoke again. 'Reached my limit. Knew

I wouldn't make it home if I took one step more. But you know all about pushing yourself, don't you, Simon?'

'Huh?'

'If you can do the *Eiger* then you can do this.' He gave me a shrewd glance. 'What year were you there again?' *Shit. Careful, Si.* I knew I'd been too slick with my Eiger-dodging tactics. Malcolm, like Wanda, knew people here – it probably wouldn't be hard to prove I was bullshitting about the climb if he asked around.

A trickle of blood crept out of his right nostril, saving me from having to change the subject. Like headaches and nausea, Ireni had told us nosebleeds were common up here. He wiped the blood away with the back of his glove. 'Ach. Not again. Third time this morning.' He stood up and clapped me on the shoulder. 'Won't let the mountain beat me this time, son.'

Juliet had said much the same thing in her journal, but it had beaten her, hadn't it?

I caught a flash of red weaving through the tent city – Wanda's jacket. She grinned and waved at me. Mark lagged behind her, stumbling on the uneven surface. He was finished; his lips crusted with dried saliva. *Hopefully he's too knackered to pick up that someone's been in his tent.*

'How did it go?'

'He did very well.'

Mark gave me a watery smile.

'Hope you don't mind, Mark, but I went into your tent after all and grabbed something to read.' I made sure I sounded casual, blasé, *nothing to see here.*

A flicker of anxiety, then, 'No. That's fine. Bit of a headache. Need to lie down.' He crawled into his tent. I wanted to call after him, give him a hug. I tried and failed to put myself in his shoes. If my mum had disappeared on a mountain when I was a kid, and the only record of her fateful climb was a looney-tunes account of being stalked by a ghost, I'd be a miserable bastard too. *But you* should *be able to put yourself into his shoes, eh, Si? You lost a parent, too.* Dad's death wasn't as glamorous as Juliet's

– his sixty-a-day habit was more than likely the cause of his stroke – but there was an argument to be made that Dad's unhealthy lifestyle was as dangerous and suicidal as Juliet's. I shook this off. I didn't want to go there. I didn't want to identify with Mark. I couldn't afford to.

Wanda gestured for me to follow her to the edge of camp and out of earshot.

'I think he will be okay.' She didn't sound convinced. 'Good *pied en canard* technique, but he must learn to breathe on his rest step. The altitude is bothering him very much. He must eat more calories – he does not have the energy to do this otherwise, I think. How are you feeling?'

All the better for seeing you. It was true. There was something about her that made my heart lighter, but I was fairly sure if I said this out loud she'd probably punch me in the head. 'Getting there.'

She took off her pack and sat on it, and I squatted next to her and watched as she demolished two energy bars.

'Hungry?'

'I cannot have just one.'

I watched as she smoothed out the wrappers. 'Why?'

'It is a thing I do. You'll think I'm crazy.'

'No I won't.'

'It is something I do from a child. Everything needs a companion. So I never eat just one thing, always two, and then throw away the wrappers together.'

'You have two because one would be lonely?'

'Yes.'

Weird. OCD. But cool. 'That's actually quite sweet.'

She gave me a 'don't patronise me' look.

Time to dig. 'Did Mark say anything more to you about Juliet when you were up there?'

'No. You know what it is like when you are moving. He had no energy to speak.'

'I was wondering, did she usually climb alone?'

'She did her five solos of course, including the Eiger, the

Jorasses and the Cima Grande, but no. Not always. She was on Broad Peak with Walter Evans, who was her climbing partner.'

'What was he like?'

'I think he was well-respected, but not as accomplished as she was. I have not read much about him. You must ask Mark.'

'You know a lot about the history of mountaineering, don't you?'

A shrug. 'I like the stories. Every mountain has them. And also I was named after Wanda Rutkiewicz.'

'Oh right.' *Who the fuck is that?*

She laughed, seeing straight through me. 'She was a very famous Polish climber who died on Kanchenjunga three years before Juliet. You know about Polish climbing history? There are many great mountaineers, Kukuczka, Kurtyka, Wielicki – a very long list. Wanda was the first woman to climb K2. My mother admired her very much. You know that Wanda trekked all the way to the Karakoram, almost one hundred miles, on a broken leg?'

That put the hike up to ABC into perspective. 'Wow.'

'Yes. Imagine doing this in those days, when the equipment was not so good. Incredible. And like Juliet, and also Stefanie Weber, there was much controversy about her. She was known as a difficult woman. All bullshit. She did what she had to do to succeed.'

'Talking about women pioneers, Eri Aka was pretty incredible as well, wasn't she?'

'Ha! See you do know things.' A pause. 'How is it you know about Eri Aka but not Wanda or Juliet? Eri is not as well known to westerners, I think.'

Stupid. 'I don't know much about her, not really. She summited Everest, didn't she?'

'Yes. And of course Eri was on Juliet's expedition. Did Mark tell you about her before?'

I gave a non-committal shrug. 'Not sure where I heard about her.' Lying to Wanda made me feel dirty. But I couldn't very well admit that I'd sneaked into Mark's tent and stealth-read his dead mother's journal – not now she thought I was 'kind'.

'It is so sad what can happen on the mountains. So many men

and women who died before they completed their goals in life. Eri, of course, was trying to climb all fourteen of the eight-thousanders. I think she did six before she was killed on Manaslu.'

'*Fuck*.' Eri's calm presence while Juliet was basically losing her shit had made me like her, and I almost felt as if Wanda had just broken the news that one of my friends had died.

Wanda gave me a strange look. 'You did not know this?'

'Yeah.' *Change the subject*. 'So this Polish climber, Wanda . . . Wu . . .'

'Rutkiewicz.'

'Yeah, cheers. You want to follow in her footsteps?'

'Yes. I have goals. If I make this summit, I will get more sponsorship. Like Eri Aka, I plan to do all of the fourteen eight-thousanders, but without oxygen.' A rare touch of uncertainty. 'Do you think I can?'

'Yes. If anyone can, it's you.' I meant it. This wasn't just the usual Charming Si smarm. If I'm honest, I envied her. She had a goal, a life's ambition. All I had was a vague hope that the website would take off, and then what? I'd have more time to play *The Legend of Zelda*? Perhaps this was why I was so attracted to her: she was ambitious, driven, focused, full of integrity – everything I wasn't.

Reading my mind, she said: 'And you? What is it you want to do with your life? Make movies?'

'Something like that. Me and my mate have this website we're trying to get off the ground.' *Careful, dude.*

'What sort of website?'

'Nothing major. Just silly stuff. It won't go anywhere.'

'So how do you make your money?'

'Part-time jobs mainly, you know.' I was wandering dangerously close to the truth. 'Truth is, Wanda, this trip has wiped me out financially. Sold my car and everything to pay for it.'

'There are many camera crews on the mountain this year. I am surprised you do not think about doing this type of work. If you can climb, and use a camera, you will get work. I have some contacts I can give you if you need.'

'Really?'

'Of course.'

A surge of hope. *You could have a future, Si. A cool future.* 'Thanks. You're the best.'

It was the one and only time I saw her embarrassed. She stood up. 'I go now to listen to music.'

I followed her back into camp, brain fizzing.

I should have been finished after my bout of illness, and the emotional gut-punch I'd felt after reading Juliet's diary, but I was too wired to return to my sleeping bag cocoon. I wandered into the mess tent, almost pleased to see Robbie sitting at the table, shovelling fried eggs into his gob.

'Hey, Simon,' he said with his mouth full. 'Heard Mark and Wanda hit the col today.' One thing I will say about Robbie: he could be a dick, a major dick, but he didn't bear a grudge. Most blokes I knew would still be smarting about my stupid small penis comment.

'Yeah.'

'Good to see Mark is manning up.'

'What have you got against him, Robbie?'

'Nothing.' He looked genuinely nonplussed. 'I've got nothing against him.'

'You always seem to be on his back.'

'Don't think he should be here is all. Don't think he's got what it takes.'

I couldn't argue with that.

'Don't let him become the albatross around your neck, Simon. He's an okay guy, but bit of advice, it's everyone for themselves when the going gets tough.'

What a prince.

'Stand up and walk in a straight line for me.'

I peered into the mess tent's medical wing. Two Korean climbers were in the cramped space with Ireni, and she was instructing the older of the two to walk back and forth in front of her. He was unsteady on his feet, and despite the sub-zero temperature, his face was sheened with sweat.

'Tell him that he has the symptoms of ataxia,' she said to the older guy's companion. 'Tell him he must go down.'

His friend translated her advice, and the sweaty man slurred something in Korean.

'He say, can he rest and then climb later?'

Ireni sighed and tugged a hand through her hair. She was a couple of decades younger than Tadeusz, who was somewhere around his mid-forties, but today she had the air of someone far older. 'No. Don't stay up here. Tell him that if he does this, then he will die. Is that clear?'

The two men spoke amongst themselves. The older man nodded resignedly.

'Don't stay up here,' Ireni repeated. 'Go down. Go down to base camp where there is more oxygen. You understand?'

'Yes.'

They gave Ireni a small bow, thanked her, and squeezed out past me.

Ireni waved me onto the chair to take my blood pressure and test my oxygen levels.

'What was that about?'

'A climber who has come to the mountain unprepared and does not want to admit that he is sick. We get lots coming through here.'

'Doesn't he have a doctor on his team?'

'Not all expeditions have doctors. It can be a problem.'

'And you can't very well turn them away.'

'I can, but it is too dangerous.' She tried for a smile. 'How are you feeling, Simon? You are ready for the col tomorrow?'

Was I? Tadeusz had given us a limit of five hours to climb the steep ice wall that led to Camp I – another one of his tests. I'd seen the multicoloured dots of other climbers heading up there, and they moved at a snail's pace. Most of them would have trained for months. I was doing it on the fly. 'Sure.'

Tadeusz's voice floated in from the communications section next door. He sounded agitated.

'Problem?'

'Logistics. Mingma and Dorje are on the mountain helping to fix the ropes. It is always a worry that the weather up there will change. They are like family to Tadeusz, but they will be back in a few hours I think. How is Mark? I know that he has told you about his mother.'

'He's okay.'

'What he told you, you know, it is not for everyone, Simon. People gossip up here.'

'I know. Wanda and I know how to keep our mouths shut.' *Bullshit.* 'You think Mark can handle it?'

'I think so, yes. He will climb with Mingma, who is very experienced, and of course he will not be going to the summit. But . . .' she smiled sadly. 'Tadeusz does not think he will locate his mother's body. The conditions are different to those in September when she was last seen.' She paused. 'If indeed it is she.'

'Tadeusz knew her, didn't he?'

She stiffened. 'Did Mark tell you this, Simon?'

'Yeah.'

She removed the cuff from my arm. 'Good. You are in good shape, Simon. I am pleased. You have acclimatised well.'

Tadeusz appeared, a rare smile on his face. 'They are coming down now. All is good.' A nod in my direction. 'You are better now, Simon?'

'Yes thanks.'

'Simon was asking about Juliet,' Ireni said.

'Ah yes. Mark has told you.'

I couldn't help myself. 'What was she like?' *Did you think she was mental?*

The smile disappeared. 'Very focused. A very good climber. Strong.'

'Mark said you were worried about her.' He hadn't said anything of the sort. *Juliet had though.*

'No. That is not true.'

I couldn't let it go. 'Oh right. Do you think she ran into trouble because she refused to use oxygen?'

'Many climbers choose to do this.' His face shut down. 'The

last time Joe spoke to her on the radio, she sounded very strong. That is all I know.'

'Do you think she made the summit?'

'No.'

I wondered if he'd suspected she was losing it and felt guilty for letting her climb. I waited for more. It didn't come. Tadeusz knew how to keep his cards close to his chest.

Ed's voice came wafting in: *Pathetic. Weak. That's what you are, lad. A mewling mess, a fucking pillow-biting—*

'Do not put so much weight on the ropes, Simon,' Mingma said, appearing behind me like a ninja. He wasn't even slightly out of breath.

'Okay,' I huffed, reattaching the jumar, aware that he was watching me carefully. My heart was thudding like an out-of-control jackhammer. My head had turned into a pus-filled sphere. The sun rocketing off the snow was cooking me in my suit. I felt like an ant beneath a magnifying glass.

I stopped for the thousandth time to kick snow off my stupid fucking crampons and peered up the steep ice wall that made up the col – it didn't look like I'd made any progress. A multi-coloured caterpillar crept ahead of me. No one seemed to be moving. I thought about taking out the camcorder and filming it, but I couldn't be arsed. *Thierry probably wouldn't use it anyway: these climbers are alive, aren't they?*

The only way to do it was to splay my feet, take two steps, slide the rope up, splay, splay waddle. Of course Wanda managed to make this inelegant shuffle-slide look elegant. Her red blob and Mark's yellow shape were way ahead of me, and I'd lost track of Robbie, Malcolm and Howard. *If Mark can do this, so can you.* It had taken me a while to find a rhythm. Juliet's mantra helped, with each two-step shuffle I thought: *this is shite, this is shite, this is shite.* A queue was forming directly in front of me, climbers dropping like flies as the heat caught them. I unclipped to step around an anonymous climber who was vomiting into the snow. *Slowly, slowly.* If I slipped, the only way to arrest myself would be to use the ice axe. It was nothing like the type of climbing I was used to. You needed a different kind of mental strength (the type I'd lost at Cwm Silyn) to lunge for a flake knowing you might not make it. This required dogged determination. *Juliet did this with all her gear on her back. You can too.*

'Hot,' I said to Mingma, pointlessly.

'Yes.' How many times had he shepherded tedious wankers up this slope? It was ridiculous. After spending days working their arses off in the death zone, he and Dorje had sauntered into camp last night, looking as if they'd done nothing more strenuous than take a leisurely stroll. Wanda called them the 'rock stars of the mountain', and she was right. None of us would have a chance of making it anywhere near the summit if it weren't for them. They did all the heavy lifting, pitched the tents, picked up the slack. 'Make sure you drink water, Simon.'

'Yeah.'

'I go now, check on the others. You are doing good.' He stepped to the side and stormed off up the slope.

Fuelled by Mingma's words of encouragement, I slogged on. Besides, I didn't want to look weak in front of him. Unlike Dorje, who was laid-back and smiled constantly, Mingma was reserved and watchful, with a similar take-no-shit vibe to Tadeusz's.

This is shite, this is shite, this is shite. Juliet was my invisible, dead cheerleader.

And then: *It was here that she first felt IT.*

I half-expected to feel a tickle at the back of my neck, a poisonous sense that something was following me, but there was something worse to worry about. Worse even than the skyscraper-sized lump of ice that loomed over the col.

'Oh Jesus.' I sank onto my bum a couple of metres away from the main drag and looked up to where several aluminium ladders were strapped together, forming the world's shittiest bridge over a huge crevasse. *Nope. No way, dude. I'm done. Thierry can get fucked.*

This would have been a one-sentence aside in Juliet's journal.

Fuck Juliet.

Knew you didn't have it in you, Pretty Boy.

Wanda was nearly at the top of it, Mingma close behind her. She made it look easy. Mingma scaled down the rungs without using the ropes, and helped Mark clip himself onto the safety line.

Mark took his time, clinging on for dear life, his legs wobbling. Below the ladder's rungs, the gap went all the way down to hell.

Just fucking do it.

I joined the queue at the bottom, unable to tear my eyes away from the dark scar in the snow.

'You need help, Simon?' Mingma asked. I hadn't even noticed him approaching me.

'No, I'm fine. Thanks Mingma.'

It was time. *Come on, Chris Bonington, let's see what you can do.*

I didn't look down. I focused on my boots as I clumped up each rung; it was like climbing with concrete blocks on my feet. The ladder shifted greasily, and fear and bile rushed into my mouth. *You're clipped onto the safety ropes. It's less dangerous than what you did down in the caves.*

I was too buggered to feel any triumph when I made it to the top and stepped onto semi-solid snow. I sidestepped up to a narrow ledge where Mark lay on his side, panting. *He must have dug way deep inside himself to make it, Si. That's how you beat this thing.* But Mark had a mission, didn't he? A *real* reason for being on the mountain. It would pull him through. Camp III and Thierry's Ukrainians were still an impossible distance away.

I flumped next to him and gave him a weak fist pump, trying not to dwell on the fact that we'd be doing this again the next day. Only next time, we'd be staying the night at Camp I.

Juliet's Third Man hadn't pitched up, but I couldn't shed the feeling that it was biding its time. *Who is the third who walks beside you?*

'I have to pee,' Mark said in my ear, sounding like a child.

'So go. You've got a bottle, haven't you?' I coughed the words out, raising my voice to be heard over the squall raging outside. The tent's flimsy nylon sides were shaking epileptically. It wasn't exhilarating; it was terrifying. We hadn't had to contend with the sun on the way up the col this time, but the traverse across the Ladder of Doom was every bit as brutal as it had been the day before.

'But . . . what about Wanda?'

'Wanda won't care.'

'What is this?' Wanda said. She lay on her back, an inch away from me. I could've reached out and touched her, but all I cared about was getting enough breath into my lungs. My ankle wasn't too bad – if anything it was throbbing at a lower wattage than after the hike up to ABC – but my back felt like a yak had rolled on it; the snow beneath us, melted by our body heat, had compacted into a lumpen bowl.

'Mark needs to pee.'

'So go, Mark,' Wanda said. 'I have seen much worse, I promise you.'

I should have been thrilled to be sharing a tent with her – Camp I wasn't roomy enough for us all to have a separate tent – but I had a bad feeling about what the night would bring. Both Wanda and Mark had their head torches on, and already the dancing shafts of light were too close a reminder of what I'd experienced in the caves with Ed. Crazy. I was seven thousand metres above sea level: the claustrophobic hell that had been Cwm Pot had no place here.

A nasty skin had formed on the roof of my mouth, and I inched my water bottle out from beneath the sleeping bag and knocked back two ibuprofen, aware that if it wasn't for Wanda, Mark and I probably wouldn't have anything to drink. We were responsible for our own food and drink in the high camps, and as the only one of us who wasn't a wreck, she'd taken charge, gathering snow in a nylon bag for us, firing up the stove, making tea and soup, reminding us to drink enough, and doing all of it without whingeing. Neither Mark nor I had managed to eat anything, instead we'd watched, nauseated, as she demolished two packets of chicken noodles, even up here disposing of the empty packets together so that they didn't get 'lonely'.

'All done,' Mark said.

'Thanks for the running commentary, Mark,' I tried to say.

Wanda clicked off her headlamp, and Mark did the same.

Hello darkness my old friend. A dizziness, a sense of unreality. My fingers tingled. I shut my eyes and concentrated on the sound of the wind.

And then, with no surprise, the whoomp of the storm became the gush of water, and I was back in the caves, back in the mausoleum, back in Ed's clutches. I felt no fear; I knew it was inevitable. I'd been waiting for it. Everest, Wanda, Mark, Juliet, it was all a story I'd been telling myself while I waited to die. The water's whispery voices hissed in my ears.

'How are you feeling, lad?' Ed asked, squeezing me gently.

'We won't die, will we Ed?'

'Yes, lad. We will.'

I couldn't breathe – choking, I was choking.

I lurched awake, patted the space around me. Touched Wanda and Mark's sleeping forms. The lack of oxygen had confused my swollen brain. The tight band across my chest that had made my subconscious latch onto Ed, that was all it was. I felt around in my sleeping bag for my water bottle.

'Head hurts,' Mark gasped next to me. I could hear him clearly now – the wind had died.

I unearthed the water bottle, drank, and passed it to him. 'Here.'

'Thanks.'

He drank then handed it back. 'My mum walked . . . she climbed up here with . . . with all her stuff. How did she . . .' He had to keep stopping to cough. He harrumphed and slammed his fist on his chest.

'Calm down, Mark.'

'I'm okay. How . . . how can Wanda sleep so well up here?'

'No idea.'

I lay back and shut my eyes, assuming – and hoping – that I

wouldn't drop off again. But I did. And this time, I was lying amongst the Cwm Pot lads' bones, no – I *was* the bones, watching dispassionately as Ed cradled Mark between his thighs, rubbing at his flesh. The angle shifted, and I realised Mark was dead, his hands and feet chipped and flaking as if they were made of coal, his mouth hanging open.

'Can't get him warm, lad,' Ed said to me matter-of-factly. 'It's his fingers, see. The fingers in his heart.'

Coddled in layers of fleece, Gore-tex, down, gloves and goggles, I made myself leave my tent, which was banked by an arc of fresh snow, and huddled on my camp chair, burrowing my chin in my collar. I shut my eyes. In two days' time we'd be heading up to Camp II, and I had to get my head straight. I had a serious case of Miserable Bastarditis; it wasn't the physical strains that were bothering me now, rather the images my brain kept latching onto.

Rappelling and glissading down the col after our stormy night at Camp I had given me a welcome adrenalin kick, but it hadn't erased the vile aftertaste left by the Ed nightmares. I knew the dreams were brought on by low oxygen levels, exhaustion, subzero temperatures and overspill from my sneaky read of Juliet's journal, but rationalising them didn't help; the images lingered like the echoes of Cwm Pot's watery choir.

And added to this was a smidgen of guilt. I still hadn't bothered to ask around for any more info on Thierry's Ukrainians – or any other leads for that matter – and the camcorder was still lodged in the bottom of my pack. *What the fuck are you doing here, dude?*

'Hi, Simon.'

Shit. Mark was making himself comfortable next to me. I was too raw, and I didn't have the energy to talk to anyone. The sky was clear, the nagging wind had blown itself out, but I might as well have been swathed in shadows. *It's just a mood swing, common at altitude. You'll be fine tomorrow.* Juliet had written that life on the mountains was more intense; it stripped people to their core and revealed their true selves. I believed it. If anything, Wanda was more determined and frank than she had been at the start; Howard had squirrelled further into his shell, Mark prevaricated between being steely and needy, and for the last two days as the going grew tougher, Malcolm had shed his paternalism and become almost monosyllabic. Robbie was the only one who appeared to be on an even keel: once a dick, always a dick. I just wished I knew who I was. Charming Si was fighting to stay in control, but Simon Newman, Time Waster Extraordinaire and Exploiter of the Dead was chopping through the veneer with his secret defeatist weapons. I didn't want to be him. I wanted to be Kind Simon, someone who was worthy of hooking up with Wanda.

'Did you hear me, Simon?'

Oh just fuck off. 'Sorry, Mark. Say again?'

'I said, I've got something to tell you.'

'What?'

'Last night, when you went back to sleep, you put your arms around me.'

This snapped me out of it. 'I did not!'

'You did. You wrapped them around my chest and squeezed.'

Fingers in your heart. I forced myself to smile. 'Sorry, Mark. I don't fancy you, honest. You're not my type.' Hiding the chill with lame humour. Mark grinned, his eyes shining as if he was being lit from the inside. He was a completely different person to the sulky sop Wanda and I had helped on the hike up to ABC.

'Do you miss your girlfriend, Simon?'

'Don't have one.'

'Me neither.'

Oh there's a fucking surprise.

Stop being such a shit. Then, something Ireni had said in Kathmandu came to me. 'Who was supposed to come with you to Everest, Mark?'

'How do you know someone was coming with me?'

'Ireni mentioned it.' I shrugged. 'You don't have to tell me if you don't want to.' In any case, the black cloud was blunting my usual nosiness.

'A guy called Tom Baskin-Heath.'

I bit my tongue before I blurted, *Posh Tom? Evil Tom?* and gave away that I'd guerrilla-read the journal. *Careful.* 'Family friend?'

'Sort of. He was on the expedition with my mother in 'ninety-five. He didn't get on very well with her then, but he came to see my father after she died to give us his condolences, and kept in touch with me over the years. He felt bad about some of the stuff that had happened on the mountain.' *Yeah, like adding to her stress because he'd gossiped about her.* 'When I told him that her body had been found and that I was thinking of coming here, he offered to join me. He failed to summit in 'ninety-five and wanted another shot at it.'

'So why didn't he come?'

'He got sick. Pancreatic cancer.'

My first thought was: *karma.* But that wasn't fair – at least he'd tried to put things right. 'Shit. Sorry, Mark.'

'You say that a lot to me.'

'What: "shit"?'

'No. Sorry.'

'Sorry.'

We shared a grin.

'Do you have a photo of your mum, Mark?'

'Yes.' He rummaged in his jacket's inside pocket and took out a crumpled Polaroid. 'Here. It's one of Juliet and me at my grandparents' house.'

Juliet was stocky, with reams of ginger hair – a contrast to Mark, who was dark. I liked the look of her. She had the same take-no-shit direct gaze as Wanda. A mini, toothy version of Mark clung to her legs. They were both smiling and posing in front of a climbing frame, acres of lawn stretching behind them.

'She looks cool.'

'Yes. Only . . . can I tell you something, Simon?'

'Sure.'

'It's going to sound awful.'

Christ, get on with it. 'I'm a pretty hard person to shock, Mark.'

He lifted his chin. 'I hated her. I hated her for years. I hated her for dying. It was only when I . . .' he caught himself. 'Does that make me a bad person?'

'No. Course not. That's understandable, Mark.'

'Is it?'

How the fuck would I know? Did I hate Dad for dying? No. Whatever my mum thought, I didn't go off the rails because I was fatherless; I went off the rails because I could. Because I was bored.

'She didn't even say goodbye to me. I didn't even know she was going back to Everest. And then . . . and then a parcel arrived for me from Kathmandu two months after she died. Can you imagine that? That was the first time I really got upset.' He gave me a rueful smile. 'Sorry, I'm venting.'

'Vent away, mate.'

'I don't want to bore you, Simon.'

'You're not. Do you think . . . do you reckon that this trip will give you the closure you're after?' *Christ, Simon, hark at you being all sensitive and shit.*

'I don't know. Her . . . I read some stuff she said about her last trip. She said she was doing it for me, to make a better life for us. For years I thought she didn't care; that she'd left me to do what she wanted. But she climbed for me.' He said this weirdly dispassionately.

'What does your dad think about you being here?'

A shrug. 'Didn't want me to come. He and my mother had problems. Big problems. He doesn't like to talk about her. He hasn't . . . he's never actually bad-mouthed her, but after she died, it was as if she'd never existed.' He mentally shook himself. 'Enough about me. It's always about me. What's your family like?'

Oh you know, dead dad, estranged mum, a sister who's a borderline sociopath. The last thing I wanted to do was get into all that. Thankfully, Wanda emerged from the mess tent and headed our way, saving me from answering. My heart gave its usual puppyish leap at the sight of her.

'Hello, boys. I have bad news and some good. The good news is that Tadeusz is very happy with our progress. You too, Mark.'

'And the bad news?'

'Gyaluk has made us a cake.'

Mark laughed, thumping his chest as it turned into a cough.

She grabbed a chair and squeezed in next to me. 'What have you been talking about? You have some gossip for me?'

'We were talking about family,' Mark said. 'What's yours like, Wanda?'

'Close. Very close.' She grinned. 'Maybe too close. In fact, I live next door to my parents.' She told us that her family had fled Poland in the eighties, lived for a while in a refugee camp, and then relocated to France, where her mum and dad found work as guides. She'd grown up around mountaineers; it was in her blood.

We drifted into a discussion about Robbie's continuing dick-ishness. 'There is always one on every team,' Wanda said. After their showdown on the walk up here, she couldn't glance his way without giving him a black look. 'You must not take to heart the things he says, Mark. I hope he gets frostbite on his very small penis.'

Mark turned red and laughed.

The black cloud had drifted away.

It was only when I was edging around him that I realised the climber lying slumped at the top of the col was Malcolm. It was another of those pressure-cooker days, and people were constantly flumping down to rest. I'd passed Claude and Elodie on the way up here. They'd been lying on their backs on one of the narrow ledges like a pair of down-suited starfish. We swapped weary waves and mimed sipping espressos.

Just walk around him. You don't have the energy to help. After the col, reaching Camp II felt like a cruel cosmic joke. It seemed to shift further and further away from me. Ridiculous to think that I'd had a mental image of swanning up to Camp III as if it was a walk in the park, snapping some pics of the corpsicles up there and then wafting my way down. But I couldn't just leave him. I dug in my ice axe, made sure my crampons were securely staked, and bent down to shake his shoulder. It was a precarious position; I knew the slope wasn't much more than forty degrees, but it felt vertical. My stomach dropped as I glanced at the elevation below.

'You okay?' He was lying face up, still clipped onto the rope and huffing like a racehorse, but I couldn't see his eyes behind his goggles. The radiation cream crusted around his nose made him look like he'd been snorting a vast quantity of coke. 'Malcolm!'

He shook his head and sat up.

'Let me help you.'

'No.' He mumbled something else I couldn't catch.

'What?'

'. . . want them to know.'

'Huh? Know what?' I shook his shoulder again. 'Malcolm!'

He tapped his goggles. 'Eyes . . . black spot. It'll pass, it always does.'

'You can't *see*?'

'I can see . . .' – something, something – '. . . compromised.'

'I'll go up and get Mingma.' He and Dorje were waiting for us at a point just below Camp II to provide us with oxygen if we needed it. Or maybe I could ask one of the other Sherpas on the col to radio them.

'No.'

'You can't stay here.' The bright light was deceptive of course; the lack of movement was stealing my warmth, and I was losing sensation in my feet. My gullet was an ice block.

I slipped off my pack and retrieved my flask. It was a fucker twisting off the top with over-mitts. 'Here. Drink.'

He took a few sips. 'Better.' He got up onto one knee, swaying like a drunk, then stood up. 'Going down now.'

'I'll help you.'

'No.'

'You have your figure of eight?'

A numb nod. 'Don't tell anyone, son. Please.'

'Ireni needs to know.'

'No. It'll pass. Please, son.' He gave me a fake, savage grin. 'I'm fine. Dandy. Just a wee problem.'

'You sure?'

'Be better when I . . .when I rest down at base.'

Moving with painful slowness he clipped back onto the safety line – at least he could see well enough to do that – and began a faltering rappel down the slope.

I watched him for five minutes, but he seemed to find a rhythm. He may not have been my favourite person, but I didn't want anything bad happen to him. *Why not? You could feature him on the site, save you schlepping up to Camp III.*

It was a killer to get going again; a large part of me desperately wanted to follow him down.

I caught up to Mark, who was stopping to rest every two steps, and together we stop-started our way to where Dorje and Mingma were waiting. Wanda was already way past them, climbing swiftly, oxygen-free. I caught my breath for a minute, then said to Mingma: 'Problem with Malcolm.'

'Big problem?'

And here it was. I knew if I grassed Malcolm up, Tadeusz might kick him off the summit team. He might kick him off anyway for not making Camp II. I compromised on: 'Not sure.'

'He go down?'

'Yes.'

He nodded, but didn't hurry off, taking his time to make sure my oxygen canister was in my pack and that I knew how to check the pipe to make sure it didn't bend and restrict the flow. I took in my first breath of the tinny, artificial air. Tadeusz had made those of us using oxygen practise with it at ABC, but I hadn't yet tried the mask on with goggles. It felt like my entire head was swathed in plastic. After ten minutes or so, I could feel the effect of it: warmth flooded through me, and a shred of optimism came back. Mingma held up two fingers, meaning two litres a minute. I had to ration my oxygen; we'd only been able to afford two bottles. I gave him the thumbs up.

Last push. Let's go.

This time I led, Mark moving in time behind me.

This is shite, this is shite, this is shite.

I found my rhythm again, so much so that we overtook Robbie and Howard – Mark somehow finding the energy to do a small victory bum wiggle as we clipped back onto the ropes. And then, something clicked. I stopped focusing on the burn in my thighs, the cramp in my ankle, my stinging, sand-blasted cheeks. Juliet, Mark, Thierry, Malcolm and the Ukrainians, even Wanda was pushed out of my brain. It was just me, my body, and the mountain.

I was in the zone. I'd felt something akin to this when Chris and I had done the Aiguille Verte, but it wasn't anywhere near as intense.

This is why Wanda does it. This is why Juliet did it.

I paused to check out the view from all sides. I had a perfect sightline of Pumori and Cho Oyu, which looked dinky in comparison to where we were going. I traced the bumps and nicks on the north-east ridge which ran up to the summit pyramid. *You can do it. You can summit Everest, Si.* So similar to the creepily seductive voices I'd heard when I was escaping the clutch of the caves. *You can do it, Si.* I knew it was still a vertical mile above me, but I *could* do it. I knew I could. And I wanted to. It was attainable.

Malcolm's words about his own summit fever came to me: *There's a thread that attaches itself to you when you're up there.*

Was this what I was feeling?

No. You're not here for that.

That dream was part of someone else's life.

The wind picked up as Mark and I took our last zombified steps, spitting spindrift into our sightline. The snow had petered out up here, blasted away by the wind, leaving bare rock as well as the traces of earlier climbs – the ancient scraps of nylon that Juliet had seen, revealing themselves after years of being buried beneath ice. *Maybe some of the scraps belonged to her.* Again, our camp was set up far above the others and in the crappiest, most exposed position, but Wanda came out to guide us, and once again we used her red down suit as our homing beacon. The second we reached our tent, Mark took off his mask and promptly threw up.

Wanda and I helped him crawl inside, and then she left to collect snow for us – not easy as the little there was was riddled with urine stains. When she returned and I had my breath again, I told her that Malcolm had turned back.

'He is sick?'

Don't tell anyone, son. 'He's okay, I think. Will Tadeusz let him try for the summit if he hasn't managed to get to Camp II?'

'I do not know. I hope so.'

That night, once again unable to face eating even a crumb of chocolate, Mark and I watched in fascination as Wanda put away two packets of vegetable soup.

Exhaustion rippled through me, but I didn't want to sleep. I didn't want to be revisited by the altitude-induced Ed nightmares. *And let's not forget this was where Juliet had her own close encounter with her special friend, Si.*

Taking gulps of bottled oxygen every so often, I drifted in and out of consciousness, but this time I didn't dream. I woke to find the tent flushed with a golden glow. Wrapped in my layers, bookended by Wanda and Mark, I felt connected to something for the first time in ages. The three of us had a bond. I'd pushed myself further than I thought possible. I'd made it. And I hadn't lost the flush of longing I'd felt when I'd gazed up at the summit.

Once again I'd forgotten why I was on the mountain.

I was about to get a rude wake-up call.

The man's eyes were bulging like hard-boiled eggs, froth bubbled at the corners of his mouth, but it was the sound of his breathing that would haunt me: a low growl like a lawnmower failing to start. He was lying at the edge of camp, at the point where we were about to peel off to begin the trek down to base camp, surrounded by people barking into radios.

Mark stared down at him, body rigid, and Wanda grabbed his arm. 'Come on, Mark.'

She dragged him away towards the path. I hung back.

As if drawn by invisible strings, others were gravitating towards the drama. A couple of the American team's film crew arrived at a jog, panting hard, their cameras balanced on their shoulders. No one shouted at them to stop being callous. Everything seemed to happen in slow motion and under a light that was artificial in its brightness. I stepped back as a group of grim-faced men clustered around the prone figure. When the crowd parted once more, the man was slotted inside a red bag attached to a foot pump.

'What's that?' someone asked.

'A Gamow bag,' another voice said. 'It'll artificially lower altitude. Probably cerebral oedema. Anyone know which team he's from?'

'Think he's one of the Japanese hikers.'

Film it. Get your camera, get your camera, this is what you're here for.

I could have done so easily. I even removed my pack intending to take out the camera. But something stopped me.

Instead I walked away, picking up my pace to catch up to Mark and Wanda, again forgetting that running is a seriously bad idea at altitude. The exertion left me gasping. They'd disappeared, and I was alone in one of the stony gullies, the air filled with the stink of yak shit. My stomach flip-flopped, but I somehow held onto this morning's fried potato breakfast.

Dizzy with the onset of a panic attack, I stopped, gagged, and made myself drink some water. I stood for another five minutes, staring up at the grey talus slopes around me. Behind me loomed the summit. *Still want to go there?*

A tug in my gut. *Yes.*

Now clammy despite the cold, I walked on, fingers numb. There was someone ahead of me – a man half-hidden behind a rock, clutching his chest with one hand, wildly waving the other. *There's something wrong with him.* My gut clenched. *What the fuck is this now?* There was something clinging to his back, and he was trying to slap it off. A creature of some sort – multi-limbed, tentacled. *Not real, not real.* I squeezed my eyes shut, seeing stars, opened them, and it dawned that the man was actually just a strangely shaped rock, the play of light on it giving it the illusion of movement. My pulse thumped in my ears.

I walked on, but now I couldn't shake the sense I was being watched. There was a definite heaviness in the air around me.

Bullshit.

Maybe sensed presence was contagious.

Bullshit. You're seeing things because you're tired – you've barely eaten anything for three days, burned up thousands of calories. And no doubt I was still affected by Juliet's account, which had horrible parallels with what I'd experienced down in the caves. That was all.

Wanda and Mark were waiting for me over the next rise. Mark was picking at a sore at the side of his mouth. He'd lost the lightness he'd found on the mountain.

'You look bad, Simon,' Wanda said.

'Thanks.' That poisonous sense was fading, thank God. *See?*

'The man up there, will he be okay?'

For a second I thought she was talking about the Lovecraftian thing I'd hallucinated. I glanced at Mark who was still worrying at the sore. 'Yeah. Looks like it's under control.'

He smiled in relief. 'Good.'

I found out later from Claude and Elodie that the Japanese hiker, a chain-smoker with a history of stroke – pretty much the last person who should be at altitude – had been airlifted to Zangmu, but hadn't made it.

He was my first death on the mountain. You know what I'm going to say next: *He wouldn't be my last.*

It took me a full day to get back on an even keel after what I'd seen – and hallucinated – on the walk down to base camp. The thicker air helped. After all that time spent above seven thousand metres, my body drank it in, and my appetite came raging back.

I knew one thing for sure. I no longer wanted to have anything to do with Thierry's plan. It wasn't just the dubious morality of it, or my failure to capitalise on what should have been the perfect *Journey to the Dark Side* scenario. The lure of the summit was still strong, and I needed every ounce of my energy to haul myself up there. The high camps were freezing, nausea-inducing hell pits, but now that I was safely down I wanted to go back up. Everywhere else – here, home – felt like it was made of cardboard in comparison with the intensity I'd experienced up there.

In the first of what was to be a long list of dumb decisions, I decided I owed it to Thierry to let him know I was done with the plan. I emailed him, and immediately felt about six stone lighter.

When I returned to my tent, Juliet's climbing journal was sitting on my sleeping bag, along with a scrawled note saying: *Please read this. M.*

I didn't. I didn't want to. I didn't dare. I looked at it for a while, weighed it in my hands. Riffled to the ripped out pages at the end. Then I lay in my sleeping bag for an hour or so – about the time it would take someone to read it.

Mark leaped out of his tent the second I called his name. The sore on his mouth was bleeding. I handed the journal to him. 'Why did you give me this to read, Mark?'

He shrugged. 'I guess I'm tired of doing this alone. I wanted your opinion. Can we go for a walk?'

As we hit the edge of camp, I regretted not stopping to retrieve my down jacket. The wind picked up, and spindrift spun and danced, finding its way into crevices I didn't know I had.

'So what do you think?' he said when we were a hundred metres or so outside camp and well out of earshot.

'Your mum was hard core, Mark.' Lame, but I didn't know what to say. 'You should be really proud of her. She was tough.' *And possibly as nutty as a fruitcake.*

'I don't think she was mad, Simon. Just because she saw something strange doesn't mean she was insane.' I hadn't said it did, but it was clear that he was actually trying to convince himself, not me.

Snug in their gloves, my fingers were tingling. I bit the inside of my cheek, which was now as raw as a bloody piece of meat.

He paced around me. 'Sensed presence is really common, Simon. It usually occurs when there's sensory deprivation of some kind, or monotony, and when stress levels are extremely high.' This came out stiffly, as if he was quoting from memory.

'It's fair to say your mum was stressed.'

'Yes. She had loads of pressure on her.' He wiped his nose. 'I've read some of the articles about her, Simon. They were cruel.' I stamped my feet. I was losing sensation in my toes. 'And the Third Man factor has links to altitude and hypoxia of course.' He didn't seem to feel the cold.

'But don't people also sense it when they're not at altitude? Like that Shackleton guy.' *Or people who have gone into caving systems with crazy ex-soldiers.*

'Yes. Like I said, it can be a reaction to extreme stress. A desire not to be alone. It's actually really interesting. It could also account for other stuff too. Alien abductions, ghost sightings, the early evidence for angels. And most religious prophecies were heard on mountains. At altitude.'

'Altitude sickness is the basis for all religions?'

'Good a reason as any. Some people are more susceptible to it. Hey, did you know that centuries ago people couldn't differentiate between their inner voice and so-called reality and thought that what they were hearing were gods speaking to them?'

Are you there, God? It's me, Simon. My inner voice never shut the hell up. 'Your mum wasn't showing any other signs of altitude sickness, was she?'

'No. Well, she says not. You know, according to what I've read, the Third Man could also be a phantom double.'

'A what?'

'Like an extension of yourself. A projection. It's like a coping mechanism so that you don't feel like you're alone. Some psychologists believe you can assign other identities to it. See what you want to see in times of stress.' He took a deep breath and puffed out his cheeks. 'Sorry. I've been talking at you, haven't I?'

It wasn't just the Third Man stuff that was disturbing. There were parts of the journal that implied Juliet knew she wasn't going to make it, and had accepted this (in a couple of the crossed-out sections, it sounded like she'd *wanted* this), but no way was I going to bring this up with Mark. *That would mean she'd chosen to abandon Mark, just like Dad abandoned me.* Where the hell did that nasty thought come from? I gave myself a mental pinch. 'A couple of pages at the end were ripped out. Did she do that?'

He looked down at his feet. 'Yeah. Maybe. I don't know.'

Perhaps she'd looked behind the mask and written what she'd seen on those ripped pieces of paper.

'How did you get the journal? Was it found in her stuff?'

'Yes. Tadeusz and Joe sent it back with the things she left at Camp II after she disappeared.'

'Has Tadeusz read it?'

'No! I don't think so. He isn't that kind of person, is he?'

No. He isn't. Not like some people I could mention. He was getting agitated now, perhaps because he'd revealed so much of himself. He was like a scrap of fabric buried in the ice at Camp II, gradually emerging as the wind scoured away the layers covering it. *Bollocks.*

'Your mum was pretty messed up about Walter, wasn't she?'

'Yes. They were really close.'

'What was he like?'

'Uncle Walter? I didn't see that much of him. He didn't get on with my father, so he didn't come to the house very often. He was a bit like Malcolm, I suppose. Tough, a real bloke. Oh! He didn't have any teeth. Wore false ones. When I was little, he used to take them out and scare me.'

Sounds charming.

'What does Tadeusz say about your mother?'

'Positive stuff, mostly.'

'Mostly?'

'He admitted that she was having a few problems health-wise, but that's normal. Being up here takes its toll, doesn't it?'

'Did you speak to anyone else who was on the expedition apart from Tom?'

'Couldn't.'

'Why?'

'They're dead.'

'What, all of them?'

'Most of them.'

He reeled off the list: Eri Aka (killed in an avalanche on Manaslu); Pauline Zierzinger (a fall on Denali); Evil Tom (cancer); Joe Davis (haemorrhage after a head injury); Dawa Sherpa (accident in the Khumbu Ice Fall); Lewis, the Canadian skier (snowboarding accident).

The only surviving expedition members were Tom's sidekick Wade, Tadeusz, and Andrej Danielsen. Sem, Andrej's brother, had committed suicide in 2001. And Stefanie Weber, the German alpinist who'd being racing Juliet to the summit, had been killed while ice-climbing in British Columbia.

'Bloody hell.' Not all had died on the mountains, but it was sobering how many of those who kept on climbing had eventually run out of luck. *Maybe we only have a finite amount of luck.* 'Are you going to show the journal to Wanda?'

'No. She thinks my mother was some sort of hero. I don't want her to think she was crazy.'

'I don't think she'd think that.'

I didn't think that. But only because what Juliet had been through was so close to what I'd experienced down in the caves. *Juliet and Simon, the psycho twins.*

'Wanda's so cool, isn't she?'

'Yeah.'

He tried to smile. 'I think she likes you.'

My heart gave a little blip. 'She likes you too.'

'Not in *that* way though. Thanks for reading Juliet's journal, Simon. Thanks for listening to me ramble.'

'Hey, we're mates, aren't we?'

'Yeah.'

Yeah. 'Let's go and see if we can convince Tadeusz to let us at the beers.'

'I'm saying, it's not as easy as that, T. You don't know what it's like here—'

'I'm counting on you, Si. You're not there for a fucking vacation.'

'I know that, T, but I can't pull dead people out of my arse. What do you want me to do, push climbers down the fucking mountain? Mess with their oxygen?'

'If that's what it takes, yeah.'

It was my own fault for sending him the email. He'd written seven replies, each one more vitriolic than the last, insisting that I phone him, even though satellite calls from base camp were outrageously expensive. I couldn't put if off forever. I'd waited until the mess tent was empty, then slipped into the radio room and dialled our home number, hoping he wouldn't answer. He had, and although there was a slight time lag, his voice was clear. 'I borrowed thirty thousand dollars from my folks, Simon. I didn't do that so you could make some new pals on a goddamned mountain. You think I *want* to go back to the States?'

'Yeah, I'm so sorry you had to dip into your fucking trust fund, Thierry. What, so your folks are going to kidnap you and drag you back to the US are they? We've got six months, we can come up with something else to—'

'What about those Ukrainians you were telling me about?'

Shit. 'What about them?'

'You said they were at the last camp before the summit. You can film them on the way up, right? My arse is on the line, Simon. You *owe* me.'

'I *owe* you? What the hell does that mean?'

'I've built up the site, put in most of the work. I do all the writing.'

'Are you fucking kidding me? What about Cwm Pot? Who did that? Who almost fucking *died*? Not you and your fat fucking arse, that's for sure. I *told* you this was a bad idea, but no, you insisted I come here. You pushed me into it. This is not a long walk up a big hill, T. It's fucking exhausting. It's hard enough trying to breathe and walk at the same time, never mind do anything else.'

'So you're giving up, is that it? Leaving me in the shit. Thanks a lot, dude.'

'Fuck you, Thierry.'

I hung up. I wanted to kick something. Or hit someone. When I left the communications section, Malcolm was sitting at the mess tent's table, his hands folded in front of him. How much had he heard? I'd barely seen him since he returned from the col. 'Hi Malcolm,' I said, testing the water. 'How are you feeling?'

'Fine.'

'Any word on whether Tadeusz will let you try for the summit?'

'Aye. It looks positive.'

'Good.'

'You were raising your voice quite a bit there. Problems at home?'

'Kind of.'

'Sit down, son. Think we should talk.'

Shite. I doubted I was in for some of his old-timer's advice on safe mountain practice this time.

'You were the boy who was pulled out of Cwm Pot.'

Double shite. 'You know about Cwm Pot?'

'Aye. Used to be a caver myself, once upon a time. Knew I'd seen you somewhere before.' I'd thought that the press pics were too blurry to make out my face clearly, but then I hadn't seen all of them – I'd employed my usual Simon Newman avoidance tactics on that score. 'The guide you were with died, didn't he?'

'Yeah well, he happened to be a psycho.'

'That's no way to speak of the dead.'

'You didn't know him.'

'Why were you down there? Something to do with filming those lads who died down there, wasn't it?'

'Yeah.'

'And you haven't climbed the Eiger, have you?'

'No.'

A self-satisfied nod. I thought about telling him that to be fair, this lie wasn't strictly mine but Thierry's, but couldn't see the point. 'There's no place for being reckless underground *or* on a mountain, Simon.'

'Yeah? You're one to talk. What about you, Malcolm? What happened to you up there on the col?'

'That's nothing.'

'You said you were having trouble with your sight. Did that happen last time? Is that why you didn't make the summit?'

'Don't try turning this around now.'

He stared at me with his watery blue eyes. I stared right back. 'Are you going to tell Tadeusz?'

'No.'

I knew why he wouldn't. He was hiding something himself, wasn't he? He was hiding something, I was hiding something. Mark was hiding something. We were all hiding something.

An hour later I checked my emails. There was one from Thierry of course: *Sorry, dude. I pushed you into this. Came on too strong. I guess I just wanted to push JTTDS to the next level, you know? Anyhoo, you must do what you think is right. Just be safe and look after yourself.*

Bastard.

He knew how to get to me.

A ripple of anticipation ran through camp as Tadeusz called us into the mess tent. Most of us crowded around the table, but Mingma, Ireni and Dorje chose to stand at the back.

'I have met with the other teams,' Tadeusz began. 'The Chinese will summit first. Much earlier than perhaps is wise, but that is their business. After that, we have permission to attempt. We will go up to Camp I on May sixteen, where we should have a weather window of two days. The others will be the Polish guys, the International Team, and Mountain Conquest.'

Robbie put up a hand, but Tadeusz ignored him.

'We will do this quietly. We do not want to alert the other teams waiting at ABC that we are ready. We do not want hold-ups on the Second Step. Is that clear? We must avoid a bottleneck. The ridge can hold maybe sixty climbers. More, and there will be issues. You want to queue to get to the summit like you queue at a supermarket? So please, this I would say to you. Those of you who have friends in other camps, even the independent climbers, please do not mention the summit date.'

Everyone glanced at me – Mr Sociable.

Robbie put his hand up again, and this time Tadeusz gave him a curt nod.

'Will we all be going together? I like to climb at my own pace. Don't want to wait for others who may be slower.'

I rolled my eyes. 'You know Mark and I arrived at Camp II way before you did, right, Robbie?'

'Yeah, well, had an issue with my regulator.'

'Bullshit,' Wanda said.

Robbie ignored her. 'I'm thinking maybe Mingma could come with me, Howard and Wanda, and Dorje could guide Malcolm and the other two.'

'Mingma and Mark will not be climbing with us,' Tadeusz said. 'Mark will not be going to the summit with the rest of us.' No surprise to Wanda and me of course, but Robbie, Malcolm and Howard were dumbstruck. 'We will be ready to leave for our summit attempt at eleven p.m. Mark and Mingma will leave at four a.m.'

'I'm not getting you, Tadeusz,' Robbie spluttered.

Tadeusz looked over at Mark, who was drawing circles on the table's surface with his glove. Mark gave him a small nod. 'Mark will be taking a detour.'

'Huh?'

'He is going to pay respects to a family member who died on the mountain.'

I could almost see the cogs whirring in Robbie's mind, trying to assess how this would affect him. There was no 'Gee, Mark,

I'm sorry for your loss', or curiosity about who Mark's relative might be. Instead he said: 'So he gets Mingma all to himself? Is he paying extra for that?'

Howard had the grace to look embarrassed.

'You are disgusting,' Wanda said matter-of-factly.

'Just want things to be fair, is all. I gave up a lot to do this again. Why should Mark have a Sherpa all to himself?' *A Sherpa all to himself*, as if Mingma was a Happy Meal or something. 'You promised a far higher Sherpa to climber ratio, Tadeusz.'

'This is the way it will be. If you want to drop out, then please do so, Robbie.'

Robbie's hair plugs practically burst out of his scalp in indignation. 'That's not . . . No! I'm going.'

'Fine. To repeat: Wanda, Robbie, Malcolm, myself, Howard, Dorje and Simon will be on Team One. Mingma and Mark will be on Team Two.'

Robbie sat back in his chair. He might have lost Mingma, but it wasn't all bad. He'd got what he'd wanted all along: Mark, who he thought of as the weakest link, shunted out of the way. He could afford to be magnanimous. 'I'm sorry if I sounded harsh, Mark. I'm sorry about your relative. Where on the mountain did he die?'

'*She*.'

'Huh? A *woman*?'

Wanda huffed. 'You do not need a penis to climb a mountain, Robbie.'

Or to die on one.

'I know that. What was her name, Mark?'

'None of your business.'

Go Mark.

'Well I wish you the best of luck.'

'Thanks.'

'Yeah, buddy. Jeez. Sorry to hear about your relative.' This from Howard, bringing up the watery rear as usual. The skin around his mouth was peeling so badly he looked as if he'd been snacking on maggots.

'And I would ask you not to tell anyone else about what Mark is going to do, please,' Tadeusz said, fixing his eyes on Robbie in particular. 'It is a private matter.'

'Of course. You can count on me, Tadeusz.' He stood up and clapped his hands together. 'Let's get this thing *on*.'

Malcolm caught my eye. I couldn't read his expression.

The next day, in a futile attempt to end the cold war between Mark, Wanda and Robbie, Howard suggested a hike to the touristy enclave known as the 'tented camp' – an oblong of makeshift hotels and bars situated a mile outside base camp – for a change of scene and a few beers. I talked Wanda and Mark into it for his sake. Ireni, Dorje and Tadeusz elected to stay at base, as did Malcolm (thank fuck), but Mingma accepted Howard's invitation to join us.

Robbie fell into stride with me as we passed the mountaineering association's miserable building and headed along the Rongbuk road. Wanda and Mark, who weren't thrilled at the prospect of hanging out with Robbie, walked ahead with Mingma. A clutch of Chinese tourists milled around, sucking at disposable oxygen canisters and posing in front of the base camp sign. The ground was littered with cans, old prayer flags, scraps of toilet paper and snack food wrappers.

With no preamble Robbie said: 'It's Juliet Michaels, isn't it?'

Shite. 'Huh?'

'Don't play dumb, Simon. Malcolm said she'd had a son who'd be around Mark's age. He changed his name, right?'

We were too far back for Mark to hear us, but Wanda turned around all the same and shot Robbie one of her dark looks.

'My lips are sealed, Robbie.'

'Okay, okay. It's not as if I'm planning to blog about it. You think he'll make it? Camp III is still a helluva way up the mountain.'

'Not this again, Robbie.'

'Look at him, Simon.'

'What?'

'He looks like a goddamn skeleton.'

'We've all lost weight, dude.'

Robbie shrugged. Like all of us, Mark was always swathed in mummyish layers of Gore-tex and down, but it wasn't hard to see that Robbie was right: already skinny, Mark had lost far more weight than anyone else. His wrists were as fragile as a child's.

Howard caught up to us, and talk turned to the best way to tape our ice axe handles to stop them freezing in the high camps and other scintillating topics. Robbie didn't mention the subject of Mark's relative again. He was in the throes of his summit countdown, so the self-obsession meter was cranked to 'high'.

Mingma waved us through the carpeted door of one of the larger tents, which he said was operated by one of his mates. We sat down on a U-shaped bench upholstered in colourful fabric and cushions. A dung fire pulsed in the centre of the space. The place stank of yak shit and sour butter tea, but it was warm, snug and luxurious in comparison to our mess tent. Mingma's mate, who was good-looking in a retro matinee idol way, with Elvis hair and natty turned-up jeans, handed us each a bottle of Lhasa beer.

Mingma and I ended up sitting next to each other, Howard and Robbie on Mingma's side, Wanda and Mark on mine. I had the feeling I always got with Mingma, that he was studying us, as if we were some sort of anthropological experiment that he couldn't decide was amusing or a failure. We knocked back our first beer in minutes, and Elvis brought us another round.

'Have you always wanted to climb Everest, Mingma?'

'No.'

'But you've summited it like, nine times, right?'

'Yes. It is a good way to make money. I need to support my family and my sons.' Perhaps it was the beer that loosened his tongue, or perhaps he'd decided that I wasn't a total arsehole. He told me his family had fled to Nepal from Tibet a couple of decades earlier, when he was a child. He'd started out like Ngima, as a cook's assistant, then worked his way up the ladder. He was the only one who was working full-time, and his entire family all counted on him. *Like Ang Tsering – the Sherpa who'd saved Juliet's life after Walter died.*

'Have you ever had any really difficult clients?'

'No.'

The beer was going straight to my head, making me mouthy. 'C'mon. Tell me the truth. It won't go any further.'

A shrug. 'Most people are nice. Sometimes they say they have to get up the mountain when they can't. We turn them away. *Ban dai* Tadeusz is good like that.'

'Tadeusz is a good boss?'

'Yes. He is a good man. We worked together before, on the other side, when he was a guide. Very fair, pays good money.'

'Which do you prefer, the north or the south side?'

'The north. No Khumbu Ice Fall. This is very dangerous and many Sherpas die there.'

'You guys believe that disasters are caused by the mountain goddess getting angry, right?'

Another casual shrug. 'Some Sherpas do. Dorje, he takes precautions. He sprinkles *channe*, which is like rice, to stop the avalanches. It's not so bad on the north side.'

'But still dangerous, right? Lots of people die.'

'Yes.'

'You don't have to answer this, Mingma, but why don't Sherpas like to touch the dead climbers?' *Jesus, Simon. Way to be culturally sensitive.* I was treading on toes here, I knew that, but Mingma didn't appear to be offended.

'Only a lama is supposed to touch a dead body first, Simon. If a person is not guided to the afterlife, she can become angry and take it out on the people who are living.'

'What do you mean take it out on someone?'

'Bring bad luck to them.' Far as I knew, no one had guided Ed to the afterlife. But if what Mingma was saying were true, the whole world would be filled with ghosts of the angry dead, wouldn't it? 'The father of my mother lives in a very small village, and his doors are very low down so that the angry spirits will not come inside his house.' He tapped his forehead. 'They will hurt their heads.'

'Say you do touch a body, how do you get rid of an angry ghost?'

'You make a blessing at the monastery. Burn the butter tea, ask the lama to do a puja. But it is not about trying to *hurt* the bad spirit, only to send it on its way to a better place.'

Mingma's mate brought us a third round. Was I going to keep digging? *You might not get another chance.* 'I heard there were a couple of climbers who died last year up in Camp III. Two Ukrainian guys.'

'Many die last year.'

Careful. 'Yeah. But I've heard they're still up there.'

'Eh?'

'Their bodies.'

'Sometimes the Sherpas who fix the ropes are paid to throw the bodies down the East face. There are no bodies at Camp III.'

And there it was. *That's Thierry fucked, then.* I was swamped with a mixture of dismay and relief. *Even if you wanted to film them, you couldn't.*

'We must get back to camp, I think,' Mingma said. 'It will be dark soon.'

Next to me, Wanda stretched and yawned, her arm brushing against mine. She looked at me and smiled. 'What is the word for being warm and comfortable?'

'Cosy?'

'Yes. I'm cosy.' She wasn't the only one. Lulled by the fire, Robbie and Howard were lying back on the cushions, their eyes closed. *Peace at last.*

'Mingma says we'd better get back.' I realised that the space next to her was empty. 'Where's Mark?'

'He has gone to the bathroom.'

'I'll go get him.'

I mourned the tent's warmth the second I stepped outside and the wind smacked me around the head. The light was turning blue, and tourists were crunching their way across the moraine to film the golden glow fading over the summit ridge. I followed a rubbish-strewn path to the toilet block – a brick building sitting precariously above an open pit of raw sewerage.

A couple of shadowy figures were standing next to it, head to head, one of them in a yellow jacket. 'Mark!'

He waved. 'Coming!'

I turned to look at the summit as he approached me. *You could be up there in a week, Si. All the way up there*. Ukrainians or no Ukrainians, I was going to do it. We'd make another plan for the site.

Mark tapped his gut. 'Stomach's bad. Have I held you guys up?'

'Nah. Hey, who were you talking to?'

'Huh?' He turned away to cough. 'When?'

'Outside the toilet block.'

He gave me a strange look. 'No one.'

The stony ground shifted under my feet. There *had* been someone there with him – hadn't there? Perhaps it was just a tourist or a hiker who'd wandered off.

You know better than that.

'How come your mum doesn't haven't a memorial here, Mark?'

'I think my dad was against it. I think he was worried that if there was one, then I'd want to see it some day.'

'You're doing something a bit more radical than just visiting base camp now though, aren't you?'

'Yes. I think he—' He coughed, the force of it doubling him over. It sounded far too close to the ailing hiker's lawnmower growl for my liking.

'Jesus, Mark.'

'I'm cool.'

He didn't sound cool. He didn't look cool. In less than a day, the cough had rooted itself in his lungs. And it would only get worse from here. Ireni hadn't spared us the gruesome details. *Up above eight thousand metres, your blood turns to syrup, your muscle mass gets gnawed away, turning your body into a flabby skin suit.*

'Has Ireni checked you out?'

'I'm fine. I've told her I'm fine. And I am.'

I cast around the stone humps and chortens, some of which were draped in prayer flags, for any names that could conceivably belong to Thierry's Ukrainians. Mark had asked me this morning to accompany him to the memorial site, but I wasn't in the mood for this. *This is where she saw IT the first time.*

'I'm thinking that I might come back here next year. Try for the summit.' He smiled, his skin stretching across his bony skull. 'You could come too. You could make a documentary about it.'

'Really?' *Why not? You're a filmmaker, aren't you, Eiger Boy?* And I could actually picture it. If Hollywood movies tended to be father-and-son tales, this was a corker of a mother-and-son story. Thierry could edit it, adding a tear-jerking soundtrack to manipulate the audience. *Only you don't have to wait until next year, do you? You have a juicy story right here.*

A pressure began to build in my chest. I knew what it was. I tried to ignore it.

'Really. There's no way I can keep this quiet forever. People will find out I've been here. And I am serious about trying for the summit. I could achieve what my mother never achieved.' He cleared his throat. 'Don't think my father would like that much. I'll also put up a plaque to Juliet. She deserves one, doesn't she?'

'Yeah.'

'She wasn't mad was she, Simon?'

'No, mate.' The pressure in my chest was growing.

'But . . . but if it wasn't for me then she wouldn't have been here.'

'That's not true. You've been up there, Mark. You can't go through that for anyone else but yourself.' *Was that true? No idea, but it sounded good.* 'Anyway, if you want to blame anyone, blame those journalists who gave her a hard time and spread lies about her.'

'Yeah. *Yeah.* You're right. I just wish I knew exactly what happened up there.'

'We might never know. It's the way these things go.' *Simon Newman: sage extraordinaire.* 'There are always those pieces of paper.'

'Huh?'

'The ones from the back of the journal. Maybe she ripped them out to take up to the summit, save her carrying the weight of the book. She could have written something on them when she was up at the high camps.' *They could still be on her body.*

He shrugged. 'Maybe. It's just . . . what if . . . what if she really was seeing what she wanted to see?'

'Not getting you.'

'Her gut was telling her she was climbing for the wrong reasons. I think it was trying to warn her. The thing – *It* – had frostbite. Her worst nightmare. Maybe, like Walter, she knew . . .' Another hacking cough took him over. He flapped a mitted hand. 'I don't know what I'm saying. All that stress she put on herself when she didn't need to.'

'She was trying to redeem herself.'

'Yeah. Repair her reputation.' He spat this out.

'Time sorted that out for her, didn't it?'

'Yeah. It did. People admire her now. Simon . . . I can do this, right?'

Don't do it. But the words burst out before I could stop them. 'I'm going to go with you, Mark.'

Had I planned this from the moment I heard about Juliet's body? Maybe. But at that moment, it just felt *right.* Mark was my friend, but I also had a bond with Juliet. I knew she wouldn't want Mark going alone.

Or maybe it was simply too good an opportunity to pass up. Mark was in need of closure. I was in need of something to give to Thierry. *You owe me.*

But what about the summit?

Mark was staring at me, mouth half-open. '*What*?'

'I'm going to go with you. To see your mum. To see Juliet.' *Take it back. It's not too late.*

No.

'Why?'

Yeah, Simon, why? 'I don't think you should do this by yourself.'

'Mingma will be with me.'

'Yeah, I know . . . it's just, after reading Juliet's diary, I almost feel I know her.' This was as close to the truth as I could get.

'You'd really do that? Come with me?'

'Yeah.'

'But then you might not get a chance at the summit.'

'The summit will always be there, and like you say, we can come back next year.'

He sniffed. 'I don't know what to say.'

'Say yes.'

'Yes.' Then he threw his arms around me.

That night, I was back in Mission:Coffee, working with Ed, both of us cheerfully grinding up our fingers in the coffee machine to serve to people. Then *zip*: I was back in the flat, lounging on the couch, and Thierry was rushing up to greet me on all fours like a dog, a copy of *Into Thin Air* in his mouth. In my bedroom, Ed, my dad, Kenton and Mark were sitting side by side on the mattress, sniggering and paging through a skin magazine. They held up the centrefold – a photograph of Juliet. Panicked, I tried to warn them that they had to hide it – Wanda was on her way, but I couldn't get my words out.

My subconscious couldn't be more literal if it tried.

Tadeusz looked from me to Mark. As usual I couldn't tell what he was thinking.

'I have spoken to Mingma. Simon, he is okay with you going with him and Mark, but you must listen to him. He is the leader, you understand?'

We both nodded meekly, two boys in the headmaster's office.

'If he tells you to go back, you are to do so. Is that clear?'

'It's clear.'

'You will be ready to leave at four a.m. You will follow the fixed ropes above Camp III, and then split off from the main route. Mingma knows where to go, I have traced a route to the approximate site of the coordinates. Here you must be very careful. The climbing will be mixed. There will be much ice and rock, loose scree. I cannot be responsible for you, do you understand this?'

'Don't worry, Tadeusz,' I said.

'You will rope up with Mingma. There is no guarantee that you will find your mother, Mark. You have to understand this. I am giving you one chance, and that is all.'

'I know. I'm grateful.'

'Okay.'

As we stood up to leave, Tadeusz called me back. 'You have said this because you are his friend?' It was inconceivable to him that I'd give up my chance at the summit. I hadn't even told Thierry about my change in plans. And I had no intention of telling him. Not yet.

'It's partly that. It just feels like the right thing to do.' This was partially true.

'You are a good climber, Simon. Mingma also says you are strong. Perhaps you come back next year and join the team again.'

My heart swelled. 'Thanks, Tadeusz.'

'In your opinion, you think Mark is strong enough to do this? It will be easy for me to say no. Ireni is not confident with his health, but climbing is more about' – he tapped his forehead – 'what is here.'

'I think so. He's determined.'

'Good.'

Malcolm cornered me outside the toilet tent after lunch. I was waiting for it. The news had spread fast. Robbie had been as incredulous as Tadeusz, unable to believe that I'd give up my chance at the summit for any reason, never mind for a weed like Mark. Howard had been more supportive, shaking my hand and saying, 'Good for you.' Only Wanda had kept her distance.

And now here was Malcolm, eager to give me his two cents. It would be the last conversation we'd ever have. 'Heard what you're doing, Simon.'

'So?'

'Make sure you're doing it for the right reasons.'

A flash of irritation. Who the hell was Malcolm to give me advice? Malcolm, toeless Malcolm, someone who had experienced what the death zone could take from him in the most visceral sense, someone whose body had explicitly warned him not to climb above eight thousand metres, and yet he was still determined to do it. 'What are the right reasons?'

'You know what I'm talking about.'

'Yeah? Well make sure you follow your own advice.' I turned to leave.

'You should tell that lass of yours,' he called after me. 'About the Eiger.'

'She's not my lass.'

'You should come clean with her. She'll find out. Women always do.'

Nothing like a touch of old-school sexism.

'I will.'

And I would. But not then.

That night, as I was lying wrapped in my sleeping bag, trying to get comfortable and failing to get my head around what I'd committed myself to, Wanda came into my tent.

She crawled in and lay next to me. I barely dared to breathe. I rolled onto my side to face her.

'What you do, going with Mark. It's very kind.'

'It's what anyone would do.'

'Ha! You think Robbie would do this? You think Malcolm would do this?'

'Well, to be fair, Robbie is a special case. Being a wanker takes up all his spare energy.'

'You know, I am glad you are going with Mark. I am worried about him. I don't think he will be able to do this without you. It is so good of you to help him like this.'

'You've also helped him.'

'Yes, but you are the one who is giving up his dream for a friend. I would not do this.'

But summiting the fucking mountain wasn't my dream – or maybe it was. I don't know.

'Listen, if you do not get a chance at the summit this season then I will come back with you next year.'

'You will? Mark said the same thing.' *The Three Mountaineering Musketeers. Jesus.*

'Yes. We will all do it together. Whatever it takes.'

The tent could have blown away then, Ed could have appeared, and I wouldn't have cared.

I freed my arms from their cocoon and pulled her closer to me. And then I kissed her.

There was no going back now.

When you die, if you're allowed to go back to one moment in time and relive it over and over again, I know exactly where I'd want to be: lying curled with Wanda in her tent, her leg hooked over mine, sharing headphones and taking it in turns to play a track from our respective playlists. Not even Wanda's charms could stop me balking at *Titanic*, but I secretly enjoyed *Les Miserables, The Wiz, West Side Story* and the soundtrack to *Chocolat*, although I would have died rather than admit this to Thierry. And she didn't complain when I made her listen to my nineties classics and old Stevie Wonder tunes. But music, like the sense of smell, is a bastard when it comes to igniting memories. I can't hear any of these songs now without being swamped in a mire of sadness and regret. Sometimes the feeling lasts for days.

I had plenty of time before we were due to head up the col to dissuade Mark from carrying on, or to tell Tadeusz and Ireni that I was worried about his health. But then he'd go and 'seem normal' for a while, and I'd tell myself that he'd be fine. That he *had* to do this. That Ireni knew what she was doing and wouldn't let him go any higher if she thought his body wouldn't take it. That it wasn't my call.

Besides, any energy I had left over after hiking back to ABC was channelled into spending time with – and daydreaming about

– Wanda. I had a plan. After Mission Juliet was completed, I'd go back home for long enough to pack a bag, then move to France to be with Wanda. She'd help me find filming work. Maybe I'd document her attempts to climb the fourteen eight-thousand-metre peaks, sometimes climbing with her, sometimes providing base camp support. Thierry could run our website and help us secure sponsorship. We'd write an amusing blog about our adventures, maybe a book. We'd only have kids much later. We'd be like Claude and Elodie, living large.

I'm not joking. I really did think like this.

And like Juliet, I made a list of goals:

- Help Mark.
- Get Thierry off my back.
- Move to France to be with Wanda.
- BE HAPPY.
- I CAN DO THIS.

I told myself that Wanda need never know the real reason I'd come to the mountain. She had integrity and morality, and I knew from watching her dealings with Robbie that once you pissed her off, there was no coming back from that.

I somehow mustered the energy to shuffle out of the tent, ensuring that I was clipped on to the safety rope at all times. The tents at Camp III – a desolate slab of tattered old canvas and wind-blown rock – clung implausibly to the steep slope as if they'd been stuck there with Velcro; a misplaced step out here could mean a tumble all the way to the bottom of the col. Sucking in a deep gulp of oxygen, and ignoring my ankle, which had chosen this moment to start screaming, I pushed clumps of snow into the nylon bag, making sure it was unsullied by urine or worse. Then I limped back in, fumbling for the zip. Mark had thrown up in our tent's doorway the second we'd arrived, and the pool of puke was now a solid frozen disc. I kicked it out into the night.

It took me six tries to fire up the stove, watching as the snow melted with painful slowness. Sitting there, facing out, but seeing nothing but the tent's flimsy nylon door, I felt very small. I wanted to crawl into my sleeping bag and hide. *You can't sleep until you've drunk at least two litres.*

I shook Mark's leg. He lay on his back, his eyes open, breathing raspily through the oxygen mask, occasionally removing it to cough. 'Don't pass out yet. Got to drink.'

Wanda, our guardian angel and champion snow-melter wasn't around to help us. She was bunking up with Malcolm and Dorje, readying for their earlier departure.

Malcolm and I had avoided each other on the slog up to the high camps, but as far as I was aware, he'd made it here without any issues. Perhaps, like Mark, he was able to draw on some kind of inner battery that kept him chugging upwards. Robbie had finally shed his cockiness, and Howard had crawled all the way back into his shell. But all of us were suffering in one way or another: gaunt where we shouldn't be gaunt; swollen-faced; puffy-eyed and raw-skinned.

I made Mark sit up and drink a few mouthfuls of tea. I wasn't going to bother making any food.

'I can do this, right?' he wheezed. 'I'm strong enough, right?'

Last chance. 'Course you are, Mark. Course you are,' thinking: *Simon Newman, you total and utter fucking bastard.*

I lay wrapped in my sleeping bag listening to the crunch, crunch, crunch of cramponed feet marching past our tent as the others set off for the summit, trying to ignore a wave of regret that I wouldn't be joining them. I'd thought that the thread to the summit that Malcolm had spoken about had snapped. I was wrong.

If it wasn't for Wanda's promise that she'd return to the mountain with me, I reckon that right then, I might have gone after them.

I took a deep draught of oxygen and shut my eyes, certain that I wouldn't be able to sleep. But I must have dropped off, because then Mingma was shouting at us to get ready. Mark and

I moved as if we were on a space station, hindered by lack of gravity. Finding boots took on the enormity and concentration of performing brain surgery with a spoon. I had a special pair of merino wool socks that I'd been saving for today, and it took me ages to unearth them, groggy mind unable to figure out where I'd placed them last night when I was organising myself.

Mingma had boiled us up some snow, and I slid two bottles of water inside my down suit. Putting my crampons on seemed to take hours: the buckles were frozen, the icy metal nipped at the fabric of the gloves. Someone had poured concrete into my limbs.

Wordlessly, we joined Mingma outside. And *Jesus*, the cold. It sucked the life and warmth right out of me, taking me – just for an instant – back to the caves. Mingma helped us secure our oxygen bottles in our packs, and then we set off.

In comparison to the other climbers, we weren't going far. A stroll compared to their marathon. But at this altitude, even a stroll could be deadly. It would take us three hours to reach the Exit Cracks, where we'd diverge from the normal route and inch our way along to where Juliet lay. With no fixed ropes, the danger of hidden crevasses was our major concern. And for the first time we'd be heading into the death zone. *The place where the body starts to die; where the mind starts to crack.*

Sight restricted by my oxygen mask, hood and goggles, I let Mark go ahead of me, and concentrated on following the beam of my head torch. For a while, until daylight started to drift in, this became my world.

I didn't think, *this is shite, this is shite, this is shite.* I didn't have the energy for that. I nudged my heavy feet forward and focused on trying to breathe. It took my sloopy synapses a couple of seconds to register that we'd reached a rocky slope, and I fought to recalibrate my body to cope with this new terrain. *Careful.* It was akin to walking over roof tiles – I wanted to get down on my hands and knees and crawl.

Mingma pulled his oxygen mask aside to shout, 'Slowly, slowly,' at us, the wind snatching at his voice.

And slowly, slowly was the only way to do it.

Then he stopped and held up a hand. He removed his oxygen mask and said something into his radio. ' . . . going now, over.' He turned to us. '. . . trouble.'

'What?' *Christ*, it hurt to talk.

'Climber in trouble. Need to take up oxygen. Stay here.'

A time lapse delay while my brain processed this, and I thought: *Wanda. Don't let it be Wanda.*

'Stay here. You understand? Don't move.'

What I really wanted to do was grab Mingma and force him to tell us what the hell was going on, but neither Mark nor I did anything but stand there, watching as he moved upwards and away from us. Mark unclipped his jumar from the rope and sat. I followed suit, although it wasn't easy finding a position where I didn't feel hopelessly insecure. Below us lay Tibet's alluvial plains, now bathed in a monochrome light; above us loomed the summit. The spine of the Himalaya and the tips of the pinnacles shone as if they'd been plated in chrome.

We waited, kicking our boots to get the circulation going in our toes.

How long did we sit there before Mark spoke up? An hour maybe? He tapped me on the shoulder, and unclipped his mask so that I'd be able to hear him. 'We should go.'

'Back down?'

'No. To mam.' *Mam*. Not Juliet, or 'my mother'.

'*What?*'

'Might . . . might not get another chance. Mingma might not . . .' He'd run out of puff.

'Do you know how to get there?'

'Think so. Not far.'

'You sure?'

'Yes. It'll be . . . fine. Got . . . radio. You coming?'

Would he go if I said I wouldn't? I didn't know. *He's in no condition to go anywhere. He's a fucking walking skeleton. Say no.*

I nodded.

The wind pushed at us now, spindrift speckling my goggles. Using our ice axes as walking sticks, we started the traverse across the cracks. Mark was moving slower now, and so was I. *Your body is dying up here, Si.* The crampons scraped over an awkward mix of snow, ice and rock. At a normal elevation, it would be an easy scramble, here it was like – it was like climbing Mount Everest. The elevation seemed to tug at me, and I was glad of my restricted vision. *Don't look down.* Above us, Wanda could now be taking her last steps to the summit. *Please don't let it be her.*

Time is different up here, Malcolm was right about that. It seemed to lose all meaning as we inched over talus and rock, the light playing tricks and making the ground seem flatter than it was. My eyes were fighting to differentiate between the never-ending undulating rock and patches of stubborn snow. We'd made a fundamental mistake. The search area was too big. The chances of finding Juliet were zero. She could be hidden beneath a mound of snow and ice; we could have already stepped over her. In my mind's eye I'd been picturing her lying within easy reach, perfectly visible and looking as peaceful and well preserved as George Mallory. *Fucking stupid.*

Mark stopped, bent over, pulled his mask aside and vomited. Nothing much came up. I made him sit, removed the water bottle from inside my suit and handed it to him. He waved it away.

'Bad,' he said.

'Back?'

'No . . . on.'

'You know where to go?' *How could he?*

'Think so.'

I checked his oxygen. It was still on four bars. He drank, coughed and I helped him get to his feet, the exertion leaving me frighteningly breathless.

He walked a few steps, then slipped onto his side. I grabbed for him, my reaction, despite the surge of adrenalin, far too slow. He flailed out with his ice axe, but didn't slide more than six feet.

And then, twenty metres below him, I saw it: a flash of colour in a mound of snow. Cloud was wisping in now. I blinked to clear my vision and looked again. *Pink. It's pink. It has to be her. It has to be.* But I couldn't see how she could have fallen from the ridge, which was far to the right and way above us.

I wasn't sure how to feel. 'Mark. Found her.'

He gave a weary nod and got onto his hands and knees.

I edged my way closer to her, stopping for a breather after ten metres, not wanting to get too close without Mark. Partially covered by a snowdrift, she was lying face down, her legs splayed, her right arm trapped under her, her hood covering the back of her head. She was smaller than I'd been expecting and was still wearing her boots, one of her ankles cruelly twisted inwards. A wash of sadness: *Hello, Juliet.*

Then: *Film it. Film it now. Do it, do it, do it. Film it. Quickly, before Mark catches up.* Mechanically, as if someone else was now in control of my actions, I put down the pack, careful not to dislodge the oxygen bottle, and took out the camcorder. *You don't have to use it.* I removed the bulky over-glove, letting it dangle on its safety strap, and pressed record. Nothing happened. I tried again. Still it wouldn't work. *Fuck.* I pulled my oxygen mask aside and breathed onto it, and finally the red light blinked.

I looked up from the viewfinder as a shadow fell across her. There was a figure standing over her, a dark silhouette with a misshapen head. I huffed and fell onto my haunches, the impact driving the breath out of me. *Not there, it's not there. Seeing things, that's all.* I sucked in a whistle of air. Looked up again. It hadn't moved. It was still there. I wanted to say: *You're Juliet's vision, not mine.* Ed*'s mine,* but instead I just sat there, stunned, until cloud drifted in, obscuring it and Juliet's body.

I tried to get up, but couldn't. Something was very wrong. *What?* Then it hit me: the camera was dangling from my right wrist, but I couldn't feel my hand. My *gloveless* hand.

Oh fuck, Simon, oh no, what have you done? Shaking, I slid it back into its mitt and banged it on my thigh. *Wood, it's turned to wood.* Panic swirled in my gut. *It's okay. It'll be okay. Get out of here, now.* One handed, I shoved the camera back into my pack and shrugged it onto my shoulders, forgetting to check that the oxygen pipe was attached properly. I tried to stand once more, but my thighs were cold slabs of jelly. And Mark. Where was Mark? *He was right behind you.* I turned my head, but the cloud was thicker now – *how could it blow in so fast?* – and I couldn't see any sign of him.

The panicky, sick feeling in my belly grew.

Get the radio. Call for help.

Mark's got the radio.

My brain was telling my body to move, twitch, fart, anything, but it was as if the hard-drive that sent the signal had been hacked, and nothing was getting through.

The sky split open like a rotten fruit and then I was staring straight into what looked like an immense airport waiting lounge, filled with rows and rows of seats, people bustling back and forth. *You can go there if you want to, Si.* It looked warm, busy, and comfortingly banal. Part of me knew that my brain had pillaged its store of pop culture to conjure this image – *Beetlejuice*, *Defending your Life*, Christ knows what else. *Here's where you'll see Dad. Dad will come and invite you to join him.* But Dad wasn't there. Everyone looked perfectly content. Not happy exactly, but *fine.* The muffled tones of a tannoy burred in the background: I couldn't make out the words. Three men wearing bomber jackets and caving helmets strolled past my sight line.

The Cwm Pot lads.

I said a silent sorry to them. I said a silent sorry to Thierry's Ukrainians.

Too little too late, lad.

I tried to get up, step towards them, but something was pinioning me from behind. Ed. *Of course.* Ed. It had to be Ed. Ed was clutching me. *What the fuck are doing on Everest, Ed?*

Squeeze.

The eye into the airport lounge world closed, and cloud wisped back in.

Cold. I was so cold. *Too* cold. *You need to get out of those wet clothes, lad.* I willed myself into the fuzzy, fuggy warmth of Mission:Coffee. And then the cloud tore once again and I saw a warm glow to the right, shining through the whiteness. Three women wearing long colourful skirts and headscarves were crouching next to a campfire, feeding it with wood that looked like bones, and laughing.

Get to the fire. Warm up. But Ed wouldn't let me. One of the women lifted her skirts. Her legs weren't . . . they weren't human. They were spindly, hairy, like spider legs.

Ed squeezed me tighter, although really my pack should have restricted his grip. I couldn't breathe. 'Stop that, Ed,' I said, or thought I said. 'Ed, I can't breathe.' *You're killing me.*

The pain came then, with a mighty roar. My right hand, once again snug in its glove, was burning – it was defrosting, blood rushing into the extremities. I thrashed, howling and Ed loosened his grip. I lurched to my feet.

Move. Move or die. You can't rescue someone when they're this high on a mountain, Simon. You're on your own.

I teetered, realising for the first time that there was a crevasse a few feet in front of me. I'd been so fixated on Juliet that I hadn't noticed it.

I stumbled in what I hoped was the direction Mark and I had taken to get here. *And just where the fuck was Mark?*

Just move.

I walked like a drunken sailor, one leg longer than the other, concentrating on my feet. *Keep going. Don't stop.*

I caught a glimpse of yellow in my peripheral vision. Was it Ed, in his yellow exposure suit, showing me the way? *Is that you, Ed? It's me, Simon.* I headed that way anyway.

Another flash of colour; red this time. Then it began to dawn that the colours I was seeing were the down suits belonging to climbers making their way down from the summit. *You can make it. Reach the fixed line, and use it to guide you back to Camp III.* Easy. But when I made it over to the cracks, all the strength deserted me, and promising my nagging inner voice that I'd only rest for a few minutes, I flumped down.

I was there for four hours.

I sat there while climber after exhausted climber wove around me on their return from the summit. Half the time I wasn't sure if they were real, or simply a conga line made up of Juliet's insectile-faced spectral mountaineers. *In out, shake it all about.*

A masked Sherpa bent to shout at me. 'Where is your Sherpa? Where is your radio? Where is your Sherpa? Where is your radio?'

The sky was blue, the whiteout – if there'd even been a whiteout – was gone. Some sensible part of me had put on my sun goggles, saving me from searing my eyes in the brutal high-altitude light.

Another Sherpa stopped. I noticed idly that he was wearing a head-cam. He smacked me on the shoulder. 'What is your name?'

'Si . . . Simon Newman.'

'Where you from?'

'England.'

'No, no. What company?'

I couldn't remember. All I managed was: 'Tadeusz.'

He shouted something I couldn't understand into his radio, then tapped me on the shoulder again. 'One is coming.'

I felt a thump at my back, and then my throat, which had shrivelled to the size of a pinprick, widened. I could breathe again. The Sherpa – I never found out his name – had reattached my oxygen line after I'd dislodged it shrugging on my pack. It was this that saved me from slipping fully into hypoxia or freezing to death.

Yet another crew of exhausted, hunched climbers zombied past me. As I looked down, trailing them with my eyes, one stumbled, his knees concertinaed, and he flopped onto his side. His companions stepped over him. The blue-suited figure bringing up the rear of the snake, presumably the team's guide, bullied him into moving again. Down, down they went, moving as slowly as astronauts on the moon, attached to the fixed rope lifeline.

You could do that too. You could get up and move.

I couldn't. I'd run out of juice. There was nothing left in me. Out of gas, out of time. My feet were forgotten memories, stubborn blocks of ice. My right hand, which had been burning just minutes – hours? – ago, was now numb; it might as well have been made of wood again. I tried to lift it to shake it, but nothing happened. That unbearable cold ache I'd felt down in the caves was nothing compared to this. And then, without fanfare – almost casually, actually – my mind detached and rose, floating up to join the invisible spirits in the sky. I looked down at my body, sitting pathetically next to the fixed ropes that wound past the dirty snow and rock, and felt a mixture of pity and contempt for it. Floaty Simon was the real one; that was just a meat puppet. It was really relaxing, like being tickled with feathers. I took in the view, but I didn't really marvel at it; I'd slid beyond even that dissociative state that had saved me when I was trapped in Cwm Pot. I wondered what would happen if Meat Puppet Si below died. Would I stay floating up here forever? Perhaps I'd be sucked in like a vacuum cleaner and emptied out into that bland waiting room for the dead.

Someone was scrambling up towards the Meat Puppet. A silly-billy wearing a red suit and Herman Munster boots who was going up when he should be going down. The new arrival sidestepped to where my body was slumped. Tapped it on the shoulder. Oops. Meat Puppet Si had pulled off its oxygen mask. No gas. *Simon sans gas*. Bye-bye, Si. *Nothing but meat and two veg*. Nonsense words. I wondered if I could flit my way back to where I'd last seen Mark, locate him, check up on him, see if he needed anything. *Off to the shop, fancy a Diet Coke?*

With that same sense of idle detachment I wondered where Ed had gone. He wasn't up here with me, communing with the invisible spirits. Nor was he down below with Meat Puppet Si, clutching its body in his spidery arms.

The red-suited figure was shaking my body now. Then he hit it with the handle of his ice axe.

Thwack. Thwack. *Jesus, steady on, mate!* That had to hurt. And then, *whoooosh*, I dropped, letting out a mew of misery as I was forced back into the meat puppet me. I couldn't breathe. It hurt, everything *hurt*.

'Simon, get up!' Red Suit was Mingma. 'Where is Mark?'

'Gone.'

'Dead?'

'Don't know.' Was he? He'd been in a bad way the last time I'd seen him, just after I'd spotted Juliet. Once again my brain had slowed right down, and I was back outside the caves again, being asked about Ed. *You left another one behind, Si, how remiss of you.*

'Simon. You do not come down the mountain now, you will die.'

Too late.

Mingma made me take a few sips of tea, but I couldn't swallow. He wiped my mouth. 'Come. We go now.'

I stood on wobbly legs. My vision was blurring, I could only make out vague shapes. I blinked frantically and it gradually cleared.

'Ready?'

The terrain ahead of me was steep, and I desperately hoped that the sense of calm that had saved my life while I was in the caves would reappear. It didn't, but my brain remained fuzzy, shielding me from the full impact of what I'd been through. Mingma helped where he could, clipping my karabiner onto the safety line at every junction. Clumsy from hypoxia and exhaustion, I kept snagging the tines of my crampons on the rope. At one point I tripped, slipped on a rock slab and fell several feet, my frozen hand slamming against a boulder, the jolt of agony shattering through my entire body. After that, Mingma short-roped me.

Down and down we went, past the windblown shell of Camp III, where we'd spent the night a million years ago. Down, down to where the oxygen was thicker.

Whenever I flagged, Mingma would tug on the rope from behind like a cruel dog trainer. 'No rest, Simon. Dark soon.' I peed inside my suit.

The light was turning pink as Mingma shepherded me into a tent at the top of the col. I blacked out straight away, waking briefly as he tried to make me drink some juice. This time I managed to swallow it, feeling every centimetre of the liquid sliding down my dry gullet. I didn't dare take off my gloves. I didn't want to know. I passed out again.

After what felt like ten seconds of sleep, Mingma shook me awake. 'We go down now, Simon.'

'Down where?'

'ABC.'

As my brain woke up, fed by the richer oxygen, the shock of losing Mark really started to hit. Mark was gone, and Ed . . . don't. *Just don't.* 'Is there any news about Mark?'

'No, Simon. We must go down.'

'Is he still up there?'

'I don't know.'

'Why isn't anyone trying to rescue him?'

Mingma sighed patiently. 'There is no one to rescue him.'

I remembered that Mingma had left us at the Exit Cracks for a reason. Panicked, I asked, 'Is Wanda okay?'

'Yes. She is back at ABC.'

Thank God. 'Did she make the summit?'

'Yes. Wanda, Howard and Robbie make the summit.'

'And Malcolm?'

'Malcolm is very sick. Had to be taken down. Come. We go.'

My boots were still on, so I didn't need to do more than shrug out of the sleeping bag. Even that took up more energy than I had.

Still reeling with shock, I managed to step-shuffle the rest of the way down the col, somehow even navigating the ladder of death. The worst part was the relatively easy hike from crampon point into camp. Sensing it was close to home, my body started to shut down.

I was led into the mess tent where Ireni was waiting. She sat me in a chair. I'd never seen her looking so grim.

'I see you later, Simon,' Mingma said.

'Thanks for everything, Mingma.' I owed him way more than just thanks. 'Mark?' I asked Ireni.

A shake of the head – confirmation that he was still on the mountain. *But you knew that, didn't you? You left him there.* 'What happened, Simon?'

'I lost him.' *You left him behind. You didn't even look for him. Tell the truth for once in your life.* 'When Mingma left, he wanted to go and find Juliet.'

'Did you try and stop him?'

'Of course. But I couldn't let him go alone.' I paused to get my story straight. 'We found Juliet, but then the cloud came down and I lost him.' At least that part was true.

'Lost him? You think he fell?'

'I don't know.'

She nodded.

'Will Tadeusz send someone up to rescue him?' *Tadeusz is going to kick your fucking arse, Si. And you deserve it.*

'No. We have asked other teams up there to contact us if he manages to make it to the fixed ropes, but Tadeusz is now preparing to evacuate Malcolm.'

'Malcolm's that bad?'

'Very bad. He collapsed on the Second Step with impaired vision and I think the beginnings of cerebral oedema.' *Another one for the guilt bank.* If I'd told Ireni about the issues Malcolm was having with his vision then he wouldn't have run into trouble and Mingma wouldn't have left us. I had no doubt that Mark would still be alive if Mingma had been with us.

'He going to be okay?'

'He will be airlifted to Zhangmu when he gets down to base. Dorje short-roped him all the way down. He saved Malcolm's life.'

And Mingma had saved mine. Ireni told me that after helping Dorje guide Malcolm down from the Second Step, he'd made his way to where he'd left us. Assuming we'd ignored his instructions to wait for him and returned to Camp II, he helped Dorje coax Malcolm safely into camp. And then, after doing all this, when he heard another team's Sherpa reporting that I was in trouble at the Exit Cracks, he hauled himself back up to me. It was an incredible feat.

My right hand was thrust into a bowl of warm water, but it was too late. My fingers had defrosted by then. My vision was still compromised, but I could see enough to make out that they were turning the black of rotten bananas. Gyaluk brought me some tea. All he said to me was 'sorry, sorry, sorry', over and over again.

'I need to take your boots off,' Ireni said, her voice softer.

I sat like a child while she hauled them off my swollen feet. They were as bloodied and crunched as a prima ballerina's, but they'd somehow escaped the frostbite.

Next she cleaned and bandaged my dead banana hand. 'Go rest, Simon.'

'I'm sorry about Mark, Ireni.'

She managed a small smile. 'It is not your fault. People make their own choices. And I also feel bad. I should have stopped him from going. I was worried about his health. Tadeusz and I spoke about making him stay at ABC, but we chose to let him go as we knew that Mingma would look after him.'

Unlike you, you fucker.

I went straight to Wanda's tent. The door was open, and she was lying on her stomach, her gloved hands curled over her head, as if she was about to ward off a blow.

'Wanda?'

She didn't look up. She seemed to be smaller than I remembered.

I crawled in and lay next to her.

She turned to face me. She'd been crying. 'What happened?'

'I lost him, Wanda. One moment he was there behind me, and then he was gone. Maybe he was trying to get back to the ropes and fell.'

'Ireni says you and Mark went without Mingma.'

'Yeah.'

'But Mingma told you to stay where you were and wait for him.'

'He wanted to go. He was desperate to say goodbye to his mum.'

'There is still a chance he could be found. Many people survive nights out on the mountains.'

'Yeah.'

'Did you find Juliet?'

'Yes.' *And I also found Ed.*

She opened her arms and together, united in grief, we slept.

The weather came down the next day, the wind a brutal force that made even a nip into the mess tent a major trial. Tents on the high camps were whipped away and thrown down the col; climbers stuck at Camp II could do little else but pray that they'd make it through the night. Wanda and I didn't need to speak. We knew what it meant. If Mark had still been alive when I last saw him, he wouldn't be now. There was no way he would survive the plummeting temperatures. Tadeusz monitored the radios, all of us hoping against hope that the teams now ensconced higher on the mountain would report a miracle.

They didn't.

'I am sorry, Simon,' Mingma said, looking down at my fingers. 'But chop chop.'

Ireni gave me a sympathetic glance. 'They might still be saved, Simon. Do not worry too much.'

'I'm not worried.' I wasn't. I didn't quite believe they belonged to me any more. They were crudely swollen, the tips capped with black blisters (now I really did have fingers for eyes – or obscene black eyes on my fingers). Mingma and Dorje liked to gather round whenever Ireni changed the bandages, curious to see how they were progressing. I'd had to learn how to depend on my left hand, which made even the simplest task – getting dressed, spooning rice into my mouth, wiping my arse – a monumental mission.

'There is a good hospital for this in Kathmandu,' Ireni said. 'We will be there soon.'

'Any news on Malcolm?' I didn't really care; I just wanted to divert the focus away from me.

'Yes. He is stabilised. They will fly him home soon.'

'Good.'

Hand swathed back in its mummy-ish covering, I left the mess tent and went to find Wanda. Other teams were preparing to pack up and head home, trucks constantly grumbling in and out of base camp. I didn't remember much of the walk down from ABC, except that I was almost glad of my throbbing hand and screaming ankle; they stopped me obsessing over what had happened up there.

Wanda was waiting for me outside her tent. 'Tadeusz asked me to pack up Mark's things to send to his family.' Tadeusz had barely said two words to me since we'd arrived back at base camp. I didn't think he and Ireni blamed me for what had happened to Mark – if anything, they blamed themselves – but he kept his distance all the same.

'I'll help.'

'You are sure?'

'Yeah.'

She nodded.

I couldn't let her do it alone – I wanted to, but I couldn't. As we dumped his bags out onto her sleeping mat, everything I'd seen up there just before Mark disappeared – Ed, that sterile waiting room, the women with the spidery legs, and the figure standing over Juliet's body – came dribbling back into my mind. My hands shook, and I made a shallow fist with my bandaged hand – the searing pain helping to push the images away.

'What happened to Mark, it's not your fault, Simon.'

'Yeah.' And I might have shared the same fate if the pain of my defrosting hand hadn't snapped me out of my stupor. *If Ed hadn't stopped you from falling into that crevasse.* Don't go there.

'Listen to me. You were his friend. You tried to help him. You gave up the summit for him.'

A twitch of anger at her. *The summit isn't everything, Wanda.* 'I should have tried harder to stop him.' *You should have at least* tried. 'When he disappeared, I should've tried harder to find him.'

'There was nothing you could have done, Simon.'

'How do you know? You weren't *there*.' She flinched. 'Sorry.'

'It is fine. Let's continue.'

We picked through his clothes and books in silence – it suited us better that way. Among them was a copy of T. S. Eliot's *The Waste Land*, inscribed to Juliet – some sort of school prize – and an iPod that I'd never seen him use. The battery was almost dead, but it had just enough juice for me to scroll through the playlists. Most were classical in nature, but he'd included the odd old-school pop song – the Beatles, the Stones, Peter Gabriel. Sad. Amongst his clothes, Wanda uncovered a teddy bear, a small map of Nepal embroidered on its tummy, and another photograph of Juliet, the Alps in the background. She looked young and happy, her brown sturdy legs poking out from blue climbing shorts.

And then, in the side pocket of the pack he'd left at ABC, I unearthed a piece of familiar-looking folded paper:

Dear Marcus,

I'm writing this safe and snug in my sleeping bag at Camp II. Up to Camp III and the summit push tomorrow. Bit of a cough, but I'm feeling strong. It's really just the altitude and cold I have to worry about as usual!!

Did you know you've actually been on an 8000-metre peak? Walter and I were about to leave for our first trip to the Himalaya, an ascent of Cho Oyu (a trip we'd been planning for months), when I discovered I was pregnant. Two months pregnant. I didn't tell anyone, not even your father, and went anyway. I told myself that I'd turn back the second I felt any ill effects, but I was strong that year, almost as if you were giving me extra energy. I climbed. I summited. You clung on, and I knew you were a fighter. I knew we would be great friends.

When I returned I broke the news to your father. He was elated. I'd never seen him so happy. I promised him that I wouldn't climb any more until you were born.

I kept that promise. And I did more than that. I stayed at home with you for years, do you remember? But when you were six, when your father insisted we sent you to boarding school, I didn't argue. I'd given you six years of my life. No, that sounds like I resented it. I didn't, Marcus. I didn't resent it. But I'd watched as other climbers snapped up the sponsorships and that stung. Walter had also put his life on hold, and it wasn't fair to him. I suppose I became depressed. I wasn't getting any younger. I'm sorry. When we dropped you off at school, I cried all the way home, and I never cry. I will put this right, I promise.

Perhaps when you're older we can come back here together. I'll show you base camp. You'll like it.

I'm going to give this to Davide, one of the Italian climbers who is here at Camp II, just in case.

If anything happens to me, and it won't, be strong, and never let the bastards grind you down. But I want you to know, I am doing this for you, and you are always with me.

See you soon!

I love you,

Mam

Why hadn't he told me he had it? *Why should he?* Juliet sounded strong, sane, on top of things. And at least he knew that she'd been thinking about him as she left for the summit.

I would do almost anything to take back what I did next.

The same chest-bursting pressure that I'd felt just before I offered to accompany Mark to find Juliet came over me. And then I found myself telling Wanda the real reason I was on the mountain – the crazy plan to capture footage of the mountain's dead. Why did I do it? Was it some sort of self-flagellation, that old self-destructive impulse kicking in? *Quick! Wreck this relationship before it makes you happy, Si.* The damning words came vomiting out, and I didn't try and stop them, despite knowing that there was only one conclusion Wanda could come to: that I'd encouraged Mark to put himself in danger for my own selfish motives. That I'd ignored Tadeusz and Mingma's instructions so that I could film Mark's dead mother for a salacious website.

Wanda listened in silence, her face blank. Then she pocketed the teddy bear and left the tent. *Bye-bye lovely dream life in St Gervais-les-Bains. Farewell future filmmaking career and brilliant sex life.* Perhaps she'd never meant any of that. I'd never know.

Without thinking too deeply about what had just happened or what I was doing, I slipped Juliet's journal into my pack.

It would be two years before Wanda spoke to me again.

The long drive back to Kathmandu had the aura of a funeral procession. Wanda made it very clear that under no circumstances was she prepared to endure a twelve-hour drive sitting next to me, so I huddled in the corner seat on the back row of the minibus, dozing fitfully and letting the pain in my hand fill my mind. Occasionally Robbie or Howard would try and initiate conversation, but I wasn't capable of more than a grunt. I couldn't bear to listen to music, simply rested my head against the window and breathed in the acrid odour of the driver's butter tea and my own shame.

A chanting crowd of men wielding placards surged around us as we reached the city, forcing us to backtrack to avoid the blocked-off streets. I barely took it in. I had four days to get through before I was due to fly home – four days in the same hotel as the others. I'd been looking forward to this part of the trip, spending time with Wanda in Kathmandu, exploring the city with her, planning for the future. *But you screwed that up, didn't you?* If Juliet was the Angel of Death, then I was the devil himself. Overnight Ireni became an ice queen – Wanda had clearly told her the real reason I was on the mountain. She organised an appointment with the high altitude medical clinic in Kathmandu for me, but other than that, she could barely look at me. Thankfully Tadeusz had stayed behind in Tibet with Mingma and Dorje to deal with the bureaucratic mess of losing someone on the mountain, so I didn't have to face his ire right then.

I avoided the mirror in my room at first, after catching a glimpse of my ragged reflection and thinking, *Oh, hello, Ed.* But I couldn't put it off forever. For the first time in years my ribs were prominent, the skin on my arms and belly felt baggy, as if I was wearing an over-sized pair of long johns. It took me an hour to shave with my left hand, and showering was no easier, soaping up with one hand, the other wrapped in a plastic bag to protect the bandages.

The doctor at the altitude hospital in Kathmandu, a no-nonsense woman in her fifties, was slightly more optimistic than Mingma about my finger situation, although she looked at me as if she'd never seen anyone so stupid in her life when I told her I'd removed my glove at eight thousand metres. Good. I deserved it.

After my consultation, and unable to face the loneliness of my room, I sat in the hotel's courtyard, listening to the sounds of life in the streets outside and plucking petals off the bougainvillea. I'd got into the habit of waiting until the others had eaten before sneaking into the restaurant and ordering my own food. I was putting off calling Thierry. I wanted to blame him, just like I had when I was down in Cwm Pot. *It's all his fault. Thierry* made *me do it. Guilt-tripped me into it. Mark would be alive if it wasn't for him.* Not true. Mark had insisted we grab the chance to look for Juliet. He was in a bad way before we even set off from Camp III. *Yes, but you could have tried harder to stop him.* Losing Mark like that, the things I'd seen up there, Wanda and Ireni's disgust, I had to keep them locked away.

I jumped as a voice said: 'Buy you a beer?'

It was Robbie, Howard hovering behind him.

Tears stung my eyes and I looked down at the table.

'C'mon, Simon. Let's get out of here. Looks like you could do with a change of scene.'

Why the fuck not? I swallowed, tasting salt. 'Sure.'

'Not me. I'm gonna take a nap,' Howard said. I didn't take it personally. The climb had emptied him out. The skin sagged around his face and neck, and there were hollows where his cheeks used to be. I wondered what he'd do now that his boyhood dream had been realised. Go for harder peaks? Buy a Porsche? Get divorced and marry a twenty-year-old stripper? He gave me a small sad smile and a nod. It made me want to cry again.

I trailed Robbie through the streets, my misery streaming behind us like a cloud of exhaust, and followed him into a tourist trap bar. Everything was coloured sepia for me now.

He sat me at an outside table as if I was an elderly relative, then grabbed a couple of bottles of San Miguel from the bar.

I waited for him to speak.

'Keep meaning to find the right moment, but I'm truly sorry about Mark, Simon. Know you guys were close.'

'Yeah. Thanks.'

He wasn't acting as if he was aware of my dodgy backstory for being on the mountain. Or if he was aware of it, he didn't care.

'So Juliet Michaels really was his mom, huh?'

'Yeah.'

'Guessing you don't want to talk about it. Here if you do.' He looked like he meant it. He drank, cleared his throat. 'Feel kinda bad for giving him such a hard time up there.'

'Yeah.'

'It got to me up there. It's intense, you know?' He was on the defensive now. *Don't mind me, I'm just an arsehole.*

But I nodded. I did know. Juliet knew as well. She'd written about this in her journal. Base camp and mountain life were like concentrated reality. Addictive, because even when you were bored out of your skull, you felt alive. But really, Robbie had been a dick from the start. He'd been a dick to Mark especially, but he'd been right all along; Mark shouldn't have been on the mountain.

I made myself take a sip of the beer. It was warm and tasted like bile. 'Congrats again on your summit.' We clinked bottles.

'You think you'll be back, Simon?'

'To Everest?'

'Yes.'

'No. No way.' I was unequivocal. Sure, I'd felt that tug, that strange lure to get to the top, but I'd seen other things too, other things that were far harder to explain and if I tried, I suspected I might do the mental equivalent of a tumble down the North Col.

'Sorry you and Wanda didn't work out.'

A shrug. The real pain of that was weeks away. I'd been punched, but the ruptured organs were yet to make themselves known.

We lapsed into silence. I gazed numbly at the other people in the bar. A solo South Asian tourist, drinking from a portable water bottle and pretending to read the menu; two bearded white men, who looked as grizzled as we did; a gang of blonde hiker-type girls, dressed in shorts and sandals and Nepalese shirts. They kept eyeing my heavily bandaged hand and mountain-blasted face and then whispering among themselves.

I fished for something to say. I needed distracting. 'Do you have to go straight back to work when you get home?'

'No. I'm on sabbatical. Perks of being attached to a university.' Not only was he the world's most unlikely scientist, he was also the world's most unlikely academic. 'Six more months of freedom. Promised my fiancée I'd take her to Hawaii. I'm gonna need it as well.'

'You're a doctor, right?'

'A neuroscientist. Mainly research.' A touch of that old superiority.

It was worth a shot. 'Do you know anything about Third Man syndrome? You know, like Shackleton felt in the Antarctic.'

'I know what it is. Why? You experienced this when you were on the mountain, Simon?'

'Not me. Someone I know.'

'Mark?'

'No. Someone else.'

'Who? Malcolm? Hey, you know he had serious medical issues that he didn't disclose to Tadeusz and Ireni? He shouldn't have been anywhere near the mountain. Go figure. All those lectures he used to give us on climbing for the right reasons. All bullshit.'

'Look, it doesn't matter who it was. I was wondering, could it be caused by something else? I dunno, like a brain tumour or something?'

'Where are you going with this?'

'Could it be caused by this, though?'

'Simon, I really think—'

'Could it?'

He recoiled. *Tone down the intensity.*

'From what I've read it's usually a reaction to altitude, stress or loss.'

'Loss?'

'Yeah. Like the Widow Effect. You heard of that?'

'No.'

'There was a study done, Christ, when was this? Seventies, I think. And in the UK if I remember correctly. A group of women and men who'd been recently bereaved were interviewed, and something like thirty per cent reported that their spouses – or the spirits of their spouses – had returned to see them. You know, appeared in their armchairs or in their favourite place on the couch.' He took a contemplative sip of beer. 'There are many explanations for the Third Man factor, Simon. Messner, Fiennes, Buhl, all the greats have felt it. I wouldn't give it too much weight. For them it was a positive experience. Got them through difficult situations.'

'Hypothetically, what if the presence you're sensing feels evil?'

He put his hands up. 'Simon, I'm not an expert on this. It's not my field.'

'But what *if*?' I was leaning towards him. He shifted warily.

'Voices in your head, you mean? Telling you to do things? Simon—'

'No. Not voices.' *Oh really? 'Fingers in your heart', anyone?*

'It could hint at some sort of mental disorder. Listen, I know you're going through a hard time, but these things happen on the mountains.' He slid a business card out of his wallet. 'Take this. My email address. Look me up if you're ever in the Bay area.' He downed his beer and stood up. 'And see a therapist when you get home. Trust me on this, you need it.'

After Robbie left, I took my time finishing my beer. I couldn't buy another as I'd come out without my wallet, although I wouldn't have minded getting wasted.

I ran into Tadeusz, who'd just returned from Tibet, in the hotel lobby. He didn't speak to me. I didn't speak to him. We locked eyes, and in those two seconds I found out everything I needed to know about myself.

I lasted three hours before I called Thierry. I knew it was a mistake, but I did it anyway. Robbie's uncharacteristic kindness towards me, and running into Tadeusz like that had exposed a nerve, and I was desperate to talk to someone who was on my side. I needed to vent. And vent I did, spilling my guts about Mark and Juliet, whining that it wasn't my fault and that the others were treating me unfairly. I waited for him to say: 'Tell me you filmed it, dude,' but he didn't. I knew he wanted to, but he could hear the state I was in. He was biding his time on that one.

After that, I barely left my hotel room until it was time to head to the airport. I didn't say goodbye to anyone.

PART THREE

Simon

Thierry looked up from his laptop. 'Site's being going crazy all morning. That link in the *Daily Mail* has really kicked things off.' He gave me a sly glance. 'Imagine how many hits we'd be getting if we had some actual footage.'

Not this again. 'I *told* you, T. I tried, but the bloody camera froze.'

'Yeah, yeah. And then you dropped it on the mountain.'

'That's right.' *Liar.* I'd hidden it, and the memory card, under my mattress. I should have thrown it away, dropped it in a dumpster somewhere, but something made me cling on to it.

'I still don't believe you, Si. I can tell when you're hiding something.'

I held up my bandaged paw. 'What more proof do you need? And why the hell would I lie?'

'Because for some reason you feel guilty about that guy dying.' *Bingo.*

'Bollocks. Anyway, you're one to talk about hiding stuff, T. You should have bloody well told me about the advertisers.' While I'd been away, the website had turned a corner. It had happened almost overnight – one day it was doing fairly well; the next, it reached critical mass, and garnered the magic number of hits to start attracting advertisers. It was generating enough for us to scratch a living, which was fortunate as I could hardly serve cappuccinos with *fingers for eyes*, could I? With cruel irony, it's likely the site would have taken off without the controversy surrounding my involvement in Mark's death.

'Yeah well, I didn't want you to get distracted. The whole reason you were up there was to boost the site, Si.'

'And I've done that, haven't I?'

Thanks to Thierry, the story had broken in a huge foul-smelling wave.

I knew when I called him from Kathmandu that he wouldn't be able to resist exploiting Mark and Juliet's story. I knew what he was by then. He wasn't Ray, Dan Aykroyd's endearingly geeky character; he was a nastier version of Peter Venkman: selfish and opportunistic. To be fair, he'd have been crazy not to point out that the Simon Newman who'd left a dead body in Cwm Pot was the same Simon Newman who'd misplaced one on Everest. People couldn't get enough of it. It had everything: pathos, hubris, a dead national treasure, a tragic mother-and-son reunion, and a villain – an opportunistic time-waster who got his kicks filming dead people. Self-righteous arseholes were flocking to the site in their droves to leave 'die you sick bastard' comments.

Thierry sighed. 'Look. Let's try and move on, Si, okay? The press attention will die down soon. I get why it's stressing you out with your fucked hand and all, but we gotta ride this wave. We're doing good. We're getting thousands of unique hits every day. That's all that counts.'

The site might have been 'doing good', but I wasn't. As far as my mental health was concerned, I was on seriously shaky ground, but I hadn't even attempted to deal with the fallout of Mark's death, Wanda's disgust and my guilt and shame. It all stayed locked in its box. For now.

I lurched awake, overcome with a powerful sense of déjà vu and dread, my heart racing. I checked the time: three a.m.

The light was on in the lounge, and I padded through to it. Thierry was sitting at his desk, his headphones on, staring at his laptop. And next to him lay the camcorder – the camcorder that should have been hidden under my mattress.

I crept up behind him. 'You *bastard*.' Forgetting I basically had mush for fingers, I lashed out at the back of his head with my bandaged hand. The pain zigged through my arm like an electric shock. '*Fuck*.'

Thierry cringed and put his hands up. '*Shit*, dude! What the hell did you do that for?'

'When did you find it?'

'While you were at your doctor's appointment this morning.'

'You searched through my stuff?'

'Yeah.'

'You utter *shit*.'

He huffed self-righteously. 'I *knew* you were hiding something.'

I tried to swallow. Failed. I didn't have any saliva. 'And? Did you watch it?' *Did you see Juliet, did you see it?*

'Yeah. Don't know why you hid it, dude. Nothing on it. Just a few seconds of audio.'

'No visuals?'

'No. You were right. Camera's fucked. It's our own fault for not buying a better one. So dumb. Spent all that cash on the trip and didn't splurge on the most important thing.'

'You said there was audio.' I put the headphones on. 'Play it for me.'

'It's pretty boring, Si.'

'Do it.'

He rolled his eyes, and I had to stop myself from lashing out at him again. 'Okay, okay.'

I bit the inside of my cheek as the hiss of high-altitude wind filled my ears. I shivered. There was a crackle – the camera rubbing against my down suit? – then another twenty seconds of hissing. That was it.

'Play it again.'

'Jesus, Si. Chill.'

'Do it.'

I listened again, ears straining. But there was nothing apart from the familiar sound of Everest's slipstream. No *fingers in your heart*, no voices from beyond the grave. Nothing.

After several hour-long sessions in a hyperbaric chamber, and X-rays to determine the extent of the damage to my fingers, I got the bad news on a rainy Tuesday afternoon, sitting in my specialist Dr Grewal's consulting room. He told me in his perennially cheerful voice that I would lose two-thirds of my pinkie, and a third of both my ring and middle fingers, leaving my thumb and forefinger intact and pincer-ish. Sitting in that beige office, with its benign watercolours and stain-proof furniture, all I could think about was Malcolm and his toes in a jar.

Chop chop. Fingers in your jar, lad, fingers in your heart.

I'm not going to go into the details of the operation itself; there are pictures up on the site if you want to see them, along with the 'five gross things you didn't know about frostbite' listicle Thierry convinced me to write. I will say that I was horribly self-conscious about my mutilated hand at first. I hated doing simple tasks like handing over change at the corner shop, but eventually, in true Simon Newman fashion, I ceased giving a shit. I tried to laugh along with Thierry's jokes about my inability to do a Vulcan hand salute – black humour had always been our way of dealing with the crap life threw at us – but my sense of humour had gone the same way as my fingers.

And as my injuries healed, the self-loathing crept in. I would find myself drifting off, locking onto 'what if's. *What if you'd chosen to summit with Wanda, would Mark still be alive? What if you'd grassed up Malcolm, would Mark still be alive? What if you really are a truly awful human being? What if everything you saw up there was real? What if you've gone mad and should be sectioned?*

The public gradually lost interest in the story, but the site continued to grow. A week after I'd been for the finger chop, Thierry slid a mound of paperwork under my nose – a contract stipulating our ownership of the *Journey to the Dark Side* company, with sixty per cent of the shares going to him, forty to me.

'Reason it's sixty-forty is because of the cash and time I've put in, Si.'

I waggled my recently mutilated right hand at him. 'Whereas I've only put in a pound of flesh.'

Zing. He grimaced. 'If you want to go fifty-fifty, just say so, Si.'

'No. It's fine. I'm happy with that.'

I was. I didn't really care.

He'd be the one who'd live to regret it.

Rationalising that we could hardly schmooze advertising execs in our damp lounge, Thierry sub-let a warehouse space in fashionable Hackney from a trio of trust-funded 'artists'. Resourceful and sharp as ever, he hired a dedicated salesperson who worked solely on commission, and a couple of freelance writers and interns who appeared to be happy to churn out content for a pittance. He was happy to take the reins – it suited him to be in control – and I slipped into the role of silent partner.

My heart wasn't in it, and it showed. Eventually I was given the job of answering emails and moderating the comments. After what I'd been through, after what I'd seen, it just seemed puerile and pointless. Some days I didn't even bother looking in the inbox. Some days I found myself scrolling through the site's comments without actually seeing them, deleting them at random.

I didn't follow Robbie's advice and see a therapist.

At some stage during this period – and I really don't recall doing this, I'd created a file labelled 'WHY I SAW THE STUFF' and written the following:

Trauma after the caves
some sort of psychotic break
Maybe the Death Zone is a porous gateway into another world.
No. Bollocks. I don't live in a J-horror movie (but Ed is DEAD and you saw him up there what next you going to say that Ed is an angry mountain ghost?)
I am mad
Juliet is mad
We both have PTSD because seeing a presence or having flashbacks is v common after traumatic events
We both have head injuries we don't remember getting
We both had hypoxia (but then why no other symptoms?????)
lots of reasons for third man factor it could be monotony, the

brain reacting to extreme cold and stress, loneliness, trauma, loss (widow effect although I wasn't mourning ED was I?)

You see what you want to see

Something in my subconscious was trying to tell me that if I unearthed a rational explanation for what had happened to me on the mountain and down in Cwm Pot, then I'd snap back to normal. Like Juliet, I wanted to believe it was just hypoxia, but my gut wasn't buying it.

I carried Juliet's journal everywhere with me. I didn't read it again. I didn't dare. Instead, I decided to shake her life and see what fell out.

There were corrective, glowing accounts of her climbing life in several 'pioneering women' anthologies, but the older cached articles were as vicious as Mark had implied. One of them, a nasty screed entitled 'An Unfit Mother?', was written by a woman who was now a high-profile television chef. There were only a few pictures of Walter – these showed a hatchet-faced man with piercing blue eyes and a ropey, Iggy Pop physique. The pics of Graham, Juliet's unfaithful husband, revealed him to be smaller than I'd imagined, though every bit as suave as she'd described. His eyes were hard.

There were no photos of Mark.

I dug up some cached footage of Juliet sitting on a panel at a mountaineering conference (probably the 'disastrous' one where she'd met Pauline Zierzinger). She bristled with energy, spoke with the trace of a Yorkshire accent, and like Wanda, looked older than her years, her skin scored with deep lines. I liked her, although it was a shock seeing her 'alive' – I couldn't reconcile this tough, vital woman with the forlorn shape I'd seen on the mountain. The idiot moderator asked her about the morality of 'putting oneself in peril when one has a child', and she answered snappishly, making the point that climbers who were fathers were rarely asked this question. *Good for you, Juliet. Don't let the bastards grind you down.*

I ordered a copy of *The Waste Land* and one of those idiot's guides to it – I knew my limitations – and discovered that Juliet had misquoted the poem. She'd written, *Who is the third who walks beside you?*, when it was actually – and more chillingly – *Who is the third who walks ALWAYS beside you?* And three lines later, *There is ALWAYS another one walking beside you.* According to my crib notes, the Third Man in the poem alluded to a scene in the bible where two guys ran into a recently reanimated Jesus. Far as I was concerned, Eliot's shadowy, hooded figure was way too creepy to be J.C. To me, it was the grim reaper; a hardcore version of Terry Pratchett's DEATH character.

Next, I pootled around on the Internet looking into sensed presence. Malcolm, Mark and Robbie had all emphasised how common it was, and they were right. There were thousands of accounts reporting the phenomenon, and it wasn't culturally specific: people who'd survived the Twin Towers collapse, the Holocaust, earthquakes in China and Japan, and atrocities in Somalia all reported sensing a similar benign spirit who gave them the strength to carry on. But here was the thing: the *its* that Juliet and I had picked up weren't benign. They were malevolent. And while the benevolent presences felt by explorers or those in peril were known as saviours or guardian angels, the other type, the *nasty* type, were classified as destructors, and were usually only experienced by people who were mentally ill, or who didn't believe they deserved to be saved.

So Juliet and I were mental or wanted to die. Awesomefuckingtastic.

Perhaps Ed is *your guardian angel. He saved you, didn't he? Stopped you from falling into that crevasse.*

No. Mingma saved me, not Ed. Ed had been holding me there, waiting for me to freeze to death.

Desperate to latch on to a less disturbing explanation, I remembered that Mark had mentioned that the Third Man could be a 'phantom double', a projection of the self, an inner voice brought to life. *Some psychologists believe you can assign other identities to it. See what you want to see in times of stress.* But if that was the case, why the fuck had I chosen Ed? And why had Juliet chosen a creepy-as-fuck frostbitten ghoul? Still, that dislocation of self

I'd felt just before Mingma had saved me, that floating above myself, went hand in hand with this. It had been pleasant in the same way that the calmness that had come over me in the caves was pleasant.

But bottom line, Juliet and I hadn't just 'sensed a presence', had we? We'd seen our respective Third Men, large as fucking life. Ed had clutched me on that mountain; I could still feel his grip. And Juliet's spectre had come into her tent and forced its frostbitten fingers into her mouth.

Back in your box, join the other forbidden things in the box, throw away the key.

After I'd exhausted my ad hoc research, my brain decided, *fuck it, I'm done*, and switched itself off. I began crawling out of bed later and later each day, sometimes only rocking up at work at lunchtime. Some days I couldn't eat. Other days I couldn't stop. I went through a few weeks of being constantly drunk, after stupidly believing a 4Chan post saying that being pissed was a great way to ward off panic attacks (it wasn't).

As my only remaining friend, reluctant roommate and business partner, Thierry tried cajoling, bribing and then threatening me to 'snap the fuck out of it, Si, and get some professional help'. At his wit's end, he arranged an intervention, roping in my mother and sister Alison via Skype. The message was clear: 'Get help or get out.' Lacking the energy to fight, I caved in and went to see a psychologist. Unsurprisingly, I was diagnosed with severe post-traumatic stress disorder and depression. I didn't mention Ed or what I'd seen on the mountain to Dr O'Dowd, a brusque, somewhat self-involved woman with ropey arms like Madonna's. I wasn't stupid; I wasn't ready to be sectioned, and I was good at telling her what she wanted to hear – it was easier that way. I let her delve into my past and pontificate about my 'daddy issues'. I agreed with her assessment that Dad's death had left a wound that had festered and infected every facet of my life and poisoned my decision-making, despite knowing this was bullshit. She kept pressing me to admit that I was angry at him for dying, just like Mark had been angry at Juliet for choosing Everest over him before he read her diary. I paid lip service to her assertions, but I wasn't angry with Dad. How could I be? If there's anyone who understands the urge to be self-destructive, it's me. Maybe this element of my personality was his legacy. We tried cognitive behavioural therapy, but it didn't help – or maybe I didn't want it to. The first round of pills didn't help either; they just made me sleep. She suggested different doses, and eventually, in desperation, put me on tricyclics – a type of anti-depressant that was usually the last port of call. But as the song goes, 'The drugs don't work'. I was too far gone for that.

Sitting on the floor of the flat in a pair of pants that I hadn't washed for a week, I vaguely contemplated ending it all. Jumping off a bridge, or taking an overdose of heroin (both of which I decided against after seeing 'after' pictures on the dark web). No. I didn't have it in me – not then, at any rate.

There was only one course of action I could take in order to hold it together, and it came so naturally I couldn't believe I hadn't tried it before: I put on my Charming Si mask, and I screwed it on tight.

It worked for a while, at least on a superficial level, which is all anyone really cares about, right? But the cracks were there from the start. Occasionally, I'd be swamped with the same sense of detachment I'd felt when I was looking down at Mingma saving my life: *There goes Meat Puppet Si snorting a line of coke in the bathroom of a Shoreditch pub; there's Meat Puppet Si sitting in on a sales meeting and laughing at Thierry's crap jokes; there's Meat Puppet Si trying to maintain an erection while screwing one of the freelancers.*

'It's great to have you back, dude,' Thierry would say at least once a week, and I'd fire something amusing back at him. *Oh, how we laughed.*

But a mask can't be worn forever without chafing. Two things hastened my next spiral into the shadows. The first was Thierry's announcement that he was moving out of the flat. I was relieved at first. We'd been manoeuvring around each other like a married couple that knows deep down their relationship is doomed. But the flat's emptiness rankled. Sure, he'd pissed me off, he was a heartless git in a lot of ways, but it had been comforting to have someone around, especially in the killer early morning hours.

The second nail in the coffin came in 2009, almost two years to the day since I'd returned from Everest, when I accidentally clicked on a spam newsletter sent to me by the climbing store where I'd bought my crampons. Only there are no accidents, are there? It was advertising a series of talks by mountaineers and authors, and one of them was, 'Top Female Alpinist, Wanda Florczak, who is planning to climb all fourteen of the eight-thousand-metre peaks'.

A lump formed in my throat. I was going to go. I *had* to go.

You can see her and explain.

Explain what?

That you're not a monster.

Thanks to inactivity and comfort eating, I'd put on weight, but I didn't examine myself too closely in the mirror before I left for the event. I didn't want to lose my nerve.

Palms clammy and heart thudding, I slid into a seat at the back of the store's basement room where the talk was being held. The place was packed.

A ripple of applause, and then, there she was. She hadn't changed much; she was still slender, her skin was slightly more lined, and her hair was an inch or so longer than I remembered. She still had that *thing* about her.

She started with a series of slides, documenting her first three ascents. She spoke well, with a dry sense of humour and a self-deprecating wit I hadn't really picked up on during our short weeks together.

'. . . then, in two thousand and seven, I joined an expedition, headed by Tadeusz Bacik, to climb the North Face of Everest.' She paused, swallowed, and for an instant I was certain that she'd seen me, lurking there at the back of the room. 'The mountain that year had a record number of ascents, after a terrible year before with much controversy. Yet this year was not without its controversy, and I was almost in the middle of it.'

Her voice faded into the background as I took in the images on the slide screen. *Click.* A shot of Juliet after her successful summit of Broad Peak, dressed in her pink Tally High suit. *Click.* Another of Juliet, baby Mark in her arms. *Click.* A photo of Mark sitting outside his tent at base camp, holding up a cup of tea and grinning at the camera. My vision tunnelled into a pinprick.

'. . . Tadeusz was unfairly criticised for the loss of Marcus Michaels's life. It was not his fault. No one can be entirely responsible for another climber's decisions.'

She didn't mention me.

She moved on to her latest endeavours – back-to-back ascents of Broad Peak and Gasherbrum I. She'd made it to the Karakoram after all, following in her namesake, Wanda Rutkiewicz's footsteps. She was doing it, fulfilling her life's dream. And in each summit photograph, she was holding up a small brown teddy bear – Mark's bear. The bear Juliet had bought for him in Thamel. I dropped my head, hoping my neighbours wouldn't notice the tears plopping onto my hands.

There was a Q&A session afterwards. Someone asked how she dealt with fear and the prospect of death when she was at altitude.

'I have fear, it is important to keep that edge. But I do not let it take me over. I listen to my body.' She tapped her belly. 'If I don't have the right feeling here, in my gut, I will not go. And I do not allow myself to be pressured by others.' Next followed a predictable question about how she handled being at the forefront of such a male-orientated sport. She repeated her putdown to Robbie: 'You do not need a penis to climb a mountain,' which elicited a laugh and a smattering of applause. 'The people who know me are wonderful, but sometimes I will meet outsiders who will assume that I am being carried up the mountain by Sherpas, or that I have got someone else to cut steps. I ignore them because they are idiots. Juliet Michaels had the same thing. It is a jealousy and spitefulness that comes from insecurity.' Someone else asked her why she didn't use supplementary oxygen. 'For the same reason why some people choose to ride up a steep slope on a bicycle, and others prefer a motorbike. Remember, it was not until Messner reached the top of Everest without using gas that people really believed it could be done. For me, climbing without gas is a purer way to climb, it is more of a challenge. But I do not judge people who choose to climb in other fashions. It is their choice.'

I sat in my chair, sweat pooling in my armpits, and waited for the hangers-on to drift away. Then I stood up and approached her.

'Hi, Wanda.'

Her face remained expressionless. 'Simon.'

'How are you? Congratulations on all your achievements.'

A stiff 'Thank you'.

'What's next for you?'

'Simon, I do not want to talk to you.' Direct as usual. That hadn't changed.

'Wanda, can I just explain—'

'Explain what? That you were on the mountain so that you could take pictures of the dead? Is that not what you told me?'

'Yes, and there's no excuse for that. I didn't use any of the—'

'I do not want to know.'

'There a problem here?' A man had appeared out of nowhere. American, tall, blond, fit. Of course. *Of course.*

'No problem, Aaron. I am ready now to leave.'

Aaron, Wanda's boyfriend, husband, climbing partner, friend, whatever, looked just like the kind of guy I assumed she was seeing when I first met her. He held out a hand. 'Aaron Wright.' I googled him later. He was basically America's Andy Kirkpatrick, a bouldering technique pioneer who'd done the impossible and climbed the Cerro Torre Southeast Ridge without aids.

'Simon Newman.'

'Oh. You're the guy. The Everest guy.'

'Yeah.'

'Let's go, Aaron.'

Aaron gave me a rueful grin before departing with my career, my future and the love of my life.

I wanted to have a tantrum, lie on the floor and slam my fists into the carpeting. *Not fair.* But of course it was fair. Far as Wanda was concerned, I'd used Mark. Maybe I had. In her eyes, I was a monster. Maybe I was.

It was all fucked up.

I headed out into the June evening, weaving my way through the Covent Garden crowd, shoving past a group of tourists watching a juggler. I was halfway down Long Acre, still seething with self-loathing, when I saw him: Ed.

He was standing next to a *Big Issue* vendor, his hands hanging down at his sides, dressed in his yellow exposure suit. I blinked, and he was gone.

I ran towards Charing Cross, but there was no sign of him. Of course there was no sign of him. *Just in your head. He's just in your head.*

When I got home, I sat on the couch and drank half a bottle of Cutty Sark. I took out Juliet's diary, and flicked through to the end of it, running my thumb along the rough edges of the ripped-out pages.

I was on tenterhooks for the next few weeks, certain that I was going to see him again. And now I couldn't shed the feeling that I was being watched; a shadow skulked permanently in my peripheral vision. The sense was at its strongest in the narrow alleyway next to our building, where the interns huddled to smoke.

It unravelled quickly after that.

I discarded the Charming Si mask. I didn't return phone calls, ignored emails, lost my appetite for sex, drugs and booze, although I still found a modicum of comfort in high-calorie junk food. Thierry suggested a change of scene, and bought me a ticket to Australia. I refused to go. The freelancers, salespeople and interns who flexi-timed for us tiptoed around me. I was the office weirdo; the freak with missing fingers who wandered into the office wearing mismatching clothes and reeking of sweat.

Eventually, Thierry had enough. He was working his arse off to build up the site, and despite doing sod all except lose my shit, I was trousering almost half the profits.

'Better if you don't come in from now on, Si. You'll still get your share.'

There wasn't a showdown. There wasn't a fight. I simply grabbed the hoodie draped over my chair and walked out. As anti-climaxes go, it was right up there.

I dribbled along, getting by. I got into World of Warcraft, devoured endless *Take A Break* puzzle books, sat slumped in front of daytime TV, mainlining anti-depressants and anxiolytics. Did anything that kept my mind from straying to where it shouldn't go. It's incredible how much time can get eaten up doing nothing.

Occasionally Thierry's lawyer would contact me and offer to buy my shares. I refused. I was smart enough to do that, at least.

In early 2011, a conglomerate offered us an outrageous amount of money to add *Journey to the Dark Side* to its stable. Thierry sent me the news in a stilted email. He didn't ask me if I wanted to sell. He took it for granted that I didn't give a shit either way. He was right.

Being rich didn't 'fix' me. Naively I thought it would at first, but the adrenalin kick of buying things, expensive things, *outrageous* things, was little more than a distraction, the equivalent of using a plaster to stem a severed artery. I gave loads of cash away, to Mum, to my sister; to random charities – donkey sanctuaries, Help the Aged, Save the Children, cancer research. Sometimes I donated it in the names of the Cwm Pot lads – Nigel Rowley, Robert King and Guy McFaul; sometimes I donated it in the memory of Adam Romanyuk and Kostyantyn Sirko, aka Thierry's Ukrainians (it took me less than ten seconds to unearth their names on the Internet). I hired a solicitor and instructed her to track down Mingma and Dorje and set up trust funds for their kids (*see, world, I'm not such a bad person after all*).

I bought the first place I saw – a white 'executive unit' in a soulless, newly constructed block on Canary Wharf; designer clothes by the bushel-load; a membership to an exclusive gym (which of course I only went to once). Gadgets galore. But really all I'd done was exchange my grotty prison for a more upmarket one. My 'job' basically became sitting on a designer leather suite that cost twenty thousand quid, playing *Call of Duty* and watching box sets. It was six months before I met a neighbour; most of the apartments were investment properties. I ordered in most of the time. I could go as long as a week without talking to another human being. Mum and Alison checked in occasionally, but they'd given up trying to persuade me to visit them.

The sense that there was something lurking in my peripheral vision never went away, but it had weakened – or maybe I just got used to it. But I knew something had to change. I needed to kick-start my life.

It was an email from Howard that did it in the end. He was a rabid group emailer – instead of dumping his personal baggage on Facebook like a normal person, he preferred to update everyone via Gmail. It was obvious that each missive took hours, possibly days to put together. It was through him that I learned what everyone who'd been on my expedition was up to. Mingma was now working for an environmental project, facilitating hikes that highlighted the devastating impact of global warming on the Khumbu Valley. Tadeusz and Ireni had shed the iniquity of losing a climber, and were back running their operation on Everest, along with Dorje and Gyaluk. Ngima had moved up the ladder to become a guide. Malcolm had recovered from his life-threatening episode on the mountain, and had taken up fell running. Robbie had also moved on, focusing his energy on technical climbing and bouldering. With the exception of Wanda, who was gradually working her way through the world's highest peaks, everyone else had turned away from the death zone.

Howard had patched things up with his wife, got into sailing, and a seam of naive joy ran through his emails that I was fairly certain was genuine. This latest mail was entitled: 'My

Life-Changing Moments' and included a wedding pic, a shot of his newborn son, a photo of him aged around thirty (*Hannibal Lecter, the Early Years*), a blurry pic of him and Robbie at the summit of Everest, and then, at the end, the group photo that Ireni had taken at base camp after our first recce to ABC. It took me by surprise, and a wash of sorrow flooded through me. I looked fit and happy and cool. Wanda was standing next to me, laughing. I still thought about her every day, although I knew there was no hope. My life wasn't a Hollywood movie where love always wins the day. But the worst of it was seeing Mark. He was taller than I remembered, his eyes hidden behind his glasses, an uncertain smile on his lips.

A tentacle of shame wormed its way out of the lockbox in my mind.

It wasn't my fault.

It doesn't matter whose fault it was. He was your friend, wasn't he?

And then I had it. I knew what to do. I would return to base camp and badger the China Tibet Mountaineering Association to let me erect some kind of memorial plaque to Mark and Juliet. For all I knew, someone had already done this, but I didn't bother to check – I was too fired up and wary of losing my momentum.

In a fever pitch I booked a first-class private Tibetan tour online. I'd fly to Lhasa, and from there I'd be escorted to Shigatse and then on to base camp (I wasn't keen to experience Nyalam and Tingri again). After that I could always cross the border into Nepal and spend a week hiking through the valley with Mingma – why not?

Perhaps I thought that facing the site of my trauma would reboot my brain, erase the peripheral Third Man glitch. *Nothing like a bit of closure eh, Si?*

After the wide skies and rolling grey-green expanse of the Tibetan alluvial plateau, the rows and rows of concrete high-rises on the edge of the city came as a rude shock. The glass and doors in most of them were yet to be added, and the blank black holes only added to their grimness. They couldn't have been more at odds with the intricate, multi-layered architecture of the monasteries we'd passed after we left the airport, or the homely Himalayan homesteads I'd seen last time I was in the country.

Reading my mind, Kunga turned around in the passenger seat. 'These buildings are for the Han Chinese. Many are coming now that they build the train.'

I knew why they were being relocated here – to dilute Tibet's cultural pool. Signs of what Juliet had called the Chinese government's 'stranglehold' were everywhere. In the hour-long drive from the airport, we'd driven through two military checkpoints, and Kunga told me there would be plenty more along the way to Shigatse. *Here are some people with real fucking problems, arsehole.* I didn't remember the oppression being this blatant last time I was here, but I'd been out of it for most of the journey from Kathmandu, and base camp was pretty much its own separate universe.

The driver, Phurba, fiddled with the radio, and the drone of the Tibetan mantras he'd been listening to segued surreally into the thump and bump of TLC, the bass line beating in time with the pulse at my temples. Lhasa was a good thousand metres lower than base camp, but the altitude had smacked me round the chops the moment I'd walked out of the airport building. I was leaden-limbed, heavy-headed and faintly carsick.

Still, it wasn't all bad. I'd hit it off with Kunga, who'd be my guide for the next five days, straight away. A laid-back guy with Converse sneakers and slicked-back hair, he reminded me of Mingma's retro-minded mate at the tented camp. Phurba didn't speak much English, but had a similar easy-going vibe about him, which sadly didn't extend to his driving. He mashed the brakes and accelerator like a maniac, murmured under his breath whenever we overtook as if he was cursing the other drivers on the road, and liked to speed up around corners.

'You want to go to the hotel now or go see Jokhang monastery?' Kunga asked me.

'I wouldn't mind a coffee.' Probably not the best idea if I was suffering from altitude sickness, but caffeine withdrawal could only be making my headache worse.

'American coffee?'

'Not fussy.'

'I know a place. It is new.'

The traffic was picking up; Lhasa's taxi drivers and bikers were as suicidal as their counterparts in Kathmandu, slicing in front of each other and drifting across lanes without checking for blind spots. Phurba now drove with one hand pressed on his car horn – he may as well have stabbed a corkscrew in my brain – slamming his foot on the brakes every few metres. We bunny-hopped past an incongruous mix of western-style shops selling branded tat, Chinese supermarkets and open-fronted butcheries, where men whacked at hunks of bloody raw flesh.

'Look,' Kunga said, as we jerked to a stop behind a tour bus waiting at a red light, pointing up and to his left. 'Potala Palace.'

'Whoa.' How could I have missed it? A truncated white, red and gold blocky pyramid, it loomed defiantly above the city, its sides melding into the cliffs around it. The pavements below it were teeming with a shuffling crowd of elderly people all waving prayer wheels and wearing large-brimmed straw hats.

'That is the Potang Shakor,' Kunga said, doing his mind-reading trick again. 'People walk around the prayer path all day, circling the Potala. My grandmother does this every day, only stopping for some tea.'

'Every day?'

'Yes.'

'Why?'

'For the Dalai Lama. Also, it is like Mount Kailash, the most sacred mountain in Tibet, walk around it enough times, then all your sins will be forgiven.'

How many times would I have to walk around it to atone for my sins? A fuck-load, that was for sure. *Imagine doing that all bloody day*. At least the people circling the palace had a purpose. At least they weren't sitting on their arses all day getting pissed and watching *Storage Wars*.

Then we were off again. Hand stuck to the hooter as if it had the power to ward off death, Phurba sliced through a phalanx of kamikaze bikers, and dropped us off on the corner next to a Chinese supermarket. Still woozy from the altitude, I followed Kunga down a wide street lined with touristy shops selling jewellery, gold Buddhas and mountain gear. The pavement beneath my feet felt like sponge, and I had the same hitch in my breath I remembered from ABC. A spectacled monk trip-trapped fastidiously past me, holding up his robes; a tiny raisin-faced woman swathed in long skirts twirled a prayer wheel. A sour meaty odour slapped me in the face as we passed an open-fronted butchery, the counter heaving with hunks of meat, forlorn yak hooves attached to most of them. Stepping over two well-fed stray dogs taking a nap, Kunga led me down an alleyway, and through an anonymous side door. It led straight into a bright space filled with generic coffee shop décor – we could have stepped into a Starbucks or a Mission:Coffee. *Awesome, Simon, you come to Tibet and go straight to a chain store.*

I handed over a wad of notes, and Kunga ordered for us while I collapsed into a chair and got my bearings. A middle-aged monk, wrapped in his robes, sat at a corner table, sipping a latte and tapping at his smartphone's screen. An attractive smug-looking woman sat opposite him, doing the same. *Maybe they were texting each other.*

Kunga pushed my Americano towards me. I took a sip. Not bad. 'Thanks.'

He glanced at my missing fingers. 'My cousin is like you.'

'Huh?' For a second I thought he was going to say, *he's a mentalist too.*

'He has no fingers.' Suddenly self-conscious, I slid my right hand into my pocket. 'You have an accident?'

'No. Lost them on Everest. Chomolungma.' *Chomolungma? Jesus, could you be any more patronising?*

Kunga didn't look that impressed. Like Mingma, he seemed to take everything in his stride. 'You climbed the mountain?'

'I tried. Is your cousin a climbing Sherpa?'

'No. He lost his fingers and some parts of his feet when he crossed the border in the winter. There are many people like him.'

'The border into Nepal?'

'Yes. He had to leave Tibet.'

The solid floor under my feet still felt gooey, and my breath only seemed to sit shallowly in my lungs. 'Is he okay?' *Okay? He's got no fucking feet.*

'Yes. He lives in Kathmandu.'

Sweat spidered down my cheek. The texting monk got up, giving me a nod and a smile as he drifted past my table. Perhaps this was my chance: *I've got a dead guy bothering me, can you help?* Mingma had said the only way to get rid of an angry ghost was to hold a puja and basically think good thoughts. It wouldn't hurt to light some butter lamps or whatever when I did the touristy thing with Kunga tomorrow. 'Are monks allowed to drink coffee?'

Kunga took the question seriously. 'Of course. You know that the monks who are here are the ones who are approved by the Chinese. The others have gone.'

'Gone where?'

'Exile. To India or Nepal.' I noticed he was keeping his voice low. 'Please do not talk about this in front of Phurba. He is Tibetan, but he has a son in the military. I had one tourist, an American, who put on his Facebook about the Chinese, and I was taken in for questioning.'

'Jesus. I didn't know it was that bad.'

'Yes.' He shrugged resignedly. *What can you do?* 'We go to the hotel now?'

I drank up – the caffeine kick doing sod all to blunt the headache – and Kunga and Phurba dropped me at the hotel, a gold-gated concrete box full of artificial flowers and gloomy carved furniture. A gift shop selling a huge variety of plastic tat, and a glass-fronted altitude clinic flanked the reception area. While I waited for my key card to be processed, a clutch of grey-haired Europeans clad in walking boots and K-Way khaki thronged out of the lifts. Several of them nodded a collusive hello to me – *look at us in this strange city, aren't we brave?*

Stranger in a strange land, arsehole in a hotel lobby. My fuzzy mind was babbling nonsense again.

My room smelled faintly of cigarette smoke, and someone had clearly been a bit clumsy with their butter tea at some point. I tried and failed to nap – *told you coffee was a bad idea.* The room's carpet, a lurid mix of green and purple, swirled in front of my vision. The ceiling felt as if it was too low.

Unable to settle, I took my laptop to the lobby, the only place with adequate Wi-Fi. No one was at the reception desk, but a white-coated doctor in the altitude sickness clinic was bustling around, grinding powder. He gave me a David Lynchian slow wave.

Gmail was blocked in China, but I bypassed it to get to my emails, eager to see if Mingma had any updates about my upcoming hike with him. There was nothing from him, but there were several mails from strangers with .com addresses, the subject lines variations on 'care to comment?', and one from Howard titled, 'FYI'.

What the fuck is this now?

I clicked on Howard's email. There was no text, just an attachment. It downloaded slowly, revealing itself centimetre by centimetre like the cyber version of an elderly stripper.

Bit by bit, a block of black text – a tabloid headline – came into view: *Reunited At Last.*

The top of a grainy photograph started to appear: a teasing patch of dirty white snow, then the familiar grey of a talus slope.

Shut it down.

A flash of pink.

Don't look.

A peek of yellow.

I slammed the laptop shut.

Mark hadn't stumbled into a crevasse, or tumbled down the face, after all. He'd made his way down to where his mum lay and curled up next to her. It was possible I'd walked straight past him when I drunken-sailored my way back to the fixed ropes.

I found out later that an opportunistic climber – *sound familiar?* – had taken several photos of the bodies and sold them to a tabloid.

I stood up, walked stiffly along the corridor to my room, went into the bathroom, and threw up.

Then I pulled the curtains, turned off the lights, lay on the bed and breathed in the spectre of stale smoke until I stopped trembling.

I shut my eyes.

Cold arms wrapped around my chest and squeezed.

I didn't go back to base camp. I didn't go and visit Mingma, and experience a life-affirming hike through the Khumbu Valley.

I went the fuck home.

Only I didn't go home alone.

Ed came with me.

The human brain can get used to anything. And I got used to Ed. *The dead don't haunt us, we haunt them.*

Okay, that's not true. I *want* it to be true.

He reappeared on the third day after I returned home from Lhasa. I was slumped in my designer chair, working my way through a bucket of KFC and trying to numb my brain with *Escape to the Country*, when I looked up to see him standing in the corner of my sterile lounge, dressed in his yellow exposure suit, dirty water streaming from his fingers.

I didn't lurch out of my seat and scream. I'd known all along he was going to be back. I carefully placed the chicken bucket on the coffee table, stood up and approached him, expecting him to blip away. He didn't. His head was drooping slightly, but I could see his eyes: they stared straight ahead, didn't follow me when I moved, and were chillingly expressionless.

'Hi, Ed.'

He didn't speak or react. He just stood there.

I reached out a hand to touch him, expecting my fingers to slide through him as if he were a ghost, or for him to disappear. Instead I encountered a surface that felt like a slab of cold, raw pork. I snatched my hand away, then backed up to the couch.

He stayed there for two hours before disappearing in the blink of an eye.

After that, he'd appear at random moments; sometimes days would go by before he'd show up again, and I'd feel a small press of hope that he was gone for good. And he didn't restrict his appearances to my flat. He'd pitch up anywhere: on the street, in the corner shop, on the tube. No one else could see him. I knew that for sure.

Once, when I was on the Central Line and he appeared in an almost deserted carriage, I said to the woman next to me, a sensible-looking office worker who was fiddling with a Kindle. 'God, look at that guy.'

'What guy?'

'That weirdo in the yellow rubber suit, standing next to the door.' I pointed at him.

She got off at the next stop.

I experimented by spending a few nights in strip clubs, and all-night casinos, hoping that the cacophony and pulse of humanity would dilute him. It didn't.

His expression was always the same: blank, like someone who'd just had a stroke; as empty as my dad's face had been at the end. He didn't harangue me, or verbalise an inner monologue. He never spoke. And while being around him caused a buzzing sensation akin to standing too close to a microwave door, he didn't *do* anything.

The only thing that changed from time to time was his attire. Because he didn't always appear dressed in his dirty yellow exposure suit. Sometimes he would be naked, the scar across his chest a vibrant pink, his penis a grey slug in his damp pubic hair.

Later, I'd find out that there were two exceptions to his stand and stare shtick. On the rare occasions when I drove, Ed would sit in the front seat, dribbling invisibly over the upholstery (he never sat in the back like a normal ghost, readying itself for a 'boo' moment). And after a month of this, he came to my bed for the first time. It wasn't the last. Almost weekly I'd wake with the knowledge that I wasn't alone, dreading the slow creep of those arms around my waist, his flesh cold and unyielding, echoing the woodenness I'd felt in my hand after it had been exposed to the mountain's freezing temperatures. It was pointless to struggle against him, although I tried at first; I had to let it play out, lying for hours, or seconds, or minutes – it was never the same length of time – while he squeezed and caressed. Eventually I gave up sleeping in bed and took to napping in my chair during the day.

Why was he back? The most obvious answer was that seeing the photographs of Mark and Juliet together had triggered his appearance, a side-effect of my lingering PTSD. But why Ed? Why not Mark, or even Juliet? Why had I chosen Ed to be my Third Man? And I couldn't use the 'suffering from a hypoxic delusion' excuse. I may have seen him first on the seventh floor of my executive high-rise, but I wasn't at altitude.

Maybe you've brought an angry ghost back from Lhasa. God knows he'd been an angry fucker when he was alive.

I didn't go back to the psychologist. There was no point. I knew what she'd say: *Get thee to an asylum – or rather, a secure mental health facility – matey.*

No. I couldn't tell anyone about Ed – not without proof.

I ordered a clutch of security cameras from an online specialist shop, paying extra for expedited delivery, and set them up all over the flat, *Paranormal Activity* style. As if he knew what I was up to, Ed didn't appear for almost two weeks, and I started sleeping in my bed again. On the third night I was woken by the cold band of his arms around me. The footage showed me scrunching into myself and keeping my body very still, eyes wide and terrified, but no Ed. There was never any Ed. He was like a vampire that had no reflection.

More proof that he's just in your head, you fucking nutter.

But there was other footage, wasn't there? Thierry had seen something disturbing on the unedited Cwm Pot footage. Had he seen Dead Ed – or whatever it was that had fingers-in-your-hearted me out of there?

We hadn't spoken since the company had been sold, but I knew he'd stayed on as 'creative director'. I rang the office number, half-expecting to be bounced from personal assistant to personal assistant, but I was put straight through to him.

'Simon. Great to hear from you.' He sounded over-cheerful. *Over-compensating.*

'Hey T.' In the background I could make out the sounds of business and busyness.

'How are you, Si?'

'Great.'

'Listen, I want you to know I wasn't the one who signed off on those pics.'

'Huh? What pics?'

'Of your friend. What's his name – Mark. The ones of him and his mother on Everest. I had nothing to do with that.'

I hadn't known they'd been featured on the site. But of course it was just the sort of thing JTTDS's readership would lap up. *A slice of death with your celebrity nip-slips?* Twitchy, I walked over to the picture windows and looked down at a security guard having a cigarette break in the courtyard. 'I'm not calling about that, Thierry. Listen . . . I know you're busy, so I'm going to get straight into it.' I was sweating; my face had grown hot. Sensing Ed was near – (sometimes he brought with him a heaviness in the air, like the onset of a thunderstorm) – I turned around. He was naked today, and was facing the wall, unusual for him. The hair coating his back and thighs was damp with dirty water.

'I'm listening.'

'Do you still have the Cwm Pot footage?'

A pause. 'It's still up on the site and on YouTube, Si.'

'Not the edited clip. The other stuff. Do you still have it?'

'Christ. I don't know.'

'Remember back when you edited it? You said you saw something weird. Something that creeped you out.'

'I did?'

'I need to see it, Thierry.'

'I don't think I have it, Si. In any case, the formatting is out-dated.'

'What did you see on it? Did you see Ed?'

A pause. 'Si . . .'

'Thierry, I need to know.' *Calm down, act rational.* 'Sorry, I know this sounds strange. It's to do with my therapy.' *Nice one – you've still got it.* 'My shrink and I are working on getting closure.'

His voice relaxed. 'Dude, I'm so pleased you're getting help.'

'Yeah. It's really helping.'

'Ed's the guy who was down in the caves with you, right? Sure. He was all over the footage. You know . . . I think it'll still be on my old laptop. Listen, things are hectic right now. Why don't you come over to my place this weekend? You can meet Jen and Danny. You know I had a kid, right?'

'No. I didn't know.' I'd deliberately avoided prying into the other areas of his life. 'Congratulations.' I couldn't have cared less if he'd repopulated the earth. All I could think was: I needed to see it *now.*

Too bad.

Unable to completely mask the smugness in his voice, he gave me the address – he'd moved to a millionaire's row in St Albans – and hung up.

'Si!' Thierry appeared at the front door, a bulbous child in his arms. He'd lost weight, lost his glasses, lost any trace of insecurity. If anything, he looked younger. 'Rough night, dude?'

I looked down. My T-shirt was inside out. I hadn't changed it for three days. Nor had I shaved. 'Something like that.'

'Well hey, it's good to see you.' The baby stuffed a hand in its mouth. 'This is Danny.'

'He's cute.' He wasn't. He looked like a mini version of James Gandolfini.

I followed him through a hallway bedecked with mirrors and into a sprawling oak and stainless steel kitchen. A woman came waddling up to me and gave me a couple of air kisses. She was short and round, with dyed black hair, and a not unattractive pug face. She reeked of perfume.

'This is Jen,' Thierry said.

'I've heard so much about you, Simon,' Jen said in a posh, very English voice. I had to hand it to Thierry; with his cash he could have gone full footballer's wife and snagged himself a lingerie model. Jen looked like a normal person.

'Your house is beautiful,' I managed.

'Oh bless you. We love it.'

'I bet.'

She offered me a coffee, gesturing at a machine the size of the Millennium Falcon.

Some awkward small talk followed. I learned that she and Thierry were planning to get married next year (I was promised an invite; I immediately started planning my excuses); she was in IT, and they'd met when she tried to sell him some sort of software security upgrade. It had been 'love at first sight'. Like Tadeusz and Ireni. Like Wanda and me (almost).

'C'mon,' Thierry said when the banalities had run dry. 'Let me give you the grand tour.' He didn't relinquish the child.

All I wanted to do was watch the footage and get the fuck out of there, but I dutifully trailed him through a dining room, lounge and downstairs wet room, while Danny the James Gandolfini baby watched me over its dad's shoulder, a glistening strand of drool snail-trailing over Thierry's vintage ACDC T-shirt.

'This you gotta see, Si.' We trudged down a carpeted stairwell and into a huge basement. 'This is my space. My man cave.'

It had all the clichés, a billiard table, a huge screen, racks of games, red leather furniture, and one unexpected addition: in the corner, dripping invisible water over Thierry's state-of-the-art gaming chair, was Ed. I know I was imagining the look of contempt in his eyes at this display of excess, but it still made me smirk inwardly. 'It's awesome, Thierry.'

'Yeah? You think?'

The baby swivelled its head and fixed its eyes on Ed.

Jen appeared with our coffees, gave me the kind of supportive smile usually bestowed on someone who's been recently bereaved (Thierry had clearly filled her in on my mental health issues), then glided off with the baby. Its eyes stayed glued to Ed until the last second, after which it started squealing.

'Great to see you, Thierry, but I'm in a bit of a rush.'

'Huh? But you're staying for lunch, right? Thought we could break out the beers for old time's sake.'

I gave what I hoped was a regretful smile. 'My therapist says I have to stay off the booze.'

'Pity. Si . . . can we talk?'

Please God no. 'About what?'

'I feel bad about how we left things.'

'It's fine, Thierry.'

'I had to do what was best for the business. You were—'

'I know.' I was suddenly exhausted. I'd admired his perfect life, what else did he want from me?

'And you've done all right for yourself out of it, haven't you?'

'Yeah.'

'Where are you living now?'

'Thierry, I understand what you're trying to do, but I just want to see the footage and get the hell out of here.'

He winced. *Zing*. 'Okay. I've got it all set up for you.'

I sat down at a vintage desk and he leaned over me and tapped at the keyboard.

'You want me to stay?'

'Do what you want.'

I forgot about him as I gazed at the screen and fast-forwarded through the footage, pausing every so often. I'd caught Ed here and there, even though he'd told me not to film him. My Ed, the one who was still looming over the gaming chair, was taller, broader and balder than the one on the screen. The caves themselves looked smaller than I remembered; the traverse steeper, the Rat Run tighter. I gave the inside of my cheek a sharp bite to ward off a potential panic attack, and fast-forwarded to my last words.

I really did look terrified; my eyes seemed to be unfocused, my skin too pale. And then I saw something shift in the background, a ripple of movement in the darkness above my left ear. A bulbous, lumpen shadow lurked behind me. Whatever that was, it wasn't Ed. Ed was dead by then.

'Got you,' I whispered.

'Got what?' Thierry said.

I rewound it, and sat back so that Thierry could see the screen.

'Look.'

'What?'

'You see that?'

'Yeah. It's you, looking freaked out as fuck.'

'No. Behind me. Look *behind* me.'

I pressed pause.

'There's nothing there, Si.'

He was right.

I watched it again. And again to be sure. The Third Man was gone. Because that's what the fucker *did.*

'Gotta go.'

I fled his bat cave without another word, a panic attack nipping at my heels.

'Are you leaving already?' Jen called after me as I fumbled with the front door.

'Yes. Thanks for the coffee. Cute kid.' *And by the way, you should probably know that you're married to a complete cunt.*

I ran away from Thierry's immaculate house and perfect life, Cwm Pot's watery voices whispering in my ears. *Fingers in your heart, fingers in your heart, lad.*

I could have called in an exorcist, maybe returned to Tibet and paid a lama to help me pray away Ed's bad spirit, but Ed wasn't a ghost, was he? I wasn't being haunted in the conventional sense. Either my conscience was punishing me by building a hyper-realistic 'doppelganger', I'd brought something back from the death zone that needed another trauma – in my case being confronted by the photograph of Juliet and Marcus – to manifest itself, or I was in the midst of a schizoid delusion.

If Juliet and I had experienced a malevolent Third Man – a destroyer – and were perfectly sane (*ha*), then there had to be someone else out there who'd experienced the same thing. I scoured the web. There were thousands of accounts of 'evil entities' and hauntings of course, as well as blogs and articles about similar delusions reported by people suffering from head injuries, epilepsy and Alzheimer's, but nothing that fitted my particular set of criteria.

It was Robbie who came through for me in the end. I came up with a semi-plausible story and emailed him, saying that I was planning to make a documentary about Mark's search for his mother in order to 'put things right', and that Mark had been the one who'd sensed a malevolent presence on the mountain just before he died. As this particular kind of Third Man would feature in my research and seemed to be quite rare, I asked him if he could point me in the right direction. I also said that I'd followed his advice about seeing a therapist and thanks to him, I was as right as rain. He seemed weirdly pleased to hear from me, and after shooting the shit for a while on Google Chat, sent me a password that would allow me to access an academic site that specialised in archived material relating to psychology. 'This kind of thing took up a lot of ink in the seventies,' he wrote. 'So I'd start there. Good luck.'

It took me less than a day to unearth what I was looking for in an article entitled, 'The Angel Beside Me: The Third Man and Wartime Trauma', which had been published in a peer-reviewed psychology journal in the seventies. Drily written by a 'Doctor A. D. Meechum', one of the case studies included in it immediately grabbed me. The subject, a navvy named George Kendrick, had picked up his 'Ed' in World War II after his destroyer was hit, and he and twenty other survivors were cast adrift for two weeks off the coast of North Africa. One by one the survivors succumbed to delirium and thirst, but George had a reason to cling on: 'On the fifth day, I became aware of a presence sitting beside me. Gradually, I realised it was my older brother Philip, who'd died five years previously, and a nastier individual you'd be hard-pressed to find. He'd made my childhood a living hell. Philip stayed with me for the next ten days until we were rescued. He never spoke, but I knew he meant me harm. I couldn't let him see that he was troubling me, so I kept calm and refused to die like so many of the other lads. I couldn't let him win.' When George returned home, he didn't mention his brother's apparition to anyone. 'Thought it was just one of those things. And Philip didn't come back with me. I thought I'd left him behind on the raft.' George found work as a carpenter and got married. 'But I always knew something wasn't right.' In the nineteen sixties, after he was involved in a car accident that resulted in the death of a motorcyclist, Philip returned. 'He would sit in the corner of the room, knees up to his chest, just like he used to sit in the boat. I could tell he was still evil, mind.'

George started drinking heavily, his wife left him, and eventually his family had him sectioned, which was where Dr Meechum came in. The doctor's conclusion was that George was exhibiting signs of schizophrenia, noting that he wasn't responsive to ECT or medication. Dr Meechum was long dead, but George wasn't. Half a day's online sleuthing revealed that, aged ninety-two, he was living in an 'elder care' facility in Essex.

'Saddle up, Ed. We're going on a road trip.'

I'd been steeling myself for some sort of underfunded hellhole, but in fact George's residence was an inoffensive single-storey building surrounded by a crescent of soft lawn.

I'd called ahead, making up a story that I was a distant relative, and I was met at reception by an efficient care-worker with a Nigerian accent. He led me into a lounge area furnished in floral fabrics, which faced onto a pleasant courtyard garden. A white cat slept on a cushion. A TV hummed somewhere in the background. It smelled faintly of Sunday lunch and expensive air freshener.

The care-worker pointed at a crumpled hobbit sitting in a wheelchair next to the window, a slant of dust-mote light shining down on his pate. 'That's him. That's George. Call at reception before you leave to sign out.'

'Thanks.'

I approached the hobbit. His hands, lumped with arthritis, were twisted in his lap. His eyes were open and stared straight ahead. 'Hi George. My name is Simon.'

His gaze flicked towards me, then away. His mouth moved, but no sound emerged.

An equally tiny woman with less hair than Ed came walker-shuffling up to me, a glint in her eye. 'He don't talk, love. Stopped last year. Had a stroke and gone doolally. You a relative?'

I drew on the stale vestiges of Charming Si. 'No. I wanted to ask him some questions. About . . . about his life during the war.'

'Historian, are you? *I* could tell you some stories about the war.'

Shit. 'No. I'm a medical student. Um, psychiatry. I was interested in George's . . . mental health issues.'

'His brother you mean?'

'You know about it?'

'Oh yes, love. He was always talking about it before his stroke. Quite open he was. Said his brother had been following him for years like a bad smell. Saw my Ken after he died too. Sat right in his armchair, clear as day. For months he used to come.'

There's a term for that, I thought, but didn't say. *The Widow Effect.* 'Did George ever mention what his brother wanted with him?'

'No, love. His niece used to come and visit, said the poor old soul had been in and out of institutions since his wife died, but he wasn't mad. Just saw things. Ruined his life. Wouldn't travel, couldn't work.'

'And it never went away?'

'Could be there right now for all I know, love.'

George's eyes had drifted to the lounge's left-hand corner. The cat bolted out of the room. I didn't bother looking over; I knew what I would see.

Half an hour later I was sitting in a pub, a pint of Guinness and a whisky chaser in front of me. *That could be me. I could be George.* Was that the future I had to look forward to? Sitting in an old-age home, not knowing what Ed wanted? He could be with me forever. If Juliet had come home, maybe she'd now be sitting in an institution, haunted by a black-fingered fiend. *Who is the third who walks* always *beside you?*

Something had saved me in the caves. Something had tried to kill me – or save me – on the mountain.

'Saviour or destroyer. Which is it?' I'd spoken aloud, and the landlord gave me a dubious look.

Ed could be biding his time before he struck. Or he could be watching over me, keeping me safe. Forever.

Or it was neither.

I wasn't sure which was worse.

There's something I haven't mentioned. Something that's hard to talk – or write – about, because I'm a coward and let's face it, an all-round shit, but when I returned from Everest, Mark's father attempted to get hold of me, and more than once. I was too locked inside my own selfish misery to talk to him, and Thierry fielded the calls. He must have read the articles naming and shaming me – let's not forget that Mark died while in the company of Simon Newman, Exploiter of the Dead – and no doubt blamed me for not doing enough to save his son. After a couple of weeks he gave up, although for a while I half expected him to show up at the flat, and later, at the office.

He never did.

But now, diseased by Ed's almost constant presence and tormented by the image of George's living hell life, I needed to see him. It wasn't just the lure of redemption – I've never believed Ed is some sort of karmic manifestation that will leave me the fuck alone once I've put things 'right'. No. I wanted to know definitively if Juliet had a history of being mentally ill or not. And there was an infinitesimal chance that Mark's dad might have ripped out the last page in her journal when it was returned to him. It was a long shot. She could have scrunched the paper up and blown her nose on it; she might not have written anything on it at all. But in my defence I couldn't believe that our experiences weren't connected, however tenuously. The answer – *saviour or destroyer* – could be on that scrap of paper. *I'm going to look behind the mask.*

It took me seconds to track down Graham Michaels's address and phone number. It took me two days to get up the gumption to make the call. I was like a nervy teenager attempting to build up the confidence to ask a girl out on a date; I must have dialled and hung up over thirty times. It was the sight of Ed, who made one of his unheralded visits while I was in Waitrose buying a batch of ready-meals that finally spurred me to do it. I limped over to an empty space next to the flower display and tapped in the number. After three rings a cut-glass voice answered: 'Yes? To whom am I speaking?'

I said who I was. Several seconds of silence followed, then: 'What do you want?'

'I'd like to come and see you.'

'When?'

'Whenever suits you, sir. I know how difficult this is.' Ed was still lurking next to the lasagne. Shoppers unconsciously wheeled their trolleys around him.

'Wednesday next, ten-thirty.' He hung up.

The next five days dragged; I barely slept, and my attempts to eat up the time, mostly by getting stoned and playing Spider Solitaire, didn't do anything to dilute my nervousness about meeting Mark's father face to face.

Finally Wednesday rolled around. I hired a car and a GPS and set off. Ed had been absent for a couple of days, and he didn't show up on the front seat, although it was unlike him to miss an outing.

Juliet had described Graham's family home as a festering pile, and she wasn't wrong. It sat like a defiant old pariah on the fringe of a new housing estate – one of those hastily built cookie-cutter developments – and was flanked by a croissant of orange-bricked 'elegant country homes'.

Ten minutes early, I parked outside the gates and ate two Kit Kats, folding the wrappers carefully so that I could throw them away at the same time – that way they wouldn't get lonely.

Hurry please it's time.

Ragged grass and dead leaves smothered the driveway, which led to a courtyard fronting a forbidding, L-shaped stone building. Moss the colour of dead skin colonised its stone façade, its leaded windows cried out for a ghostly face in the glass, and the surrounding lawns were balding. In the far corner sat a rotting summerhouse and a rusted swing set. Goosebumps rippled across my skin – I'd seen them before, in the background of the photograph Mark had shown me a millennium ago when we were at ABC.

The slam of my car door sounded too loud and made me jump. It was quiet here, too quiet as if the house was surrounded by an invisible force field that inhaled the sounds of life from the estate and the nearby A-road. I was about to head for the front door – a wooden monstrosity studded with black iron, when a smaller side door opened, and a chunky grey-haired man in a baggy brown cardigan and trousers tucked into green boots bustled out. 'This way, please.'

'Mr Michaels?'

'Yes. This way.'

He was far smaller, older and fatter than I expected. He waved me impatiently through a dim boot room that reeked of wet dog, and into a cavernous kitchen dominated by a table covered in a grubby oilcloth. An armchair, a frayed shirt draped over it, squatted next to a grumbling Rayburn stove. An old television was wonkily placed on top of a rusting microwave, an aerial piercing its top. An elderly dog, the source of the smell, farted and raised a disinterested ruby-rimmed eye at me from its basket. It was the loneliest room I'd ever been in. And that included my own.

He waved at the table. 'Sit.'

'Thanks. And thank you for seeing me.'

'Tea, coffee?'

'Coffee would be great, thank you.'

Graham's hands were dirty, the fingers as swollen and bulbous as overstuffed sausages. He fumbled with a cheap plastic kettle and a tin of no-name brand instant coffee granules.

'Amazing house,' I said.

'Can't heat it. Developers want it.'

He placed a crusted sugar bowl in front of me, his hands shaking slightly, from Parkinson's or grief or anger or nervousness. He sat opposite me. I tried and failed to find a trace of Mark in him, or connect him with the suave Jeremy Irons character in the web pics.

'What do you want?'

'I'm . . . I wanted to give you my condolences, for Marcus.'

'Bit late for that, isn't it?'

'Yes. I'm sorry I haven't spoken to you sooner. I've had some problems.'

He waved this away with a contemptuous gesture and took a sip of his coffee. 'Did he die easy or hard?'

'He . . . I don't know for sure. I wasn't there . . . you know, at the end.'

'But you must have some idea, some sense?'

'Sir, I don't think you really want to hear—'

'Don't tell me what I want to hear, you *fucker*.' He slammed his fist on the table, sending my coffee spilling across the oilcloth. 'He was my son.' The elderly dog struggled to his feet and limped to his master.

And then I told him. Not the truth, but a version of the truth. My sanitised version. That it had a been a joint decision to head off along the moraine after Mingma left us, worried that we wouldn't get another chance to locate Juliet. I told him that one minute Marcus was there, one minute he wasn't.

He listened silently. 'Thank you.'

'I want you to know, my motives for accompanying him weren't as' – what? *speak* – 'weren't as self-serving as you might have heard. He was my friend. I liked him a lot.'

'Are you saying you didn't film his last moments? That's what you were there for, wasn't it?'

'No. No. I didn't.' I wanted to say: *I'm not a monster*, but that would be a lie.

The dog whined and turned its head to the corner of the room. *Oh, hello Ed.* 'I read her journal. Juliet's journal.'

He jerked. '*What*?'

'The account of her last days on Everest.'

'How did you get that?' He'd gone white.

'Marcus had it. Didn't you know?'

'No. I . . . wait.'

He got up and shuffled to a door in the corner of the room. As he disappeared through it, I caught a glimpse of the darkness beyond, and thought I could smell a gust of cold, stale air. The house was a mausoleum.

I delved in my memory to retrieve what Marcus had said about the journal. I was certain he hadn't mentioned that his dad didn't know he had it. Christ.

Losing his mum had scarred Marcus and changed the course of his life. The psychologist I'd seen a trillion years ago had wanted to delve deeper into my own parental loss with a Freudian fervour, but I'd parroted what I knew she wanted to hear. Would it have made a difference if I'd allowed her to poke around in that particular hole? Maybe. Maybe not. I tried to picture Dad's face, but Ed's kept coming up.

I was – *am* – an armchair psychologist's wet dream.

Graham returned, wiping his hands on his trousers as if he'd been touching something odious. 'It's gone.'

'Listen, Mr Michaels, I'm really sorry. I shouldn't have mentioned it.'

'I meant to destroy it all those years ago. Should have thrown it on the fire when it was first sent to me. So Marcus found it, did he?'

'Yeah.'

'I should have known. A year before they found Juliet's body, he started asking me about Ang Tsering's family, you know, the man who saved Juliet's life after Walter died. I suppose I assumed Marcus had been in touch with Joe, or a journalist had told him.

Periodically one would ring the house. We fought, you know, Marcus and I, before he left. Said some unforgiveable things to each other. When he told me what he was going to do, that he was going to go to that blasted mountain, I admit I lost my temper. Something was burning inside him. I should have guessed what it was.' A shrewd glance. 'Where is it now?'

'I have it. I should have sent it back to you, only . . .'

'I don't want it back. But you must promise never to share the information in it. That will only tar her reputation.'

'I promise.'

'I suppose if you were going to publish it, you would have done so by now.' He sighed and closed his eyes. 'She was right about me, you know. I wasn't exactly faithful. I did resent her success. But only because it took her away from us, from Marcus and I.'

'You don't have to explain yourself to me, sir.'

'I know.'

He got up and dug out a pair of dusty crystal glasses and half a bottle of Glenfiddich. 'You want?'

'Please.'

'It's the only thing I refuse to cut back on. There's no excuse for drinking cheap whisky.'

He handed me a glass. 'Did Marcus tell you anything about Walter?'

I blinked. 'No. Not really.'

'I wanted to blame Walter for dragging Juliet back into that life. I didn't like him, I don't mind telling you that. Complex, but you wouldn't know it from looking at him. Came across as salt of the earth. Juliet refused to believe he was troubled. Wouldn't hear a bad word said against him. He had a terrible temper, held a grudge.'

'In the journal he sounds like a saint.' No – that wasn't true, was it? She was critical of him as well, although she'd crossed out those lines in her journal in one of her acts of self-censorship. But still, I wasn't sure if I was prepared to take Graham's word for anything. Part of the reason she'd been on the mountain was her desperation to be out of his clutches.

'To Juliet, he was. He was a father figure of sorts. She met him when she was sixteen, shortly before her father passed away. He was one of the older fellows who used to climb where she and her friends started out. He saw her potential. Hitched his wagon to hers. I've never been able to quite nail down what drew them together. He came across as a drifter. One of life's untethered people.'

An Ed. Only Ed truly was evil when he was alive. Saviour or destroyer?

'Do you think Walter's death might have caused her some mental problems?'

'Yes. Yes, of course. When she returned from Nepal after he died, she was a shadow of the person she once was. Broken. And all the bad press she received after it didn't help. Terrible. Often she was her own worst enemy where journalists were concerned. All that mattered to her was the climbing. She didn't know how to play the personality game. Came across as rude more than once in interviews.' He sat up straighter. 'The breakdown of our marriage didn't help. I'm aware of that. And I know what you're getting at. That Third Man stuff and nonsense. It was so unlike her. She wasn't a spiritual person. She didn't have a history of being . . . unstable.' He paused. 'I told her not to go in 'ninety-five. She hadn't been training, you see. Wasn't fit enough. But she was determined to go when she found she could get a place on an expedition. Climbing is always what she turned to, you see. She was like Walter that way. Didn't show emotion, used it on the mountains.'

'There were a couple of pages missing from the end of the journal.'

'Yes. She wrote a letter to Marcus when she was in the high camps.'

'I saw it.'

'He showed it to you?'

'No. I . . . found it. Later.'

'I only gave it to him when he was twenty-one. Held it back when he was a child, didn't want to upset him. Blame myself for that. Maybe if I hadn't given it to him he wouldn't have gone. When they discovered her body, it did something to him.'

'By any chance, did you remove the other page when Joe sent you the journal?'

'Me? Why would I do that?'

How to word this? 'I don't know. Some of the things she wrote about you . . . they weren't exactly flattering.'

He drained his glass. 'It should be sipped, but there's a time and a place for everything.' I glanced at Ed, half-hidden in the shadows. Dirty water poured out of his mouth. The dog whined again. '*Quiet*, Philip.' Graham scowled at it. 'But no. I didn't deface that book. If I was worried anyone would read "unflattering" things about me, I would have destroyed the whole thing. And in any case, they would only need to look at some of the tabloid stories that came out at the time. She must have ripped them out before she made the final push for the summit, as she did with the page she used for the letter. Every ounce of weight counts up there, as I'm sure you know. It would have been normal practice for her to do this so that she could make notes while in the high camps.'

'So the page could still be on her body.'

'What on earth do you think is written on it, and why does it interest you so much?'

'When I was up there . . . I had a similar experience. I sensed something.'

'Not uncommon, I believe, in those circumstances.'

'Yes.' Only what I'd experienced was somehow worse. But I couldn't say any more without sounding like a complete fruit loop. 'It's just . . . I was wondering if she'd written any more about her own experience.' *If she'd looked behind the mask after all and written down what she'd found.*

'It's not likely, is it?' He drifted off somewhere, then shook himself. 'I've heard that the Chinese military are cleaning up their side of the mountain. Removing the bodies that are up there.'

A hitch in my chest. 'Who told you that?'

'The man who was running your expedition.'

'Tadeusz?'

'Is that his name? Yes.'

You should know his name. He was on your wife's expedition as well as your son's. 'He keeps in touch with you?'

'Sporadically, yes.'

'Do you blame him for what happened? For letting Marcus climb?'

'No.' Was he lying? Hard to tell. We locked eyes. 'Marcus's death shook me badly, of course. But it comforts me to think of them up there together. At least they're not alone.'

And if it was true the Chinese authorities were cleaning up the mountain, then it might only be a matter of time before Juliet and Marcus disappeared into a crevasse.

Ed was gone. The dog allowed his head to flop back onto his bed, no longer needing to be vigilant.

Graham's chin wobbled again. 'That mountain has taken so much from me.' He topped up our glasses. 'We might never know what happened to them. At least they've found peace.'

We both knocked back the whisky in one gulp. We were both thinking the same thing: Marcus and Juliet might be at peace, but we sure as hell weren't.

It was time to do something about that, once and for all.

The lane looked exactly as it had the last time I was here. Same overhanging branches casting fingerish shadows in the mud, same aura of desolation. I parked the hire car exactly where I'd parked Thierry's Ford Focus seven years ago, then sat for a few minutes taking small, gag-inducing nips from the half-jack of brandy I'd bought en route from an Aldi in Newport.

My backpack contained a pair of bolt cutters, a bacon roll, spare batteries and a flask – *that* flask, Ed's flask – of Johnny Walker Black that I planned to drink when (*if*) I made it into the mausoleum cave. I was wearing a red state-of-the-art over-suit and fleece Babygro I'd bought online, kneepads and the same old wellies I'd worn the first time around. I took another swig, feeling the burn of the cheap alcohol, then waved the bottle in Ed's face. 'Want some?' He was slumped in the front seat, his hands folded primly in his lap, his fingernails black with dirt. 'No? Afterlife got your tongue?'

Would my plan work? 'Who can say,' I muttered to myself, taking another gulp. A rivulet spilled over my chin, burning the chapped skin around my mouth. A line from an old Coldplay song drifted into my head. 'We're going back to the start,' I sang to Ed.

It would probably go horribly wrong as soon as I tried to grip the ladder's rungs with my mutilated hand. The rational side of my brain bleated at me to go the fuck home, but I couldn't. I needed to know. *Saviour or destroyer?* It was this or end up like George, a husk of a person sitting in a wheelchair, forever staring at my deeply creepy imaginary friend. And returning to Cwm Pot to get answers was a better alternative than my only other option. 'Whatcha think, Ed? Should I stay or should I go?'

I reached out to touch him, drawing my hand back at the last second. The cold, unhealthy feel of his flesh would stay with me for hours afterwards, and I didn't want that visceral memory to haunt me as I embarked on my semi-suicidal mission.

Hurry up please it's time.

I made myself leave the hire car's comforting Korean cocoon, and collected the rest of my hastily bought gear – a rope, helmet and headlamp – from the boot. No helmet-cam this time around – this trip was just between Ed and me. I dug in my pocket to check I still had the map. In lieu of a guide, I'd managed to locate an outline of the system on one of the caving clubs' websites. It was little more than a hand-drawn sketch, and its folksy lines made the obstacles look easier and friendlier than I knew they were. Whoever had done it had added a grimly inappropriate exclamation mark to the 'Rat Run' label. *Hey, why not spend a day exploring the Rat Run! Fun for all the family.*

The sky was almost obscenely clear, the air chilly but not uncomfortably so. As I jumped over the stile and crossed the first field, I picked up my pace, and my trepidation about the climb down the ladder started to fade. Maybe it was the numbing effect of the brandy, or maybe I honestly didn't give a shit any more if I lived or died. I checked to see if Ed was lurking somewhere. He wasn't. He'd show up though, I was sure of that. He'd show up when it counted.

The cracked 'No Entry' signs I remembered from my last trek here had been replaced with newer, more aggressively worded ones. I paused for breath next to a barbed-wire fence and took another sip of booze. The fence's tines caught on the suit and bag as I crawled through the wires, the brandy affecting my balance and coordination. *No biggy.* I huffed my way up and down the next couple of paddocks, clouds of sheep bunching together, and then gusting away from me. In the distance I could see the beginnings of the rocky pathway that would lead down into Cwm Pot's fetid guts.

The gate was padlocked twice, a thick chain wrapped around it. This time around, there was no sign attached to it. I peered at the sky. It didn't look like it would rain, but what did I know? The test would come, but I was fairly sure that this time, it wouldn't come at the hands (*fingers*) of the whispery water.

I raised my face to the sun's weak rays and closed my eyes.

So, dude, you going to do this thing or what?

WWJD? What would Juliet do? I knew what she'd do. She'd face it head on. She wouldn't namby-pamby around; she'd get her arse into gear.

One more for the road?

No. Dutch courage was all very well, but the bottle was almost empty and I was well past half-cut. I chucked the bottle away from me, hearing it clunk against a rock. *Tsh, tsh, don't be a litter-bug.* I had the high-end booze in Ed's flask to top me up if I needed it.

The bolt cutters slipped the first time, jarring my wrist. I couldn't grip them properly with my damaged hand. I gave it another go. It was only when the chain finally gave way with a resigned *ping* and I was staring into the entrance tunnel's maw that doubt came dribbling in again. Did I honestly think this outing would give me the answer? That I'd run into trouble and he'd save me? *Super Ed, world-class psycho and child molester to the rescue.* Or perhaps he'd try and trap me down there, while above me storm clouds gathered, and the caves filled with muddy, blood-coloured water.

Whichever way you looked at it, embarking on this death-wish mission meant that my status as a mental case was assured. And what had my outing to question Graham Michaels achieved? Fuck all. There were no answers there either. Juliet was either as mad as I was, or we'd both caught a ghost like a virulent strain of flu. *The Third Man virus.*

Stop whining and get to it.

It was then that I realised I'd forgotten to buy any gloves. *Tough shite, boyo.*

I rolled onto my belly and let my legs drop over the edge with the reckless abandon of the pissed and stupid. Grateful that the alcohol blunted that stomach-dropping vertiginous lurch I'd felt the first time around, I scrambled down, taking it in turns to grasp the rungs with my good hand, and the weaker pincer-grip of Ol' Stumpy.

Down, down.

Dark, it was too dark. Why was it so dark?

Turn on your headlamp, arsehole.

Down, down, down, the backpack and rope dragging on my shoulders. As I descended, I ran through the obstacles I'd have to master in order to reach the mausoleum: the boulder choke, the narrow mouth and its slippery chain, the climb down the vertical wall into the abyss, and then the Rat Run (!). If I conquered them, defeating each one like an old-school hero on a quest, would my reward be Ed waiting for me in the cave? His body would be there at least. It must be. Who could forget the old adage, *You can't take a body out when it's this far underground, lad.* Not me, no siree. Maybe once reunited with his corporeal form, Ed would leave me the fuck alone. The story would be neatly wrapped up. A happy horror-movie ending.

I sped up, taking the rungs two, then three at a time, the booze making me cocky. When my foot hit nothing, I clipped the rope onto the rungs. If I chickened out (or sobered up) and decided not to risk cramming my bloated body through the Rat Run, then I could come back this way.

See, Ed, there ain't no flies on me.

See, Si, you don't really want to die.

At the tunnel's base, I squirmed through the aperture, moronically forgetting to take it slowly and landing with a crump on my coccyx again, the bolt cutters in the bag digging into my lower back. I got to my feet and blearily took stock. I half expected Ed to be waiting for me there: *What took you so long, lad? Knew you'd be back.* Way back in the sands of time, I'd been impressed with this section, thought it cavernous and church-like, but now it appeared to be smaller, the ribbed walls lower, reminding me of the bony insides of Monstro, the whale in *Pinocchio*. 'Someday you'll be a real boy, Si,' I said aloud, belching out a giggle and tasting brandy. It was probably due to a trick of the light. Without the additional bloom of Ed's head torch, the chamber had a claustrophobic cast to it. The specialist headlamp I'd bought had cost a packet, but it wasn't as bright as I remembered Ed's being.

I stood there for a while, listening to the discordant, drunk-pianist sound of dripping water, letting my head torch's beam dance across the space. *Plinkety plonk, the soundtrack to your very own biopic, Si.* An alien splash of colour caught my eye. Someone had sprayed an arrow in green fluorescent paint on a curve of rock. I was almost certain it pointed the way to the tunnel Ed and I had taken the first time.

Had the rescuers who'd hauled me out of the sewerage pipe left a fluorescent breadcrumb trail? Or perhaps the original Cwm Pot footage had attracted other salacious spelunkers, keen to do a spot of their own death tourism.

A wave of profound loneliness came crashing down. This time, no one knew where I was. There would be no rescue party. No Thierry making middle-of-the night jaunts down from London to help me. No gruff, dry-humoured chaps risking their lives to save me. *Just me, and if I'm lucky, my friendly neighbourhood ghosty.*

My inner little boy whined, *Don't wanna. Wanna go home.*

Pussy, the Ed voice said.

I retrieved the map. Far as I could tell, the arrow did seem to correlate with the sketch of Cwm Pot's guts. It was hard to be a hundred per cent sure as the booze was really hitting me now, and I was almost at the stage where a good bartender would cut me off.

Follow the yellow brick arrow. There was more than one – every twenty feet or so another pointed the way. They were comforting, shiny cheerleaders, egging me on. Perhaps it was their presence – their illusion of safety – that contributed to the fact that I still wasn't feeling a 'normal' level of fear. Every so often I bent to touch the ground, testing it for dampness, as if I were some sort of Bear Grylls type figure, able to sense if the weather had changed up top.

And there it was, obstacle number one. On the map, this had been unimaginatively labelled: 'the boulder choke' (it hadn't warranted an exclamation mark), and the jumble of rocks was just as unreal and Indiana Jones-ish as I remembered. I'd followed Ed closely the last time I'd squeezed myself through it, but this time around I was out of shape, with sagging muscles, a bowling ball of a stomach, hands already cramping from cold, and I was hindered by the bag. I couldn't jettison it; it contained the bolt cutters, which I'd need to cut through the padlock at the other end. As I scrambled inelegantly through each fissure, guided by dots of fluorescent paint, sweat trickled into my eyes, and my helmet became a microwave on top of my head. It helped that I could be as noisy and as ungainly as I liked, huffing and wheezing and swearing as I corkscrewed my body through places it shouldn't strictly have been able to fit, nudging the bag ahead of me.

I paused to dig out Ed's flask for an unwise booze top-up before I tackled the next bit. Fighting the loneliness, I kept myself company, talking to myself, singing whatever tunes popped into my head. I ran through, 'You'll Never Walk Alone', making up the words when I forgot them, 'Tiptoe through the Tulips', and

'Smack my Bitch Up', making percussion sounds deep in my throat.

Still no Ed. Well, I'd hardly put myself in danger yet. That would come.

Following my arrow friends, and humming 'let your conscience be your guide,' I didn't pause for breath until I reached obstacle number two – the narrow mouth through which I'd have to post myself feet first while clinging to the chain. The facetious cartographer had called this 'the slot'. I didn't hesitate. I couldn't give Whiny Little Boy a chance to talk me out of it. Thanks to the booze, the hairy scramble up the face, the leap for the chain, and the clumsy flail to slot my toes inside the gap went smoothly – *too* smoothly. Each manoeuvre had a curious, dream-like quality to it, a distant cousin to the feeling I'd had just before Mingma rescued me after Mark's death. A flare of panic as I realised I didn't have enough room for both the bag and my arse in the squashed space, which called for a series of awkward moves, but hey ho. Done. Tick. Next?

I was seconds away from the abyss – the steep face that had put the fear of God into me the first time around.

I peered over the edge of it. *'Come on then, Chris Bonington, let's see what you're made of.'* The memory of Ed's words when we were first here was so strong I turned to see if he was behind me.

'Ed?'

I stared into the shadows below, half-hoping, half-dreading that he'd be lurking there, water dribbling down his face.

No Ed.

My rescuers or Fluorescent Guy had attached a rope to a load-sharing anchor that looked solidly embedded in a crack. I tugged on it to be sure. I didn't clip onto it, but used it as a guide as I scaled the face. *Always let your conscience be your guide.*

And then I was down. Easy-peasy lemon squeezy. It shouldn't have been that easy. *Why not, Eiger Boy? Remember, Si, you've been to Everest, the highest mountain in the wooooorld.* Bullshit. That meant nothing. When I was slogging my way up to ABC that first time, I'd used my hellish experience in Cwm Pot to prove to myself that I could do it. But now, back in the damp depths, I couldn't let the mountain and its ghosts muscle their way in. They had no place here.

This is all about Ed and me.

Three obstacles down. One to go.

I stood in the exact spot where Ed had attacked me. I took out his flask and shook it – a talisman to lure him in. I knocked back a gulp. 'Ed? Look what I got.'

Come on you motherfucker.

Dizziness roiled, my vision was beginning to blur. The booze sloshed in my gut. That last sip had been a bridge too far. *Idiot. Sober up.* I ripped into the bacon roll, a lump of bread and rind sticking in my gullet. I choked it down. It didn't take the edge off the dreamy, greasy feeling of being pissed, but only added to the nausea. I thought about sticking my fingers down my throat, but it was too late. The alcohol was already in my blood.

Have a little lie-down.

No. I wasn't going to sleep down here. No. Not after last time. I knew what would happen if I did. I could picture it in 3-D clarity. While I slept the batteries in my headlamp would die. I'd wake up in pitch darkness, disorientated, terrified, and while I was trying to change the old batteries for new, I'd drop them, and they'd dribble into a crack in the cave's floor. I'd blindly feel around for them, trip and stumble into a crevasse. The fall would be sudden and jarring. I could almost hear the crack as my femur broke, feel the agonising jolt of bone and sinew snapping. I could taste the panic and despair, hear my screams. Hear the answering silence.

Fucking stop it.

Move.

Rat Run. That's what you should be thinking about, lad.

I'd forgotten about the next bit – the first encounter with Cwm Pot's watery arteries – although the stream's loud whisper had been part of the background for at least half an hour. Following the signs, I tiptoed over scree to the water's edge.

Check the water level, lad.

It barely lapped over my ankles. Far lower than last time. I bent at the waist as if to listen to it – almost over-balancing – then stepped in. This time it wasn't high enough to over-boil into my boots, and someone, maybe the phantom fluorescent guy, had criss-crossed several plastic pipes across the sinkholes, which made the going far easier, even for the stupidly pissed. God knows how they got them down here. Taking the traverse across the stream with the care of a geriatric with brittle bone syndrome, I let the light drift up to the geological marvels dripping from the ceiling. A fair few of them had been snapped off.

Sloshy, slosh-slosh. I paused, straining for any signs of the watery choir in the background burble. The voices weren't there. *Is that a good or bad sign?*

And then there it was, the aperture leading to the Rat Run. The puckered stone around it gave it the look of a petulant arsehole, although I don't recall getting this impression last time. This image wasn't helped by the fact that the phantom spray-painter had surrounded it with four arrows pointing inwards.

You can do it. You did it last time.

But now I'm fatter. And drunker.

Not true. I was sobering up, my future hangover starting its woodpecker drill at the base of my neck.

Turn back. You don't have to do this.

While I was hunting down the map, in a fit of masochism I'd googled caving disasters, and I'd read an account of a bloke who'd got himself jammed in a fissure. They'd had to cover him in oil and butter to wheedle him out. My swollen gut would jam me in there. A cork in a bottle. A fist in an arse. How long would it take to die like that? There was that guy who'd had to cut off his own arm to survive when he was trapped in a rocky prison. But you can't hack through your own fat, can you?

And you haven't even brought a knife along.

'Oh bollocks.'

Ready for the Rat Run, lad?

'I was born ready, Ed.' But saying it aloud didn't make it true.

First there was the teasing ease of the hands-and-knees scramble. Then the toe-crushing hell of the crawlspace, made more gruelling this time around as I had to keep nudging the bloody bag ahead of me, and I couldn't pull myself along with my fingertips – I didn't have enough of them to make it effective. Without gloves, the scree tore into my flesh. Tasting the ground beneath me, that bitter dirt coating my teeth, Juliet's mantra filled my head, *this is shite, this is shite, this is shite.*

Scrape, scrape, shuffle, push. *Inch worm, inch worm.* I emptied my mind. Tried not to think about Ed wrapping a hand around my ankle, holding me down here, holding me down here until . . .

Round a bend, past the point of no return.

The light cruelly illuminated just how tight the next section was. The ceiling and floor seemed to pincer together.

Bile flooded into my mouth. I spat it out.

'Ugh, ugh, ugh.'

Then, straight after this, the place where I'd been wedged last time. I pushed the bag through ahead of me. This time I made sure both of my arms went through together. *Shoulders through, check, you're doing it. Good. Scrabble, scrabble with your fingertips, heave, heave with your toes.*

You're doing it!

I stopped moving to draw in a breath.

Big mistake.

Stuck. I was stuck, my barrel chest and gut jamming me in.

You're not stuck. Relax.

I let myself go limp. Tried again to prod and pull myself forward, stones razoring the tender stumps on my right hand.

Stuck.

The panic came then, hot and fresh, my drunken defences useless against it. I flailed, whipping my head back and forth, the helmet clunking on the rock. I screamed. I sucked in a breath and I screamed my lungs raw: 'Ed! *Ed*!'

The acres of rock above me pressed down. The band across my chest tightened its anaconda grip.

You wanted this, Si.

Welcome to being stuck, your worst nightmare.

I prayed for the watery voices to come and tell me what to do.

'Ed! Thierry! Mum! *Anyone*!'

My bowels loosened. *Don't you* dare.

How long would it be until anyone came? Déjà vu. I'd thought this exact thing when I was in the mausoleum cave the first time around. *No one is coming. You're on your own, lad.* No. Someone will come. Someone will find the hire car. Perhaps after two or three days the farmer who owns the property will realise that it's been there too long.

Three hours for air, three days for water, three weeks for food.

And say they do find you. How will they get you out?

They'll smear me with butter and oil. They'll pull me out with a rope, they'll dig at the stone around me, they'll . . .

But what if it rains, Si? What if it floods? What if you're lying here, trapped, and the water rises, slowly, slowly. You'll be able to hear it first, that burble, that gush. Perhaps by then you'll even be grateful. Perhaps by then you'll be begging to die.

No. Ed will come.

Those lads died down here. In this exact spot. Bet you can't remember their names. Bet you've already forgotten.

'I know their names.'

Bullshit.

I waded through the clamour in my mind.

Nigel Rowley, Robert King and Guy McFaul.

Nigel Rowley, Robert King and Guy McFaul.

'Nigel Rowley, Robert King and Guy McFaul!'

I let myself go limp again, and then I shoved with my toes. Like last time, I shifted a centimetre.

'Ha! Nigel Rowley, Robert King and Guy McFaul!'

Another centimetre. The stone band crept over my gut, cruelly squeezing against it, and then I was through.

I lay face down on the dirt, breathing and panting, then scrabbled to the end of the bowel.

I didn't have the energy to sob with relief. I dropped down into the water – now it did lap over my boots, but I was glad of this, the water's cold embrace soothed my aching toes. My legs were shaking. I gagged. Nothing came up. My nails were jagged and torn. The stumps were embedded with black stone diamonds.

The worst is over.

I let the light cruise across the walls that led into the tunnel where I'd almost drowned in 2006. Instead of the maelstrom that had swept me along last time, the stream burbled benignly into the tunnel's blackness, as harmless as the start of a theme park ride.

The arrows pointed up to where I knew the mausoleum cave was.

If Ed's going to be anywhere, he'll be there.

I ran at the wall as best I could, slurping through the stream to get purchase on the slippery rock. I fell back, and tried again. This time I managed to grip an outcropping with my left hand, wincing as the ripped skin on Ol' Stumpy was pierced again by rock as it did its best to help. My unused shoulder muscles and biceps came to the party, and I wriggled my chest and torso onto the ledge, crawling towards the too-familiar entrance tunnel.

Only . . . something was wrong.

No.

It can't be.

It was.

It was blocked.

It was sealed in with rocks, concrete poured around them. The phantom spray painter had scrawled a sad face emoji over it. I pushed against it. It wasn't going anywhere. I'd need a stack of C4 to shift it.

No, no, no. This can't be how it ends.

I wouldn't get to gaze upon Ed's bloated corpse after all. Or be reunited with my old sleepover pals, Nigel Rowley, Robert King and Guy McFaul.

I let my body slide back down feet first into the water, the force of the drop making my jaw click.

I'd been through all that for nothing. It was a staggering anti-climax.

Now what?

Get the hell out of here.

I waded down the former tunnel of death, the nubs of my missing fingers thumping in time to the sick pulse in my head. I stared up at the grooved ceiling. The last time I was here I'd pulled myself along with my *fingers for eyes*. I'd accepted death, felt a cold calmness that had saved my life, a calmness that hadn't arrived when I needed it most on Everest.

The water gushed over the tops of my boots again, mixing with the blood-warmed puddles drenching my feet. It was almost up to my knees. Wait . . . was it rising? I couldn't be sure if the floor was sloping imperceptibly and if this accounted for the higher water level. I paused. Was its gush and grumble louder? Paranoia nipped: was it rising?

It can happen in an instant.

I picked up my speed. Sloshing through the current at a slow-jog, heart rate picking up, too scared to look behind me in case I saw a wall of water crashing towards me, B-movie style. I caught my left boot in an underground sinkhole and then I fell, crashing onto my side. The helmet dug into my ear and I got a mouthful of water that chilled my teeth.

That'll sober you up, lad.

Legs as fragile as glass, I stood. The water hadn't slipped through the collar of the over-suit, so that was something. I looked down. The stream now lapped at the tops of my boots again. It hadn't risen after all.

Dumb-ass.

I carried on. There were no arrows down here – they'd died out with that pathetic emoji. The tunnel seemed to stretch on and on. Had I really managed to scrape my way this far along it using just fingers for eyes?

Slosh-slosh.

The tunnel's ceiling opened out, and ahead of me, the conduit split into two. *No. That's not right.* I dragged out the map, but it came apart in my hands. Water had sneaked into the bag. *Fuck.*

I glanced around, searching out the suitcase-sized opening I remembered from last time. I'd clambered up a rocky incline to reach it. I remembered that clearly.

Retrace your steps.

I carefully swung the light around. I passed an outcropping, but no aperture. Then another. To my left, the light caught another one, which did have a small eyelet at the top of it – but was this the one that led to the exit route? I wasn't sure. It looked too small.

My guts churned. It was getting hard to swallow.

Try again.

Thighs protesting against the effort of wading against the current, I retraced my steps. Nothing looked familiar.

Okay. Be logical. What now?

You're at a crossroads here, matey-boy.

Was this the test I'd been waiting for?

I could take one of the unfamiliar-looking routes and hope that Ed – or the whispery voices – would come and save me before I ran out of juice. I had a fistful of spare batteries, but they wouldn't last forever. Or I could retrace my steps. That would be the safe option.

Would it though? You really want to go back through the Rat Run! And then backwards through 'the slot'?

Sophie's choice, dude: the joys of the Rat Run, or risk wandering around Cwm Pot in the dark.

I shivered. For the first time the cold was getting to me. *Time to get out of those wet clothes, lad.*

'What should I do?' I said aloud.

Well, that depends how badly you want to know the answer. Ed's had a million chances to finish you off down here already. Do you want to give him a chance to save you?

No.

Then move it, arsehole.

I didn't allow myself time to back out when I reached the Rat Run's orifice. Instead I channelled my inner Mingma, and became calm, stoical, accepting of whatever life wanted to throw at me. And I had my magical-thinking mantra this time: *Nigel Rowley, Robert King and Guy McFaul.* Chanting this aloud, I got to it and delved into the sweaty bowel. Did I get stuck again? Yes. But I took it slowly, and didn't allow myself to panic. I'd chucked the bolt cutters, and all I had with me in the bag were the batteries and the flask.

I didn't worry about the water rising and filling the channel this time.

Nor did I feel any triumph when I made it through. Exhaustion and disappointment loomed too large. My feet dragged like a toddler's when I reached the foot of the abyss. I didn't bother calling for Ed. Everything ached, my dehydrated brain was having a tantrum and I would have sold my soul for a Red Bull.

As I climbed up, using the rope like an amateur, my legs began to jitter – 'doing an Elvis' Kenton used to call it. I felt around for a toehold, but there wasn't one. My broken fingers couldn't hold me; my biceps were shot. And then, with a casual inevitability, I fell. I didn't have time to think, 'this is gonna hurt'. My life didn't flash before my eyes. I landed on my back, *whoomph*, whacking the breath out of my lungs, the force of the landing dislodging the helmet with a vicious crack, instantly killing the light.

Can't breathe.

Dead.

Am I dead?

'Ug.'

That sound. Did I make that sound?

'Ug.'

Don't move. Back broken. I think your back's broken.

Ed!

There's no Ed.

It can't end like this.

I don't know how long I lay there, convinced that I was dead or dying. I'd forgotten how pure the darkness could be down there. I blinked my eyes rapidly – seeing a flash of stars, but nothing else.

Ed could be here right now, and you'd never know it. Creeping closer, perhaps moving in stilted jerks like a J-horror schoolgirl.

Did this scare me? Yes. Although this was what I'd wanted, wasn't it? I'd wanted Ed to pitch up. And where were the voices that had saved me the first time?

They aren't coming this time, matey-boy. You're gonna die in the dark, like you should have done the first time around.

No.

I felt around with my damaged hand for the helmet and headlamp. Couldn't feel it anywhere. If it was smashed, that was it. I'd die in the dark, no question. Slowly, carefully, I sat up, and promptly vomited. I pressed my fingers against my spine and hips, half expecting to feel jagged shards of bone. I rolled onto my hands and knees and vomited again, tasting the sour poison of brandy, whisky and the remains of a half-digested bacon roll.

But I could move. That was something.

I tentatively waved my arms in the space around me, the pure blackness now disorientating and nauseating. I half-expected to reach out and touch cold skin, the sandpaper stubble on Ed's face, maybe.

The pain in my back still raged, but breathing was becoming easier. I touched my hair, feeling for a hairline crack. My fingertips came back wet. I brought them to my mouth. They tasted salty – blood or sweat?

Does it matter?

I pushed away the image I'd had on my way through here. I wasn't going to fall in a crevasse. I could do this. That curious, life-saving calm didn't come over me, nor was I floating above myself looking down, but I inched methodically back and forth on my hands and knees, spidering my fingers over the rocky floor.

My fingers touched plastic. The helmet.

I held my breath.

I could feel the rough strap of the headlamp.

If the globe was smashed, that would be it.

Do it.

I clicked the switch. A second of horrible nothingness, and then: *let there be light!*

Huzzah!

I got to my feet.

You know what this means, don't you?

Yes. I'd done it. I'd faced the demon head on. I'd done my own version of shock therapy, called Ed's bluff and come out on top. He hadn't come. The voices hadn't come. He was all in my mind, and now I knew that for sure. He hadn't tried to harm me; my fall was just a result of exhaustion. I'd been my own saviour, and my own destroyer. I'd banished him by proving to myself that I was a nutter after all. He wasn't an angry ghost; he wasn't anything but a figment of my imagination.

The exhilaration of banishing Ed smothered the ache of the bruises that would cover my spine like Rorschach blots in the days to come. Not even climbing back up the rope, and returning through the skinny mouth could shake me. I did it blithely, wriggling on my gut feet first, reaching out blindly for the chain, then swinging across. Back through the boulder choke, carelessly slamming my elbows on the sulphur-stinking limestone nodules, and even the leap and lunge of scrambling up the rope to reach the last rung of the ladder felt effortless. Each step on the rung was – and this is going to sound vomitous – life-affirming.

I fought the law and I won.

I practically danced back through the chamber and out into daylight. The late afternoon sun greeted me like a conquering hero. How long had I been down there? *I didn't fucking care!* I sank to my knees next to the stream and drank, flushing away the taste of bile, relishing the sting of the freezing water on my lacerated hands. I splashed my face with it, over and over again.

Time to begin the next stage of my life. What would I do? The world was my oyster. I could start a charitable organisation, *The Simon Newman Home for Impoverished Welsh Spelunkers* maybe. Get myself a girlfriend, maybe even breed and produce my own Gandolfini baby. Retrain to be a doctor, join *Médicins sans Frontières* or whatever the fuck they were called. Volunteer at a dog sanctuary. Do something that actually helped the world instead of making it a murkier place.

The growl of a distant tractor, the twitchiness of the sheep, the sting of the nettles jostling for space around the stream – all of it was supremely, impossibly beautiful.

'Cheers, Ed,' I said, holding up the flask and taking a sip. *Hair of the dog, why not?* I gagged, but it stayed down.

Onwards!

Too late, it hit me that the engine noise I'd heard earlier was now filling my ears. I turned to see a figure zooting towards me on a quad bike – a balding guy dressed in an anorak and boots, a shotgun looped over a shoulder. There was nowhere for me to hide, and besides, he was on me in seconds, skidding to a halt just feet away from me. 'Can't you read?' he gruffed in a thick Welsh accent. 'This is private property. No trespassing.'

'Sorry about that,' I slurred. 'I was going for a ramble. Must have got lost.'

'Always go for a walk dressed like that, do you?' He eyed my wellies, the caving helmet still balanced on my head, the nicks and cuts on Ol' Stumpy, the over-suit which was sodden and smeared with Cwm Pot shite.

'Are you going to call the police?' I didn't care if he did or not, and this must have shown on my face. I was invincible. I'd escaped Cwm Pot, vanquished Ed, and yeah, once upon a time I'd climbed fucking Mount Everest. His eyes strayed to the pieces missing from my right hand. *Pieces. Yes. That's how I should think of them. Not fingers. Not hands.* I waggled the bloodied stumps at him and smirked. *Don't fuck with me or I'll pincer you to death, boyo.* I didn't mean to laugh, it just happened. Great booming gusts exploded out of my mouth. The force of them didn't help my throbbing spine, but I couldn't stop until they doubled me over and I was gasping for breath.

The farmer – if that was what he was – just stared at me warily until I finished. 'Sorry,' I said, wiping the tears from my cheeks. 'Sorry – I'm not crazy, I promise. It's just . . . me and Cwm Pot, we've got a history.'

'Oh yes?'

'Yes. Friend of mine died down there.'

'Did he now?' He was still staring at me guardedly. I didn't blame him.

'I was paying my respects.'

'And that's a laughing matter, is it?'

'No. I guess I'm just . . .' *Just what? Drunk, certifiable, or both. No. Neither. I'm happy. I'm* done.

I fumbled in my bag for the flask and took a swig. There was sod all left, but I wiped the spout and offered it to him. He hesitated, then took it and drank. 'You'll be on your way then, will you?'

'Yeah. You going to call the police?' I asked again.

'No point, is there? Place is going to be sealed over. Blocking it up for good. Kids keep getting lost down there, see. There's something on a website about the bodies down there that draws them like flies to shit. Caving clubs have been fighting it for months, but we've had enough. Already capped the main exit.'

Even if I had made it through the network of tunnels to the sewerage pipe, I couldn't have made it out. 'Thanks,' I said. 'I appreciate that.' To my ears I sounded normal, sober.

'Not driving, are you? If you are, best you take a nap first.'

I gave him a bright grin and a double thumbs-up, turned and made my way back towards the car, still on a ridiculous, irrational high.

Yes. It was all fine. It was all going to be good.

Going back down there, down to where it had started had been just the ticket. I'd unwittingly performed my own version of immersion therapy.

Cured.

I'd risked my life, and he hadn't come.

A niggle. *But Si, are you sure that your life was even in danger when you were down there?*

What do you mean?

If you were never in danger, then why would Ed pitch up as your saviour? You took the easy option, remember. You retraced your steps.

I fell. How is that the easy option?

Did Ed push you?

No. And he didn't push me because he doesn't exist, dumb-ass. He's dead. I got myself out of the bad situation. No whispery voices, no Third Man, none of that bollocks. Ed is – *was* – just in my head. A blip, a physical manifestation of PTSD.

You sure, dude? What if you let yourself fall?

Why would I do that? SHUT UP SHUT UP SHUT UP.

I approached the car like a bird approaching a tiger. This would be it. If Ed was in there, waiting for me, then the whole Cwm Pot enterprise would have been a massive waste of time.

No Ed.

The relief was potent, but it washed away the last of the adrenalin buzz and euphoria that had pulled me out of the cave. I wasn't in any state to drive. I lay back, the seat pressing into my tender back and torn muscles, and closed my eyes.

I was out in seconds.

I woke to darkness, fine rain spattering the windscreen. Every inch of me had seized up. The back of my head roared with agony. My mouth was full of foul-tasting glue. I needed water.

A shadow blipped in the corner of my eye.

No.

No.

I didn't need to look.

'What do you want from me, Ed? *Why are you here*?' I wanted to punch him, but the tender skin where my fingers once were wouldn't take it. I was sick of pain.

'But I fell, Ed. I fell.' I was keening, begging, whining, a little boy again.

I collapsed against the steering wheel, breathing in the smell of fake leather and other people's palm sweat, and sobbed. Ed merely sat there beside me, mud-coloured water spilling out of his mouth.

I was crying for Juliet, for Mark, for Mark's awful dad, for George, but most of all I was crying for me.

Because I knew what I had to do next. There was only one thing *left* to do.

That's it. *That's all she wrote.*

Tadeusz won't let me join his team again, but there are others who will. I have the cash, and this time I have the motivation. And I have to do it soon. Graham was right. The Chinese are clearing the mountain of its dead, and it could only be a matter of time before Juliet and Mark are tumbled into a crevasse. Maybe I *am* seeking redemption or fucking closure after all. Maybe Juliet does have the answer. Maybe I'm putting far too much store in that ripped piece of paper.

One thing I know for sure, the question isn't: Who is the third who walks always beside you? It's: What the fuck does he *want*?

JOURNEY TO THE DARKSIDE

(2.07.2018)

The Five Freakiest Real-Life Found Footage Clips Ever! (Number 5 Will Make You SHIT Yourself!)

1. The Curious Case of Simon Newman

You've all seen this one, but we're showing it again as it's close to our cold, dark JTTDS hearts.

It starts like this . . .

Simon Newman, who used to work for this very site way back in the sands of time, headed off to Everest in 2007 where he met a dude called Marcus Michaels, the son of Juliet Michaels, a kick-ass mountaineer who wait for it, died on Everest in 1995. While searching for Juliet's body together, Marcus disappeared and Simon almost bought it too. He escaped death but lost a bunch of fingers (check out this link to Five Gross Things You Didn't Know about Frostbite!).

Here's where it gets *really* fucking freaky.

Simon returned to the mountain in 2013 for messed-up reasons of his own (basically, the dude was batshit insane), and set off for the summit with the rest of his team. He never made it back. A year later, his body was discovered lying next to Juliet and Marcus's corpsicles, and his camera, along with a few seconds of footage, was sent to his next of kin, Thierry Andre (aka our beloved creator T Cakes). This clip, which has now had over twenty-eight million views, shows Simon looking into his GoPro's screen, and basically *shitting* himself.

The wind is too loud for you to hear the audio, but this is what a lip-reader reckons he's saying: 'My name is Simon Newman. He hasn't come. He hasn't come. He hasn't come. *He hasn't come* . . .' [here he stops and smiles] '*Oh—*'

2. The Cat-Killing Nanny Cam

Juliet

at camp III leave in an hour pen keeps freezing joe wrong about the weather its bad but he's here and he took off his mask and its Walter it's Walter IT'S WALTER and I know he will be with me no longer alone. Shuld have known it was him all along but why the fear was he pushing me testing me? his fingers his fingers
Donesnt matter
all going to be ok. He'll make sure I'm safe he'll lead out this time and I know that I will get back to Marcus

<u>I CAN DO THIS</u>

Glossary

AMS: Advanced Mountain Sickness.

Ataxia: The loss of control over body movement and balance. Can be one of the symptoms of HACE (High-Altitude Cerebral Oedema/ Edema).

Belay: A rock, bush, or aid sturdy enough for a rope to be passed around it to secure a hold. Can also refer to the protection/safety technique of exerting tension on a rope so that a climbing partner won't plummet to her death if she falls.

Bivouac: A temporary camp in which purpose-made 'bivvy-sacs' or bags are used.

Chorten: A monument to a distinguished Buddhist, usually a lama.

Crampon: Metal plates with spikes that can be attached to boots to aid in gripping ice or snow.

Crevasse: A deep open crack found in ice fields or glaciers (these are sometimes hidden under snow and can be extremely hazardous).

Col: The lowest point between two mountain peaks.

Didi: Nepalese word for sister. Used as a term of affection or respect.

Exposure/Over-suit: A protective suit usually made out of PVC and neoprene worn when caving in wet and muddy conditions.

Figure-of-eight: Metal device shaped like the number 8, usually used when descending but sometimes as a belay.

Free-climbing: Climbing without use of aids, gear or protection.

Gamow Bag: An inflatable pressure bag large enough to fit a person inside. It simulates lower altitude conditions in order to help alleviate the symptoms of AMS, HACE and HAPE.

Glissad(e)(ing): A controlled slide used when descending a steep slope (can be done on the feet or buttocks).

HACE: High-Altitude Cerebral Oedema (or Edema). Fluid on the brain caused by hypoxia (oxygen deprivation). Can be fatal.

HAPE: High-Altitude Pulmonary Oedema (or Edema). Fluid on the lungs caused by shortage of oxygen at high altitudes. Can be fatal.

Hypoxia: A condition in which oxygen supply is insufficient.

Jumar (or ascender): A clamp attached to a fixed rope that tightens when weight is applied and relaxes when it is removed. Used as a tool for ascending.

Karabiner: An oval metal hoop with a spring-loaded gate for attaching to a belay. Can also join two ropes together.

Moraine: Rocks and sediment carried down and discarded by a glacier.

Oedema (UK) Edema (US): An excess of watery fluid collecting in the cavities or tissues of the body.

Rime: A granular frost formed by the rapid freezing of water vapour.

Serac: A pinnacle, ridge or block of ice on the surface of a glacier. Some can be house-sized and unstable.

Seven Summits: The highest mountains of each continent. Summiting all of them is a popular mountaineering challenge.

Spelunking: North American term for caving.

Spindrift: Loose powdery snow.

Traverse: To move left, right or diagonally across a rock face or slope, rather than heading directly upwards.

VS (route): An abbreviation of the traditional UK climbing adjectival grade 'Very Severe'. The adjectival grading system denotes how challenging or well climbed a route may be, and runs from Moderate (M) to Extremely Severe. (These grades can be controversial, as some climbers may find a moderate climb a nightmare and vice versa). Adjectival grades are usually coupled with a numerical 'technical grade' (with 4a being the easiest, and 7b the hardest), which indicate how difficult the hardest move on the route may be.

Mountain Glossary

Aconcagua (6,961 m) (22,838 ft): Located in Argentina, it forms part of the Andes and is the highest mountain outside Asia.

Annapurna (8,091 m) (26,545 ft): Forming part of the Himalayas (Nepal), it has an alarmingly high summit to fatality ratio (one in three climbers who attempt it are killed).

Ben Nevis (1,346 m) (4,414 ft): An ancient volcano and the highest peak in the British Isles.

Broad Peak (8,051 m) (26,414 ft): The twelfth highest mountain in the world, it forms part of the Karakoram Range in Pakistan.

Cerro Torre (3,128m)(10,262 ft): Situated on the border between Argentina and Chile, it was once thought to be the world's most difficult climb.

Changste (7,543 m)(24,747 ft): Connected to Mount Everest via the North Col.

Cho Oyu (8,188m)(26,864 ft): The sixth highest mountain in the world, it forms part of the Himalayas (on the border of Tibet and Nepal), and is the easiest of the 8,000 metre peaks to climb.

Cwm Silyn (734m)(2,408 ft): A popular climbing destination in Wales.

Dhaulagiri (8,167 m) (26,795 ft): Part of the Himalayas and the seventh highest mountain in the world.

Denali/McKinley (20,310 ft) (6190 m): Located in Alaska, it's the highest peak in North America.

Eiger (3,970m)(13,020ft): Located in Switzerland, it forms part of the Bernese Alps. The North Face of the Eiger is infamous for being the site of many tragic deaths and has earned the nickname 'The Murder Wall'.

Gasherbrum I (8,080m)(26,510 ft): The eleventh highest mountain in the world, it straddles the border of Pakistan and China and forms part of the Gasherbrum Massif.

K2 (8,611 m)(28,251 ft): The second highest mountain in the world, and the highest point of the Karakoram, K2 lies on the border between Pakistan and China. Known as 'The Savage Mountain', it is the second most dangerous of the 8,000 metre peaks to climb.

Kanchenjunga (8,586 m)(28,169 ft): Part of the Himalayas (Nepal and India), and the third highest mountain in the world.

Kilimanjaro (5,895 m)(19,341 ft): Located in Tanzania, it's the highest mountain in Africa.

Manaslu (8,163 m)(26,781 ft): Part of the Himalayas (Nepal), and the eighth highest mountain in the world.

Mount Cook/Aoraki (3,724 m)(12,218 ft): The highest and deadliest peak in New Zealand.

Mount Rainier (4,392 m) (14,411 ft): Situated in Washington State (U.S), it's the highest mountain in the Cascade Range.

Nanga Parbat (8,126 m) (26,660 ft): Located in Pakistan, it's the ninth highest mountain in the world. A dangerous and difficult peak, it has earned the nickname 'Killer Mountain'.

Pumori (7,161 m)(23,494 ft): Part of the Himalayas (Nepal and Tibet), it's affectionately known as 'Everest's Daughter'.

Snowdon (1,085 m) (3,560 ft): The highest peak in Wales.

Vinson Massif/Mount Vinson (4,892 m)(16,050 ft): A mountain range located near the base of the Antarctic Peninsula, and the highest point in Antarctica.

Acknowledgments

In order to research this book, I decided I had to go underground. This meant finding someone prepared to guide a claustrophobic couch potato down a big hole. After trawling through YouTube clips documenting arse-clenching caving expeditions, one name kept popping up: Keith Edwards of The Dudley Caving Club (Keith isn't just a highly skilled caver; he's the Spielberg of the caving scene). Keith and his fellow cavers, Brendan and Mark, bravely agreed to guide my husband Charlie and me through the Cwm Dwr caves in South Wales, and did so with skill, dry humour and unshakeable patience (there's a clip of me hanging off a ledge and having a cry somewhere on YouTube if you want a laugh). A better bunch of people it would be hard to find and I can't thank them enough for their generosity.

Also invaluable were the high altitude mountaineers who gave me a peek (peak?) into their world and provided valuable insights into the commercialisation of Everest, especially Thomas Vermaak (who summited Everest twice at a ridiculously young age), and Gyaluk Sherpa of Asian Trekking (who has summited the mountain an incredible six times).

All mistakes are mine.

Many thanks also go to Phurba and Kunga who accompanied us through Tibet and to Everest base camp at very short notice, answered endless tedious questions and were all round brilliant guys. I'm also indebted to Karina Szczurek (for allowing me to steal her integrity), Tadeusz Bradecki (for allowing me to steal his name), Simon Walters (for allowing me to steal some of his personality), Savannah Lotz (for pulling my arse out of the fire yet again), Helen Moffett (who caught me when I fell off the page), Paige Nick (for hauling me out of plot holes), Alan Kelly, Alan and Carol Walters, Lauren Beukes, Nishma Khadgi, Rob 'Flexible' Sandy, Kate Sinclair and as always, Charlie Martins, who has learned the hard way that living with a writer sometimes means getting dirty.

My agent Oli Munson and fantastic editor Anne Perry were superhumans as always – thank you both. Many thanks also go to Joshua Kendall for his superb editorial insights, and to Veronique Norton, Hélène Ferey, Jennifer Custer, Fleur Clarke, Ben Summers, Vickie Dillon, Oliver Johnson and all the brilliant people at A.M Heath, Hodder & Stoughton and Little, Brown.

Bibliography

I became a mountaineering literature addict after reading Joe Simpson's peerless *Touching the Void* in the early nineties. After that gateway drug, I couldn't get enough, and below are listed the books and blogs that were invaluable resources (most are best read sitting next to a fire while the weather rages outside):

Andrew, Jamie, *Life and Limb*, Portrait, 2005.

Anker, Conrad and Roberts, David, *The Lost Explorer: Finding Mallory on Everest*, Robinson, 1999.

Arnette, Alan, alanarnette.com

Blum, Arlene, *Annapurna: A Woman's Place*, Granada, 1980.

Blum, Arlene, *Breaking Trail: A Climbing Life*, Scribner, 2005.

Bonatti, Walter, *The Mountains of my Life*, Penguin Modern Classics, 2010.

Boukreev, Anatoli and DeWalt, G. Weston, *The Climb: Tragic Ambitions on Everest*, Pan Books, 2002.

Breashears, David, *High Exposure: An Endearing Passion for Everest and Other Unforgiving Places*, Canongate, 2014.

Bowley, Graham, *No Way Down: Life and Death on K2*, Penguin Viking, 2010.

Burgess, Adrian and Alan, *The Burgess Book of Lies*, The Mountaineers, 1998.

Cave, Andy, *Learning to Breathe*, Hutchinson London, 2005.

Coburn, Broughton, *Everest: Mountain Without Mercy*, National Geographic Society, 1997.

Coffey, Maria, *Where the Mountain Casts its Shadow: The Personal Costs of Climbing*, Arrow Books, 2004.

Curran, Jim, *K2, Triumph and Tragedy*, Hodder & Stoughton, 1987.

Da Silva, Rachel, *Leading Out: Mountaineering Stories of Adventurous Women*, Seal Press, 1998.

Davis, Wade, *Into the Silence: The Great War, Mallory and the Conquest of Everest*, Bodley Head, 2011.

Dickinson, Matt, *The Death Zone*, Arrow Books, 2011.

Diemberger, Kurt, *The Endless Knot: K2, Mountain of Dreams and Destiny*, Vertebrate Publishing, 2013.

Douglas, Ed and Rose, David, *Regions of the Heart: The Triumph and Tragedy of Alison Hargreaves*, National Geographic Society, 2000.

Douglas, Ed, *Chomolungma Sings the Blues: Travels Round Everest*, Constable and Robinson, 2001.

Eicher, Donnie, *Dead Mountain: The Untold True Story of the Dyatlov Pass Incident*, Chronicle Books, 2013.

Eyre, Jim and Frankland, John, *Race Against Time*, Lyon Books, 1988.

Falvey, Pat and Sherpa Gyalje, Pemba, *The Summit: How Triumph Turned to Tragedy on K2's Deadliest Days*, Beyond Endurance Publishing, 2014.

Gammelgaard, Lene, *Climbing High: A Woman's Account of Surviving the Everest Tragedy*, Seal Press, 1999.

Geiger, John, *The Third Man Factor: Surviving the Impossible*, Canongate, 2009.

Hall, Lincoln, *Dead Lucky: Life After Death on Mount Everest*, Tarcher/Penguin, 2007.

Hall, Lincoln with Fear, Sue, *Fear No Boundary: One Woman's Amazing Journey*, Hatchette Australia, 2005.

Hargreaves, Alison, *A Hard Day's Summer*, Coronet, 1995.

Harrer, Heinrich, *The White Spider*, Harper Collins, 2005.

Heil, Nick, *Dark Summit*, Virgin Books, 2009.

Hemmleb, Jochen and A Johnson, Larry and R Simonson, Eric, *Ghosts of Everest: The Authorized Story of the Search for Mallory & Irvine*, Macmillan, 1999.

Hemmleb, John and R Simonson, Eric, *Detectives on Everest: The 2001 Mallory & Irvine Research Expedition*, The Mountaineers Books, 2002.

Herzog, Maurice, *Annapurna*, Vintage, 2011.

Holzel, Tom and Salkeld, Audrey, *The Mystery of Mallory & Irvine*, Jonathan Cape, 1986.

Horrell, Mark, *Denali Nights: A Commercial Expedition to Climb Mt McKinley's West Buttress*, Mountain Footsteps Press, 2014.

Horrell, Mark, *In the Footsteps of Mallory: A Journey to the North Col of Everest*, Mark Horrell, 2013.

Horrell, Mark, *The Ascent of Manaslu: Climbing the World's Eighth Highest Mountain,* Mountain Footsteps Press, 2013.

Horrell, Mark, *The Chomolungma Diaries*, Mark Horrell, 2012.

Horrell, Mark, *Thieves, Liars and Mountaineers: On the 8000 Metre Peak Circus in Pakistan's Karakoram Mountains*, Mountain Footsteps Press, 2012.

Hoyland, Graham, *Last Hours on Everest: The Gripping Story of Mallory & Irvine's Fatal Ascent*, Collins, 2013.

James, Tori, *Peak Performance: The First Welsh Woman to Climb Everest*, Accent Press, 2013.

Jordan, Jennifer, *Savage Summit: The Life and Death of the First Women of K2*, Harper Collins e-books, 2005.

Kirkpatrick, Andy, *Cold Wars: Climbing the Fine Line Between Risk and Reality*, Vertebrate, 2011.

Kirkpatrick, Andy, *Psychovertical*, Arrow Books, 2009.

Kodas, Michael, *High Crimes: The Fate of Everest in an Age of Greed*, Hyperion e-books, 2008.

Krakauer, Jon, *Into Thin Air: The Illustrated Edition*, Villard New York, 1998.

Lovelock, James, *Life and Death Under-Ground*, G.Bell and Sons LTD, 1963.

Macfarlane, Robert, *Mountains of the Mind: A History of a Fascination*, Granta Books, 2008.

Mazel, David, *Mountaineering Women: Stories by Early Climbers*, Texas A&M University Press, 1994.

Mcdonald, Bernadette, *Freedom Climbers*, RMB, 2011.

Noble, Chris, *Women Who Dare: North America's Most Inspiring Women Climbers,* Falcon Guides, 2013.

O'Dowd, Cathy and Woodall, Ian, *Everest: Free to Decide*, Zebra Press, 1997.

O'Dowd, Cathy, *Just for the Love of it: The First Woman to Climb Mount Everest From Both Sides*, Crux Publishing, 1999.

Perrin, Jim, *The Villain: The Life of Don Whillans*, Hutchinson London, 2005.

Ralston, Aron, *Between a Rock and a Hard Place*, Pocket Books, 2005.

Ratcliffe, Graham, *A Day to Die For*, Mainstream Publishing, 2013.

Reinisch, Gertrude, *Wanda Rutkiewicz – A Caravan of Dreams*, Carreg LTD, 2000.

Rowell, Galen, *In the Throne Room of the Mountain Gods*, Sierra Club Books, 1986.

Schultheis, Rob, *Bone Games: Extreme Sports, Shamanism, Zen, and the Search for Transcendence*, Breakaway Books, 1996.

Simpson, Joe, *The Beckoning Silence*, Vintage, 2003.

Simpson, Joe, *Dark Shadows Falling*, Jonathan Cape London, 1997.

Simpson, Joe, *Touching the Void*, Heinemann, 2009.

Tasker, Joe, *Everest the Cruel Way*, Vertebrate, 2013.

Tenzing Norgay, Jamlin and Coburn Broughton, *Touching My Father's Soul: A Sherpa's Sacred Journey to the Top of Everest*, Ebury Press, 2002

Trueman, Mike, *The Storms: Adventure and Tragedy on Everest*, Baton Wicks, 2015.

Tullis, Julie, *Clouds From Both Sides*, Grafton, 1987.

Venables, Stephen, *Everest: Alone at the Summit*, Adrenaline Classics, 2000.

Venables, Stephen, *A Slender Thread: Escaping Disaster in the Himalaya*, Hutchinson London, 2000.

Vernon, Ken, *Everest '96*, Ken Vernon, 2015.

Viesturs, Ed with Roberts, David, *K2: Life and Death on the World's Most Dangerous Mountain*, Broadway Books, 2009.

Viesturs, Ed with Roberts, David, *No Shortcuts To the Top: Climbing the World's 14 Highest Peaks*, Broadway Books, 2006.

Weathers, Beck, *Left For Dead: My Journey Home From Everest*, Little, Brown and Company, 2000.

Willis, Clint, *The Boys of Everest: Chris Bonington and the Tragedy of Climbing's Greatest Generation*, Portico, 2006.

Yates, Simon, *Against the Wall*, Vintage, 1998.

Yates, Simon, *The Wild Within: Climbing the World's Most Remote Mountains*, Vertebrate Publishing, 2012.

Zuckerman, Peter and Padoan, Amanda, *Buried in the Sky: The Extraordinary Story of the Sherpa Climbers on K2's Deadliest Day*, W.W. Norton & Company, 2013.